The Sea & The Sand

CHRISTOPHER NICOLE

The Sea & The Sand

This first world edition published 1986 by
SEVERN HOUSE PUBLISHERS LTD of
4 Brook Street, London W1Y 1AA

Copyright © 1986 F. Beerman BV

British Library Cataloguing in Publication Data

Nicole, Christopher
  The Sea And The Sand
  I. Title
  823'. 914[F]   PR 6064. 12/

  ISBN 0–7278–1350–1

Printed in Great Britain

Chapter 1

The Caribbean and Long Island – 1800

'Sail ho,' came the cry from the masthead.

'Where away,' replied Second Lieutenant Tobias McGann, standing on the quarterdeck of the United States Ship *Constellation.*

'Bearing three points off the starboard bow,' was the answer.

Toby McGann moved to the rail, levelled his telescope to the south-east, at the distant cluster of canvas emerging every second above the horizon, white against the lush green slopes of the island beyond. It was February in the Caribbean Sea, in the year 1800, and in this best of tropical seasons the water gleamed a brilliant blue in the noonday sun, with only the odd breaking crest, whipped up by the north-easterly trade wind, to splash against the bows of the United States' frigate as she beat towards St Lucia. Clouds were gathering above the island peaks, and there would certainly be a rainsquall within a couple of hours, but this was normal midday convection – it would do no more than cool the air slightly.

Sailing such waters, where his father, the famous Harry McGann, had first learned about fighting at sea, could not help but stir Toby's blood, even if, at nineteen, he had already seen far more action than had Harry when such an age. But the Caribbean was where all the great sea battles had been fought over the past century; he was just fortunate that events had transpired to give him the opportunity to sail this sea in time of war.

'Where is she, Mr McGann?' Captain Thomas Truxton spoke quietly, but with brisk authority. Ashore, when visit-

1

ing the McGann family home on Long Island, he might call his second lieutenant Toby, and exchange a quip as well as a glass, for he had sailed as lieutenant to Harry McGann, and had known Harry's son almost since birth. But at sea he preserved his growing reputation for being a disciplinarian, and also as a fighting skipper whose men would follow him anywhere.

'Bearing east by south, sir,' Toby replied. 'Just clearing the shadow of the island.' A note of excitement entered his voice. 'I make out four of them.'

Truxton, tall and spare, although giving three inches to the young giant who stood beside him, levelled his telescope. Toby waited for his captain's evaluation of the situation; he counted this man as almost a second father. But he was a true son of Harry McGann, six feet four inches in his stockinged feet, and made to seem even taller by the blue bicorne hat he wore. His heavy shoulders and slim hips were set off by the blue tailcoat and white breeches of his uniform, so that the sword slapping his thigh seemed hardly larger than a dirk. His hair too, straight and black, was that of his Irish father, but he had the blue eyes of his English mother. His heart pounded with a pleasant anticipation at the thought of a possible action, even against what promised to be considerable odds. He had been born to the sea, as had his father before him. And he had accumulated, even at his tender age, sufficient experience to make the possible terrors of action or storm nothing more than vague apprehensions, which he was confident of taking in his stride.

'They're English, out of Castries,' Truxton remarked, closing his telescope with a snap, his voice laden with disappointment. He could not yet make out the nearest vessel's flag, but he could discern from the shape of her bow and the cut of her foresail, or jib, not less than from the yellow-varnished hull with its row of black gunports, as the ship steadily came closer, that she was not the Frenchman he sought. 'A frigate, I'd say, escorting three merchantmen.'

'Ahoy the deck,' came the call from the masthead. 'She is signalling.'

Truxton and Toby, now joined by John Rodgers, the first

2

lieutenant, hastily cramming his hat on his head as he came up the companion ladder, again levelled their glasses.

'She wishes to speak with us, sir,' Toby said.

'Aye, well, we'd best heave to. She may have news of importance. Perhaps even an end to this senseless war.'

'She could also be looking for men,' John Rodgers remarked. The Royal Navy, in the course of its long war with Republican France, sought to impress able seamen wherever it could, even off American vessels – claiming they were British deserters.

Truxton gave a grim smile. 'She can be looking for all the men in the world, Mr Rodgers,' he said. 'She'll not take any from my ship.'

He had total confidence in his thirty-six-gun frigate, and his men. With reason: he had proved their worth in battle.

'We'll hear what he has to say. Heave to, Mr McGann. But have the guns loaded, just in case.'

'Aye-aye,' Toby acknowledged, and gave the orders. The frigate's sails were sheeted hard to bring her up directly into the wind, and secured there, so that whenever she sought to gather way she was again turned into the wind to check herself. Thus held, she danced gently over the waves. The *Constellation* did everthing superbly, because she was a superb ship, and a beautiful one, from her snow-white decks to the sheath of copper that plated her hull and keel to repel the teredo worm; from the three tall masts to the Stars and Stripes fluttering proudly at her stern. One of the six frigates authorised by Congress in 1794, when it had become apparent that the young republic had to possess some kind of navy in order to protect its overseas trade, she had been built in Baltimore, and commissioned for sea only eighteen months previously, in June, 1898, the first of the six to be completed, and just in time to fight the French.

That the United States and France, who had fought shoulder to shoulder against the British less than twenty years before to secure American independence, should now have gone to war with each other was one of the absurdities of human nature, as both Harry McGann and Thomas Truxton agreed, and Toby acknowledged. But the fault lay with the Republican Government of France, which had taken offence because President Adams had at last signed a peace treaty with Great Britain, and had then insulted the Americans by attempting to bribe the United States' representatives in Paris. And whatever the reasons, the conflict had provided the infant United States Navy, and especially the USS *Constellation*, with an opportunity to show the world its mettle; an opportunity the officers and men of the *Constellation* had certainly grasped.

Now the sailors moved like the well-drilled crew they were, every man carrying out his allotted task with hardly an order from the officer.

'She's putting down a boat,' called the masthead.

The British ship was now within a few hundred yards, and they could clearly see what was taking place.

'Prepare to receive an officer, Mr McGann,' Truxton said. 'Full honours.'

'Aye-aye,' Toby acknowledged. The boatswain's whistle cooeed, and a guard of honour of twenty men fell in at the waist of the ship, while the port gangway was opened and the ladder put down.

The British frigate had also hove to, although the ships of the convoy, under shortened sail so as not to leave their escort behind, continued to make slowly north-west, approaching every second. Toby could see that the decks of the merchantmen were crowded with people, amongst whom were a considerable number of women and chldren. But then, to his surprise, he saw that there was at least one skirt fluttering on the quarterdeck of the frigate as well. He had no time to look more closely, for already the British gig was bouncing across the gentle waves, to come in under the side of the big American ship.

'Boatswain,' Toby commanded, drawing his sword and standing to attention, as the guard of honour did the same.

The man who came through the gangway, dressed in blue frock coat and white vest and breeches of a British naval officer, was not many years older than Toby himself, and if lacking an equal height, was still tall and decidedly thin, with a somewhat cold, narrow face, built around a prominent nose and determined mouth. He raised his tricorne hat, replaced it, saluted the quarterdeck, and then again, as

4

Truxton and Rodgers advanced to meet him; like all the American frigates, the *Constellation* was flush-decked. 'Lieutenant Jonathan Crown, at your service, Captain Truxton.'

Truxton raised his eyebrows. 'You know my name?'

'Every sailor in the Caribbean knows the name of the captain of the USS *Constellation*, sir,' Crown said. 'Your victory last year, over the *L'Insurgente*, why, sir, it has become a classic of the sea. Did she not carry the heavier metal?'

'Slightly, Mr Crown. Slightly.'

'And was it not in these very waters?'

'It was north of here, Mr Crown. Off the island of Nevis, but just a year ago. And I hope, sir, that you did not request this meeting merely to flatter me?'

'No, sir. You'll be aware that there is another French man-of-war in these waters?'

'I have heard rumours, Mr Crown.'

'We have positive information, sir, brought to us by a Vincentian fisherman, that she arrived in Fort Royal a week ago. Her name is *La Vengeance*, and she carries fifty-two guns, sir.'

'The devil,' Rodgers commented. 'Fifty-two guns? If that information is correct. . .'

'It is correct, sir,' Crown insisted. 'She is at present lying in Fort Royal, Martinique, taking on fresh provisions after her Atlantic crossing.' He looked over his shoulder at the large island lying immediately to the north of St Lucia in the Windward chain, and which he would have pass, with his convoy, in the next twelve hours if he continued to the north. 'Fifty-two guns, sir. She is all but fit to take her place in a line of battle, sir. And she is loose, here in the Caribbean, with not a Navy ship south of Jamaica capable of offering her battle.'

'Hm,' Truxton commented. 'You'd best come aft, Mr Crown, and we'll discuss the matter. Dismiss your men, Mr McGann, and join us.' He led the way down the companion-way into the great cabin of the frigate, where Toby followed them, along with the senior midshipman, Thomas McDonough, a keen young man only a year the younger and with whom he had struck up a close friendship. There they were offered lemonade by Tuxton's steward, and shown to chairs around the table.

'Now, sir,' Truxton said. 'We are grateful for your information, but would appreciate knowing the reason for your co-operation.'

Crown was sipping his lemonade with a somewhat quizzical expression; clearly he was used to something stronger. 'Why, sir,' he replied. 'Are we not allies against the French?'

Truxton frowned. 'Allies, Mr Crown? I know of no alliance between Great Britain and the United States.' His tone implied that he would not believe it even if he had heard of it.

'Well, sir,' Crown acknowledged. 'Perhaps no treaty has been signed. But as we fight the same enemy . . .'

'For different reasons, sir,' Truxton interrupted. 'You seek to reimpose a monarchy on the French Republic, as I understand it. Or certainly to put an end to that republic. We merely seek reparations from our *sister* republic, for certain insults and damages offered to our flag and our citizens.'

Crown finished his lemonade, set the glass on the table, gazed at his host. 'I am truly sorry, sir, that such is your attitude. I had thought, my captain had hoped, that we could make common ground here, sir. May I point out that it would be to both our advantages? We mount but twenty-eight guns on board *Lancer*, Captain Truxton. Our duty is to convoy those three ships you see out there to the safety of Kingston, Jamaica, where there is a large escort waiting to see them and others safely to England. Now we are informed there is a fifty-two-gun French ship hovering on our flank, waiting to dash out and destroy us, and against whom we would be very nearly helpless. You, sir, whether you agree with our reasons for fighting this war or not, are yet also at war with France. It is your duty to do what damage you can to your enemy. But that is a fourth-rate ship, sir. What damage can you, with your thirty-six guns, do against such strength? And he will be seeking to avenge the loss of *L'Insurgente*, you may be sure of that. But together, the pair of us may well give him a bloody nose.'

'And ensure the safety of your convoy,' Rodgers remarked.

'Indeed, sir, that would be a most satisfactory outcome of our endeavours. Those ships are crammed with innocent women and children, who have no part in this conflict.'

'And would you, Mr Crown, engage upon our side if *we* were the convoying vessel?'

'I, sir, and my captain, would most certainly engage an enemy ship on sight, where there was the slightest prospect of victory, as we shall in this instance, without such a prospect if we have to, in defence of our charge.' He flushed. 'My own family is on board these ships, sir, *en route* back to England. In fact, my father and mother and sister are guests of my captain on board *Lancer*.'

'Is that so?' Truxton raised his eyebrows. 'Your family are planters?'

'No, sir. My father was Chief Secretary to the Governor of the Windwards. He has now been reassigned, after leave in England, to Gibraltar, and is thus on his way home.'

Truxton smiled and nodded. 'And you would not wish them to fall into the hands of the French.'

'Would you, sir?' Crown asked. 'If they were yours?'

Truxton cleared his throat.

'May we ask, sir, what would your captain do, had we not been sighted?' John Rodgers enquired. 'Would you have put back to Castries?'

Crown flushed. 'I have already indicated, sir, that we understand our duty. Those ships must reach Kingston by the end of next week; the main convoy will not wait after then. But as you *have* been sighted . . .' His flush deepened. The mission on which he had been sent was obvious to all present, yet it went against the grain of an Englishman to have to come out and ask the help of upstart Americans.

As Truxton understood. But he understood much more than that. He gave another cough. 'There is some mystery here, Mr Crown, which I would appreciate your explaining to my officers and myself. You say you knew of the Frenchman's arrival in Fort Royal some days ago, and thus prudently postponed your departure. Yet now you have departed while he is still there and, indeed, his replenishment has no doubt been completed. Even to rendezvous with the Jamaica convoy that was a remarkable risk to take.'

'Well, sir . . .' Now Crown's face was almost purple.

'Or did you in fact have additional information,' Truxton suggested. 'From a fisherman, perhaps, bound for Castries, two days ago, with whom we spoke, and who therefore was able to tell you there was a United States ship on patrol in these waters? A ship which, her topsails sighted, your captain thought might make common cause against the French?'

Crown gazed at him with his mouth open, unable to think of a suitable rebuttal.

Truxton smiled. 'Your captain was mistaken, Mr Crown. I will not fight alongside a ship flying the flag of the Royal Navy. I fought against such ships for too long to change my principles now. But you have reminded me that it is my duty to seek out and destroy the enemies of my country wherever they may be, and in whatever strength. This I shall now do, acting upon your information. While I am doing so, I would recommend you escort your precious charges as rapidly as possible to Jamaica.'

Crown's face cleared. 'Sir, that is spoken like the man we knew you to be. We expected nothing more. We shall, of course, assist you.'

Truxton pointed. 'You will do no such thing, sir. We require the assistance of no Royal Navy ship. I will make this plain, Mr Crown. If you approach within gunshot while I am engaging the Frenchman, I will fire into you.'

Crown frowned at him. 'You will seek battle with a fifty-two-gun ship on your own?'

'Now that I know where he is to be found, sir, I shall certainly seek either to restrict him to his port or to damage him beyond his ability to harm the United States or her ships at sea. I will tell you, sir, that we had supposed the Royal Navy, indulging in its principle of close blockade of all French seaports, had rendered impossible the escape of any large French vessel from Europe. Now that I see we have been mistaken in that assumption, we must take steps to remedy your comrades' neglect.'

Crown's flush returned. 'Accidents do happen, Captain Truxton. Well, sir . . .' he stood up and saluted. 'I will report your intention to my captain.'

Truxton nodded. 'Do so, Mr Crown, and wish him good fortune.'

Crown looked from the captain to Rodgers to Toby to McDonough. 'You'll challenge a fifty-two-gun ship,' he remarked. 'Gentlemen, if I may say so without causing offence, you are mad, stark raving mad.' He saluted again and left the cabin.

'Fifty-two guns,' John Rodgers mused, watching the gig pulling into the side of the British frigate to be taken up. 'The young fellow could be right.'

'We'll not fight in harness with any Britisher,' Truxton growled. Like many American seamen, such as Harry McGann himself, he had once been impressed on board a Royal Navy ship, and bore no happy memories of the harsh discipline and inflexible rules he had experienced. 'And fifty-two guns, Mr Rodgers, even fifty-two guns, are only as powerful as the men who serve them. You'll make sail, Mr McGann. Course is east-north-east, for Fort Royal. We'll show ourselves, and the flag, and see if this Frenchman comes out.'

'Will I beat to quarters, sir?' Rodgers asked.

Truxton shook his head. 'You'll beat to dinner, Mr Rodgers. And join me for the meal. We won't come to blows for several hours yet.' He looked at the sun, which was just past noon high. 'Maybe not until dark. That might not be a bad thing.'

'Fifty-two guns,' Tom McDonough muttered, leaning on the rail to watch the mountains of Martinique looming against the darkening horizon, dominated, to the north of the island, by the active volcano of Mount Pelée, more than three thousand feet high. St Lucia was now on the starboard quarter, but both the islands were becoming indistinct as the sun sank in the west; they could already make out twinkling lights ashore. The afternoon rainsquall had long passed and the air was almost cool. Although there was no moon due, as was common in the Caribbean they could anticipate a clear, bright night.

'That'll be a big ship,' the midshipman mused.

9

'You heard the Britisher,' Toby said. 'She's a fourth-rate, fit to take her place in a line of battle.'

The navies of the world divided their vessels into two broad categories: those big enough and sufficiently well armed to fight in the line of battle, and thus known as line-of-battle ships, and those regarded as too small to take the battering of a fleet action, and therefore to be used for scouting and reconnaissance and patrol, and convoy duty – these included frigates such as the *Constellation*. Line-of-battle ships were further divided into rates. Thus the very largest warships, those carrying a hundred guns and more, were called first-rates; second-rates carried eighty-four guns or more; third-rates seventy or more, and fourth-rates fifty or more. Ships, such as the *Constellation*, carrying between thirty-two and fifty guns were called fifth-rates. Normally only those of the first three rates were ever included in a battle line, but it was not unknown for fourth-raters to be so used, and certainly no naval officer would doubt the superiority of a fourth-rate over a frigate.

'But you reckon we can beat her?' McDonough asked.

'I reckon the captain's right,' Toby said. 'A gun has only the strength of the man serving her, as a ship has only the purpose of the man in command. The French Navy is still suffering the effects of the revolution. They don't have many trained officers, and they have no traditions. Oh, aye, we'll beat her, if we're determined enough.'

Yet, for all his confident words, his heart pounded and the adrenalin flowed into his veins. They were accepting immense odds. And he knew, for all the gruff refusal of Truxton to help the British as an ally, that his captain certainly meant the convoy, and its passengers, to escape, by keeping himself between Martinique and the British ships until they were out of danger. Even if the Frenchman did not immediately come out, it might be a lengthy operation, for the British remained close at hand, as the wind had dropped with the dusk. The frigate, *Lancer*, had also moved to the east of her charges, placing herself between them and Fort Royal. Both warships had lit their stern lanterns, and others besides; if the Frenchman was going to come out, they each wanted him to know where they were. To the west, the three ships of the convoy were in darkness; the passengers on board would be praying they would pass unnoticed by the French.

Toby wondered what it must be like, to be in the position of Jonathan Crown, and know that he was not merely seeking to do his duty by his profession and for his country, but actually in defence of his own family. Would that strengthen, or weaken, a man? And to have that family on board one's very ship . . .

'There, Toby,' McDonough said, forgetting their respective ranks in his excitement. 'There!'

Toby levelled his telescope at the headland which protected the port of Fort Royal, and caught his breath. Even in the gloom of the dusk he could make out the tall masts and white canvas of the Frenchman, slowly coming into view. 'You'll inform the captain, Mr McDonough,' he said quietly.

Truxton was up a moment later, hat askew on his head, telescope levelled before he reached the rail. Across the water behind them they heard a drum roll; the British had also seen the enemy.

'He'd best not get in my way,' Truxton growled. 'You'll watch him, Mr McDonough; I meant what I said. Beat to quarters, Mr Rodgers. Shorten sail, Mr McGann, and come about on the port tack.'

'Aye-aye,' answered both officers, and went about their duties. McDonough remained on the quarterdeck to relay any additional orders his captain might need to give, while the junior midshipmen hurried about their gun duties on the main deck.

Toby had the topmasts sent down for stowage, the nets rigged at once to repel boarders and to catch falling spars. Under her working canvas alone the *Constellation* moved quietly across the water towards the Frenchman, who still carried all possible canvas in the fair offshore breeze. His intention was clear: to burst past the warships and reach the convoy.

Aboard the *Constellation* the drums began to beat, a sound always prone to quicken the blood, while the fife men were playing *Yankee Doodle Dandy* as the ports were dropped and the guns run out, sixteen thirty-two-pounders

11

to each broadside, all on the single main deck; the four long chasers were mounted two in the bows and two in the stern. Powder and ball were brought up from the orlop deck below the waterline and heaped beside each gun, while the gunners themselves, stripped to the waist and with bare feet to aid them to grip the deck when it became slippery with blood, their heads wrapped in bandannas to keep the sweat from their eyes, quipped and chatted as they prepared their deadly work.

The rest of the crew busied themselves with stacking muskets and cutlasses for use if it came to close work, and scattering sawdust over the deck to absorb any blood which might be spilt. This was the province of Mr Rodgers, who commanded the main deck during any action.

Toby made his way right forward to the forecastle, where the opening shots would be fired. Now the darkness was sweeping across the sea at increasing speed; the lights on Martinique gleamed ever more brightly, but those on the French ship had been doused as her captain had seen the United States ship making towards him. The range between the two vessels was perhaps four miles, and closing every second.

Tom McDonough joined Toby. 'The captain says to show him we mean business, Mr McGann,' he said, just the faintest of trembles affecting his voice. They had both taken part in the encounter with *L'Insurgente*, but that had been a year ago, and *L'Insurgente* had only carried forty guns, four more than the *Constellation*, to be sure – but a long way short of fifty-two.

'Raise your elevation,' Toby commanded.

The wheels were turned, and the long barrels of the culverins slowly crept towards the sky, while the frigate plunged onwards, close hauled now, spray breaking against the bows as they went down, and being thrown high into the air as the bowsprit came back up. Although the seas were gentle, it was still necessary to time the shot very accurately, or it would merely plunge harmlessly into the waves. Toby waited for one dip and rise to be completed, and then the next; behind him it seemed that the entire ship, giving off a demoniacal red glow from the battle lanterns strung fore and aft, also waited: even the fifers had ceased their tune.

On the top of the next surge he gave the command, 'Fire!'

The huge gun roared and leapt; she fired only a twenty-four-pound shot, as opposed to the heavier weight of the main armament, but she could throw that ball for twice the distance of the cannon. And in the darkness the watchers could clearly see the splash of white as the ball entered the sea, some quarter of a mile ahead of the Frenchman.

'Try again, Mr McGann,' Truxton's voice boomed; he was using a speaking trumpet.

The first gun was being reloaded; the second was ready. Again Toby chose his moment, and this one brought a cheer; it entered the sea much closer to its target and some of its spray clearly scattered across the French decks.

'Good shooting, Mr McGann,' Truxton called. 'Keep at her.'

Toby obeyed, but the French captain, realising he had a fight on his hands, was already altering course, to come directly towards his impudent opponent, and thus not only present less of a target but use his greater strength to its best advantage. Toby straddled the approaching giant with two more shots, and suffered several in return, but these were well wide.

'She must not pass us unscathed, Mr Rodgers,' Truxton called.

'Aye-aye,' Rodgers agreed, prowling up and down the deck between the two rows of cannon. Should the bigger, and therefore faster, ship get past them, they would hardly catch her again. They had to hit her, hard enough to cause some damage, and then outmanoeuvre her by superior sea-manship. But no one on the American frigate doubted their ability to do that.

'Stand by the guns,' came the order, and Toby left the chasers to go aft; the culverins would be of little value in the coming work, as they lacked the weight to smash stout timbers – that was the job of the main battery of carronades, 'smashers', they were called. His job now was to mount the horseblocks – little platforms let into the bulwarks on either side of the helm – and take over the responsibility both of conning the ship, as the helmsman could not of course see over the high rails and cluster of masts and sails, as well as keeping the sails filled, giving a quiet order to the attentive boatswain to harden a sheet whenever he saw the canvas flapping. Fighting an action was the reverse of ordinary sailing; in the latter, the ship was usually steered to gain the maximum value from wind and sails; in the former, the ship was placed where it could do most damage to the enemy and receive least damage itself, and it was the business of the sails, and those who manned them, to find the wind where they could.

'You'll fire as you bear, Mr Rodgers,' Truxton called, looking down on the waist.

'Aye-aye,' came the response.

'Bear away, if you please, Mr McGann,' Truxton said.

'Starboard your helm, coxswain,' Toby said. 'Free those sheets, Mr Barclay,' he called to the boatswain.

The *Constellation* swung to the south-east, away from the wind, and the sails, allowed to balloon by the freed sheets, filled and bulged as she gathered speed. The frigate crossed the bows of the Frenchman, now just a dark mass in the gloom, even as his chasers exploded again; he was so close that the flashes of light and the whistle of the balls seemed almost as one; there came a crack from above their heads and one of the mizzen spars crashed into the netting.

'Aloft there,' Toby snapped at his repair squad.

The seamen swarmed into the rigging to make the necessary running repairs.

'Fire!' John Rodgers called.

The ship exploded into smoke and flame, heeling even farther away from the wind before coming upright again.

'Bring her about, Mr McGann,' Truxton called. 'Bring her about.'

'Hard to port, coxswain,' Toby bawled. 'Hand those sheets now, smartly.'

Even before the smoke had cleared to let them see what damage they had done to *La Vengeance*, the *Constellation*, flawlessly handled, was coming about once more, intending again to cross the Frenchman's bows even at this close, and closing, range, and hit him again before he could bring his own broadsides to bear. And the main deck gunners were giving a cheer as, despite the gloom, they made out the

14

shattered bowsprit of their adversary. The Frenchman's fire was desultory, and the Americans delivered their starboard broadside as they surged past, within a hundred yards now, while the port guns were run in and reloaded.

At last the Frenchman came about, and the *Constellation* had to take his fire in return. Only some, because the Americans were again wearing ship with all the expertise of hours of practice, presenting the smallest of targets as they did so. Yet several of the huge balls smashed home, splintering the bulwarks and dismounting one gun while reducing its crew to so much carrion.

'Swab those decks.' Toby stepped down from the horse-block and went forward to supervise, instinctively ducking as another spar thudded into the netting immediately above his head. 'Easy, lad, easy.' He knelt beside a moaning seaman, whose right leg had been blown off at the thigh and who was clearly bleeding to death. 'Help is on its way.'

He assisted the orderlies to lift the dying man on to a stretcher, then wiped the back of his hand across his forehead as he stood straight. Even when faced with the horrible effects of being hit by a cannon ball, you still always felt, you knew, that it would be the next man to go down, never yourself, until the fatal moment. But what must it feel like to look down at your body, and know that however strongly your heart still beat, you were going to be dead in a matter of minutes?

At least the poor fellow would have felt no pain; the shock would have seen to that.

He returned aft.

'Hot work, Mr McGann,' Truxton said. 'Your father would have enjoyed it.'

'No doubt he would, sir,' Toby agreed. But he was happy enough that the old man was not here today, however often he had wished he could have sailed with him – because now it was hot work. The broadsides of the French vessel filled the night with flying ball, and although the American ship was far faster, and far better handled, delivering three broadsides to every one of her enemy's, she had yet to stay too close for comfort if she was to stand any chance of inflicting a mortal or even crippling blow.

But their first objective had been attained. The Frenchman was damaged, and more important, he wanted to settle this matter. The convoy should be safe by now. Toby cast a hasty glance to the west, and could see the lights of the British frigate, some distance away to be sure, acting as a second line of defence should the Frenchman break through, but obeying Truxton's command not to interfere, and beyond . . . the lights of the convoy. Because now they, too, had set lights, no doubt to inform their escort of where they were. But yet they hardly seemed to have moved in the light airs.

It was time to concentrate once again, as the *Constellation* delivered another broadside, to the accompaniment of cheers as *La Vengeance*'s mizzen mast trembled and then went by the board, crashing over the side in a welter of sails and cordage. Now the stars were gleaming in the cloudless sky, and visibility was quite good; the Americans could see the French seamen frantically trying to cut the encumbering wreckage free.

'We have him now,' Truxton shouted, slapping his thigh with delight.

'Will you board, Captain?' Midshipman McDonough asked eagerly.

'No, sir,' Truxton said. 'He'll have twice our numbers, and marines, too. No, sir, we must batter him into submission.'

Which was going to take time, Toby knew. There was a lot of fight left in the Frenchman yet. He watched men still hacking away the fallen mast and ropes, and the French guns were continuing to belch smoke and flame. As were the *Constellation*'s as round she came yet again. Toby ceased to be aware of the passage of time, as he gave the various changes of course to the helmsman, ordered the necessary adjustment of the sails time and again, sent repair parties fore and aft to cobble up the damage being done by the French shot. Balls whistled about his head, and twice men on the quarterdeck were hit, while the waist was a bloody swamp, and all the men he could spare from trimming the yards were hard at work carrying the wounded down to the sickbay where Dr Lamming would be waiting – what the cockpit was like did not bear consideration. But the firing never ceased, as they hammered the huge French ship again and again, sailing round and round her like a dog attacking a bear.

'Mr McGann, sir.' The boatswain stood to attention before the helm. 'The forestays are shot away. I've doubts about the mast, sir.'

'You go forward, Mr McGann,' Truxton said. 'I'll con her. Don't lose that mast.'

'Aye-aye,' Toby agreed, and accompanied the boatswain forward; the foremast was essential to manoeuvre the ship, especially to windward. Now it was necessary to pass between the gun batteries, keeping his footing with difficulty as he tried to avoid stepping on dead or dying men or slipping in their blood, while there was a continuous cloud of heavy white smoke swirling about his head to make breathing difficult. The guns slid back and forth on their restraining cables as they were fired, recoiled and reloaded, and the noise was an unending peal of thunder, through which the cries and curses of the men could dimly be heard.

He gasped with relief when he emerged on to the foredeck, and could look up at the mast, which was indeed swaying dangerously as it lacked all support, and still carried the weight of the sail and the jibs; indeed, the fore halliards were acting as auxiliary stays to keep the mast up, but the next time the ship went about and the wind came from aft, the timber would undoubtedly snap.

'She'll not hold for long without guying, Mr McGann,' the boatswain said, confirming his opinion.

Toby nodded. 'I'll inform the Captain,' he said. It was not an order he dared give himself in the midst of battle, to take all the foresails off the ship. He hurried aft, listening to an immense cheer, blinked into the darkness as he gained the quarterdeck, and saw that the Frenchman's mainmast has also gone; she was down to foremast only, and in addition there were several fires burning on her deck.

'She'll not escape,' Truxton said, snapping his fingers with satisfaction. 'Damage, Mr McGann?'

'The foremast will not carry sail before the wind, until we've rigged some fresh stays, sir.'

Truxton considered for a moment, then nodded. 'Very

17

good, Mr McGann. Hand your foresails and make your repairs. Smartly, now.'

'Aye-aye.' Toby went forward again, but had not yet reached the forecastle when he heard the cry, 'Cease firing,' from aft. He jumped on the bulwark the better to see, and saw a lantern being waved to and fro on board the Frenchman, not a hundred yards away: *La Vengeance* also had ceased firing.

'Ahoy, USS *Constellation*,' came the call over the water, the accented English booming through the speaking trumpet. 'We 'ave struck our flag, sir. You are too quick for us.'

An enormous burst of cheering rose from the deck of the *Constellation*.

Toby leapt down from his perch and continued forward. 'Get sail off her, Mr Barclay,' he told the boatswain. 'And smartly. Retain one jib as a support until we can rig some jury stays.'

'Aye-aye,' Barclay acknowledged. 'Aloft there, lads,' he told the seamen he had assembled. 'Carry those lines up. Haste, before she goes.'

'Heave to,' Truxton was calling form aft. 'You'll accept a boarding party, *La Vengeance*. Any treachery, *monsieur*, and I will resume firing.'

'We 'ave surrendered,' the French spokesman replied with dignity.

'Break out a boat, Mr Rodgers,' Truxton commanded. He still would not risk going alongside the larger and more heavily manned vessel until she had been totally disarmed. 'Muskets, pistols, and cutlasses. And remember that we will be covering you.'

'Aye-aye,' Rodgers acknowledged, and issued the necessary orders.

'Christ!' Barclay muttered.

Toby felt the breeze at the same instant, blowing on the back of his neck as he gazed up at the foremast. 'Oh, damnation,' he cried.

For the helmsman had allowed the *Constellation* to turn too far away from the wind, and it was filling the foresails from aft; and none of the auxiliary stays had yet been secured.

'She's going!' Barclay bawled.

From above Toby's head there came an enormous crack, and then a splintering sound. The seamen, swarming up the rigging, were thrown left and right as the mast snapped, well below the first cross trees, and went crashing forward, carrying sails and stays and men with it.

'Fetch those men back,' Toby shouted. 'Axes, Mr Barclay, we must cut her free.'

For a moment following the collapse of the foremast there was almost silence, the crew of both ships being bemused by this sudden change of fortune. Then it was the French turn to cheer.

'God damn and blast the treacherous rogues,' Truxton bellowed. 'They are reneging.'

Toby looked across the chaos on his own foredeck to that of the enemy; the Frenchmen were hastily resetting their foresails.

'Abandon that boat, Mr Rodgers,' Truxton called. 'Recommence firing.'

'Aye-aye.' Rodgers called his gunners back to work. But where the *Constellation* could no longer work to windward without her jibs, the French, having only such sails, could, and was now steadily drawing forward. Nor could Toby load and aim the chasers, covered as they were in the debris of the fallen mast.

'Wear ship,' Truxton shouted. 'All hands wear ship. We'll give him a broadside. By God, we'll have him yet.'

But all the manoeuvrability which had been the American's great strength was gone. By the time they had come around to deliver a broadside, *La Vengeance* was two thousand yards away, and escaping every moment. Yet she was escaping. She was running from a ship not much more than half her size. The Americans had won a clearcut victory, even if they had not been able to take possession of their prize.

Truxton himself came forward to inspect the damage, and to stare after the disappearing enemy. 'Treacherous rogues,' he growled. 'Damned Jacobins, I'll be bound. Well, Mr McGann, what are you standing about for? I want a jury rig, and fast.'

It was dawn by the time Toby's crew had managed to cut away the last of the wreckage and bind a spar firmly enough to the stump of the foremast to take at least a single sail and restore, in some measure, the *Constellation*'s windward capacity. By then he, and all his men, were grey-faced and exhausted, and even then there could be no rest, as they assembled in the waist to attend the service, read by the captain, and watched the dozen men killed by the French shot being sent over the side, their weighted bodies slipping out from beneath the flag-shrouded biers to plunge into the clear blue waters and slowly sink from sight.

Yet already the ship had been largely put to rights, the decks swabbed clean of blood, the carpenters patching the various shot scars on the bulwarks, the sailmakers stitching away at the torn canvas. And the guns remained run out; they were still only a few miles off Martinique, although during the battle they had drifted north and were by now almost as close to the mountains of Dominica, there was still a chance the Frenchman might return. But he had made back to the safety of Fort Royal, to lick his wounds. He had had enough.

'Permission to come aboard, sir,' came the cry.

They had been so busy they had not noticed the approach of the *Lancer*, which had again put down a boat.

'What does he want?' Truxton growled, looking down at the British sailors. 'We have a deal to do, sir.'

'My captain but wishes to offer his congratulations, Captain Truxton,' Lieutenant Crown called. 'We have seldom witnessed a braver fight against odds, nor a more successful one. Had you been prepared to accept our help we'd have got him.'

'Or blown each other to bits,' Truxton said. 'But I thank you, sir. We would have had him but for an unlucky stroke.'

'Acknowledged, sir. My captain would take it most kindly if you and your officers would breakfast with us.'

'Breakfast, by God,' Truxton muttered. Then his face broke into a grin as he looked at Rodgers and Toby. 'Why not?' He knew he had won a remarkable victory. Outgunned by sixteen cannon he had yet to all intents and purposes captured the Frenchman, as he had certainly outsailed and outfought him. Had that foremast snapped but a few minutes later, or had the French captain been more punctilious and less revolutionary, *La Vengeance* would even now be flying the American flag. And the British were witnesses to the deed. More important, they could be of value. 'Aye, Mr Crown,' he said, 'it will be a pleasure. If you will share some of your fresh provisions with my crew.'

'That, sir, will be our pleasure,' Crown replied.

'Then you may expect us in half an hour,' Truxton said.

Rodgers and Toby tossed a coin, and Toby won. He was not sure he was pleased about that. For all his experience, it was still not sufficient for him to enjoy being alive on the morning after so many brave men had died, or been wounded or maimed; their cries continued to rise from the cockpit, where Dr Lamming was still hard at work. In addition, he was as exhausted as any other member of the crew. But it was necessary to match the British insouciance, and so he shaved and washed the battle grime from his face, donned his spare uniform, made sure his sword hilt was adequately polished, and joined Truxton and Midshipman McDonough in the waist, where eight smartly dressed seamen were already manning the captain's gig.

Like the *Constellation*, the *Lancer* was hove to, nodding in the low seas and gentle morning breeze provided by the protection of Dominica. Obviously they could clearly be overseen from the Martinique to the south. But equally obviously the crew of *La Vengeance*, even had they been able to effect repairs by now, would have to reckon that the two Anglo-Saxon ships might well fight together the next time around, so there was little danger from that quarter.

Toby found himself staring at the tumbled peaks of Dominica, the last Caribbean stronghold of the still-feared Carib Indians. The *Constellation* had passed this way before, several times during her two tours of duty in this sea, and his nerves had never failed to tingle at the sight of those green-clad mountains. His father had been shipwrecked on that island, had spent a year living with the cannibals in the shadow of the Boiling Lake, as they called their active volcano, at the end of the famous Valley of Desolation. By his size and strength and vigour, as much as by his intelligence, Harry McGann had become one of their leaders, rather than one of their breakfasts.

Toby wondered if the Caribs had listened to last night's cannonade. But that was a sound and a spectacle they must be getting used to; just north of Dominica, for instance, had been the scene of one of England's greatest naval victories, over the French during the War of the Revolution.

He took his place beside Truxton on the transom as they were rowed towards the Royal Navy ship. The British gig had been taken up, and a petty officer stood in the bows to oversee their approach. 'Who comes there?' he called.

Truxton smiled. He had not served in the Royal Navy for nothing, and had no intention of being caught out by British etiquette. 'Reply, *Constellation*, Mr McGann,' he said in a low voice.

'USS *Constellation*,' Toby replied. He also had been taught naval etiquette, by his father. The reply, 'Aye-aye,' would have indicated that although there was an officer on board, he was not a ship's captain; 'No-no,' would have meant there was no commissioned rank on board at all; and 'Flag' would have indicated the presence of an admiral. But there were no admirals in the United States Navy, and the name of the ship conveyed the information that the captain himself was present.

As the British understood. Whistles cooeed, and there was a guard of honour of red-jacketed and tall-hatted marines drawn up for them to inspect as they went on board.

The three officers saluted the quarterdeck, and then the short, brisk little man who was awaiting them. 'Captain Truxton,' he said. 'William Phips, at your service, sir. And may I be the first to congratulate you on a most brilliant action.'

'We were unlucky, Captain Phips,' Truxton said.

'Oh, aye, but not so unlucky as that Froggie, eh, in catching such a tartar when he must have supposed himself on the verge of an easy victory. Oh, aye, this'll make splendid gossip in Kingston, that it will. Now, sir, I'd have you meet my old friend Charles Crown, and his wife Julia; you already met their son, my first lieutenant.'

Truxton saluted the civilians, and presented his officers in turn. The Crowns were very obviously the parents of the lieutenant, tall, thin, and sharp-featured.

'And their daughter, Miss Felicity Crown.'

'I am charmed,' Truxton said, again raising his hat.

While Toby felt quite bemused, and suddenly more awake than for some time. Undoubtedly the girl was the daughter of the two people he had just met, and the sister of the lieutenant: she was tall and slender. But on her the suggestion of gauntness which shrouded the other members of the family was absent, and her face, far from being of the hatchet variety, was full-cheeked and red-lipped, although she certainly had somewhat aquiline features, which in repose might be a trifle severe. But when, as now, she was smiling, the wide mouth, longish nose, and pointed chin came together to make a most attractive picture. Her eyes were grey and cool, her hair a deep brown and straight and, as it was at present undressed, lay like a shawl beyond her shoulders. She wore a muslin day gown, with but a single chemise beneath, he was sure, and although manners forbade more than a glance in that direction, he was equally sure she possessed a figure to match her face.

'You'll take a glass,' Phips was saying, and Toby discovered that a marine steward was standing at his elbow with a tray of glasses. 'Rum punch, sir,' Phips explained. 'Rum punch. Nothing like it for warming the blood.'

Toby looked at McDonough, who looked at him, and then they both looked at Truxton, who had gone red in the face.

'Harrumph,' remarked the captain. 'Well ... on this occasion, gentlemen. But remember that we have a great deal of work to do.'

'Ha ha,' Phips said. 'I had forgotten that strong liquors are not permitted on board United States' ships. But you are my guests, gentlemen. My guests. And now to breakfast.'

Or luncheon, or dinner, Toby supposed; it was only a name. As Truxton had surmised, unlike the *Constellation*, several weeks at sea with few friendly harbours into which she could put for provisions, the *Lancer* had just departed a British port. Here was succulent fresh pork, or as an alternative, equally fresh chicken; here were yams and sweet potatoes, dug but two days earlier; here were okras and pumpkins, fresh as daisies. And here were mangoes and pawpaws, without a bruise or a discolouration. And here, too, continu-

23

ously served, were the glasses of the heady brown punch, in which floated slices of oranges and tangerines. All the goodness of the Caribbean, accumulated beneath an awning on the quarterdeck of the *Lancer*.

Toby used his rank to have himself seated next to Felicity Crown, McDonough having to be content with a place opposite.

'I had never seen a battle at sea before last night,' Miss Crown confessed, smiling at each young man in turn. 'It was perfectly dreadful. And yet, somehow splendid as well. I will admit I did not retire all night, but remained on deck to watch.'

'We are very flattered, Miss Crown,' Toby said. 'And may I say that your summation, dreadful but splendid, is admirably accurate.'

'It must have been horrible to experience, though, and terrifying.'

'I guess we were too busy to notice,' he said. 'And I suspect it was more horrible and terrifying for the French.'

She gave a mock shudder. 'You men can joke about it. We women find that impossible.' She sighed. 'It seems that we have been at war almost since I can remember. Certainly since I was ten years old.'

Toby gazed at McDonough, aware that each of them was making the same rapid mental calculation. Great Britain and France had gone to war in 1793: she was seventeen years old. Old enough to be betrothed or even married. But the absence of any rings on her straight white fingers proscribed that. And was it any business of his?

He thought it would be very pleasant if it was.

'And now that Bonaparte has seized power, there is no saying where it will end,' Felicity continued, revealing a seriousness unusual in one so young. 'They say his ambition is to conquer all Europe.'

'And Great Britain will continue to oppose him?' McDonough asked.

'Of course,' she replied, without hesitation.

'Will you be accompanying your father to Gibraltar?' Toby asked.

'Of course,' she said again. 'Should I not?'

24

'It is just that I would have supposed Gibraltar, the gateway to the Mediterranean, would be in the very thick of the struggle.'

'Why, so it is, Mr McGann,' she replied. 'But those are naval affairs.' She gazed at him. 'Will your duties ever take *you* to the Mediterranean?' Suddenly her cheeks were pink at her own boldness.

'Now that I doubt, Miss Crown. We have no part to play in opposing France's ambitions, so long as they do not extend up the Delaware or the Hudson, to be sure. It is the avowed intention of my country to turn its back on the squabbles of the Old World.'

'Squabbles you call them.' Her flush faded and her grey eyes struck sparks. 'It is the life of our nation, sir.'

'Then I apologise. But still, it can be no quarrel of ours.'

She nodded. 'I understand that. Yet you are fighting the French.'

'That is a private matter, between our two countries, which will hopefully soon be resolved.'

As she continued to gaze at him, and as McDonough had been distracted by the English midshipman seated beside him, he ventured on a mild flirtation. 'But I would like to make you this solemn promise, Miss Crown, if you will not take offence: should my duties ever take me to Gibraltar, or anywhere else that your father may be stationed, I should like to call ... upon your family. With your permission, of course.'

She did not reply for a moment, although she did not lower her eyes, either. Then she said, 'Why, Mr McGann, I shall look forward to that day. Very much.'

Their eyes held each other's for several seconds; it was a moment when they could either go forward, perhaps faster than either wished or had intended, or could withdraw entirely from the situation. But before either of them could come to a decision, the meal had ended.

'We shall sail in your company,' Phips was declaring. 'At least as far as Jamaica. Although there are no worlds left for you to conquer.'

'There is always the sea, Captain Phips,' Truxton said. 'But it will be our pleasure, sir. Then we had best make haste, before the weather changes and we lose that jury mast all over again. Gentlemen. Ladies.' He stood up. 'My officers and myself thank you for your hospitality.'

Toby hung back as they moved towards the ladder leading down to the waist. 'Until our next meeting, Miss Crown. Because it will happen.'

Felicity, gazing straight ahead, turned her head sharply. 'Why, Mr McGann, I never doubted that for a moment.'

'And the jury mast held until Norfolk?' Harry McGann asked.

'Just,' Toby confessed. 'We nearly lost it in a blow in the Florida Strait, but we shored it up.'

'Good work,' Harry said. 'Good work. But your entire tour of duty was good work. How I wish I could have been there.'

He sat on the porch of his house on Long Island, and looked out at the rolling acres of farmland he had cleared with his close friend John Palmer, and then ploughed and planted. John Palmer was dead now, but his son, who was married to Harry McGann's sister, Toby's Aunt Jennie, had proved as good a friend and neighbour, and business partner, as his father.

Yet for all that Harry appeared, and pretended, to have found what he really wanted from life, here in the utter peace and tranquillity of his island home, Toby knew how much he missed the sea. Harry McGann was only just fifty-one years old, a mountain of a man who looked as fit as anyone half his age, save for the shattered leg which trailed behind him as he walked, and was now propped before him on its special stool. That leg had been the result of a duel with a man he had hated throughout his adult life, and it had ended his naval career. Otherwise he might have commanded the USS *Constellation*, instead of his erstwhile first lieutenant.

'And how glad we are that you are home safe and sound, Toby,' remarked Elizabeth McGann, drying her hands on her apron as she joined the men on the porch. Elizabeth remained as beautiful a woman as she had been a girl, thirty years previously, when she had first encountered Harry

McGann. She stood straight, somewhat above average height, with a handsome face and clear blue eyes, a full figure and the most glorious yellow hair, although this was concealed beneath a bandanna – however well she could afford to employ several servants, she still did much of the work about the house herself. And she still looked at her husband with utter devotion and contentment; no one could doubt that she counted that pistol ball a fortunate event, as it had kept Harry home and free from danger. But Toby was her only son, and every time he went to sea she counted the days. Yet she had never attempted to interfere with his choice of career; she knew how much salt water there was in the veins of any McGann.

Theirs had been a strange romance and an unlikely one, possible perhaps only in the turmoil of a revolution. Harry McGann had been nothing more than an innkeeper's son who had made his living by smuggling French wines and perfumes for the benefit of the Irish gentry; Elizabeth Bartlett had been the daughter of one of New York's most prominent merchants. But the War of Independence which had ruined Bartlett's business – he had also been a prominent Tory – had at the same time raised Harry McGann, in the company of his great, and now mourned, friend John Paul Jones, to the level of a national hero, holder of a gold medal presented by Congress, and given him the prosperity he now enjoyed.

It was a solid, unchanging prosperity, except that it grew with the years. The old timber house he had built with his own hands had been extended, by means of wings and upper floors, into a rather ramshackle colonial mansion; the original dozen heifers had grown into a milch herd of over a hundred; there were chickens in the runs and pigs in the pens, just as there were fish in the streams and abounding in the Sound, only a few miles distant. There were several acres under wheat, as well as a vast apple orchard, and barrels of cider in season as well as the home brewed barley whisky. And there was New York, seeming itself to grow every day, to provide a market for the McGann and Palmer surplus produce, from which was found the cash for Elizabeth and Jennie's ribbons and furbelows, for the powder and shot for the men's muskets, for the occasional luxury – and to finance Toby into the Navy. However he might regret the abrupt termination of his naval career, Harry McGann had accomplished more solidity than most men.

Yet it had been hardly won. Although he had recognised his love for Elizabeth almost from the moment of their first meeting, more than thirty years before, the course of their romance had by no means run smoothly, Toby knew. He had himself been born out of wedlock, while his mother had been another man's wife – although there had never been any doubt in anyone's mind whose son he was – and it had taken some twelve years for them to reach the tranquillity of Long Island, together.

Toby bore no grudge for his bastardy. That had long since been set right. Indeed, he envied his parents the adventures, and misadventures, of their youths, and wondered if his own romantic career would be as uncertain – and would have as happy an ending. Whenever it commenced. It had not, so far; joining the Navy as he had done at the age of sixteen, there had been no time for the ladies, especially as he had shortly been pitchforked into the middle of a war. But in fact, he had never had the inclination.

Until now? No doubt it had been the aftermath of the battle, when his emotions had still been as tight as a bowstring, and the rum punches had been playing tricks on his overtired brain – but Felicity Crown had affected him most strangely. He could not get the image of her out of his mind, nor the strange conviction that they would one day meet again.

'And you say the British offered you hospitality?' Harry's tone was sceptical. But then, the old enemy whose pistol shot had shattered his leg had been a Royal Navy officer, quite apart from the year he had spent as an impressed man.

'Indeed they did, most generously,' Toby said. 'As well as supplying our company with much fresh fruit and vegetables. Of course, they were grateful. Without us, they'd have scarcely got past Martinique.'

'But they'd not assist you in the battle itself.'

'Well, that was Uncle Tom Truxton's decision, Pa,' Toby protested.

'Ha!' Harry commented.

Toby bit his lip. He had, of course, told his parents nothing about Felicity Crown. Ma might sympathise, but she was inclined to keep her opinions to herself where the English were concerned, and Pa had a deep-seated hatred of anything to do with England, saving the woman he had loved and married. Apart from his own experiences, it had been an English order that had caused the hanging of his father. Toby could not quarrel with that point of view, even if he regretted it. There was good and bad in every nation, and he did not think he felt that way about the English merely because he was half English himself. Besides, none of them was English, or Irish, anymore: they were Americans. Pa should remember that.

But he'd never quarrel with his father. And in truth, his irritation was only on Felicity's account. Senselessly. Why cause friction over a woman he'd probably never see again? He was well aware that his promise to her had been nothing more than fine words; he was a serving officer, and his life would be spent going where his ship was ordered, not where he personally might have chosen.

'There's a gentleman approaching, Captain McGann,' said the hired hand, standing hat in hand at the foot of the steps; his employees always gave Harry the courtesy title.

Now he shaded his eyes to look at the horseman walking his mount up the drive, somewhat cautiously, clearly happier on the deck of a ship than the back of a moving animal. 'Tom Truxton, by God!' he shouted, and heaved himself to his feet.

Truxton dismounted, rubbed his backside, shook hands with his old friend, kissed Elizabeth, slapped Toby on the shoulder, and smiled at them grimly.

'You look like a man carrying a burden of news,' Harry said. 'But also on holiday?' He frowned; Truxton was not wearing uniform.

'Aye, well . . .' Truxton sat down, extended his long legs, accepted a glass of whisky from Elizabeth. 'I've news, certainly. The war's done.'

'Now there's good news,' Harry said. 'It should never have begun.'

'I'd not argue with that.'

'But . . .' Toby bit his lip as the older men looked at him. 'Do you mean the war between France and England is done as well?'

'Lord, no, lad. They'll never stop fighting. They never have in the past. No, just our little quarrel has been patched up.'

'Little quarrel.' Harry observed. 'It was big enough to bring you all the fame a man could wish. Two victories over superior ships? There's immortality.'

'And for my crew,' Truxton reminded him. 'Toby here . . . he's a fine career ahead of him. Mine has ended.'

'What did you say?' Harry and Toby spoke together.

'I have resigned my commission.'

'But why?' Harry demanded.

'Ah, 'tis the way Congress and the Navy Board handles its affairs,' Truxton told him. 'But they are the nation's affairs as well. The moment the war with France was done, it was decided, Adams decided, but he'll have been stirred by Jefferson, there's no doubt about that, he decided to do something about Tripoli. You'll have heard of it?'

'About Tripoli?' Harry asked. 'Some.'

'What is Tripoli?' Elizabeth asked.

'It's one of the Barbary states,' Harry explained. 'You know, all those little city states along the north coast of Africa, what they call the Barbary Coast. There are several of them: Algiers, Tunis, and Tripoli as well, to be sure, as well as others inland. They are nominally parts of the Turkish Empire, and own allegiance to the Sultan, but they are in reality all but independent.'

'Their rulers call themselves deys,' Truxton told her. 'And the ones on the coast are a right load of pirates. Have been for generations. Algiers was always the worst. But it seems a couple of years ago there was some kind of revolution in Tripoli, and the Dey, Hamet Karamanli, with whom we have always got on very well, was chased from his throne, and replaced by a total ruffian, who since then has been capturing every American vessel he can lay hands on, and imprisoning the crews. You'll recall that it was part of Jefferson's election manifesto to demand a cessation of these attacks, and a return of all enslaved Americans. Well, as he won't be inaugurated until next March, Adams is doing the job for him meantime, and you know what? This dey has actually had the temerity to demand that we pay him an annual tribute. If we do that, he says, he'll leave the Stars and Stripes alone. Imagine it, the United States of America paying tribute to some tinpot pirate. The President means to refuse, of course. But he considers it best to have some strength actually in the Mediterranean to look after our interests.'

'So he's sending a squadron,' Toby cried, hardly able to believe his good fortune.

'That is the intention, to be sure.'

'Under whose command? Yours, of course,' Harry said. 'But you say . . .'

'I resigned my command. They would give me Barron as my flag captain. I'd not have it. I wanted Decatur. They'd not budge. So there it is.'

'But . . . surely there was no need to resign?' Harry was aghast.

'I lost my temper.'

Harry sighed. Whatever the fighting qualities of this new American Navy, he was well aware that its chances of success were always at risk because of the quick-temperedness and independence of its captains. Tom Truxton clearly understood the need, and approved the concept, of taking action against the pirate fleets, yet he would not take the command except with officers of whom he personally approved. 'So who will command?'

'Why, they have said Barron.'

'Ah,' Harry commented. 'I've heard it said he's a good man.'

'When driven to it,' Truxton growled. 'Anyway, there it is. Toby, I've secured you a position, second lieutenant on the *Essex*. She's Barron's flagship.'

'Oh!' Toby cried, mind spinning.

'You're to report next week.'

'The Mediterranean!' Elizabeth said. 'A long way away.'

'But only to teach a handful of pirates a lesson,' Harry said. 'The boy can come to no harm there. It'll be a holiday.'

31

The Mediterranean, Toby thought. Gibraltar! That was a singular turn of events. 'But . . . I had hoped to sail with you, Uncle Tom.'

'You'll not do that again,' Truxton said. 'I've a mind to follow your father's example, and turn my hand to the plough. 'Tis what the Good Book recommends, to be sure. But it's been a pleasure having you aboard, Toby. A real pleasure. Now mind you go straight to the top. There's no reason at all why you should not. You have the courage and the determination, and the skill. All you need now is the experience, and the opportunity to show your worth. This campaign could give you that opportunity.'

'Amen!' Harry McGann agreed.

In the Mediterranean, Toby thought. Only fighting pirates, to be sure. But, in the Mediterranean!

Chapter 2

The Atlantic – 1801

The Atlantic! This was truly the ocean on which to sail, Toby thought. It was the ocean on which his father had learned his trade, and across which he had sailed to find his home in the Americas. Now, as Toby gazed at the rainswept northern horizon, he almost felt he could see the green hills of Ireland: they were only a few hundred miles away.

He had never visited the country of his forebears. Or England, his actual birthplace. Perhaps, being stationed in Europe, it could be possible . . . but a glance at the map had told him it was a very long way away from Sicily, which he gathered was to be the American squadron's main base of operations – both because the Kingdom of Naples was one of the few European countries prepared to offer them facilities and because Sicily was situated immediately north of Tripoli itself – to Ireland. Yet it was a distance which had been traversed often enough by the very Barbary corsairs it was their duty to overawe and, if necessary, chastise.

He frowned at the distant sail, appearing and disappearing through the rain mist, and perhaps five miles away. Could they have encountered their first pirate? But that was wishful thinking. The Barbary pirates had certainly raided the coasts of England and Ireland in the past, but that had been before England's Navy had reached its present enormous strength and reputation. Nowadays, if the corsairs ventured into the Atlantic at all, it was to harry the coasting trade of Spain and Portugal, and the only British ships they would dare to assault would be those isolated by weather or circumstance.

But if it could be an enemy, over there . . . the *Essex* was a fine ship, commissioned a year after the *Constellation*, but built to the same general design. And her crew were nearly all veterans of the French war, during which, under the command of Edward Preble, she had been the first American warship to round the Cape of Good Hope. While not a mile away to the south, her sister, the USS *President*, also rode the waves. Together they'd be a match for any pirate, or fleet of pirates, Toby thought.

Nor could he find much fault in his new Captain, however prepared he had been to be critical in the beginning. James Barron was no Thomas Truxton. He was a younger man, and lacked Truxton's experience, and Toby could well understand Truxton's being unable to appreciate Barron's more relaxed, easy-going style of leadership. But he had earned considerable distinction as first lieutenant of the USS *United States* during the French war, under the captaincy of John Barry, the most senior of all serving American naval officers, and it had been Barry himself who had recommended Barron for promotion. Toby did not doubt he would give a good account of himself when called upon to do so.

He was on deck now, a short, stout man with red cheeks, looking almost bearlike in his heavy oilskin coat and hat, off which the drizzle dripped. 'What do you make of her, Mr McGann? What do you make of her?'

'I would say she's a Britisher, sir,' Toby replied. He had already studied the approaching ship for some time through his glass, noting her lines even as he had allowed his imagination to roam.

'Aye, that would be right. On convoy duty. There are several behind.'

Toby brought up his glass again; his captain had keener eyes than he had supposed, keener indeed than the look-out who was only now reporting the approaching ships.

'Shall we close them, sir?' Toby asked.

Barron shook his head. 'We'll alter course to keep our distance, Mr McGann. We've no business with them. Our first destination is Gibraltar, for water and fresh provisions.

We'll likely see those very ships there; they can hardly be bound anywhere else.'

Gibraltar, Toby thought. It was less than a week away, if the wind held. In fact, thoughts of the famous rock had loomed much larger in his mind than any of Ireland or England during the Atlantic crossing, and now the sight of the sails of a convoy brought back that day, over a year ago now, after the fight with *La Vengeance*. There had been times he had desperately wished he could get Felicity Crown out of his mind; there were others when he wanted to think of no one, and nothing, else. And she would be in Gibraltar.

Would she be in Gibraltar? Well, surely her father still would be. He could only have taken up his position towards the end of last year, and he was a government servant, who would be stationed in each post for some time. But would *she* be there? She would be eighteen by now. More beautiful than he even remembered, perhaps. And if she had not been betrothed a year ago, that would surely have been because there had been no eligible young men in St Lucia. But once she had got back to England ... oh, by now she would certainly be at least betrothed, if not already married. There was gloom.

And what would he do, supposing she were not either betrothed or married? He was only just coming up to twenty-one himself, and was, besides, a sailor. He did not suppose the meagreness of his pay would present a problem. Once Ma approved, as she certainly would of such a girl, he need have no worries on that score: Ma would be able to persuade Pa to accept her, he was sure. But would Felicity wish to remove herself to the United States, still regarded in some English quarters as a revolted colony ... especially when he would be away so much of the time?

And besides, he reminded himself, his mother's English caution attempting to dominate his father's Irish romanticism, he hardly knew the girl. Indeed, he did not know her at all; he had met her but once, and then for an hour, and in most unusual circumstances. He *was* a romantic, and that was no way to approach the most serious business in life: marriage.

'Besides,' Captain Barron remarked, as the rain stopped

35

and a patch of blue sky appeared in the grey mass above them, even as a puff of wind filled their sails with unexpected energy, 'we'll have other things on our minds for a day or two, Mr McGann. Rain before wind means a blow, in my experience. You'll call up the watch below to shorten sail.'

'Ships!' cried Mistress Flemming. 'Oh, Captain, do let me see.' She waddled to the rail, scattering raindrops from her cloak and hat. 'Are they French, do you suppose? Will there be a battle?'

Captain Brathwaite willingly gave his telescope to the stout woman, and looked over her head to waggle his eyebrows at Felicity Crown. She was his favourite passenger, not only because she was the prettiest of the half dozen women on board this ship, and not even because it was her father he would have to deal with when the convoy reached Gibraltar, in order to get his papers cleared and a place in a fresh convoy allotted before he would dare venture into the war-torn Mediterranean Sea. Mainly it was because she was an experienced sailor, who had crossed the Atlantic – and who had also witnessed a battle at sea, even if from the point of view of a spectator.

But Mistress Flemming was chaperone to the girls, and had to be humoured. 'I doubt there will be a battle, madam,' the captain said. 'We are too strongly escorted. And in any event, those ships are flying the American flag.'

'Are they?' Felicity cried, suddenly interested.

'As far as I can make out, Miss Crown.'

'May I borrow your glass, Mrs Flemming?' Felicity asked.

Somewhat reluctantly, Mrs Flemming handed over the telescope. 'Of course,' she remarked, 'you have lived in America.'

'Not exactly,' Felicity said, levelling the glass. 'But I have seen American ships before.' She gazed at the two frigates, which were proceeding on a course very nearly parallel with their own. She did not think either of them was the *Constellation*, which was irrelevant, as there was little probability that Toby McGann would still be serving on the same ship as a year ago. So then ... but the odds on Toby

McGann being in the same few square miles of water as herself for a second time were extremely remote.

Yet that she should still be thinking of him ... undoubtedly the circumstances had been very strange. She had stayed up all that night, a year ago, watching men fighting for their lives. And then had actually met one of those men, unharmed, and looking for all the world as if he had just left his tailor. He had been taken with her, she knew; she still flushed as she recalled his words. She had not taken his promise very seriously, although she had thought how nice it would be if he could ever appear in Gibraltar. And then had been convinced it would never happen, especially when the illness she had contracted in England had forced her to remain behind there for several months after her parents' departure.

But now, actually to see American ships steering for the Rock, or at least the Strait of Gibraltar; they could be going nowhere else, on that course. And surely they would need to stop for water and fresh provisions, after having crossed the Atlantic. She was so excited she had to bite her lip.

'Whatever can they be at?' she asked the captain, returning the glass to Mrs Flemming so that the older woman would not notice her agitation.

'They are probably going to show the flag off the north African coast,' Brathwaite told her. 'And try to convince the Barbary pirates to cease interfering with American vessels. What with both the British and French Navies entirely occupied with fighting each other these past eight years, those Moorish scoundrels have been growing very bold. It is something to which we shall have to address ourselves before too long. Oh, yes. We shall have to bring a few of their castles tumbling about their ears.'

He was a fire-eater, who regarded the Royal Navy as the panacea for all the ills that beset the world. Nor would she argue that point. Which meant, as the convoy was under the escort of five warships, including a ship of the line on her way to join Admiral Cornwallis's squadron blockading the Spanish port of Cadiz, that as Brathwaite had said earlier, there was no risk of even a French privateer attacking them, much less any Barbary pirate who happened to have passed the Strait.

She turned away from the rail, and reseated herself in her chair on the afterdeck, alongside Mrs Flemming's daughter Margaret, a young lady no older than herself, although as she took after her mother and was thus short and plump, as well as possessing a head of brilliant yellow hair, as opposed to Felicity's brown, the contrast between them was considerable. Yet they had become friends through force of circumstances, even had they not been the only two girls on board.

The chair was still very wet, although the rain appeared to be stopping, but even wet chairs on deck were preferable to being cooped up in the stuffy, crowded cabin of the brig.

'Do you know anyone on board those American ships?' Margaret asked.

'How on earth could I do that?' Felicity demanded.

'Well ... I thought you had met some American naval officers once.'

'Oh, good Lord,' Felicity said, 'so I did. But there are hundreds of American naval officers.' Or were there? She frowned. Her brother Jonathan had told her the entire American Navy only consisted of half a dozen not very large ships. That meant there could hardly be more than fifty American officers currently serving. Of whom perhaps twelve were just over there, on one or other of the two ships. Toby McGann could very well be included in those short odds. She almost went back to the rail to borrow the telescope again. But even with a telescope she would not be able to make out the faces on board the distant ships, and she did not want either of the Flemmings to think her the least interested – because surely they were all bound for Gibraltar, and would meet there. When she would at last be free of this constant prying supervision?

The Flemmings were inclined to be busybodies. Mr Flemming was also on board, on his way to Gibraltar and thence Malta, where he was intending to take advantage of the British occupation of that island to set up a branch of his family business. His wife and daughter were accompanying him for, mysteriously, his wife's health – she did not look the least ill to Felicity.

The Crowns and the Flemmings had apparently known each other for years, although Feliclty could not remember either Peggy Flemming or her mother from their previous sojourn in England, five years earlier. They had renewed their acquaintanceship last summer, just before Felicity had come down with that dreadful attack of pneumonia, which had left her too weak to travel for several months. She had remained in the care of her Aunt Lucy, but Father had immediately arranged that, if she was well enough, she should go out to Gibraltar with the Flemmings the following spring.

In fact, her naturally strong consititution, and her determination to get on with her life, had brought a complete recovery by Christmas, and she had felt well enough to travel long before now, but of course there had been no way anyone would allow her to undertake the week-long voyage unchaperoned. And Mrs Flemming had from the start considered her as a sort of foster child, regularly calling at Aunt Lucy's house on Hampstead to take her riding in her phaeton, and just as regularly entertaining her to tea so that she could be introduced to 'nice' young men, at least in Mrs Flemming's opinion.

Mrs Flemming regarded Felicity as an unfortunate, because of her lack of wealth. Her father was a salaried civil servant, her brother a penniless naval officer; the Crowns did not have the solid substance of a family business behind them, as did the Flemmings. Yet the girl was undoubtedly good looking, and it might be possible to find her a husband more interested in looks than a dowry.

Felicity had no doubt there had been more to Mrs Flemming's interest than that. Mrs Flemming was also attempting to discover a husband for Peggy, and in that instance the form would need to be reversed, and the man more interested in the size of the dowry than in his wife's looks. Having a very attractive girl around could only enhance Peggy's chances, in Mrs Flemming's opinion.

In the event, she had been sorely disappointed. Felicity had not yet been the least interested in any of the young mem trotted out for her approbation. She had not been sure why. All of them had been perfect gentlemen, and one or two had been passingly handsome. And if the majority had been the sons of business acquaintances of Mrs Flemming, who had never left England, and who seemed entirely unable to understand the great forces at work in the world beyond the Channel and the Atlantic, there had been a couple of soldiers, and even a Naval lieutenant acquainted with Jonathan. Yet even he had failed to attract her in any degree. Could it possibly be that the romantic streak which was the curse of her nature – according to her mother, and, she suspected, in the opinion of Mrs Flemming as well – demanded that the man to attract her had to have arrived straight from the heat of battle? She had only ever met one such man. Or, rather, three. But Captain Truxton had been old enough to be her father, and Mr McDonough had been only a midshipman. Mr McGann had been a lieutenant, and so tall and yet gentle, he had fulfilled her ideal of what a man should be. Another of her recurring problems was that at least half of the men who wished to come courting were shorter than herself.

It was not a point of view she had confided to anyone. Mother and Father might have been graciously pleased to meet the Americans on the morrow of their remarkable victory; but perhaps because they were not out of the very top drawer of society themselves, they were the most utter snobs, who by definition regarded Americans as upstart rebels with the breeding of peasants. She presumed the Flemmings held the same opinions. In any event, any suggestion that she might actually know and be interested in someone on the American ships would be disastrous. Even supposing Mr McGann could actually be there. And he couldn't, possibly.

'Who's a bear with a sore head, then?' enquired Peggy Flemming.

'It's the weather,' Felicity complained. 'It really is terrible.' It had now been raining for a steady twenty-four hours.

'But the rain has stopped,' Peggy pointed out. 'Look ... there's blue sky. I do believe the sun is going the shine.'

'Briefly, ladies, briefly,' Captain Brathwaite remarked. 'If I were you,I'd go below and make sure everything you value is properly stowed. There is going to be a blow.'

Mrs Flemming was properly impressed by his prognostication, and had to fortify herself with a tot of gin. They, and all the ten passengers carried by the *Poseidon*, as the brig was rather grandly named, shared the great cabin, so there had been little encouragement to unpack anything more than was strictly necessary – the ladies had in fact worn the same clothes since leaving Plymouth five days before. But that was an accepted part of the discomforts of sea travel, and now they quickly closed and locked their various boxes, and stowed them as best they could, while above their heads they heard the scurrying of feet as the ship heeled to the sudden increase in wind, and the seamen were sent aloft to shorten sail.

'A storm at sea,' Mrs Flemming groaned, sitting on the bunk she shared with her husband – an uncomfortable business, as the bunk was narrow and Mr Flemming was nearly as plump as his wife – and clutching her gin bottle as if it were a lifebelt. 'A storm at sea! Oh, what shall we do?'

'I am sure there is no need for us to do anything,' Felicity suggested, pulling on her cloak. She had every intention of returning on deck. 'This is a well found ship, and Captain Brathwaite is a capable man.'

And besides, she had been in a storm while crossing the Atlantic the previous year, two in fact; the first had frightened her, but she had taken the second in her stride. And here they were within five hundred miles of the Portuguese coast.

She climbed the companion ladder, and held on to the main shrouds to peer across the water at the Americans. The patch of blue sky had disappeared again, and in its place great black clouds were scudding up out of the ocean. The brig had already reduced sail, and there were two men on the helm in anticipation of the hard work ahead; now she watched the American ships also reefing their sails, as were the Royal Navy vessels to either side.

'You'd be better off below, Miss Crown,' Captain Brathwaite told her. 'This is going to be a strong gale.'

'How can you tell?' she asked.

'Well, miss, there are several bad signs. The glass has been dropping for three days, pretty steadily. That's bad. Long foretold, they say, long last. Then, the rain came before the wind. There's an old saying about that too: when

41

the wind comes before the rain, soon you shall make sail again; but when the rain comes before the wind, then your sheets and halliards mind. And lastly, we're on a lee shore.'

'But land is five hundred miles away,' she protested. 'That's what you said at breakfast.'

'Five hundred miles ain't all that far in a westerly gale. And that's an iron-bound coast, no place to get too close to in bad weather. We're going to have to beat out against it.'

'Then you mean we won't get to Gibraltar on Friday?'

'Well,' he said, 'it may delay us for a day or two. But so long as the *Poseidon* has sea room, Miss Crown, we've naught to worry about. Save being washed overboard. Now do as I ask, and go below. Up here is for men.'

Felicity cast a last look at the Americans, but they were obviously also preparing for the storm, and even more efficiently than the brig. Then she obeyed his command and went below, where Mrs Flemming was still drinking gin and Peggy was being seasick, as were two of the other women. How she wished she were a man and could stay on deck.

But she changed her mind as the wind rose, and the ship began to heave and plunge and roll as well; as she listened to the orders being shouted above her head, and the creaking of the wheel being turned to and fro; and as the waves struck the wooden hull, it seemed only inches from where she sat, with tremendous crashes. Up there really was man's work. And there was sufficient to do in the cabin, coping with the alarm of the women, and of the male passengers as well. Mr Flemming sat with his arm round his wife's shoulders, but was clearly just as terrified, and soon took to the gin bottle himself.

It became one of the longest days that Felicity had ever known. It was of course impossible for the steward to serve a proper meal, and they had to exist on biscuits and snaps of brandy, while the wind howled and the seas battered the ship. In the cabin it was impossible to tell what was really happening outside, but when Felicity could stand her confinement no longer, or the sounds and smells which went with it, and attempted to return on deck, whatever the risk, she found that the companion hatch was locked and battened. My God, she thought, we are trapped down here.

A feeling which grew as she listened to the clacking of the pumps, suggesting that the hull was making water. Yet even that soon became commonplace, as the day faded into darkness, and she found that she dozed off, her arms around Peggy Flemming, to be awakened in the middle of the night be a tremendous crack.

'Oh Lord!' Mrs Flemming shrieked. 'Oh, God in heaven, have mercy on us, for we are lost.'

'That was a mast snapping,' said Major Britton. He was on his way to join his regiment, and up to this moment, as befitted a soldier, he had been the calmest of them all, but now even he was looking pale in the light of the swinging lantern.

'We must find out,' Felicity decided, and climbed the ladder again, prepared to bang on the hatch door until someone heard her, but as she reached the top it opened anyway, and the captain peered in.

'Now ladies,' he said, shaking water from his oilskins on to her unturned face, while she inhaled great gulps of magnificent fresh air, and looked past his shoulder at the huge waves, white crests tumbling over, clearly visible even in the darkness as they surged by. 'There is nothing to be afraid of. We have lost our fore-topmast, that is all. But we are hove to, and the wind is abating. And as soon as it is gone altogether, why, we'll rig a jury and get under way. So sleep well.'

'A topmast,' Major Britton surmised. 'Well, that is not so bad, I suppose.'

'And hove to,' Mr Flemming said. 'Oh, that is very good. You heard the captain, my dear. There is nothing to be afraid of.'

Oddly, Felicity believed him. and the wind *was* dropping, she was sure. She fell into a deep sleep, curled on the bunk beside Peggy, who every so often gave a convulsive shudder, as if she was having a succession of nightmares, and awoke with a start to find the cabin almost still and filled with snores and grunts, but also with a considerable amount of daylight, finding its way in through the stern windows. Out there the seas did not look half so terrifying as during the night, and the terrible whistle of the wind was gone.

Cautiously she pushed herself up, straightened her clothes as best she could, drew a brush through her hair, and tiptoed past the various sleeping bodies, to gain the ladder. The hatch was open. She stepped out into the waist of the ship, and the most beautiful morning, with the heavy clouds of yesterday quite disappeared, and the sea, if still splashed with the occasional whitecap, no more frightening than at any previous time on the voyage. To her dismay, however, the other ships of the convoy, together with the warships, British or American, had all disappeared. The *Poseidon* was no longer hove to, but sailing quietly before the wind under a storm trysail only; her foredeck was a mass of disordered rigging and canvas, and the fore-topmast hung like a broken bone from its lower section.

'Where is everyone else, Captain Brathwaite?' she cried.

'Scattered by the storm,' the captain replied. 'I imagine they're not too distant, though. There's one in sight back there ...'

He pointed astern, and Felicity shaded her eyes to see a ship several miles behind them, carrying only a single sail, and appearing to roll heavily in the swell.

'She's been dismasted, I reckon,' Brathwaite said. 'Once we get our foremast jury-rigged, and can work to windward again, we'll beat back to her and see if she needs assistance.'

Felicity swept the horizon with the captain's telescope. 'And there's another over there,' she cried, vastly relieved as she made out the sails. 'She looks quite all right.' Because the ship was carrying all sail, and was approaching quite fast; she was coming from the direction in which the *Poseidon* was at the moment sailing, and thus the two vessels were on converging courses.

'Now that's odd,' the captain said, and took the glass back to level it. 'Yes,' he said doubtfully, after a careful inspection of the approaching ship. 'I don't like the look of her very much. Certainly she's not one of ours.'

Felicity frowned at the stranger, which was by now quite visible to the naked eye, and realised that it was indeed unlike any vessel she had ever seen before: a long, low hull, with no discernible forecastle or quarterdeck, and fore-and-aft-rigging, like a schooner, save that the after yard seemed unnaturally long.

'That's a lateen mainsail, that is,' Captain Brathwaite said. 'I don't like the look of her at all.' He left Felicity's side and went to the rail. 'Mr Lewin,' he called. 'Make haste with clearing that deck and rigging that mast. Mr Clark, issue muskets and cutlasses to the crew, and load the guns. We've a Barbary pirate on the starboard bow.'

The crew ceased their activities to run to the bulwark and peer at the approaching vessel. Felicity's stomach seemed to give an enormous roll. They had been so safe, just twenty-four hours ago, surrounded by well-armed warships, by friends. Now. . . Desperately she ran to the stern to look back at the other ship. But they could expect no help from that quarter; she was entirely crippled for the time being. And the pirate was definitely coming straight at them.

But if perhaps they could get back to the other straggler, and form a united front. . .

The same thoughts were obviously occurring to the captain. 'Mr Lewin,' he bawled, and the first mate hurried aft again. 'Our best course will be to beat up to that fellow astern. Together we'd be too strong for the Moors.'

'She'll not do it, Captain,' Lewin objected. 'She'll only carry one foresail until that mast has been shored up, and that'll be too slow. Those corsairs are like whippets to windward. She'd haul us down in minutes.'

Brathwaite chewed his lip, while Felicity watched them anxiously.

'Our best chance is to sail past him, Captain,' Lewin said. 'Give him a broadside and get downwind of him, and then run for it. That way we'll have a better chance. And a better chance of regaining the convoy, too.'

Brathwaite continued to chew his lip for several seconds, looking at Felicity, then snapped his fingers. 'Aye, Mr Lewin,' he said. 'You're right. That's our best chance to be sure. You get down below, Miss Crown, and explain the situation to your friends. We'll lock the hatch from the outside, and mind you lock it from the inside as well, and be sure to have the men watch the stern windows. No one is to come out under any circumstances, except on my say so.'

'Not even if the ship is sinking?' she asked.

He gave a grim smile. 'It's not their style to sink a victim

45

until she's been captured and looted. If they capture us, well
... may God have mercy on all our souls. But we'll do
everything in our power to stand them off. As Mr Lewin
says, if we can get past them and make it a straight chase,
we've a better than even chance of sighting the rest of the
convoy, or land, or something, before they can catch us. It
means abandoning that poor devil ...' He looked aft again.
'But as we can't help him anyway ...'

'And if you don't get past him?' She gazed into his eyes.

He sighed, and lowered his own. 'Miss Crown, I'd not
want a dog of mine to fall alive into the hands of those
devils.'

Felicity turned away, stared at the approaching vessel.
Now she could even make out the crowd of men on the
pirate's deck; the morning sunlight was glinting from their
weapons. They counted the merchantman already theirs.
And in her heart, she knew they were right.

She went to the companionway, descended to the cabin,
where the other passengers were also awake by now.

'What's all the excitement on deck?' Major Britton wanted
to know. 'Don't tell us the damage is more severe than we
thought.'

'No,' Felicity said. 'No.' Her voice was toneless. 'We are
about to be boarded by Barbary pirates.'

She hadn't meant to put it quite like that, but she hardly
heard the commotion aroused by her statement, the screams
of Mrs Flemming, the gasps of the other women, the startled
ejaculations of the men. She went to the stern window
and looked out at the sea; from down here the other sail
was invisible. Above their heads she heard the hatch being
closed and bolted. But it hardly seemed relevant. The captain
had just told her to commit suicide if the pirates should take
the ship. She should kill herself, or have one of the men kill
her. Her! She was eighteen years old, and had everything to
live for. And now she was about to die. Because nothing was
going to stop the pirates from taking this ship. Captain
Brathwaite might be a fine seaman, and an aggressive man,
but he lacked the spark of determined willpower which
alone could save them.

She turned back to face the cabin. Major Britton and the

other two male passengers were priming their pistols and examining their swords; Mr Flemming was trying to comfort his wife. The other three women huddled together on a bunk, while Peggy Flemming sat on the edge of the one she shared with Felicity and trembled, great tears rolling over her plump cheeks.

'Don't worry, Miss Crown,' Major Britton said reassuringly. 'No darkie is going to get in here.'

Felicity drew a long breath. 'The captain suggested we should bolt the hatch from the inside,' she said. 'Then there'd only be the stern windows to worry about.'

'Good idea,' Britton agreed, and shot the bolts on the inside of the door. 'Now lads . . .' he might have been commanding his regiment, 'watch those windows.'

'Aaagh!' screamed Mrs Flemming, as the ship trembled to a tremendous roaring sound. 'Oh God, have mercy on us.'

'That's our broadside,' Major Britton said reassuringly. 'We're teaching those blackguards a thing or two.'

The ship trembled again as the guns roared. Felicity remembered the *Constellation*'s guns belching fire and smoke, and those of *La Vengeance* replying. How grand the cannonade had seemed, viewed from the deck of HMS *Lancer*. Now it was merely terrifying and deafening.

'What's that?' snapped one of the other men.

Because now there was a new sound, close at hand, a deep throated roar, 'Ul-ul-ul-Akhbar!'

'By Christ,' Major Britton shouted. 'They haven't been stopped by the guns!'

'Oh,' Mrs Flemming moaned. 'Oh!'

There was a ripple of musketry from above their heads, and then more timber-rattling cannon explosions. But these were no longer broadsides, only single shots. The women began to scream, and then more loudly as there came an ear-splitting crash which shook the ship from stem to stern.

'We're sinking,' Peggy Flemming screamed. 'Oh, we're sinking.'

'They've come alongside,' Britton snapped.

Felicity had been staring at the stern windows, half expecting to see a Moorish pirate appear there at any moment. The jar threw her from her feet across one of the bunks, and she remained sitting there, her back against the bulkhead, staring now at the hatchway, and listening to the shouts and screams from above her head, the stamping of feet, the clash of steel and the explosions of pistols and muskets.

She remained curiously detached, as though she wasn't really there at all, but merely looking down on the scene, wondering if the captain had made any attempt at all to get past the corsair, or if he had just been totally outsailed. She felt like a sleepwalker, as if this couldn't really be happening, but was merely a nightmare from which she would soon awaken. She was moving, living, breathing, feeling . . . and above her was death, coming closer every minute. It just could not be happening . . . and it was happening in such a matter of fact, inevitable fashion.

But she also thought how wonderful it could be if one of the American warships were to appear, now, and deal with the Moors. The rescuing party would of course be led by Toby McGann, who would put his arm around her shoulders and assure her that she was now safe, and she would know that she was gong to be safe for the rest of her life.

'Listen,' Major Britton said. 'Listen.'

The noise above them was dying, although the jabber of voices was growing louder.

'They've taken the ship,' said one of the other men, his voice trembling.

Even as he spoke they heard the bolts on the door being drawn, and a moment later the door itself creaked as someone tried to open it.

They gazed at each other. Britton licked his lips. 'Well,' he said, 'I . . . well. . .' He looked at Flemming. 'We seem to have no choice.'

'Oh my God,' Flemming said, understanding what the major was trying to tell him. 'Oh my *God*!'

Britton checked the priming on his pistol, while there were more thumps on the door. 'It has to be done,' he sad, growing in determination. 'If you will attend to your wife and daughter, Flemming, these gentlemen and I will see to Miss Crown and the other ladies.'

Felicity pressed herself against the bulkhead, as if trying to force it open so that she could be thrown into the sea. That would be preferable to what was happening here. She could not be about to die, killed by her own kind to save her from . . . she had no idea. She only knew she did not want it to happen.

'Now, ladies,' Britton was saying, while all the women stared at him as rabbits might stare at a king cobra. 'It is necessary for you to be very brave, and to trust us that this will be as quick and painless as we can make it, and that . . . well, we shall all meet again in a better place. Now ladies, will you please close your eyes and turn to face the bulkhead . . .'

He had delayed too long. With a crash the door gave, and men came tumbling down the steps. Felicity, flattened against the bulkhead as she knelt on the bunk, could only gasp in horror. Britton turned and fired his pistol. He hit one of the Moors, who gave a cry and fell, but before he could draw his sword was cut down himself by a swinging scimitar, his blood scattering across the dresses of the women. The other two men died a moment later. Mr Flemming attempted to stand in front of his wife and daughter and received a sword thrust in the stomach which collapsed him to his knees, blood spurting through the fingers with which he clutched the wound.

Mrs Flemming appeared to faint. The other three women were screaming. Peggy Flemming stared at the marauders, eyes wide, ample bosom giving enormous heaves. Felicity watched them coming towards her, saw their straggling beards and their grinning, remarkably white teeth. Only dimly she realised that they had thrust their swords and pistols back into their sashes.

She tried to force herself still further against the bulkhead, considered kicking at them, and did so as they came close. To her horror the first man merely caught her boot, and pulled. She came away from the bulkhead feet first, sitting down heavily, skirts flying. She gasped and screamed herself, and was picked up by her arms and legs, as if she were a sack of coal, and carried to the steps. She twisted her body and attempted to kick again, all thoughts of decorum gone, but was quite helpless in their grasps; her efforts only made them laugh the louder.

She emerged into the open air, twisting her head to and fro, gazed at dead bodies, many still oozing blood from terrible cuts, saw Captain Brathwaite lying draped over the rail, his head nearly severed from his body. She stared at the pirate ship, long and low, held beside the *Poseidon* by grappling irons, the two hulls grinding against each other as the ships rose and fell on the swell. Then she was surrounded by dark-visaged, grinning, bearded men, wearing turbans and loose robes, peering at her until distracted as the other women were dragged up from below.

And she listened to the most bestial of noises from forward, where one or two members of the crew who had survived the battle were being tortured by their captors.

Tortured! She blinked at them, saw their naked bellies and legs, the flopping penises . . . and the gleaming knives of the Moors. She closed her eyes tightly. She had never seen a naked man before. She didn't know what was about to happen to those men, either, and she didn't ever want to find out.

Then she was herself thrown to the deck, with a jar which swept the breath from her lungs; could only pant as she stared at one very well-dressed pirate, who had jewels in his turban and on the hilt of his scimitar, and wearing a fine white tunic, although this was spattered with blood to indicate that he had been in the thick of the fighting. His features were the most terrifying she had ever seen, for his nose was huge and hooked, and his chin protruding, so that he looked like the man in the moon, save that his mouth suggested the cruellest of natures, even when surrounded by beard and moustache.

Now he stood in front of Mrs Flemming, who had regained her senses, if not her wits, for she merely goggled at him, and screamed and screamed. The man smiled, and his face became crueller yet. Then he jerked his head and gave an order. His men roared with laughter, and Mrs Flemming was dragged away, to be thrown, still screaming, to the deck by the mainmast, only a few feet from where Felicity lay, while the pirates tore at her clothing and buried their hands in the plump flesh, one of them kneeling between the flailing white legs.

Felicity felt sick: now it was Peggy's turn. She gasped in horror as the pirate captain gave another order, and Peggy was dragged to the nearest cannon, and thrown across the barrel. The girl screamed and attempted to kick her legs, but these were caught and pulled apart by the eager men, while her skirts were thrown above her head.

'Oh my God!' Felicity panted. She had never seen anything so horrible in her life – and it was going to happen to her as well. She pushed herself up, wondering if she could gain the rail and throw herself over the side, but the men standing around her immediately caught her arms, pulling her to her feet and holding her between them. She didn't know where to look, found herself staring at her friend as the captain took his place between Peggy's legs, using only his hands to spread her buttocks, and very carefully look and feel between.

Felicity's legs went weak and she would have fallen, but for the men. The captain was laughing again and giving another order; his men were equally amused, and Peggy was dragged away to join her now moaning mother on the deck.

Dimly, Felicity was aware of what the captain had been doing, what he had been seeking, and also that she should be shocked, not at what he had done so much as at what he had discovered. Peggy Flemming was not a virgin. Whatever would her mother say when she found out? As if it could ever possibly matter again; a man was now kneeling between Peggy's legs in turn, and she was shrieking her fear and pain and humiliation.

Felicity realised she was being taken to the captain, who had ceased smiling as he looked at her, and then slowly up and down her. Then he did smile, and made a remark. His men agreed with him, from their shout of acclamation.

'Please,' Felicity begged. 'Please . . .' If he was somehow interested in her, surely. . . But she was being thrown across the gun in turn. She felt hands on her legs, and suddenly the morning breeze and sun on her thighs. She was naked from the waist down before a pack of men. she attempted to move, but the men in front of her were holding her wrists, and she could only wriggle; she stopped that as soon as she felt hands on her buttocks. Then they were being pulled apart. She thought she was certain to die of shame, or a heart attack, so loudly was the blood pounding in her arteries; wept and ground her teeth together as she felt fingers probing into her, very carefully and gently, but so knowledgeably, touching her where she had never even touched herself. Then she was jerked back to her feet, panting, breasts paining from being pressed into the iron of the gun barrel, but skirts mercifully falling into place.

Her ordeal was not over, for now the captain tore open her bodice, and felt inside, cupping her breasts and feeling the texture of her skin. Then he gripped her jaw to force her mouth open and peer at her teeth, before lastly driving his fingers into her hair, sifting it and evaluating it.

'English?' he asked. 'You are English?'

She gaped at him.

'Have you lost your tongue?' he asked.

Felicity licked her lips; she could still feel the touch of his hand between her legs. 'I am English.' She whispered.

'You have a degree of beauty,' he told her. 'You are too thin, but we can fatten you up. And you are the only virgin on board this entire ship. Ha ha!' he roared. 'You will fetch a good price in Algiers. And you will make some rich man very happy, in his harem.' He gave an order, and Felicity was dragged across the bulwarks on to the deck of the pirate ship.

Chapter 3

The Mediterranean – 1801

Toby McGann slowly climbed the steep street, determined not to break out in an unbecoming sweat. All the streets in Gibraltar seemed to be steep, climbing up the solid rock away from the huge, busy harbour, and although it was only March the morning sun was already warm. But if the address he had been given by the harbour master was a true one, he would soon reach his destination.

And there it was. He paused, both to catch his breath and to make sure there was no dust clinging to his blue uniform jacket and trousers; he had recently been passed by a carriage, going downhill, and the road was in no way surfaced.

But the view was in any event worth stopping for; it was quite breathtaking. Above him, the Rock continued to climb, for another few hundred feet, he estimated, although up there the houses ceased. By looking directly ahead, and therefore south, he saw first of all Europa Point down at the water's edge, the southernmost extremity of the peninsular, then the dark blue waters of the Strait, always restlessly flowing eastwards, except at the very top of the ebb tide – because of the rate of evaporation in the land-locked Mediterranean there was a constant replenishment from the Atlantic – and then at the mountains of North Africa, only seven miles away, and at one hill in particular, close to the shore – the other of Hercules' Pillars.

To the west, he could look across the long, narrow bay at the mainland of Spain, and the port of Algeciras closer at hand, while immediately beneath him the white houses of Gibraltar itself formed a series of terraces down to the waterfront. Down there was a myriad of ships, all riding safely and comfortably behind the massive breakwaters which protected the port. He could make out the *Essex* and the *President*, as well as several ships from the convoy, still engaged in making running repairs to the damage suffered in the gale of the previous week; not all the merchantmen had even come in as yet, although at least one appeared every day.

As he looked he saw a battered brig, having come up the Strait on the tide, being towed by her boats through the pierheads into the harbour. She had apparently lost both masts, and was jury-rigged. The American warships had themselves not come off unscathed, although he reckoned they had been better handled than most. He had been fortunate to be allowed this brief shore leave, but Captain Barron had considered that an officer who was acquainted with the Governor's Chief Secretary could be a useful asset to his squadron: not only did they require considerable victualling now, but they would undoubtedly have to pass this way again at some time in the future. Barron, of course, did not even know of the existence of Felicity.

Toby straightened his hat, flicked a last imagined speck of dust from his sword hilt, and climbed the last few steps to the almost English-looking cottage, set against the side of the hill, naturally, but with a brief garden in which roses and honeysuckle vines predominated. How his heart pounded. Suppose it were to be Felicity herself who opened the door to his knock. . . It was Mrs Crown, frowning at his uniform, clearly not that of a British officer.

'Yes?' she asked.

Toby raised his hat. 'I doubt you remember me, Mrs Crown,' he said. 'Lieutenant McGann, of the United States Ship *Essex*. But last year I served on the *Constellation*, and had the privilege of breakfasting with you on board HMS *Lancer*.'

Mrs Crown's frown disappeared. 'Mr McGann,' she cried. 'Of course. How could I forget such a . . . well . . . you are a strapping fellow, to be sure. But here in Gibraltar? The *Essex*, you say?'

'We are on our way to a station in the eastern Mediter-ranean,' Toby explained, 'and but stopped for water and provisions. But remembering that your husband was on his way to take up a position here, I felt I should call.'

'And how glad I am that you did,' Mrs Crown said. 'I do hope your ship will remain here for a few days yet. But come in, Mr McGann, come in. Charles will be so pleased to renew your acquaintance. He should not be late today. You *are* going to remain for a day or two?'

'Well ... that depends very much on your husband, I imagine.'

'Then the matter is settled.' She escorted him into the small parlour, rang a bell, and a maid hurried in with a tea tray. 'I do hope you can stay for at least a day or two. Felicity would be so sorry to miss you.'

'Your ... your daughter isn't here?' he asked, his stomach filling with lead.

'Not at this moment, Mr McGann. But she will be here at any moment. Sugar?'

'Oh, yes, thank you.' He wondered if Mrs Crown's tea would be anything like that his mother made. But he was impatient to hear about Felicity's whereabouts.

'She is on her way from England now,' Mrs Crown ex-plained. 'The convoy should have been here last Friday, and indeed most of the ships have arrived. But they were scat-tered by a storm off Portugal, apparently, and some have been delayed. Amongst them the *Poseidon*, on which she was travelling.'

'The convoy!' Toby cried. 'Felicity was on that convoy? Ahem, I meant Miss Crown.'

Mrs Crown sipped tea with the utmost composure. 'Were you with that convoy, Mr McGann?'

'Not exactly. But we sighted them just before the gale. Good Lord! If you'll forgive me, Mrs Crown. I had no idea your daughter was in that fleet.'

'Well, as I was saying,' Mrs Crown continued with deter-mined confidence, 'she appears to have been delayed. But we are expecting her at any moment. When she does get here, I will send a message to your ship, and you must come up to dinner. Bring your captain with you, and we will have

55

a jolly occasion. I am sure Felicity would like that. She has often spoken of that fight you had with *La Vengeance*, and our meeting afterwards. I think it made a considerable impression on her. You know, we have lived for so long in the midst of the terrible war, but it is so seldom we women actually experience anything of it, so to speak. Even as spectators.'

'Oh, quite,' Toby agreed. But he was hardly listening. Felicity had actually been within a few miles of him last week, and he had not known. Not that there would have been anything he could have done about it even if he *had* known ... but it would have made a delightful voyage even more enjoyable. Save that he would have worried for her during the gale. But it had been only a gale, and now she was going to be here in a couple of days, or hours... That last ship entering the harbour during his climb up the hill could have been the *Poseidon*.

'Well, I am most grateful for your invitation, Mrs Crown, and most happily accept; it will be a great pleasure to meet Miss Crown again. I cannot speak for Captain Barron, of course, but I will certainly relay your invitation to him.'

'Oh, he will wish to dine with my husband, Mr McGann.' Mrs Crown smiled archly, to suggest that twenty years before she must have been every bit as attractive as her daughter. 'That is politics.'

'And will your son, Lieutenant Crown, also be here?' Toby asked, desperately remembering his manners.

'Now that I cannot say, as we receive no advance notice of his arrivals. He is with the fleet off Cadiz, you see. However, we count ourselves fortunate that he is so near by, and that we are able to see him with some regularity, whenever his ship comes into Gibraltar to victual.' She raised her head at the sound of drumming hooves. 'Now whoever can that be?'

Toby was on his feet, to face the door as it burst in a moment later. He had supposed he might be being recalled to the ship to deal with some crisis, but it was Mr Crown, who stared at him in bewilderment, then looked at his wife. He was hatless, his hair windblown, his face quite pale despite the exertions of the ride up the hill.

'This is Lieutenant McGann, my dear,' Mrs Crown said.

56

'Off the USS *Essex*. You'll remember we met last February in the Caribbean.'

'McGann,' Crown muttered. He did not offer to shake hands, but crossed the room to the table in the far corner, and poured himself a glass of brandy.

'Charles?' Mrs Crown demanded, revealing some asperity at his lack of manners. 'Whatever is the matter?'

Charles Crown sat down, sighed, the glass dangling between his knees. 'Felicity,' he muttered.

'Felicity?' Mrs Crown's voice rose an octave.

'Felicity?' Toby had been considering taking his leave, as the crisis was so clearly a domestic one, but now he started forward. 'Where is she?'

'Lost,' Crown moaned.

'Lost?' Toby shouted.

'Lost?' Mrs Crown shrieked. She ran to her husband's side, and shook his shoulder so hard he spilled his drink. 'What do you mean, lost?'

'Her ship could not have foundered,' Toby protested. 'Not in a mere gale. It was hardly more than that.'

'She is lost,' Crown said again. He sighed, drank the last of his brandy, drew the back of his hand across his mouth. 'Every ship in the convoy is safe to port, save one. The *Poseidon*.'

'And that leads you to suppose she must be lost, sir?' Toby asked, relief flooding his system. 'It is early days yet, surely. Possibly she was dismasted, or suffered some structural damage. She'll be along as soon as her crew have made good their rigging.'

Crown uttered another sigh. 'The *Medway Star* made port not an hour ago,' he said. 'She was dismasted.'

'I saw her come in, sir,' Toby agreed.

'And she had news of the *Poseidon*?' Mrs Crown begged.

'Aye,' her husband said. 'She had news. She reports seeing an English ship hove to on the morning after the gale, some miles to her south-east, making repairs to a broken foremast. Then she reports seeing another ship come over the horizon, and go alongside the first. An hour later, the first vessel was in flames, and the other ship was sailing to

57

the south-east again. The crew of the *Medway Star* clearly identified her lines as that of no English or French design.'

Mrs Crown stared at her husband with her mouth open. 'Pirates?' she whispered.

'Undoubtedly. Out of one of the Barbary ports. She was seen to carry a lateen mainsail. That means she was certainly from the Mediterranean.'

'But ... you cannot be certain the burned ship was the *Poseidon*, sir,' Toby protested.

'What other ship can it have been?' Crown demanded. 'Every ship in the convoy, and every one of the escorts, are here in Gibraltar, saving only the *Poseidon*. There is no other merchant vessel known to have been in these waters at all. She is gone, sir, gone. And all those who sailed in her.' His shoulders hunched as he stared at the floor. 'Our daughter is at the bottom of the sea, butchered by the Moors. Or ...' he raised his head to stare in horror at his wife.

'Oh, my God,' she gasped. 'Not taken as a slave? Oh, my God!'

Toby caught her as she collapsed in a faint. He placed her on the settee as gently as he could, then ran to the door.

'Mr McGann,' said Captain Barron, leaning back in his chair and smiling across his desk at the young lieutenant. 'I am pleased that you have returned so promptly. You have heard the news, eh?'

'My God, yes, sir,' Toby gasped. 'And we are putting to sea? Why, sir, I am most grateful.'

Barron scratched his head. 'I had supposed you would be disappointed, Mr McGann. However, as you have observed, we are putting to sea. We must be out of here by nightfall. I intend to be off Tripoli by the end of the week.'

'Tripoli, sir?' Toby frowned at him.

'Of course.' Barron frowned back. 'Are we talking about the same things, lieutenant?'

'Apparently not, sir. Sir ...'

'You mean you are not aware that we are at war?'

'At war, sir? With whom?'

'Why, the Dey of Tripoli, of course. The news was brought to me not fifteen minutes after your departure this afternoon, by our consul. I found it hard to credit myself, Mr McGann, but the Dey of Tripoli has declared war upon the United States of America. Can you credit such effrontery? Well, sir, I can tell you, we are going to teach that fellow a lesson he won't forget in a hurry. Now, lieutenant, I trust you had a successful reunion with Mr Crown?'

Toby had paused outside the door of the captain's cabin to regain his breath and straighten his uniform, but he could tell from the way Barron was looking at him that he must appear far from normal. Now he had to try to get his thoughts under control. He had supposed, as he had returned to the dockside and seen the sea-going preparations, that in some miraculous fashion the American squadron was preparing to sail against Algiers. But Tripoli, several hundred miles to the east . . .

'No, sir,' he said. 'The most terrible thing has happened.'

'Indeed?' Barron sat up straight. 'What?'

'Well, sir, you are aware that only one ship of that convoy we sighted has failed so far to arrive?'

Barron nodded.

'That ship was a brig named the *Poseidon*, sir,' Toby said. 'And on it was the Crowns' daughter, a girl named Felicity.'

'Ah,' Barron nodded. 'I can see they will be in an anxious mood. Yes, you chose a bad moment for your visit, Mr McGann. But I hope you were able to reassure them that delays are one of the hazards of seafaring.'

'The ship is lost, sir,' Toby said, keeping himself from shouting with an effort. 'She was sighted on the morning after the gale by another straggler, the *Medway Star*, which has just arrived, being boarded and then burned by Barbary pirates.'

'The devil,' Barron said. 'And this *Medway Star* could not assist her to defend herself?'

'She was herself dismasted in the gale, sir, and counted herself fortunate the pirates were sated with the one victim.'

Barron nodded. 'It is a sad world, by God. Well, there it is. I can understand that this Mr Crown will be too distracted to be of any assistance to us now. Still, you will have offered your condolences, and we are sailing on the evening tide anyway.'

'Sir . . .' Toby placed his hands on the desk and leaned forward. 'You don't understand. Were we to be certain of Miss Crown's death it would be terrible enough. But there must be a chance that she was taken by the pirates, to be sold as a slave in Algiers.'

'That is their way with female captives, certainly,' Barron agreed. 'If they are at all attractive.'

'Then, sir, should we not attempt to rescue her?'

Barron stared at him, then slowly leaned back in his chair. 'Rescue her? Do you know this girl, Mr McGann?' He gazed pointedly at Toby's hands, and Toby stood to attention again.

'Yes, sir. We have met.'

'Ah, I begin to understand the situation. My dear boy . . .' he got up and walked round his desk to squeeze Toby's shoulder. 'Then this is indeed a tragedy.'

'But one which can perhaps be remedied, sir, if we act immediately. If we were to assault Algiers . . .'

'My God, what a suggestion. There is no possibility of that.'

'But, sir, Captain Barron . . .'

'Even if it were physically possible,' Barron went on, more firmly, 'it would be a pointless exercise. A Barbary pirate, you say? Have you any idea which port the corsair actually sailed from? Have you any idea, Mr McGann, how many ports there are which give these rascals shelter? But we can be certain of one thing: that ship was out of a western port, Algiers, or one of its satellities. No Tripoli ship has ever been reported as passing through the Strait of Gibraltar.'

'That is my point, sir. And it is certain that Miss Crown will be offered for sale in the market at Algiers. If we were to bombard the port, and demand her release . . .'

'Bombard Algiers? Commit an act of war? Mr McGann, we were sent here to deal with Tripoli. Now that the Dey has seen fit to declare war upon us, our duty is even more clearly defined. Tripoli is our enemy, not Algiers. Certainly we were not sent here to take on the whole of North Africa. With two ships? That would be quite out of the question. It is not as if this girl is even an American citizen.'

'Sir . . .'

Barron held up his finger. 'She is a young lady to whom

60

you are attracted, Mr McGann. This I accept, and I wish you to believe that I can sympathise most sincerely with your feelings. But to my knowledge you have not yet married her, or even become betrothed to her. Thus she remains a British responsibility. It is up to the Royal Navy to do something about her situation. But I am afraid they will not. For two very good reasons. One is that not even the British could consider assaulting so strongly a fortified port as Algiers with any hope of success. They would need to invest the city from the land as well, and that would require an army – every British army is engaged in fighting Napoleon.

'The other reason ... here me out, boy,' he snapped as Toby would have interrupted. 'What I am about to say is going to make unpleasant hearing for your ears. But in this life one has to face facts. Miss Crown was taken by the pirates several days ago. That ship will have regained its home port by now. Your friend will already have been placed upon the block and sold. This may very well have happened in Algiers, but that does not alter the fact. By now, Mr McGann, she will have been incorporated in the harem of some fat old Turk, who will have her maidenhead and then misuse her body most shamefully.

'I am sorry, Mr McGann, but there it is. These fellows are not Christians, and they have no concept of the proper way to treat a lady. Believe me, boy, that girl is as dead already as if they had cut off her head. We must, indeed, pray that she did perish when the *Poseidon* was taken. Certain it is that even if, by some miracle, she could be regained, there would be nothing any Christian man would ever be able to do with her again. I doubt even a convent would have her.'

Toby stared at him, unable to believe his ears. 'Sir, may I have your permission to call for volunteers and raise a personal force?'

Barron frowned at him. 'A volunteer force? With what in mind?'

'To undertake a cutting out operation against Algiers.'

'Are you mad, sir? Do you suppose you would have the slightest chance of success; of even locating her whereabouts? Oh, I understand how you feel. Quite apart from the girl herself, you are the son of Fighting Harry McGann, who was a legend in his own lifetime. Well, sir, that may well have been so. But those days of individual derring-do are finished, Mr McGann. Individual feats of glory may have been acceptable during our struggle for independence, when the Navy was an unorganised body of individual ships. But as I have said, those days are finished, thank God. We have been given our orders, and those orders we will carry out. Our task is to bring the Dey of Tripoli to heel. We will undertake nothing else, unless commanded to do so by Congress.'

His tone softened. 'I am sorry, Mr McGann. More sorry than I can convey in words. But as I say, you must face facts. You are excused duty for the rest of the afternoon. I suggest you go ashore and have a drink. Alcohol is a good healer, in the short term, and you will be excused any reprimand for returning the worse for it. You have my word on that. Just be sure you are on board by dusk, or I will have you posted as a deserter.'

Toby hesitated, then saluted and left the cabin. He went on deck, stared past the breakwaters at the African mountains. He had never felt so damned in his life. And he did not even have the pleasure of hating his captain; Barron had just given him the option of deserting, if he felt he had to. And was that not what Fighting Harry McGann would have done, if faced with the alternative of deserting the woman he loved? Of course, he did not love Felicity Crown. How could he love someone he had met only once? It was the thought of her in the hands of the Moors. . .

But he also knew that even if he had met her a hundred times, he was not going to desert his ship. It would have been nice to feel that was because his devotion to the Service was greater than anything else in his life. It would even have been nice to suppose that he was far more level-headed than his father; because he knew that every word Barron had spoken was absolutely true. He had lived all his life under the aegis of his father's name and fame, but had been cursed by it as well: no man could ever hope to equal the deeds of Fighting Harry McGann.

But worse, he knew the captain had been right about Felicity as well. He could not now rescue the girl he had met

62

on board the *Lancer*, because that girl no longer existed. After what must have happened to her, could he possibly ever look at her again without a shudder? He didn't know. Nor was there the slightest chance of his ever being given the chance to find out.

So he would do his duty as an American officer, and try to pretend to himself that he was not actually a coward. And pray that one day he might have an Algerian corsair in the sights of one of the *Essex*'s guns. One day.

The door of the little cabin opened, and Felicity blinked at the lantern. She could not immediately make out the man carrying it, but she knew who it was. The pirate captain, as the man who had examined her obviously was, had visited her several times during the days since the capture of the *Poseidon*, and although he had never touched her or offered her the slightest insult or injury, had only ever looked at her, her reaction to the sight of him was always the same; she drew up her knees and pressed herself against the bulkhead. There were no bunks in this dark pit, no furniture at all, so there was nothing behind which she could hide her nakedness.

How long had she lain here? How long was it since that unforgettably terrible morning? She thought perhaps three days, because she had been fed six times, good food, yoghurt and honey and sweetmeats and some kind of lamb stew. At first she had determined not to eat. Her mind had been filled with the horrible sights and sounds which had followed the capture of the *Poseidon*; of the screams of the young boy being castrated; of the Flemmings being raped; the splashes of the bodies being thrown over the side – Peggy and her mother amongst them? She had to suppose so, as she had not seen them since. She was the only prisoner, so far as she knew, therefore she was the only survivor. Out of all the sixty-odd souls with whom she had left Plymouth.

Therefore, why did she continue to survive? The Moors had certainly considered it a possibility that she might choose not to. When she had been brought down to this noisome pit in the very bowels of the ship, below the water-line so far as she could judge, they had stripped of her clothing. She had shrieked her horror and disgust, assuming that it was but the prelude to some bestial assault, but as they had not harmed her in any way she had realised they merely intended to prevent her from being able to smother herself. In fact, the thought had never actually crossed her mind. Life was too precious, even as a captive, for her to contemplate suicide. And besides, she did not know she was the only survivor, for certain. There might be other pits like this one, scattered all over the ship. To that hope she clung.

And the Moors had in fact treated her with great circumspection; apart from the fact that they kept her naked. Except when bathing, she had never been naked in her life before. Now her nakedness both added to and detracted from the horror of her situation. As she was never taken from the cabin, it soon became an open sewer, but twice a day the door was thrown wide and buckets of salt water were hurled in, over her and over the floor, until the place was awash. At first she had supposed they intended to drown her, then she realised there were drains in the corner of the cabin which allowed the water to flow through to the bilges, from whence, presumably, it was pumped out from time to time with all its noisome contents. The feeling of cleanliness after each of these douches had raised her spirits, but the salt water had also left her itchy and uncomfortable, and her hair as stiff as a board.

Until yesterday. Yesterday had been different. Last evening she had been taken on deck. The thought had been horrifying. To be exposed to all of those men. . . She had shut her eyes tightly until more buckets of water had been emptied over her, when the sting of the cool breeze had forced them open. Certainly there had been men, staring at her, laughing and commenting to each other; but as she had no idea what they were saying it did not really matter. She was in fact so relieved by the wind playing about her, scattering her hair, that she almost felt happy. And then she had looked past the bow of the ship, and seen the loom of the Rock. She had recognised it immediately from pictures her parents had shown her before their departure. The corsair was well to the south of it, of course, on the Morrocan side of the Strait, so that they could seek shelter should they be challenged by any British cruiser. But it was there . . . as if it would ever mean anything to her again.

It had to. Just over there, not ten miles away, was her family. There was the British Navy, the most feared fighting force in the world, every member of which would be on his way to rescue her the moment it was learned what had happened to her. She had to survive for that triumphal moment, no matter what was done to her before they arrived.

No matter what was to happen to her now.

The captain, having inspected her, lowered the lantern. Whenever he looked at her long and slow like that, her blood seemed to coagulate, her skin to grow cold, no matter how determined her resolutions. It was not just the memory of what he had already done to her, where he had touched her, where he had looked; it was also the thought of what she knew he would like to do to her, every time his gaze drifted over her naked limbs – and she did not even know what a man could do to a woman. But she instinctively turned on her side, although not too far, so that he could look at only one thigh and one buttock, while her groin was hidden, at the same time as she folded her arms across her breasts. Those movements were instinctive, and yet hardly seemed to concern him. Because she actually was quite safe. Whatever he might want from her, he wanted his profit more.

'We passed through the Strait in the night,' he said in his surprisingly good English. 'Soon we will enter the port of Algiers. You must prepare to go ashore.' He extended his hand. 'Come.'

She remained crouched against the bulkhead, and his tone became imperative. 'Come!'

He snapped his fingers, and two of his men, who must have been waiting for just such a summons, entered the cabin. Hastily Felicity pushed herself up; she had no wish to be manhandled more than was necessary. Yet they still gripped her arms and half dragged her up the ladders to the deck, where more men waited with another assortment of buckets. She had not expected another bath so soon, and somehow it was vastly different in the harsh brightness of the morning sunlight than in the gloom of the previous evening. But before she could catch her breath the water was emptied over her, while she shivered and blinked and gasped for breath, and listened to the chatter of the men, and looked past them again, hoping for another glimpse of the Rock. But instead she saw in front of her a brown sea coast, from which a range of hills, equally brown, rose sharply, while in the distance she was sure she could see mountain peaks. On the edge of the coast, and directly before the ship, she looked at a town, rising away from fortified breakwaters and up the hill behind, dominated by a fortress on the hilltop, and presenting an aspect of startling whiteness against the drab colours of the surrounding country.

'Algiers,' the captain said, standing beside her and to her consternation squeezing her buttocks. 'That is my home.'

His sudden familiarity, both of word and deed, left her brain spinning, and again before she could recover she discovered herself being wrapped in a white linen garment, more like an enormous towel than a cloak, as it lacked buttons or ties and required being tucked into its own folds, which task was carried out with great enthusiasm by the man attending to her. Enough of the material was left free, even after it had been wrapped round her body several times, and allowed to fall in folds down to her ankles, to be used as a cowl for her head. Before this was set in place a white face mask was placed over her nose and mouth and chin, and secured by means of a draw string on the back of her head. Then the cowl was draped across her hair, so that only her eyes and perhaps an inch of forehead were left exposed, together with her hands and feet. But sandals were now being fitted over her toes.

It seemed utterly incongruous, after having been kept naked for three days, to be so utterly concealed. But her immediate feelings, even her fears as her wrists were pulled together in front of her and secured by a length of velvet cord, were submerged beneath her growing interest in the port they were now entering. It was a place clearly of much trade and prosperity, judging by the number of ships either unloading or taking on victuals alongside the various quays – most of them very similar to the corsair on whose deck she stood, and no doubt also pirates – by the activity along the waterfront, the babble of voices, the dust stirred by the passage of both people and animals. The appearance of her ship caused much comment and additional interest, as the sails were handed with great smartness, the huge boom of the lateen mainsail brought inboard to be stowed, and the vessel slipped expertly alongside an empty space in the dock. Warps were hurled and caught by waiting men to make the ship fast, and people clustered the quayside to shout questions at the crew, the men all armed, the women, she was relieved to note, dressed much as she was.

But she was not left to enjoy the scene for very long. Also waiting on the quayside were three very sumptuously dressed individuals, with jewelled red fezzes on their heads and jewelled buttons on their jackets. In complete contrast to everyone else, they carried no weapons at all and, as they came on board the moment the gangplank was run ashore, she observed that although they certainly appeared to be full grown men, they wore no beards or moustaches, again in complete contrast to everyone around them. Indeed, their faces seemed entirely hairless. Their voices, too, were high and harsh, as they chattered with the captain, descending into the hold to examine what lay there.

When they re-emerged, they seemed quite pleased, but were less so when they came aft to survey herself. They made no attempt to uncover any part of her, to her relief, but frowned and spoke sharply to the captain, so much so that she did not know whether to be insulted that they thought so little of her, or hopeful that they might, so to speak, throw her back.

Her feelings were put to right by the captain himself. 'You are to go with these people,' he told her. 'They are eunuchs, who work for my lord and master, Sheikh Abd er Rahman. They will take you to his house, and there your future will be decided. They are disappointed that there is only one of you, but they know that it is rare for even a single English beauty, who is also a virgin, to fall into our possession. Now listen to me well, English girl. You will be sold, and if you are fortunate you will spend the rest of your life in the harem of some wealthy man. The life you will lead will depend upon yourself. Accept your fate, and please your lord, and you will be happy. Bear your lord a son, and you may achieve heights you have never dreamed of. But resist him or anger him, and it will be the bastinado, if you are not drowned in a sack. Remember always that your lord has absolute power over you, of life and death. Now go with God.'

She felt incapable of response, as much because of her surprise at his obvious liking for her as by the horrendous fate he had just outlined. She was going to be sold as a slave. Her parents had had three black slaves in their house at Castries in St Lucia, jolly girls who had become almost her friends, when she had overcome her initial fear of them – she had been only twelve, and straight from England, when she had seen black people for the first time. But one of them had been lazy and occasionally insolent, and Mama had at last determined to get rid of her. Felicity could still remember the girl's terrified wails and pleas for mercy when she had realised she was going to be sold to a planter.

She remembered other things, too: of visiting a plantation once to take tea with the lady of the house, and passing large wooden triangles from which there had hung the naked bodies of both men and women, their backs a mass of open cuts, some of which had been so deep she had thought she could see their bones exposed, before she had hastily looked away. There were other tales, even more sinister, of the way some planters mishandled their belongings. Because the black people had been belongings. She remembered feeling sorry for them, but in an abstract fashion. Their fates and hers were too far separated for her truly to be able to understand anything of their feelings.

Now she would have to understand such feelings. She was to become such a chattel herself. But she would understand, she determined fiercely and she would survive, too. For just as long as she had to.

Yet when of the eunuchs spoke to her sharply, and another seized her bound wrists to jerk her towards the gangway, her courage nearly failed her. Eunuchs! Once again, a phenomenon of which she had only been dimly aware in the past, but never truly recognised – the concept was too horrible. But that, too, was now a sudden terrifying reality.

She looked at the captain, now such a rock of comfort and sympathy.

'You must go,' he said.

'Your name?' she gasped. 'Please!'

'I am Mansur,' he replied. 'But we will not meet again, English girl. Now go.'

She stumbled across the gangplank and on to the quay, and nearly fell at the sudden cessation of movement beneath her feet. People stared at her as the eunuchs caught her arms to hold her up and force her forward. She was unused to the sandals and her toes kept kicking stones, most painfully. Several times she would have fallen, but for the hands holding her up. She was aware of blinding heat, as the glare of the sun reflected from the white walls of the houses, soon followed by a tremendous thirst. Her eyes were narrowed to little slits as they began to water, and the whole discomfort was too much for her to observe much of her surroundings.

She knew that she was in the middle of a crowd of men, women, and children, all talking in high pitched voices, of dogs growling and barking, and asses braying, and scents and odours tickling her nostrils, and laughter; she caught glimpses of shops, in the doorways of which hung splendidly worked carpets or bolts of materials, and in which stood men, smoking pipes and surveying the world go by. She was aware, too, that she passed people who were clearly Europeans for all their Moorish dress and sun tanned skins; several of them even looked English – but she was also aware that these were slaves, hurrying about their masters' business, and they all carefully averted their eyes from the eunuchs and their obvious captive.

But most of all she was aware of the steepness of the hill she was climbing, so that she soon ran out of breath, and could only stumble along, panting and gasping, her breathing not helped by the unfamiliar face mask, until mercifully, and quite without warning, she was pushed through an arched doorway opening off the street. A bead curtain brushed her face and head, and she found herself in blessed shade, and in surroundings of some luxury, too.

The room in which she stood was not large, but there were thick carpets on the floor and sumptuous divans against the walls, and beyond, an inner courtyard which was a place of quiet beauty, far removed from the dust and hubbub of the street, in which flower beds and palm trees surrounded a fish pond, filled with brilliantly coloured, darting goldfish.

69

She was led into this courtyard and across it, into another section of the house. The eunuchs took her down a short corridor to arrive before a door made of heavy wood. One of the eunuchs produced a bunch of keys, and after some effort, turned the lock. The door was pushed in, and Felicity followed, to discover herself in a long gallery, almost dark after the brightness of the glare outside, because there were no windows, although the right hand wall was actually a trellis-work screen, with tiny apertures through which could be glimpsed another inner courtyard, larger than the one at the front of the house, but just as beautiful, and reached by a door at the end of the gallery.

Even as she realised that this Abd er Rahman must be a man of considerable wealth, both to own a pirate ship and an establishment of this much size and luxury, she also became aware that she was in a very special place, both from the subtle, but entirely feminine scents which surrounded her and, as her eyes became accustomed to the gloom, she realised that the left hand wall was actually a series of doorways leading off the gallery into inner chambers.

From these there now came eight women, dressed in a fashion she would not have considered acceptable in her wildest fantasies. Each of them wore wide, loose silk pantaloons, clasped at waist and ankle – but utterly sheer to reveal that there was nothing but flesh underneath. Their breasts were as exposed as their crotches by the small embroidered bolero jackets which hung from their shoulders, and moved to and fro as they walked. Their feet were encased in velvet slippers, and they wore small fezzes, rather like those of the eunuchs, on top of their abundant hair.

In fact, as each of them wore a set of different coloured garments, fez, bolero, pantaloons and slippers all matching, they made a splendidly kaleidoscopic picture, of pink and yellow and pale blue and crimson, and mauve and white and green and orange, and although two of them were definitely past their first youth and inclined to plumpness, the other six were young and slender, at least two hardly older than herself, Felicity calculated, and as they did not wear their yashmaks here in the harem – where she now knew herself to be – she could see that two of them were decidedly pretty.

But she was utterly embarrassed, not merely at being in

70

their presence at all when they were in such a state of undress, but because she realised, even as she attempted not to look at them, that their bodies were utterly devoid of hair, although that on their heads was the last word in luxuriant and sweet-smelling dark cleanliness.

Even more embarrassing, however, was the appearance of several children, half a dozen girls, ranging in ages from a toddler of about three to an obvious teenager, all dressed exactly like their mothers – as at least two of the women had to be – and equally disconcertingly depilated. There were also three very young boys, the eldest of whom could not have been more than eight years old, but even so, Felicity was most relieved to observe that they were fully dressed, in tunics and breeches.

And if she was embarrassed by them, they were not embarrassed by her, or by the presence of the eunuchs, whom they greeted familiarly. They surrounded Felicity, pulled the cloak from her shoulders and let it fall to the floor to leave her naked, while they examined her with the greatest interest. With her hands still bound together in front of her, she could do nothing to stop them, and in any event she thought it safest to remain absolutely still, even as they fingered her hair, drawing it in great strands away from her head, stroked her skin, felt her breasts and buttocks and even her stomach, and pulled her pubic hair with curious comments.

The sensations induced by their presence, and her helplessness in their midst, would, she knew, have made her faint only a few days before – or should have. As she had survived everything else which had happened to her since the capture of the *Poseidon* without fainting, she began to wonder if there was something the matter with her, and indeed, she was less interested in being manhandled in so intimate a fashion than in the remarks they were making, which she could not understand, but which she decided, from the way they wrinkled their noses, were far from complimentary. But she could understand that after two days in the cabin of the corsair, following five unsalubrious days in the cabin of the *Poseidon*, she could neither look nor smell in any way attractive.

The inspection completed, the oldest of the women, obviously the senior wife or concubine, gave orders, and the eunuchs marched her forward again, through one of the doors to her left. As the woman did not look particularly unfriendly, Felicity licked her lips as expressively as she could to convey her thirst, and the woman appeared to understand, for she gave another order, and one of the younger girls hurried off and came back with a cup of liquid for her to drink. It wasn't water, to her surprise, but yet tasted better than anything she had ever drunk before, except that it made her aware of how hungry she was.

But she was apparently not going to be allowed to eat for a while. She had gathered that the women's derogatory remarks had been with regard to the length of time since her last proper bath more than to any defects in her face or figure. This they now proceeded to remedy. Felicity understood that survival entailed not resisting them in any way, but in fact she did not wish to – whatever lay ahead of her, to be again clean and sweet-smelling, something she had so anticipated on her arrival in Gibraltar, was a most attractive thought, even if she realised that the eunuchs were going to share in the operation. And the children!

For she was to undergo much more than a bath. She was escorted into what was certainly a bathing chamber, although with certain attributes she had never seen before, not all of them reassuring. The floor was on three descending levels, the lowest being in slats and drains to allow the water to run off, while on the second level there was a glowing fire, over which there was a huge pot suspended on a spit, which gave off a sickly sweet odour, akin to that of boiling toffee.

The room was quite large, but became distinctly crowded when all eight of the women, accompanied by their children, as well as the three eunuchs, filed in behind her. The women and children, including the little boys, promptly removed all of their clothing, and the eunuchs most of theirs – to Felicity's enormous relief they retained a loin cloth each.

But in fact she realised that she was temporarily inured to shock; in the past three days her nerves had been exposed to so many horrors, so many sights she would not have supposed possible. She felt very like a drunken man, staggering from support to support, always surprised and relieved to find that there was yet another support on which he could lean. Thus she would have supposed that the sight of her friends and shipmates being raped and butchered and drowned would have driven her irresistibly mad; but it had not. Similarly with her being flung across the cannon to be examined, or exposed time and again on the decks of the corsair, or being led like an animal through the streets of Algiers.

Yet she had not gone mad, and so far she had not even been harmed. Simply by bending before the irresistible forces with which she was presently surrounded, rather than attempting to defy them, and snapping like a twig.

So once again she determined to submit to whatever her new captors chose to do to her, although she could not help but shudder when she discovered she was to be shaved, most meticulously, from the neck down, including her armpits and crotch. The shaving was done by one of the eunuchs, but the women were eager to assist him, as the children were to gather round and watch. Felicity felt as if she were a huge toy, being unwrapped for their pleasure – but she kept trying to hold her breath as the very sharp razor was passed over her skin, again and again, being forced to gasp every time there was a new sensation, her breasts being touched, or her legs pulled apart.

Nor was being shaved the end of her ordeal, for her body was then coated with the toffeelike mixture, ladled from the cooking pot on to her stomach, and then spread with great enjoyment over every inch of her body by the eager assistants. The mixture was just short of boiling, and she could not stop herself giving a whimper of discomfort and anticipated agony, but the women laughed and made reassuring sounds, while they created an entirely new set of sensations as they forced the toffee into every available crevice.

In fact it did cool very rapidly, leaving her in an almost unbearable condition of half arousal and half total discomfort, while the wildest of thoughts plunged through her brain. For a moment she even wondered if these people were actually cannibals, who were preparing her for the oven.

But now she was made to lie absolutely still, while one of the eunuchs produced a length of silken cord. The women ceased their chatter, and even the children were enjoined to

73

be quiet as with the greatest of concentration the eunuch, holding the cord in both hands, pressed it into the coating on Felicity's arm, at the shoulder, and then slowly drew it down the entire length of the limb, to the wrist. Felicity found that she was again holding her breath; she did not need to be told that she could be skinned if he was careless or she made a sudden move. But he was an expert, and her arm was left absolutely smooth and white and hairless.

Then she did want to move, as she realised he was not only going to treat her arm, but now she was held still by some ten pairs of hands, while the elder woman spoke to her in quiet but authoritative tones. She obeyed with an enormous effort, closing her eyes and knowing only the tumultuous desires which raced away from her groin.

Her front completed to the eunuch's satisfaction, she was made to lie on her belly while the whole operation was repeated on her back. This was easier to accept, although once again she reflected that if anyone, a week earlier, had told her that she would one day be held naked on a cold stone floor, by eight naked women and two eunuchs, as well as a family of children, while a third eunuch drew a silken cord down the inside of her thighs, she would have slapped his or her face in outrage.

But at last the long, slow tickling sweeps were done. Then she had to endure the caress of his hand, as he made sure no hairs had been overlooked, a task in which he was joined by the two older women, while the others giggled and chattered. Then she was pulled to her feet and conducted to the lowest level to be bathed. She was soaped and rinsed, time and again, by the women, while two of the eunuchs concentrated on washing her hair. The intimacy of the bath, the sensuality of the fingers and the warmth of the sweet scent of the perfumed water, coming on top of all that had happened before, combined to make her mind wander away into a dream world she had never known before, but in which she felt she was trembling on the verge of an experience she would never forget – and which would change her forever.

But, she thought, as she gazed at herself in the full-length mirror which filled the entire inner wall of the bath chamber, actually seeing herself in the nude for the first time in her life as opposed to a hasty and self-embarrassed glance in the course of dressing, was she not already changed forever? Could anyone undergo such a physical experience and not be changed forever?

Yet when the door at the top of the room suddenly opened to admit a man, she instinctively gave a little shriek of alarm and sank to her knees, endeavouring to hide behind her hands.

The women and the eunuchs were bowing, while the children also fell to their knees; none of them seemed embarrassed by their nakedness, however anxious they might be to illustrate their servility, and Felicity realised she was in the presence of Abd er Rahman. Her new master! She allowed herself a hasty glance at him, and was decidedly reassured. Abd er Rahman was short and stout, with a flowing beard and carefully waxed moustaches, which stood away from his lips like the wings of an enormous butterfly. His dress was in keeping with everything else in his house, ornate and luxurious. The sash over his red tunic was cloth of gold, he wore an enormous jewelled pin at his throat, and the haft of the little dagger which hung from his waist, as well as the toes of his upturned velvet slippers, glittered with rubies and emeralds. Even the beard and moustache could not hide the dimples beside his mouth, the soft curve of the cheeks, and his eyes were like pools of shallow black liquid, sliding to and fro, but principally concentrating upon her.

She found it difficult to be afraid of him, as indeed down to three days ago she had never actually been afraid of any man. Yet he had the right, which he might at any moment choose to exercise, to throw her on the ground and ... she had no idea, her brain crowded with the memory of the pirates kneeling between the legs of Peggy Flemming and her mother while they had shrieked their agony and horror at what was being done to them. Therefore it could in no way approximate any of the sensations she had just experienced.

Yet whatever it was, it would have to be endured. Not only because she had no doubt at all that everyone else in the room would be anxious to assist their master, but because only by enduring, and even pleasing, as Mansur the

75

pirate had told her, could she hope to survive. And now she was more than ever determined to survive.

But she could not stop her muscles from tensing as Abd er Rahman spoke, in a voice as gentle as his appearance, and the eunuchs gripped her arms to raise her to her feet. She stood there, water rolling down her arms and legs, dripping from hair, nipples and chin, while he came down the levels to look at her, and subject her to the inevitable examination, stranding her hair through his fingers, opening her mouth to peer inside, fingering her breasts, watching her intently as he stroked a nipple into tumescence, then stooping to examine her genitals, the women making her part her legs to accommodate him.

They were also, she realised for the first time, themselves almost holding their breaths with anxiety; she might have been a rare animal, or a statue, which they had produced for their master's approbation, or perhaps angry distaste, and in fact, as she was keeping as still as she possibly could, presumably she did suggest a statue. But she was flesh and blood, and she knew she wasn't going to be able to remain still much longer, when he moved away, speaking rapidly.

The women clapped their hands with pleasure, and some relief, she thought – not only because he was obviously pleased, but because of something additional in his commands. She guessed, as he left the room and they immediately fell to work again, that they had been apprehensive that he might be going to keep her for himself, to their mutual disadvantage. Whereas now she was obviously being prepared for display. She didn't know whether to protest or not, and in any event could not, as she was carefully patted dry with huge towels, the eunuchs meanwhile wrapping up her head and hair in other towels and gently drying it, and was then made to sit on a stool while they painted her fingernails and toenails with henna. While this process was taking place, the eunuchs completed the drying of her hair, which was then brushed and combed and perfumed and brushed again, until it lay in a long dark brown sheen down her back.

Now at last she was taken from the bath chamber, still wrapped in her towels, and presented with a meal, in which

76

the women and children shared, with much good humoured chatter and laughter. Felicity was more interested in the mouth–watering food, for there was sweet tea, bread and honey, and couscous, as well as a variety of the most delicious sherbets. Nothing had ever tasted so good, and following her experiences of a very long day, as well as the repeated shocks to her senses, she wished only to lie down and sleep when she was finished.

To her surprise she was allowed to do this; escorted to a divan in one of the inner rooms, and there allowed to nestle naked amongst the cushions, a delightful sensation which was only a copy of what the other women were doing, while the children were chased out into the garden to play. She slept heavily and dreamlessly, until rudely awakened by a sharp slap on the face. She sat up, panting, for a moment unsure of where she was, and had her face covered with a wet towel before she had properly gathered her senses.

Hurriedly she suppressed her anger, as she discovered that she was again surrounded by the eunuchs as well as the rest of the tribe, smoothing her eyebrows, re-brushing her hair, applying dabs of perfume to her neck and ears and armpits and groin. She was being prepared for ... she had no idea. While the woman who had slapped her chattered at her, not scolding but certainly informing, all without Felicity having the slightest idea what she was saying.

She supposed she was very rapidly going to find out, however. At last they seemed satisfied, and subjected her to another minute examination, which seemed satisfactory. Then she was wrapped in a fresh, clean linen cloak, or haik, given velvet slippers to wear, and had her face concealed behind another yashmak, After which the three eunuchs escorted her back out of the harem.

She was desperately sorry to see the women remain behind – oddly enough, she felt that as long as she was in their company she was perfectly safe. Now she realised the truth: that she was about to be offered for sale, and her legs almost gave way. But the eunuchs held her arms to urge her onwards, and once again fear was at least neutralised by curiosity, as she discovered she was not actually being taken out of Abd er Rahman's house, but instead along a succession of corridors until she entered a very large room, like all the others in this palace, sumptuously furnished with carpets and drapes and divans of incalculable value, and where there waited two men, seated on one of the divans, smoking water pipes and conversing in low tones. Both men rose to their feet at her entrance, but she suspected that had nothing to do with manners.

One of them was of course Abd er Rahman, which was something of a relief. The other was a man she had never seen before, and she did not like the look of him at all. Where Abd er Rahman was plump and jolly looking, this man reminded her of the captain of the corsair, Mansur, save that he possessed a far greater aura of authority, and indeed wore the expression of a man of some power. Yet his dress was utterly simple, certainly when contrasted with that of the captain, while beside his simple white tunic and breeches, and his brown kid boots, Abd er Rahman glowed like a lighted lantern. There were no jewels here, save for a ruby clasp on his green turban – although Felicity suspected that one stone was perhaps worth more than all of Abd er Rahman's baubles added together – and his scimitar was clearly intended for use rather than show.

Abd er Rahman certainly held him in awe, and hastily waved the eunuchs, who had led Felicity into the very centre of the room, away to stand against the far wall. She gazed at the two men, feeling as if there was a great void where her stomach had been, for all the satisfying meal she had had before her siesta, while they looked back, conversing in low tones and obviously discussing her. Then the stranger asked Abd er Rahman a question, to which Abd clearly replied in the affirmative, as he gestured his guest forward.

The stranger advanced, and stood immediately in front of Felicity. It was all she could do to remain still as the dark eyes stared into hers, but she refused to lower her gaze. He stroked his beard, and then reached out and took the cowl of the haik from her head, before releasing the yashmak to look at her face. She had no doubt at all what he was going to do next, and tensed her muscles, but instead of removing the haik altogether, the man took her entirely by surprise by saying, in English, 'Speak.'

78

She could only stare at him.

'The Sheikh tells me you are English,' the man said. 'Are you not English?'

Felicity licked her lips. 'I am English.'

'Ah. Good. I am pleased. When the Sheikh sent to me and said he had something of great interest to show me, I was sceptical. He is given to exaggeration. But in your case he was telling the truth. Yes. What is your name?'

Felicity had to draw a deep breath. 'My name is Felicity Crown.'

'Ah,' he said again. 'I like that very much. Yes. I shall buy you, Felicity Crown. You will go with these eunuchs, and prepare yourself. We have a long journey ahead of us.'

His courtesy was most reassuring. Boldly she asked, 'Will you not tell me to whom I now belong, sir?'

He frowned at her, and then almost smiled. 'I am Mohammed ben Idris. I am the Vizier of the Dey of Tripoli, Greatest of the Faithful, Lord of the Mediterranean. That is where you are going, Felicity Crown, to Tripoli.'

It occurred to Felicity that it might not be difficult to establish at least a mental rapport with this man, perhaps even a superiority; she was well on the way do doing that already. 'And you say that you are not the greatest man in this Tripoli, my lord ben Idris? How can that be?'

Once again he frowned, and as quickly smiled, and turned to Abd er Rahman, speaking brusquely. Abd er Rahman hesitated, and then nodded, glancing sharply at ben Idris as he spoke.

Again the Vizier smiled, and nodded, and turned back to Felicity. 'I have completed the purchase.' he said, 'and paid more than perhaps I should, indeed. You are very fortunate, you see, Felicity Crown. Abd er Rahman knew of my presence in Algiers, and he also knows my tastes, and so offered you to me privately, thus saving you the humiliation of the public block.'

'And I am to your tastes, my lord?' she asked.

Mohammed ben Idris came right up to her, and now he did take the haik from her shoulders, and allow it to fall about her ankles, while he gazed at her. 'Oh, indeed,' he said. 'You are to my taste. And will be more so when you are tamed. You English women are all the same. I had another once, and she I had to drown, slowly.' He smiled, and Felicity caught her breath; she had never seen anything so unpleasant. 'I sewed her up in a sack with two cats and two rats, and suspended her over the sea. In time they all fell in.'

Felicity thought she was going to choke. And she had thought she could dominate this man.

'Now you are similarly insolent,' Mohammed ben Idris continued. 'But you are too pretty to drown. At least until you have begun to bore me. Go with these men. They will prepare you for the bastinado.'

'The ... the bastinado?' She had no idea what he was talking about, but the very word sounded highly unpleasant.

'Oh, yes,' he said, smiling at her. 'Before we set out upon our journey, I am going to cane that splendidly shaped rear of yours, that you may know who is the master here, and who the slave.'

Chapter 4

The Mediterranean – 1803–4

'Sometimes I think I am going mad.' Toby leaned on the taffrail of the USS *Essex* and gazed down into the clear blue waters of Syracuse Harbour in Sicily, then up at the low, green hills which surrounded the huge, landlocked natural haven. Syracuse surely had to be one of the most beautiful and peaceful places on earth. And over the past two years he had come to hate it.

'You don't still dream of that girl taken by the pirates?' asked his companion and immediate superior, Stephen Decatur, first lieutenant of the *Essex*. 'Did you not only ever meet her once?'

'Her? Oh, you mean Felicity Crown.' Toby gave a false laugh. 'Good heavens, Stephen, I have quite forgotten what she looked like. Although the circumstances were unusual, to be sure . . .' He bit his lip before he carried the lie too far. Because he could still see her face before his eyes every time he closed them, even in daylight, much less in the dark solitude of his bunk. Of course, after three years the features had become fuzzy – and he knew nothing else about her. Yet quite without warning, she had become the symbol of what this war was all about, helpless captives being held in the vicious maw of a heathen, desperate, despotic power.

He had been so eager to fight this war, knowing full well that it could never return Felicity Crown, either to her parents or to the world of civilised behaviour, even if she were not already dead. And surely she must be already dead. Yet there had been the prospect of vengeance, of ending the scourge of the Barbary pirates for ever, of returning to America with a sense of something accomplished ... instead of which he went each day about his duties, endlessly repetitive, endlessly boring, endlessly hot. Even in harbour they maintained the routine of a ship at sea, four hours on watch, four hours off, save for the dog watches between four and eight in the evening, when each watch had only two hours on duty, so as to rotate the duty times once every other twenty-four hours. But that was all the variety the system permitted, and whether you walked the quarterdeck from eight until midnight tonight, and midnight until four tomorrow night, made very little odds – you knew you would be on the eight to midnight shift the day after.

For the rest, there was breakfast at eight, then punishment drill. There had been few punishments on board *Constellation*. That had been a happy ship. But then, there had been few punishments on board *Essex*, until she had arrived in Sicily. The men had supposed they were going to fight. Instead, as they had nothing to do but sit around the ship, they became as bored as the officers, and began to quarrel and then to fight ... and then to suffer the cat-o'-nine-tails.

Punishment over, there were the inspections to be carried out of decks and rigging and sails and guns and quarters. Then lunch. Luncheon over, there were the midshipmen and ship's boys to be instructed in navigation and seamanship and boat handling. Then dinner. And then bed, if you were not on watch. With an exactly similar day to be anticipated on the morrow.

When given liberty ashore, he, like most of his shipmates, explored old Syracuse, gaped at the ruins of the Roman amphitheatre outside the town, and resisted the attempted flirtations of the dark-eyed Sicilian beauties – in this instance, *un*like most of his shipmates. Perhaps there he was creating his own hell, but he did not think he could ever hold a woman in his arms again without vomiting, unless he had settled with the Barbary corsairs first, and thereby, he hoped, regained a modicum of his self-respect.

He sighed. 'Two years, Stephen. Two years! I had supposed we came here to chastise the Dey of Tripoli, and rescue all those Americans held captive by him. Instead of which we have done nothing but swim and fish and paint our ships.'

Decatur's lean, saturnine features broke into a savage smile. 'Why, we have demonstrated off the African coast at least once a year, my dear Toby, and we have chased an occasional Tripolitanian vessel, without ever catching any of them, to be sure, and we have ... why, we have sat at anchor here and listened to the teredo worms nibbling at our bottoms. But I doubt not we have accomplished more than that – we must surely be the laughing stock of the world. It takes a good deal of effort to accomplish that.'

Toby glanced at him in surprise. He had never doubted that his senior felt the same frustration as himself, with more reason, as everyone knew how Thomas Truxton had asked for Decatur as his second captain and been refused by the Navy Board – or that he was as privately critical of the commodore. But he had never supposed he would hear the first lieutenant voice such opinions. Yet there could be no man in the entire squadron not aware by now that James Barron would far rather spend his time being entertained by the Sicilian magnates than navigating the dangerous shoals off the coast of Libya.

'Still,' Decatur said. 'Surely one day. . .'

He straightened as the anchor watch called: 'Vessel entering the harbour.'

Decatur levelled his telescope. 'The *Enterprise* schooner, by God! She'll have word from the *President*.' He slapped his thigh. 'I had no doubts that John Rodgers would stir things up.'

Rodgers, now promoted captain, had recently arrived to join the Mediterranean squadron, in command of the *President*, which was at least a sign that Washington was not altogether happy with their commodore's inactivity. And Rodgers had insisted on keeping to the sea as much as possible, patrolling the passage between Malta and the mainland, even if he had not been able to persuade Barron to do likewise.

The commodore came on deck now, very smartly dressed

in his shore-going uniform. 'What is the commotion, Mr Decatur?'

'The *Enterprise* schooner has returned, sir, in some haste, I would say,' Decatur reported. Indeed, the schooner had not even shortened sail until already inside the huge harbour, and now came surging by the anchored *Essex*, while her commander, Lieutenant Isaac Hull, used his speaking trumpet.

'Ahoy, the *Essex*. *President* reports a large Tripolitanian fleet standing out from the harbour, destination eastbound.'

'The devil,' Barron muttered. 'Bring your ship up, sir,' he bellowed back. 'Bring your ship up.' He lowered his voice. 'Does the fellow know no etiquette, careering about enclosed waters like that?'

'A large fleet,' Decatur said. 'And eastbound. We'll have time to intercept them, sir. This could be the opportunity we have been waiting for.'

'Intercept a large fleet, Mr Decatur? Why, that could mean the Dey's entire navy. We have two frigates, and that schooner.'

'Not one of theirs is a match for ours, sir.'

'I did not come here to hazard a third of the United States' naval strength at such odds, Mr Decatur.'

'Well, sir,' Toby ventured. 'If their entire fleet has sailed, might it not be possible to carry out a raid on the port itself? It can scarcely be adequately defended.'

'By God, Toby, but you're right,' Decatur cried. 'If we could get in there, burn his palace, free the captives...'

'I wonder, gentlemen, if either of you will ever be fit for command,' Barron remarked contemptuously. 'Assault the port, indeed. Tripoli, Mr McGann, as a glance at the chart will show you, lies at the end of a channel through a large area of sandbanks. A channel for which we have no directions. We would have to feel our way in behind our boats, and that means there is no way we could achieve any kind of surprise, as they would see us coming long before we could approach them. And you suppose it is undefended just because some ships have left? There are forts in there, sir. Ships cannot assault forts with any hope of success. That has been proved too often in the past. Besides, I have a dinner engagement with Signor Martino Pucchini. There are important matters to discuss.'

'But . . . the *Enterprise* is looking for orders, sir,' Decatur said.

Barron looked at the schooner, hove to as sail was taken off. 'When Mr Hull has properly moored his ship, Mr Decatur, thank him for his information, and then send him back to sea. Tell him my orders for *President* are that she should follow the Tripolitanian fleet, taking care not to be brought to action, and report back on its destination. That way we may well learn something of value. Why, they could be seeking allies, perhaps from Turkey itself. Now that would be an important development. Good-day to you, gentlemen.' He went to the gangway, and his waiting gig.

'Something of value,' Decatur said in disgust. 'Take care not to be brought to action, by God!'

'Without those orders, I could have nobbled up at least half a dozen,' John Rodgers agreed. 'They had not been at sea five hours, but they were straggled all over the horizon. As for the port itself, so far as I could make out there was hardly a skiff left in there. We could have penetrated the harbour, I am certain. Oh, we would have had to take some shot, I will not argue with that. And the commodore is right, historically: forts, well manned, have always proved too much for ships. But would those forts have been well manned? I suspect our cannon, properly aimed, would soon have discouraged the Moors.' He sighed. 'Ah, well, the chance is gone. The fleet is safely returned.'

'With six prizes, you say?' Decatur asked. 'Including an American?'

'Out of Athens. Aye, a sad business. With us virtually spectators.'

Toby had no opinion to offer, because he was angrier than either of the others. The American squadron *was* fast becoming the laughing stock of the world, especially now that the war between Great Britain and France, ended during their first year here, had been resumed with more ferocity than ever. In the midst of which mighty conflagration the three of them sat on the long sweep of shore which enclosed

Syracuse Harbour and fished, their ships resting quietly at anchor before them. At fishing, they had become experts, the commodore, as usual, deeming that as the autumnal gales approached, his squadron was better off in sheltered waters than tossing about south of Malta.

It felt particularly galling to be here, overlooking the scene of several of the greatest sea battles of antiquity, when fleets of seventy and eighty triremes on each side – the Athenian bent on taking the city, the Syracusan bent on defending their home to the last breath – had fought each other to the bitter end. As Decatur had so angrily said last spring, the American squadron was fighting only the Teredo worms, and that was a battle the worms would certainly eventually win, unless the ships were to move.

But what was their alternative? James Barron apparently remained the choice of Congress to command the Mediterranean squadron, and conduct the war with Tripoli. For any one of them to resign his command in disgust and go home would be to end his career. Besides, Toby at least did not want to go home. He wanted to fight. It was rapidly becoming a case of wanting to fight anybody, not just the Dey of Tripoli.

But just to sit here, day after day and week after week and month after month . . .

'Sail entering the harbour,' came the distant cry from the lookout on the *Essex*.

'That will be *Enterprise*, returning from patrol,' Decatur said. 'Hull may have news.' Their fellow lieutenant, who commanded the schooner, was the only one of them in regular employment.

They packed their fishing baskets, collected their catches, and hurried along the shore to where the liberty boat waited. And paused to frown at the entrance through which there slowly moved a very large frigate. A smaller vessel followed her.

'That's a big one, by God,' Rodgers said. 'She almost looks like *Constitution*.'

'She is *Constitution*!' Decatur cried. 'Give way, lads, give way. We've reinforcements.'

'But look there,' Toby shouted, even more excited. 'She's also flying a commodore's broad pennant.'

'Gentlemen.' Captain Edward Preble came through the gangway of the USS *Essex*, saluted the quarterdeck, and then inspected the guard of honour Decatur had hastily assembled. 'Stephen.' He shook hands. 'Good to see you.'

'Welcome, sir, welcome,' Decatur said. 'But. . .'

'You'll know Captain Bainbridge; he commands *Philadelphia*.' Preble, small and dark and intense, indicated the tall, thin man behind him. 'John . . .' he shook hands with Rodgers. 'You're a sight for sore eyes. Toby McGann, by God! I knew your father.' Another firm handshake. 'And you're a chip off the old block in more than just size, I'm informed. Tom Truxton sends you all his best regards. By God,' he said again, 'but you've a hot sun in these parts.'

'And enervating,' remarked William Bainbridge. 'Apparently.'

'I will confess, sir, that I am befogged,' Decatur said.

'I've despatches for your commanding officer,' Preble explained, and looked right and left. 'You do have a commanding officer?'

'He is ashore, sir.'

'He is returning now,' Toby said, watching the captain's gig pulling away from the beach.

'Ah,' Preble said. 'I think it would be best we awaited him in the cabin. Mr Decatur, you'll dismiss your people. Gentlemen, you'll accompany me.' Without waiting for a reply he marched across the deck to the companionway, Bainbridge following him.

Toby, Decatur and Rodgers exchanged glances, and then looked across the water at USS *Philadelphia*, a sister to both *President* and the *Essex*, as they all were to the *Constellation*, and then at the bulk of the USS *Constitution*, the biggest ship in the Navy, beyond. The fact was, whatever the mystery behind Preble's unannounced arrival, and he was second only to John Barry in seniority in the Navy, they now had a very powerful frigate squadron in the eastern Mediterranean.

'You'd best remain for the commodore,' Decatur muttered to Toby, and led Rodgers below.

Toby dismissed the guard of honour, took his place with the boatswain to whistle their commanding officer on board. Barron had obviously left the shore in some haste, and did not look very pleased; his cheeks were flushed with wine and one of his jacket buttons was undone.

'Well, sir, well?' he barked as he came through the gangway. 'That is the USS *Constitution*, Mr McGann.'

'And the *Philadelphia*, sir,' Toby agreed.

'And what are they doing here, sir? Can you tell me that?'

'Their captains are waiting for you below, sir. With despatches.'

'But *Constitution* is flying a broad pennant. There is some mystery here.'

'I am sure her captain will be able to explain it to you, sir,' Toby ventured, scarce daring to believe what was becoming more apparent every moment.

'Hm,' Barron commented, and hurried to the companionway.

Toby went behind him. He did not intend to miss a moment of the coming confrontation.

'James!' Preble was on his feet behind the wardroom table, saluting and then extending his hand. The other officers stood to attention.

Barron ignored them as he stared at his visitor. 'Captain Preble?'

'In the flesh,' Preble agreed, smiling as jovially as his tight features would permit.

'I do not understand your presence, sir,' Barron said.

'Then sit down, James, sit down. I have a communication for you from Congress.'

For the first time Barron looked at the other four officers, acknowledged their presence with a nod, then slowly lowered himself into a chair before picking up the envelope Preble had placed before him. He looked at it for several seconds before finally slitting it. There was no sound in the cabin save for the gentle slurp of water beneath the rudder.

Slowly Barron raised his head; his flush had deepened. 'I am to haul down my pennant,' he said in amazed tones.

No one spoke.

'I am accused of spending too much time in Italian ports,' Barron said. 'That is absurd. This is my home base.'

Still no one spoke.

After a moment the little man seemed to gather himself. 'Well . . . I salute you, Captain Preble. And wish you success of your new command. May I ask which ship I am to take home?'

Toby held his breath.

'I'm afraid no ship of this squadron can be spared, Captain Barron,' Preble said. 'I regret this sincerely. But if you will read further, you will see that those are the orders of Congress. You are to make your way across Europe and seek a passage from one of the German ports.'

Barron read the rest of the letter, opened his mouth, then closed it again and stood up. '.I must see to my gear,' he said, and left the cabin.

There were another few minutes of silence, then Toby said, 'I feel very much like throwing my hat into the air.'

'You will do no such thing, Mr McGann,' Preble said sternly. 'Occasions like this are the tragedies of a man's career, and should be regarded with due respect. Captain Barron has had a distinguished record, up till now. Perhaps command of a squadron was beyond his capabilities, as indeed it may prove to be beyond mine . . .' He looked from face to face, his eyes twinkling; they all knew he had already commanded a squadron, and had, indeed, in this same *Essex*, been the first United States commander to lead a ship beyond the Cape of Good Hope. 'However,' he continued, 'I must carry out my orders as given me by Congress. We are at war, gentlemen, even if your recent inactivity may have caused you to doubt that fact. Captain Rodgers, I would like a resumé of our operations against Tripoli during the past two years.'

'Yes, *sir*,' Rodgers replied. 'Each summer there has been a distant blockade of the port itself . . .'

'A distant blockade, Mr Rodgers?'

'From twenty to fifty miles off the coast, sir, according to the weather.'

'Do you consider such a blockade to have been effective, Mr Rodgers?'

Rodgers shook his head. 'Not in the least. There are

89

sufficient inshore channels which the Tripolitanians used freely to come and go.'

'I see. Continue. Have there been no actions?'

'We have pursued Tripolitanian squadrons on several occasions,' Rodgers said. 'But always without bringing them to battle.'

'Are their ships so much faster than ours?'

'No, sir. But they have always sought shelter amidst the sandbanks which encumber the coast, and into which Captain Barron prohibited our venturing for fear of stranding.'

'I see,' Preble said again. 'Go on.'

'There was one occasion, this spring, when the entire Tripolitanian fleet ventured forth, but we confined ourselves to shadowing it ...' He shrugged. 'For the rest, we have fought a continuing war with the teredo worm.'

'I see,' Preble remarked a third time, and again scanned their faces. 'Well, gentlemen, I have to inform you that I did not sail five thousand miles to fight worms. These are my orders, which are to be implemented immediately: all shore leave is from this moment cancelled, all liberty boats are to be recalled, and any man not on board his ship by sunset will be posted a deserter. All victualling is to be completed by sunset, all preparations for sea completed by midnight. This squadron will weigh anchors at dawn and proceed to sea.' Another glance around the cabin. 'Every ship and every man in this squadron, gentlemen. Now go about your duties.'

Toby and Decatur clasped hands as they reached the deck. 'Hurrah,' Toby said. 'Oh, hurrah.'

'And again, hurrah,' Decatur said. 'We are going to fight at last.'

'We need more sail, Mr Decatur,' Edward Preble said, 'if we are going to take those fellows down before they gain shelter. Set your top-gallants.'

'Aye-aye,' Decatur acknowledged, and hurried forward to give the necessary orders.

Preble had elected to transfer his pennant to the *Essex* for close work against the African coast – she drew considerably less than the far larger *Constitution* – and if this had entailed a great sharpening of discipline, it had also meant they were in

90

the thick of whatever action was to be found, which was a most pleasant change.

Standing beside the commodore, Toby swung his telescope from left to right. The four Tripolitanian ships they had sighted the previous evening, south of Malta, obviously totally surprised to find the American squadron at sea in November, were strung out in front of them in full flight towards the now visible shore. Behind them the three smaller American frigates were also sailing south as fast as they could, while *Constitution* prowled the northern horizon, Malta now long out of sight.

But with every minute they were entering uncharted waters, for them; James Barron had never allowed his ships to approach this close to the dangerous sandbanks off the Libyan coastline.

'Look at that gallant fellow Bainbridge,' Preble said. 'He outstrips us all. By God, sir, that is rank insubordination, to outsail one's commodore.' But he was clearly delighted.

'The *Philadelphia* has fewer worms in her hull, perhaps, sir,' Toby ventured.

Preble shot him a glance. 'Then we should travel even more quickly, Mr McGann, as where there are worms, there is surely less timber. That will do very nicely, Mr Decatur,' he acknowledged, as the first lieutenant came aft, having set the fine-weather sails at the very tops of each mast.

Preble looked aft, to where the *President* was bounding along in their wake; further back yet, the *Enterprise* schooner carried only her working canvas, and was almost hull down; armed only with a few light six-pounder guns, her business was fast scouting and the rapid transmission of despatches, not becoming mixed up in a fight.

Toby continued to watch the fleeing pirates, and suddenly caught his breath. 'Breakers, sir.'

'Rocks?'

'No, sir. I would say sand.'

'To either side,' Decatur commented.

Preble levelled his glass. Now the pirates were almost blanketed from their view by the billowing canvas of the *Philadelphia*, directly ahead. But to either side of the American vessel could be seen the ripples of breaking water over the sandbanks. They were now within five miles of the coast, and the houses of Tripoli could clearly be seen.

'Does Bainbridge not see them?' Decatur muttered.

'He reckons where the pirates can sail, so can he,' Preble said.

'Not necessarily, sir,' Decatur argued. 'Those fellows draw only a fraction of the water our ships require, and there will be bends in the channel which the pirates will anticipate, but which may well catch Captain Bainbridge unawares.'

'Shall I signal recall, sir?' Toby asked.

Preble continued to stare at the *Philadelphia*, biting his lip. The frigate was now very close to the corsairs, and even as they watched her bow chasers exploded, and one of the pirate masts went by the board.

'Noble fellow, Bainbridge,' he said. 'Oh, noble fellow. He knows no fear.'

'He'll still not catch them,' Decatur said. 'Sir, I most respectfully urge that you call him back.'

Preble sighed. 'It goes against the grain. Mr Decatur, the first thing we must do is put boats down and thoroughly chart that channel.'

'That'll bring the pirates back out to stop us,' Toby said gleefully.

'So it will, Mr McGann, so it will. Meanwhile ...' he shrugged. 'Set the recall signal.'

'Aye-aye,' Toby said, and hurried to the signal halliards, where a midshipman waited, book in hand.

'Supposing he's looking behind him,' Decatur said.

'Well, it's to be hoped he's looking ahead of him. Shorten sail, Mr Decatur, and signal *President* to do the same, then prepare to anchor. As soon as *Philadelphia* rejoins us, we will ... Great God in heaven.'

The glasses came up again, but even with the naked eye it was possible to discern the catastrophe which had happened in front of them, as the cries of the sailors on the main deck and the forecastle testified. For the *Philadelphia* had come to a halt, while the fresh northerly breeze still filled her sails, and as they watched, her foretopmast went slumping down as if shot away, its sails a flailing mess.

Toby and Decatur looked at the commodore, aghast.

Preble continued to stare at the stranded vessel. What thoughts must be going through his mind Toby dared not consider. The United States Navy only possessed six frigates. And now one of them was stranded. Through Preble's decision to order a general chase in the first place, and then through his fatal hesitation in ordering her recalled. Now, to get her off a sandbank in an almost tideless sea would require an immense effort, as well as certain knowledge of the surrounding water . . . and no adjacent enemies.

'Can we tow her free, Mr Decatur?' Preble asked in a low voice.

'She drove on at speed,' Decatur said. 'And we would be working to windward in very narrow waters.' He shrugged. 'We have to attempt it, sir.'

Preble chewed his lip some more. It was a horrifying decision to have to make. Send another of his precious ships in there to attempt to tow the *Philadelphia* to safety, or abandon her.

'Heave to,' the commodore said. 'And anchor, as I have instructed. Signal *President* to do the same. Mr Decatur, you'll prepare a boat party, well armed. We will cover you as far as we can, but those villains may well try to interfere with your activities. I want that channel sounded and surveyed and a plan made to bring *Philadelphia* out this evening. This is a most urgent matter, Mr Decatur.'

'Aye-aye,' Stephen cried, and slid down the ladder into the waist.

'They're coming back, sir,' Toby said.

Preble's glass came up. 'God,' he said. 'God!' The Tripolitanian ships had come about, in complete confidence as there could be no doubt that *they* knew every inch of these waters. 'God!' he said a third time. For now it could be seen that there was a perfect armada of other craft, mostly small, some hardly larger than rowboats, but every one crammed to the gunwales with armed men, issuing from the distant harbour. The Tripolitanians knew they had the frigate at their mercy. 'There must be several thousand of the rascals,' Preble muttered. 'Will our guns fetch them, Mr McGann?'

Toby licked his lips. But there was only one answer he

dared give: the truth. 'No, sir. We are two miles too distant, at the least.'

Two miles through the sandbanks. 'Then they will be overwhelmed before we can possibly assist them.' Preble snapped his fingers in despair. 'Set the signal to abandon ship, Mr McGann. And fire your bow chasers to make sure that Captain Bainbridge is aware of the order.'

'Aye-aye.' Toby hurried forward to carry out his instructions. But his belly seemed filled with lead, an increasing weight of despair as he stood on the foredeck, peering through the smoke of his guns, and watched the pirate vessels going alongside the *Philadelphia*. Even that order was going to be too late. The frigate's cannons boomed and wreathed her in smoke, but, lying as she was, listing heavily to starboard, her big guns could only fire into the sky, or into the sand. There was considerable small arms fire as well, but the crew of the American ship could not hope to defend themselves against the enormous numbers opposed to them. And indeed, the firing was already slackening.

As Preble recognised. Toby supposed this had to be the bitterest moment of the commodore's life – in attempting to carry the fight to the enemy, as instructed by Congress, in contrast to the inactivity of Barron, he had in a single afternoon suffered more casualties than his predecessor had in three years. But he would not shirk the responsibilities of his position and sacrifice yet more lives in a forlorn hope. 'Mr Decatur,' he called, as the boats were swung out. 'Avast there.'

'But, sir,' Decatur protested.

'Bring those boats back in, Mr Decatur,' Preble repeated. 'The *Philadelphia* is lost. Bainbridge is lost.'

It was not the first winter Toby had spent in the Mediterranean, but it seemed by far the coldest. He patrolled the quarterdeck of the *Essex*, wrapped in a heavy jacket, slapping his arms together to increase his circulation. The ship was anchored, but there was enough sea running to make her snub her cable with sharp jerks, and besides, it was very necessary to keep a sharp lookout in case the Tripolitanians decided to come out for a surprise assault. They had gained a great deal of confidence since their stunning victory of the previous year. They had even sent a boat out under a flag of truce, and their envoys had strutted the decks of the flagship, waxed moustaches bristling, beards thrust forward aggressively, jewelled fingers wrapped around the hilts of their scimitars, as they had presented their demands to the commodore. One hundred and nineteen sailors, they claimed, including Captain Bainbridge, lay in their prisons. And would lie there until they rotted, unless a ransom of sixty thousand dollars was paid.

Toby thought Preble would burst a blood vessel as he stared at them. But the commodore replied in a controlled voice. 'And the ship?' he enquired.

The head envoy, a tall, dark man with heavy features and a ferocious smile, who spoke perfect English and was, it appeared, the Vizier of the Dey himself, and who had introduced himself as Mohammed ben Idris, smiled. 'The ship? Ah, no, Commodore Preble. The ship belongs to Tripoli. Such are the fortunes of war.'

Preble's fingers curled into fists, but he had still kept himself under control. 'I will have to forward your demands to my Congress in Washington,' he said.

Mohammed ben Idris bowed. 'May Allah speed your messengers.' Another smile. 'For the sake of your people in our prisons.'

'Murdering cut-throats,' Preble growled, as the felucca made its way back into the shallows.

'At least they'll get no joy from the ship,' John Rodgers remarked. He had joined them in the *Essex* for the conference. Now he stared at the stranded *Philadelphia*.

'I don't agree,' Decatur objected. 'I would say they have already had a great deal of joy from her, and will have more.'

They had all looked at the distant vessel, knowing he was right. The frigate still lay, listing to starboard, and another of her masts had gone overboard. She looked a total wreck, but there was no indication that her hull had been in any way damaged by the soft sand. Certainly she had been already looted of all her guns, the small, shallow-draft Tripolitanian boats being able to get right alongside, while there had been hundreds of eager hands to man blocks and tackles and swing the huge pieces of metal out on to their decks. Since then the work had become even more intense, as the pirates, no doubt utilising slave labour, could be seen at work dredging a channel away from the sand to deeper water.

'They mean to refloat her,' Decatur asserted.

'Can they do it, gentlemen?' Preble asked. 'Can they?'

'Given sufficient time, yes, sir,' Decatur said. 'Now they have lightened her by removing her stores and ordnance, it is entirely practical. Certainly once they get that channel dug. Sir, may I respectfully . . .'

'Yes, Mr Decatur,' Preble said. 'I am giving the matter much thought. But to destroy an American warship, ourselves . . .'

'There is also the matter of the crew,' Rodgers said. 'If we assault the ship, supposing we can, will that not be to sign Bainbridge's death warrant? And all his people?'

'They are American sailors and officers,' Decatur said stiffly. 'They will have no doubts as to their duty.'

'Gentlemen,' Preble interrupted. 'Squabbling amongst ourselves will accomplish nothing. We will have to see how they progress, and make our decision when it becomes necessary. Meanwhile, we will despatch the Dey's ransom demand by all possible haste to Paris and thence Washington, and hope for an early reply. And add our recommendations. If they would send me a military force to undertake a land assault while we came in from the sea . . .' He sighed. He knew Congress would never send an American army overseas, just as he was now realising that this was an impossible war to win with merely a handful of frigates.

'You are yet speaking of a couple of months before we can hope to have a reply,' Rodgers pointed out.

'I am afraid I am,' Preble agreed. 'But we can do nothing more except wait and watch, and by remaining here, gentlemen, make sure that nothing and no one uses this port. Or the *Philadelphia*.' His smile was grim. 'I am afraid I can wish you no very jolly Christmas, gentlemen.'

Nor had it been a jolly Christmas, several weeks ago. The *Enterprise* had ploughed back and forth between Sicily and their station, bringing occasional mail and replenishments of fresh food and water, but the two frigates had kept the sea at the mouth of the channel, watching and waiting and hating their helplessness more than their enemies. But they hated the Moors, too. Mohammed ben Idris, Toby thought, as he peered into the darkness and listened to the wind howling in the rigging. The Vizier had seemed to sum up all of his feelings about the Moors, in his arrogant awareness of his power, of the victory his people had gained by a lucky stroke. At least the weather in the New Year had been so unfailingly bad there had been no question of them salvaging the *Philadelphia*. It revealed the extent of the protecting sandbanks that the frigate was still intact. This night was indeed the best for several weeks, with the wind no more than twenty knots, he estimated, and . . .

'With respect, Mr McGann,' said the duty midshipman. 'There are lights over there.'

Toby levelled his glass.

'Do you think the Moors are coming out, sir?' The boy's voice was high with excitement. 'To fight?'

'No, by God.' Toby closed his telescope with a snap. 'Summon the commodore.'

Preble was on deck a moment later, his greatcoat over his nightshirt, hurrying to the rail. 'What is your estimation, Mr McGann?'

'I would say they are attempting to float *Philadelphia*, sir,' Toby replied. 'Look, there is a cluster of lights, then a line of them, and then others at intervals all the way back into the harbour. The lights are bobbing, sir. They have their new channel marked with anchored boats, and are preparing to tow *Philadelphia* into Tripoli.'

'By God!' Decatur had joined them. 'If they succeed in that . . .' He glanced at the commodore.

Preble's voice was heavy with disappointment; once again he had underestimated the spirit of his enemies, had failed to accept that they might take a chance at the very first fine weather. 'Aye,' he said. 'They will have possession of one of the finest ships ever built.'

'She'll need to be re-rigged,' Toby ventured.

'That will cause them no great difficulty,' Decatur said. 'And they have the guns ashore already, and all the shot for them as well. You may be certain of that. Once they have her, armed and rigged and ready to put to sea ...'

'Aye,' Preble said again. 'There'll be no stopping them.' He sighed. 'I had thought to make a quick end to this war. Now it seems I may have managed to lose it.'

'What happened to the *Philadelphia* cannot possibly be considered your fault, sir,' Toby objected.

'Do you not suppose so, Mr McGann? I had signalled general chase on that fateful day. And I did not signal recall soon enough. And I am the commodore; whatever happens to my squadron is my responsibility. Well, gentlemen, we may as well turn in.'

'Sir,' Decatur stood to attention. 'We cannot allow the *Philadelphia* to be taken into the Tripolitanian service. Even if it costs the lives of Captain Bainbridge and his people, and I doubt it will do that – these fellows are too anxious for money, and will await at least the outcome of their ransom demand – we yet have a clear duty greater than friendship to our mates.'

'I agree with you, Mr Decatur,' Preble said. 'But I do not see how we can retrieve the situation now. They have outmanoeuvred us. I know you have almost completed your survey of the outer channels, but to attempt them in the dark ...'

'I accept that, sir. It will be necessary to devise a new plan.'

'What sort of plan?'

'A *ruse de guerre*, sir. A single bold stroke. It will require courage of both the moral and physical variety. But it can be done. It must be done. If you will allow me to raise seventy volunteers ...'

'You'll take me for a start,' Toby said.

Decatur clapped him on the shoulder. 'I never doubted that.' He looked at Preble. 'And if you will but humour my proposition, sir ...'

Preble gazed at him, then at Toby, then looked at the distant lights where the *Philadelphia* was being refloated. 'You had best come below, Mr Decatur,' he said. 'And explain to me what you have in mind.'

Chapter 5

The Mediterranean—1804

'Well, Felicity, what do you think of the Americans now?' Mohammed ben Idris chuckled, and put his arm round the girl's shoulders as he stood beside her on the battlements of the fortress overlooking Tripoli Harbour, gazing at the American squadron now hull down on the northern horizon. 'They have finally admitted defeat. Now we can sleep easily in our beds again.'

Felicity stared at the distant ships. Mohammed ben Idris often allowed her to walk here, on the battlements outside his private apartments – suitably veiled, of course – and from the very first time she had exercised that privilege the Americans had been there, at least one of them. By all accounts they had been there even before she had completed her journey across the desert from Algiers to . . . her home, she supposed it would now have to be called. Whatever had happened to her during the past three years, those ships had been a suggestion that she could yet hope to be rescued. She had even been surprised that it had not yet happened, when she remembered the way Thomas Truxton had accepted odds of nearly two to one to defeat *La Vengeance* . . .

But then had come that dreadful day last November when the *Philadelphia* had run aground, and Tripoli had celebrated all night long. Mohammed ben Idris had snapped his fingers, as he always did when things were going well and had said, 'We must have her here, in this harbour. An American frigate . . . oh, the world will see that to be a great

99

victory.' And he had given the necessary orders. Because there could be no doubt that Mohammed ben Idris was the real ruler of Tripoli. He boasted that he was the man, then merely captain of the guard, who had engineered the coup to overthrow the rightful Dey, and had then erected the present puppet in his place. He counted his only failure the fact that Karamanli had managed to escape with his head. Now he was content to rule from immediately behind the throne. He wanted the power, not the title.

And rule he did. If she had no contact with his decrees and judgments, she knew of them from his boasting when she was summoned to his couch. She doubted so bloodthirsty a monster had ever lived; his 'justice' was concerned solely with beheadings and impalements, strangulation and drowning, his mercy only with the bastinado and slow torture. 'That is the way to rule,' he said proudly. 'Once people are afraid of you, then all the world is yours. The secret is to keep them fearing you, then a man might rule forever.'

Until smashed by the Americans. Because surely they would seek to avenge the loss of their ship . . . But now they were sailing away, having lifted the blockade of the port they had maintained for more than two months.

So, she would survive, at least for a while longer. Because of course she had had every intention of dying in the rubble as the American cannon brought this fortress tumbling down; her only ambition was to remain alive long enough to be sure the fortress *was* tumbling down, and that Mohammed ben Idris would be buried beneath the rubble beside her. She had never truly considered rescue. That would be too terrible to contemplate. To stand before an American officer, who might even be Toby McGann, and have him look at her, look through the sheer silk of her pantaloons, and realise what was done to her once every week. He would also know what was done to her most days, or nights, as well. Or would he? Could any Christian gentleman understand anything of the lusts of a Moor? Yet he would know that she was as contaminated as a leper.

Because that was the truth. As she was flesh and blood, and as she had elected to live for as long as possible – even now she had not lost that determination, save that 'as long as possible' had come to mean until the moment of Mohammed ben Idris's death – she had to have become contaminated. Besides, she recognised it. As a man, perhaps, fearing both the taste and the effects of too much wine, is abstemious until it is forced upon him, and then gradually discovers that he likes the taste, and more, that he cannot exist without the effects, so had she come to anticipate the touch of this man's hand, and even more, the quest of his lust into whatever unholy paths he guided her.

Easy to tell herself, now, that she had surrendered to him because of sheer boredom. He was, in fact, the only spark of interest in her existence. There was absolutely nothing to do in the harem save preen oneself, play at stupid games, or form close attachments to one or more of the inmates, and if she had necessarily learned to speak and understand Arabic she could yet discover nothing in common with the other girls who shared her life. This was partly because she did not wish to, but was also partly because they were jealous of her, and sought to vent their spite in every way short of actually harming her: that could have been fatal for them, as she remained their master's favourite.

Something to be proud of? Indeed, it had not been entirely inadvertent. For all her terror, all her apprehensions of utter mistreatment, all her initial disgust when he had first made her kneel before him, she had quickly recognised that utter surrender would very soon reduce her to the level of a thing – and that she was determined not to allow. Even if she also recognised that resistance would necessarily be painful, on that first occasion, she had squirmed less with the pain of the penetration, the horror of losing her virginity to such a man in such a manner, than with the lingering agony of the fifty stripes on her buttocks, which he had himself administered with a thin bamboo cane while she had been held on the floor by Abd er Rahman's eunuchs. The bastinado! She had screamed and attempted to writhe, and she had cursed as well as she knew how, and eventually she had wept. And she had been straightaway taken to his couch, as apparently the beating of her had powerfully aroused him.

There she had been turned inside out, too terrified on that occasion to do more than obey and accept. Her lord had been pleased. If her breasts were not as large as those of the ideal Arab woman, they were high and firm; if her belly was too flat, it was hard muscled; if her pubes were not as pronounced as a man might desire, it yet seemed to fascinate him – as he was fascinated by her tight white buttocks, and the length of her slender legs. The texture of her hair, too, delighted him, as did the cool of her eyes. He had said, when he had been at last sated, 'I am pleased with you, Felicity Crown. Oh, indeed, you will make me very happy.'

She had actually been hardly less sated, less with fulfilled desire than a mixture of exhaustion, shock, and a sudden *awareness* of desire, which she had never known before. Yet even then her brain had flickered into life. She had raised her head to look at him, and had asked, 'And will you, Mohammed ben Idris, also make me pleased?'

He had been angry. And yet, amazingly, delighted as well, and if he had immediately made her weep, using the flat of his hand, she yet felt she had gained a victory of sorts. Thus she made herself dare his wrath, time and again, and suffer his anger, time and again, always keeping her insolence well under control so that he could never really be angry with her; yet always reminding him that she remained a prisoner, never either a slave or a lover. In that direction he was easy enough to goad, but he was also intelligent enough to appreciate her motivation, and in the most remarkable fashion had come to value her the more highly for it. So the surrender, the contamination, had spread, and the physical pain he inflicted upon her, always followed by a spasm of the purest passion, had become merely an aspect of their foreplay.

What he did not suspect, and could never know, was how much she now herself lusted for the touch of his fingers, the feel of him on her and in her. If her sole reason for living had to be the sexual act, then the sexual act had become all she craved. That made her angry with herself. She was angry now, for he had dragged her from his bed to bring her out on to the battlements and watch the flight of the American squadron. Thus her anger encompassed them as well, for sailing away and robbing her of her revenge. Her lip curled.

'No doubt they have decided, great Idris, that there is, after all, nothing here worth challenging. Are there not

102

hundreds of thousands of men in America? Of what value are a hundred sailors? And do they not have so many ships they can hardly count them? Should they be concerned over the loss of a single frigate? I doubt they rate your great victory as more than the sting of a mosquito bite.'

His hand tightened into a fist, squeezing her flesh and bringing a gasp of pain from her lips. Then he almost threw her at the steps leading down from the battlements. She regained her balance, and walked before him. Another victory? Or a fresh eruption of her disease?

'She is definitely a Tripolitanian,' Isaac Hull reported. Thick set and bluff featured, with hair already receding although he was still only thirty years of age, he stood at the taffrail of the USS *Enterprise* and studied the approaching vessel through his telescope, relaying his observations to Decatur and Toby, both waiting on the lower deck. Decatur would not jeopardise the success of his plan by allowing himself to appear on the quarterdeck, just in case someone on the approaching pirate had sufficiently sharp eyesight to discern there were two senior officers on board the schooner, and wonder why. He knew as well as anyone that while he could not in any way guarantee the success of this desperate venture, failure, should it overtake them, would be resounding and total.

Yet Edward Preble had agreed to the plan, his only reservation being that success would still be a failure for the United States Navy. Even if it was a failure that had to be accomplished. Thus Decatur had been given everything he wanted, even in being allowed to take Toby along as his second in command, so depriving the *Essex* of her two senior lieutenants. But he had said, 'If ever there is an occasion for McGann's strength, it will be now.'

McGann's strength, Toby thought, his nerves tightening. That size and strength had never been truly tested, the way Father's had from an early age. As Barron had perhaps truly said, deeds of derring-do belonged to history, and for all Toby's nine years in the Navy, he had never boarded an enemy ship, sword in hand, to fight for its possession. He did not even know if he would be able to.

But he was about to find out. Because this was an adventure of the purest derring-do, inspired by the courage and imagination of Stephen Decatur. And thus far the plan was working to perfection. The *Enterprise* had put to sea, and when south of Malta, had struck her topmasts, but left them hanging there, a cluster of apparently ruined rigging to the casual eye, so that it would appear she had been caught in a sudden squall and been virtually dismasted. Her mainsail had also been cut to ribbons, and left trailing from gaff and mast, while her boom banged idly to and fro, as if her crew too had been afflicted by illness or despair. Now she rolled in the Mediterranean swell, looking an utterly helpless victim of the savage sea.

She had drifted like this for three days, seeing nothing but the distant hills of Malta on the northern horizon. But at dawn this morning another ship had been sighted. And sure enough, the stranger was now approaching, too curious for its own good, perhaps unable to believe its fortune that fate would have sent another American ship, crippled, to be taken into Tripoli as a prize.

'Fall to,' Hull commanded, and his men began to work as the corsair came within range of the naked eye. Now they would appear to be frantically attempting to repair their stricken vessel, but yet unable to accomplish their tasks in time, while the *Enterprise* schooner, normally fast enough to outsail any lateen-rigged Tripolitanian, wallowed uselessly.

'Prime your muskets and pistols, but hold fast until I give the word,' Decatur commanded. He and Toby had joined the seventy men of their force in the hold, pressed shoulder to shoulder, armed to the teeth, and now feeling the adrenalin flow as the reason for their long vigil came to an end.

'Not a sound, now, not a whisper,' Decatur said, as their preparations were completed and they could hear the distant cries of 'Ul-ul-ul-Akhbar!' as the corsair prepared to board.

The schooner's guns opened fire. She had only small six-pounders in any event, and Hull, as excited as anyone at the daring of the coup they were attempting, had commanded them to be deliberately misaimed; the pirate had to be undamaged to fill Decatur's requirements.

'They will be alongside in five minutes,' he said quietly from immediately above them.

Decatur nodded, and Toby tightened his grasp on his already drawn sword. Now the noise was very loud, and the guns were barking again, almost desperately, while before he was quite ready he heard the crunch of the grappling irons, thrown from the corsair, biting into the wooden gunwales of the schooner to bring and hold the two ships together; the splintering thud of the two hulls meeting threw several men from their feet.

With a scream of anticipated triumph the Tripolitanians poured over the side of the American ship.

'Now,' Decatur shouted. 'Now. All together, boys.'

The seventy men scrambled from the hold, and the pirates checked in dismay at finding the numbers of their opponents so unexpectedly tripled.

'Present your pieces,' Decatur bawled. 'Fire.'

He himself discharged his pistol, as did Toby, while the seamen levelled their muskets and delivered a volley. A good dozen of the pirates fell, and the rest gave a shriek of dismay and endeavoured to regain their own vessel.

'Behind them,' Decatur commanded, his voice hoarse. 'Follow me.'

He was first across the gunwale. Toby drew a long breath and leapt behind him, swinging his sword. The men at whom he charged gave yells of terror, having clearly never encountered anyone quite so formidable looking in their lives before. But he was already into their midst, all thoughts of fear or hesitation disappearing in the excitement of the moment, the determination to conquer or die. Yet he paused in horror as his swinging sword, travelling with all the strength he could command, sliced into flesh and bone to bring forth spurting blood, and the nearest Moor collapsed to the deck. A pistol was discharged close by, and jerked Toby back into awareness of his situation. His sword came up as the pirate who had just fired at him now swung his scimitar; the two blades clashed and sparks flew, but as Toby's sword never moved the scimitar was sent spinning from the man's fingers. Immediately he dropped to his knees and cried for mercy, as Toby well understood – he and

Decatur had taken the trouble to learn Arabic from a Maltese schoolmaster during their weary months in Syracuse.

He looked left and right, but the battle was already over. The pirates had been totally surprised, and equally devastated by the ferocity of the assault they had received; a good thirty of them were dead and dying, and the remainder were anxious only to surrender. But now it was time for Toby to remember his instructions, as outlined by Decatur before the campaign.

'Follow me,' he snapped at the half dozen men nearest to him, and led them below to tear through the after- and then the fore-sections of the ship to rout out the several men hiding there. Fortunately not one of them had thought to carry a light to the powder magazine and destroy them all.

He regained the deck, where Decatur was surveying his victory. 'Assemble the dead,' he was commanding. He had lost his hat, but was otherwise unhurt although there were powder stains on his cheeks.

Toby put up his hand and was surprised to find that his hat was still in place – and then discovered there was blood soaking the jacket of his uniform, but it was clearly not his own.

'And the living,' Decatur ordered. 'We want their clothing. Strip them to the buff and confine them in the hold of the *Essex*. Look lively, now. Toby, talk to this fellow.'

Toby went aft, still carrying his drawn, bloodstained sword, to stand over the pirate captain, less then half his size, whose very beard was trembling with terror.

'Now listen to me,' Decatur said. 'If you do not agree to do exactly as I wish, this man, my friend, is going to eat you alive. He is a giant, who lives only on human flesh, and he is very hungry.'

The man goggled at Toby, who endeavoured to look suitably fierce. In fact, with his bloodstained visage and uniform, it wasn't difficult. He only hoped the pirate could not see how close he was to vomiting; he had just knowingly killed his first man – blowing someone apart from a distance of half a mile with cannon shot was not quite the same thing.

'Yes,' the man said 'Yes.'

'Very good,' Decatur said. 'Then let us make haste. Put a

106

guard on this fellow for the moment, Toby. Remember, if he escapes us, even to die, our plan will come to nothing.'

'We'd best tie him to the mast,' Toby decided, and summoned two of the seamen to have this done. Then he pulled one of the rich Moorish robes over his uniform. Decatur was doing the same, as were all the seventy sailors who were going to man the captured vessel. But there was no question that they were Americans.

'Toby,' Decatur said, bursting into laughter. 'We have forgotten the beards.'

Toby slapped his chin in dismay. They had indeed forgotten that essential part of being a Muslim.

'Well,' Decatur said, 'we will have to get close enough to accomplish our mission before they discern that. Keep the cowls of your haiks thrown across your faces as we enter the harbour. What is the name of this ship?'

'*Mastiko*,' Toby said. 'Whatever that may mean.'

'Well, I rename her *Intrepid*.' The men gave a cheer, and he went to the rail. 'Are you ready, Isaac?' he shouted.

'Fifteen minutes,' Hull requested.

'Then cast us free, and we'll be on our way.'

The captured pirates who had survived the brief encounter had already been locked in the hold; now Hull's crew was busy restoring their topmasts to a proper position. The grapples were cast off, Decatur's men set the sails their recent adversaries had dropped on coming alongside, man-handling the huge, unfamiliar, cumbersome lateen main boom into position, while the pirate captain, tied to the mast, wailed his fate, calling on Allah to save him from the infidels.

'Now listen very carefully, my friend,' Decatur said, standing beside him, a cutlass in his hand. 'You are going to con us into that harbour of yours. If you show the slightest hesitation, or the slightest desire to betray us, I am going to cut off your balls and feed them to my big friend here. He has balls for breakfast, every day, and alas, he has not yet breakfasted today. But if you do as I ask, I may persuade him to spare you. Understood?'

The man's eyes rolled in terror.

'So, set your course, Mr McGann.'

'Due south for Tripoli, Mr Decatur. Hurrah!'

'And again, hurrah,' Decatur shouted. 'For Tripoli!'

The course was set, the sails filled, and the corsair hurried away to the south. Hull allowed them an hour, and then followed, the *Enterprise* now restored to her full sailing capacity. So far everything was working exactly as Decatur had said it would – but the true dangers still lay ahead, as every man of his company was aware. Just as they were aware of their likely fates were they to be captured. It might please the Moors to hold Bainbridge and his men as prisoners of war – they represented both prestige and the promise of profit; those attempting to invade Tripoli disguised as Arabs could expect no such mercy.

Nor could any of them suppose that Mohammed ben Idris would allow them anything so straightforward as immediate execution; their fates would vary from castration to impalement. But Decatur had warned them of the risks they ran when they had volunteered, and so they crouched by the bulwarks, clutching their weapons and staring at the African coast-line as it came above the horizon.

Now *Enterprise* commenced firing at them, but aiming again deliberately wide. From the distant shore no one would be able to tell anything more than the essential fact: that one of their ships was being chased by an American, and was so far escaping.

'Bring that fellow aft, Toby,' Decatur commanded.

Toby signalled the two men he had guarding the pirate captain, and the Moor was brought to stand beside the helm.

'Now you are going to con us through these sandbanks,' Decatur told him. 'And remember, my friend is still very hungry. If we touch, you die, piece by piece. My friend is also very partial to toes and fingers, and lips and tongues, and eyeballs most of all. He eats them raw.'

Toby licked his lips, and pinched the pirate captain's cheeks appreciatively.

A perfect stream of sailing directions issued from the man's lips, and within seconds they watched rippling breakers to either side, while they themselves slipped through deep water. Sextant at his elbow, telescope in hand, Decatur made notes of the various courses and traverses, as the channel changed direction several times, and Toby realised how hopeless it would have been for them to attempt this passage without a pilot.

But the white walls of Tripoli were coming ever closer. Behind them the *Enterprise* ceased firing and bore away, apparently in frustration, in fact to sail north as rapidly as possible and regain contact with the American squadron, cruising off Malta. It seemed fairly certain that the *Intrepid* was going to get into Tripoli; getting back out again was not guaranteed without close support.

Decatur watched her go. 'Now, then, Toby,' he said in a low voice as the schooner dwindled from sight. 'It is all up to us. You,' he told the captain in Arabic. 'Is it deep water alongside the quays in the harbour?'

'Oh yes,' the man said. 'Oh yes.'

'Twist his prick for him, Toby,' Decatur said in English. 'Eh?'

'Come on,' Decatur said. 'You are supposed to be an ogre; act the part.'

Reluctantly, Toby began to fumble with the man's clothing, squeezing every piece of flesh he could find.

Apparently with effect. 'There is water by the quays,' the man screamed. 'I swear it by Allah. Only the south-western part is shallow.'

'I guess we can believe that,' Decatur decided, and Toby gratefully ceased his activities.

Decatur himself took the helm as they were now in a clearly marked channel, only a quarter of a mile from the pierheads. There was a fort on each head, bristling with cannon, but these were silent, while the battlements were lined with cheering Moors, welcoming them to safety from the American patrol.

'Do you see *Philadelphia*?' Decatur muttered, scanning the harbour as it opened before them.

Toby shaded his eyes; they could not risk using their European telescopes this close. Inside, the harbour was larger than he had expected, and was crowded with shipping, most alongside the quays. Behind the vessels, the housing clustered into narrow streets, leading up a shallow hill towards a larger fortress from which there flew a green flag. Up there, too, were a large number of cannon, poking their muzzles through the embrasures. And against the quay immediately beneath the citadel was the *Philadelphia*, entirely re-rigged, and with guns in her ports; she was almost ready for sea – but there were no men to be seen on board. He could hardly believe their good fortune.

'There,' he said.

'Aye.' Decatur had seen her in the same instant. 'Shorten sail,' he bellowed. 'Look lively, lads.'

The watchers on the shore were starting to shout comments as the corsair continued into the harbour at full speed. Now the huge mainsail was dropped, but she continued across the calm water far too fast, making straight for the frigate. At that moment the captain, ignored by his guards as the moment of decision approached, broke free and ran across the deck.

'Stop that fellow!' Decatur shouted.

Toby ran behind him, but was too late; the captain reached the rail, threw up his arms, and dived over the side, to the accompaniment of an enormous upsurge of amazed noise from either side.

'Well, then,' Decatur said. 'We shall have to find our own way back out, to be sure.'

The spreading noise awoke Felicity, where she lay in a heated doze. It was the middle of the afternoon, and the Vizier lay beside her, enjoying his siesta. It was a time of day when he was most sexually active, and she was his selected companion on at least four days out of every seven. He never seemed to tire of her, and in fact his siestas were gradually becoming longer and longer, as he preferred to lie abed with her, playing with her body, than attending to business.

Often, when she awoke like this before him, she wondered why she did not end it all. His clothes and weapons were on the far side of the room. It would be a simple matter to leave the bed, pick up his curved dagger, and drive it into his chest with all her force. It *should* be a simple matter. But she did not know if she could strike the fatal blow. Equally, she did not know if she would then be able to kill herself. Because not to do that ... There had been a case of a concubine

110

killing her master during her sojourn in Tripoli. The woman had been sewn up, alive, in the belly of a dead ass, and then left there. She had been fed and given water to drink, every day, while her body had slowly putrefied along with the carcass. Felicity could still hear her screams, her pleas to be strangled.

And her lord had not been Mohammed ben Idris.

In any event, the moment was past for this day at least; the noise had also awakened the Vizier. He got up and went out on to the flat roof overlooking the harbour, returning a moment later with his white teeth gleaming in a grin.

'One of our ships seems to have gained another victory,' he said, kneeling astride her naked body. 'By Allah, but I do believe you have brought me nothing but good fortune, my pretty little pomegranate. As well as much pleasure, to be sure. Now ...' He turned his head as there came an urgent knocking, and Felicity realised the noise from outside had grown even louder. 'Cover yourself,' Idris commanded, as he left the bed again and wrenched open the door.

Felicity hastily dragged the sheet across herself, for an officer stood in the doorway, gabbling almost incoherently. But she caught the word 'Americans'.

Idris seized his scimitar and his robes, and was dressing himself as he ran down the corridor, banging the door closed behind him. Felicity sat up, threw back the covers. Through the opened windows she could hear shouts and screams, and now the explosions of both cannon and small arms. The Americans! Capturing the city? That had to be an impossible dream. But if it was happening ... and something was certainly happening.

She scrambled out of the bed. To make the journey from the harem up the stairs to the Vizier's apartment she was always required to wear her haik and yashmak. She wrapped herself in the haik, but ignored the mask, then stepped from the upper doorway on to the roof. For her to be out here alone, overlooked by the guards on the other walls and with her face uncovered, would surely earn her a flogging but it would be worth it to see the end of Tripoli – and Mohammed ben Idris.

She ran to the battlements, looked down, and caught her

111

breath as she watched what was obviously a Tripolitanian ship manned, equally obviously to the first glance, by Moors, crashing alongside the USS *Philadelphia* where she lay beside the quay immediately beneath her.

The captured ship was Mohammed ben Idris's pride and joy. Visitors had come from all over North Africa to inspect the Tripolitanian prize, and stroke their beards and wonder at the prowess of men who could obtain such a marvellous machine of war. Now ... She stared at men, wearing Arab robes to be sure, but discarding these to reveal American uniforms beneath, scrambling over the sides of the big frigate. They moved with an orderly haste, some score of them, armed with muskets, taking up positions along the inner bulwarks to fire into the Moors who were gathering on the quayside, while two other parties went down the hatches, forward and aft, carrying barrels of what had to be gunpowder; those who remained on board the much smaller corsair were readying the ship to pull out to sea again, warping her about to face the harbour mouth.

Felicity found herself panting as she watched the well-drilled manoeuvres being carried out, and then lost her breath altogether as she saw two other men hurrying on to the American quarterdeck, swords drawn. One of them she had never seen before. But the other, towering above his companion, dark hair fluttering in the breeze ...

'Toby McGann!' she muttered. 'Toby McGann!' she screamed, before she could stop herself. 'Oh, my God, Toby McGann!' Her knees gave way, as the afternoon turned black.

Toby heard the shout above even the tumult around him. He looked up at the battlements and saw her there, for she had thrown the cowl of the haik back from her head. He had not seen her for four years, but he recognised her immediately. Felicity Crown! Alive, after all. And a slave, here in Tripoli. Felicity Crown!

Decatur grabbed his arm. 'Haste, Toby,' he snapped for Arabs were attempting to climb up the after topsides. Decatur drove one back with a thrust of his sword, then fired his pistol point blank at another bearded face.

Toby recovered his senses and also fell to, and the assault

was temporarily repelled, while the American sailors were hurrying back up from below, their powder trains laid and lit.

'Rejoin the ship,' Decatur bawled. 'Deck party repel boarders.'

Because now was the most dangerous part of the whole operation; they had to remain on board *Philadelphia* until the last possible moment, to make sure no bold spirit succeeded in putting out the fuses.

'Stephen,' Toby stood to attention. 'Permission to go ashore.'

Decatur, hastily repriming his pistol, cast him an astonished glance. 'Are you mad?'

'I have seen her,' Toby said. 'Up there.' He pointed at the battlements, which were now deserted.

'Seen who?'

'Felicity Crown.'

'Felicity Crown? That girl who was taken by an Algerian three years ago? You *are* mad.'

'I saw her,' Toby shouted. 'I tell you she is here in Tripoli, a slave. Stephen. . .'

'And you would attempt to rescue her? If she is indeed here, and not some figment of your imagination. Do not be a fool. Worse, do not play the traitor. If we could risk a sortie ashore with any hope of success, would you not go after Captain Bainbridge and his people, rather than a woman? But your place is here. These men are your responsibility.'

Toby flushed at the rebuke and bit his lip – but he knew his friend was right. In addition to the large Moorish force assembling on the quay, clearly meaning to charge them at any moment, the cannon on the fortress itself were being run out, and several of the corsairs had been cast off to block their attempt at escape. Every man was needed for the coming fight if they were going to survive. The entire command had had this drummed into them by Decatur before they had set out: that their mission was to destroy *Philadelphia* and escape again – not to attempt the impossible by thinking of Bainbridge, and thus give the Tripolitanians the opportunity to claim another victory.

But to walk away from Felicity . . .

'Give fire,' Decatur was shouting, and his men delivered a

113

volley into the advancing Moors, driving them back again. 'Now,' he shouted. 'Regain the ship. Regain the ship.'

The sailors ran back across the deck of the frigate and leapt the bulwarks on to the corsair.

'Get aboard her, Toby,' Decatur commanded. 'And cast off. Make sail.'

'But you . . . '

'I'll be there.'

Toby obeyed the order, scrambled across the gunwale. 'Release these grapples,' he shouted. 'Set sail. Push her away.'

He himself exerted all his strength to drive the two ships apart, then turned to look for his friend, saw Decatur, waiting on the quarterdeck for the first Moor to emerge over the side. Decatur levelled his pistol, shot the man through the head, then turned and ran for the rail. Shots whistled around him, but he made a clean jump, and Toby was there to seize his arm and pull him to safety, even as the corsair heeled to the breeze and started to come about, drifting clear of the frigate now filled with screaming Moors firing their muskets, but fortunately very wildly. In front of them was the more serious danger, as half a dozen ships sailed to and fro, bristling with men, also shouting threats and imprecations – but at least behind them, the cannon on the citadel were unable to shoot, for fear of hitting their own people.

'Straight for them, Toby,' Decatur snapped. 'It's the only way. And we must . . .' His voice was drowned in the most enormous explosion Toby had ever heard.

'A *coup de main*,' Edward Preble said proudly. 'A *coup de main*. I will write to the Board about it, Stephen, you may be certain of that. About all of you.'

Decatur winced as the surgeon removed the dressing from his burns, and applied a fresh one. There was not a man of his command, still alive, who was not burned on some part of his body by the flying cinders and flaming debris of the *Philadelphia*; the real miracle was that any of them remained alive.

'And you, Toby,' Preble promised. 'That was a right gallant deed. Your father will be proud of you.'

114

'Thank you, sir.' Toby closed his eyes as the surgeon turned his attention to him. But when he closed his eyes, he saw and heard – his ears still seemed to be ringing – nothing but the blazing holocaust which had been Tripoli Harbour. He remembered the ship being thrown on to her beam ends, remembered hurrying below to discover several timbers started and seeping water, remembered having the pumps manned and himself using his great muscles to keep them from foundering. Water below, fire above. Their masts and sails and rigging had all been burning as they had closed the Tripolitanian ships, Decatur, face blackened and uniform half blown away, clinging to the helm.

But the very fact that they resembled a fire-ship, together with the total shock the Moors had also received from the explosion, had turned out to their advantage. They had been in the midst of their enemies, their guns exploding to either side, and then through them and between the pierheads before the Moors could understand what had happened. Clearly it had never crossed their minds that the Americans would seek to destroy their own ship. Just as they had never supposed any ship could penetrate their sandbanks without a pilot.

Their pursuit had been half hearted, as they had presumed the invaders must go aground, to burn helplessly. But the Americans had got the flames under control, and the bearings Decatur had so carefully taken on the way in, properly reversed, had taken them back out, and by the time the Moors had gathered their wits sufficiently to mount a chase, the squadron had been appearing over the northern horizon. It had still been a near thing, for the pirate vessel had been slowly sinking, and Preble had had to put boats down to pluck his men from the sea as the corsair had at last slipped beneath the waves. Yet they had carried out their mission. Decatur had dared, and he had succeeded, in surely one of the most remarkable feats of arms in history.

At what cost? Why, very little, in terms of casualties. Half a dozen men badly wounded, two killed. And Toby himself? If no more than lightly burned, he wondered if he was not the most serious casualty of all. Because there was another vision, looming from amidst the flames and smoke, whenever he closed his eyes. That face, looking down at him from the battlements, and so abruptly disappearing. He did not know whether she had fainted or been dragged away to some unspeakable torture. Or had merely regretted calling out his name, had not, after all, wished him to know she was there. It was even possible that she might have been hit by a stray bullet or a burning splinter. But she had been there, and she must have been there through all of the long months he had been sitting in Syracuse. She had been there, suffering, while he had been fishing on the command of James Barron.

And she would remain there, as he realised once the euphoria of their raid had worn off. Decatur's feat had accomplished nothing towards saving her, or Bainbridge and his men. It had been a necessary gallantry, designed to prevent the Tripolitanians from utilising the advantage they had gained by seizing the *Philadelphia*. Undoubtedly they had caused immense damage; when the American squadron had returned to the head of the channel the next day, parts of the port were still burning.

But the damage had not been decisive, nor had it inhibited the Moors' determination to fight. When the frigates had attempted to approach closer, using Decatur's pilotage notes, the guns on the harbour forts and those on the citadel had opened up so heavy a fire Preble had been forced to order a retreat. Tripoli was not going to fall to an assault from the sea, that was more certain than ever.

Thus Felicity Crown was as lost as if he had never seen her at all. It was the second time she had been almost within his reach – and he had turned away.

So, once again, blockade. But now the entire war had become hateful to him. To walk the quarterdeck of the *Essex*, as winter bloomed into spring and the whistling mistrals – the strong north-westerly gales which blew, sometimes for days on end, out of a clear sky – dwindled to gentle breezes as spring eased into summer, to stare at the shore and know that perhaps she was staring back, was the most exquisite torture he could have imagined possible.

She had seen him, and he had seen her, and understood her situation . . . and he had sailed away, because he had

116

chosen the path of duty to that of chivalry. Would Father have made that choice? How that thought haunted him.

Yet equally haunting was the thought of what he would have found had he got ashore and rescued her. Had he not recognised, years ago, that she could never be regained, because the girl he had known and admired and, indeed, fallen in love with, as he now knew to be the case, no longer existed. Not after four years in an Arab harem. He attempted to comfort himself with the reflection that the girl he had fallen in love with had probably never existed at all, even before that fateful gale off the Portuguese coast. He knew nothing of Felicity Crown. He had fallen, with boyish impetuosity, for a face and a figure, for a concept rather than a human being. And fate had conspired to leave that concept imprinted on his mind. It were best forgotten. He would do best to return to America and the sanity of the Long Island farm, and drink a glass of whisky with Father, and find some homespun, apple-cheeked girl to wed, and be happy – and pursue his career in the Navy, Tripoli no more than a distant nightmare.

He wondered how many men in this squadron, separated for so long from their homes and loved ones, felt exactly like that.

'Sail ho,' came the cry, and immediately the ship sprang to attention. Tripolitanian corsairs had been scarce so far this summer; Decatur's raid had accomplished that much, at least, in that the Moors had at last conceived a healthy respect for the Americans. In any event, Toby saw at first glance through his telescope, this was no corsair, but a stout little brig, dancing over the waves as it approached, and flying the British flag.

'You'd best call the commodore,' he told the duty midshipman, and himself went to the gangway, as the brig hove to and put down a boat. But the boat, remarkably, flew the Stars and Stripes, if only in miniature.

'Ahoy, the *Essex*,' cried the man seated in the stern, dressed as a civilian, but very well dressed in the latest fashion, and with a bicorne hat, which he was now raising. 'William Eaton, United States Consul, requesting permission to come aboard.'

'Permission granted, Mr Eaton.' Toby waited at the gangway for the big, blond man to appear. 'Consul, you say, sir?' For all his broadcloth, the man had a most military bearing, and was, he reckoned, about forty years of age.

'I am United States' Representative in Tunis,' Eaton explained. 'You'll be Lieutenant McGann.'

Toby frowned. 'Have we met, sir?'

'No. But it is my business to keep informed.'

'In Tunis? One of the Barbary states?'

'Why not? Tunis is neutral in *our* quarrel, and she has never taken an American ship. 'Tis a useful place to be, Mr McGann, astride the North African world, one might say. Captain Preble.' He saluted, and then shook hands as the commodore came on deck. 'William Eaton.'

'United States' Consul in Tunis, sir,' Toby said, still mystified and a little suspicious.

Preble nodded. He seemed to know of the man, at any rate. 'You've information on the condition of Captain Bainbridge, Mr Eaton?'

'I know he is alive, sir. And his men. Little more than that. Can we talk?'

Preble led him below, summoning Toby and Decatur to accompany them.

'Have you received a reply from Congress to the ransom demand as yet?' Eaton asked, seating himself at the wardroom table.

Preble shook his head. 'It is still being debated, while Bainbridge and his people languish. As indeed do we. The defences of the port are so strong we are unable to undertake very little.'

Eaton nodded. 'Ships alone will never reduce Tripoli.'

'Do you not suppose I have asked Congress for an armed force?' Preble demanded. 'No doubt that also is still being debated.'

'While, as you say, our people languish, and undoubtedly dwindle,' Eaton said, gazing at him.

Toby's heart began to thump: this man had an idea.

As Preble and Decatur both also recognised. 'Have you an army, sir?' Stephen enquired.

'I believe I can raise one.'

'You'd best explain yourself,' Preble told him.

'Well, sir, my business in Tunis is mainly concerned with gathering information. To do this I have spread my net as wide as possible. And but six weeks ago I found the man I was looking for: Hemet Karamanli. Miserably surviving in Cairo as Mehemet Ali's pensioner, dreaming of his past glories.'

'Karamanli?' Preble enquired. 'Was he not once Dey of Tripoli?'

'Indeed. The Karamanli family have been Deys of Tunis for the past century. In fact, a Karamanli is still Dey of Tripoli, Hemet's cousin, established as ruler following the coup of Mohammed ben Idris. But he is only a puppet of this Idris.'

'Mohammed ben Idris,' Toby said. 'We have met him, sir.'

'I remember,' Preble said grimly.

'An utter scoundrel, believe me,' Eaton declared.

'As hated as he is feared thoughout the Muslim world.'

'But still *de facto* ruler of Tripoli,' Decatur observed.

'By force, because he holds the Dey in his power,' Eaton said. 'My information, reliably gained from spies I employ who take part in trading caravans to and from the city, is that the Tripolitanians bear him little love. They think back to the days of Hemet Karamanli with regret. In addition, my spies tell me that Idris is no longer the man he once was, and nowadays prefers to spend more time in his harem than at the council table.' He shrugged. 'It is a pattern one sees repeated, time and again, amongst those who seek to rule in Africa. It is even a pattern which is repeated amongst the sultans in Constantinople.'

'I begin to get your drift,' Preble said. 'But did not this Hemet Karamanli also once prey upon American shipping?'

'Perhaps he did,' Eaton agreed. 'But you may be sure that he would no longer do so, if it was an American force restored him to his throne. From that moment forth he would be the most loyal of allies, and we would have gained a signal victory. More, an important foot-hold upon the African continent.'

119

'No doubt,' Preble agreed. 'But where am I to find this American force to restore him to his throne?'

'I would suggest you leave that to me, Captain Preble.'

'To you?' Decatur frowned.

Eaton raised his head. 'Sir, I had the honour of holding a commission in the United States Army, down to ten years ago. I am not bereft of military experience.'

'And there are others like you in Tunis? Or in the desert?'

Eaton smiled, rather than take offence. 'Not enough of them, certainly. But I will raise an army amongst exiled Tripolitanians, Moorish adventurers, Egyptian soldiers of fortune . . . Cairo is filled with men who love a fight. And also with men who hate Mohammed ben Idris. I will raise an army.'

'I am sure you will, Mr Eaton,' Preble conceded. 'But it will hardly be an American army.'

'It will be recruited, and march, in the name of Hemet Karamanli, and its purpose will be the restoration of the legitimate Dey of Tripoli to his throne,' Eaton agreed. 'But I will command it, and I promise you that we shall carry the Stars and Stripes into battle along with the green flag of Islam. But more than that, sir. I do not believe it is any more possible for me to reduce Tripoli without support from the sea than it is for you to do so without support from the land. Thus it will be necessary to co-ordinate our plans. When I assault Tripoli from the land, at the same moment your squadron must assault it from the sea. There can be no question which flag *you* will be flying. And I will make Hemet Karamanli very aware that without your ships, our plan will come to nothing.'

Preble stroked his chin.

'May I say, sir,' Decatur put in, 'that as I remember the map, it is approximately one thousand three hundred miles from Cairo to Tripoli.'

Eaton nodded. 'As the crow flies, Mr Decatur. The distance is somewhat longer the way we will have to go.'

'May we enquire how you intend to go? How you mean to transport your army?'

'I intend to march my army, sir.'

'Across the desert? Because that is what it is: desert.'

'We will cross it, Mr Decatur.'

120

'A ragtag assembly of Arab cut-throats,' Decatur said contemptuously. As bold as a lion when it came to his own adventures, or the sea, he found it difficult to appreciate a similar amount of daring in others, or a similar determination, and especially to understand a foreign element, such as waterless sand.

But then, Toby thought, neither did he, even if he was consumed with excitement, and could see his way clear ahead.

Eaton continued to smile. 'It will take time, both to organise my force and to reach our destination. But it will be done.'

'How much time are we talking about?' Preble snapped.

'Ah ... several months, I would estimate. It might take less were I able to recruit volunteers from amongst your people.'

'Aha,' Decatur commented.

Preble continued to stroke his chin, while Toby could scarce contain his excitement as he realised that the commodore was going for the concept. So where were all his reservations regarding Felicity Crown, his desire only to get home and forget about her, now?

'I could allow you no more than half a dozen,' Preble said.

'One would be a great advantage,' Eaton remarked.

'Me,' Toby said.

Their heads turned to look at him.

'I do not think I can spare you,' Preble said.

'Sir ...' Toby flushed, and glanced at Decatur. They had never discussed the incident on board the *Philadelphia* just before she blew up, nor had Decatur mentioned it in his official report on the operation, for which Toby had been truly thankful ... but he knew his friend had not forgotten it, either. 'There is a personal matter involved. I would be most grateful for permission to volunteer.'

Preble had caught the glance, and now he, too, looked at Decatur. 'Your opinion, Mr Decatur?'

Decatur stared at Toby for several seconds, and then shrugged and grinned. 'It would be a gallant way to commit suicide, Toby.'

'I cannot spare *you* for that long, Mr Decatur,' Preble snapped.

121

'Nor do I wish to volunteer, sir. My forte is the sea, not the sand. But if we do not let Mr McGann go, I doubt his continued fitness for duty.'

'Perhaps you will explain that riddle, Mr Decatur,' Preble suggested drily.

'Why, sir, I suggest we let Mr McGann do that, when he returns in triumph. If he returns in triumph.'

Preble studied them both for a few moments, then shrugged. 'You have permission to volunteer, Mr McGann. And to find another six volunteers from amongst the crews of the *Essex* and the *President*. Not a man more.'

'Thank you, sir,' Toby cried.

'I hope you continue to do so when you are dying of thirst in the Libyan desert. Mr Eaton, you spoke of time, and mutual arrangements. We must be exact.'

Eaton nodded. 'It is now July. It will take me some months to recruit my force, and to persuade Hemet Karamanli that we are his only hope. Then we must make our march. That were best left for the winter months. Shall we say . . . I shall knock on the gates of Tripoli, from the land, on the first day of April, 1805.'

'All but nine months,' Decatur muttered.

'During much of which I shall be out of communication with you gentlemen, at least after I leave Cairo. I must have your assurance that you will be bombarding the city from the first day of April next.'

Preble gazed at Decatur. 'We shall be there, Mr Eaton,' he promised. 'I give you my word.'

Toby also gazed at Decatur. Hurrah, he thought, and read the same emotion in Decatur's eyes. And again, hurrah. For Felicity Crown. Come what may.

Chapter 6

The Mediterranean – 1805

'Tell me what you know of the Americans,' Mohammed ben Idris invited, conveying a grape to his mouth and appearing to swallow it whole.

Felicity raised her head in surprise. He had never asked her opinion on any matter before; the very word American had not been mentioned for several months. Not since immediately after that dreadful, tremendous day, when Toby McGann and his compatriots had sailed into the harbour to burn their own ship rather than surrender it to the Moors, and in the process left the entire Tripolitanian waterfront in flames.

Toby had seen her, and that had been too much for her. She had wanted to throw herself from the battlements then, partly in a wild dream that he might catch her, partly to kill herself, because surely the revenge for which she had waited so long was at hand. But her mind had gone black and her legs had given way and she had fallen, after seeing him, and by the time she had recovered herself, his ship had disappeared from view in the smoke of the explosion which had destroyed the *Philadelphia*.

But it had reappeared again outside the harbour. She had watched it sail away. She believed he had survived, and was still surviving. Only now he would know of her. She was so glad she had not thrown herself from the battlements. To live in the daily misery that was her life was almost acceptable, while Toby McGann knew of her. Even if she would never, dared never, think of facing him again.

She was glad she had survived for other reasons. Mohammed ben Idris had been shaken by the American exploit, and that had been worth remaining alive just to see. He had pulled his beard and stared at the sea, and muttered, 'Such men. Such men.'

And when she had remarked, 'One day they will destroy you', he had slapped her so hard her lip had burst and left her face swollen for days.

Then he had been contrite, anxious for her to regain her beauty. And to her total surprise, almost affectionate. He had held her in his arms and stroked her hair, almost as she might have expected an English, or American, lover to do, and had whispered, 'I would like to have a child by you, Felicity. He would be a man amongst men. Why do you not conceive?'

Because I hate you too much, she had thought. In any event, she had not, nor would she ever, conceive for him. Or any man, now, she supposed. She did not know why. Mohammed had certainly fathered several children by his other concubines, but that had been when he was a younger man. Perhaps he and she did not achieve the success of mutual ecstasy, however she might have learned to achieve that ecstasy, either by herself, or by the stimulation of his fingers.

His alarm at the American display of panache had not lasted, especially as the enemy fleet had taken up the onerous and largely pointless duties of blockade once again. 'They are fools,' he had said, swaggering the battlements. 'Oh, they are brave fools, perhaps. But fools, none the less. Do they suppose they can in some way starve Tripoli? Do they suppose we are frightened of them, out there? Do they think they can ever harm me? Me? I am Mohammed ben Idris. Many have tried to bring me down. None have succeeded.'

Yet he had been frightened, and in the strangest way had come to value her more highly than before. She had expected a flogging, both for going out on to the roof and because of the American exploit; instead he had again chosen to believe that she had brought him good fortune. Clearly he had realised that had the Americans really wished, had they, just for instance, known where to find him, they might have assaulted the citadel itself, as they could so easily have done, and turned their defensive coup into a remarkable victory. He had escaped that fate, and he was grateful.

Since then, several months ago, she had been required to sleep with him every night as well as attend him most days, to the obvious disgust and even anger of the other women. She had indeed insisted upon having her food tasted, for fear of being poisoned, and kept her favourite eunuch posted at the door of her chamber at all times.

Her favourite eunuch! Three years ago the very thought of the half-men had made her feel vaguely sick. Now they were her only friends. But three years ago she had been a different person. Even physically, and quite apart from the loss of her virginity. The rich food and lack of exercise had caused her to put on weight. Her mirrors confirmed that this was no bad thing; the slenderness of her girlhood had become rounded into a fetching voluptuousness. In another few years she would become as fat as any senior Arab woman. But she was more than ever determined to wait it out, and see the end of Idris. And herself? She could not now make up her mind about that. Seeing Toby McGann had weakened her resolution. She only knew that Toby McGann had also seen her. And surely Toby McGann would move heaven and earth to rescue her.

Even after several months she clung to that dream. To abandon it now would be to drive her mad. Even if she dared not contemplate what such a rescue might involve, what it could involve.

While Mohammed ben Idris's interest in her grew. Sometimes she thought it might even be developing into real affection – she could not suppose such a man could ever love. But nowadays he even, as on this occasion, chose to share his meals with her. Perhaps, she thought, having lost the *Philadelphia*, I remain his only symbol of success.

But tonight he had been preoccupied, until the sudden question. 'Why, great Idris,' she said. 'I know very little of them. I have never been to America.'

'But you are of the same race.'

'They are different people from the English, now.'

'I have read of this. How they rebelled and seized their independence, even from Great Britain. And does not Great Britain rule the seas? Or claim to do so? Yet the Americans defeated them.'

'No country can rule the seas, great Idris.'

'Ha ha! Well spoken. But yet these Americans must have been great warriors to defeat the British.'

'You have seen their abilities,' Felicity pointed out.

'And there is the riddle I wish to solve,' he told her. 'Because I do not understand them at all. They have spent years doing no more than blockade my city. That is fighting a war? And they go to war with such strange concepts. When the *Philadelphia* was surrounded and forced to surrender, it never seemed to cross the mind of this Captain Bainbridge, whom I hold in my dungeons, that I could, if I wished, have struck off his head. He merely presented his sword, and said, "The fortunes of war." This is a fighting man? And yet, those men last year who came sailing in here and all but destroyed us . . . those were demons. From the same ships. I do not understand them at all.'

Felicity bit into a pomegranate. This was the first she had heard, secluded as she was from all news of the outside world save for what Idris chose to tell her, that he still held Bainbridge and his men prisoners; she had supposed the crew of the *Philadelphia* would have been ransomed some time ago. Another reason for Toby McGann to return? Perhaps a more compelling one. But why hadn't he come?

'So tell me of them,' Idris commanded.

Felicity shrugged. 'They are certainly men who live by the law, and their laws are different to yours, great Idris. Their laws require them to treat prisoners of war with respect and even honour, and so they expect to be so treated by their captors. But I will tell you this: they are men who will never admit defeat. However long it will take them, they will win this war.'

Idris stared at her, then got up and walked to the windows, to look across the rooftops at the harbour, and beyond, at the Mediterranean across which the brilliant spring moon was cutting a white path. 'There is an American force marching on us now.'

Felicity swallowed a piece of fruit without chewing it and nearly choked.

'At least . . . it is a motley force, I am informed. But with American officers. They seek to reinstate Hemet Karamanli as dey. They are fools. Yet . . .' He stroked his beard. 'They have crossed the Libyan desert, and seized the port of Derna. That is a remarkable feat for a few hundred men. They number no more than that. Derna is some distance away from us, but still I am told they are again marching across the desert towards us; my information is that their destination is Tripoli. They are led by a man called Eaton. I know of this Eaton. He has spent some years in Tunis. He has some naval people with him, I believe, from off the ships. My scouts speak of a giant of a man . . . such a man was with those who destroyed the warships. Now he marches with this Eaton.'

Felicity could hardly breathe. Toby McGann! Marching on Tripoli. She had known he would come. Toby McGann! What did it matter if he was actually seeking Bainbridge and his men? He was yet coming.

Idris had turned, and was watching her expression. 'A giant of a man,' he repeated. 'You know of this man? You saw him, the day of the explosion? My guards found you on the roof. From there, you saw him?'

'Yes,' she whispered. 'I saw him, great Idris. And I know of him.'

'Unless there is more than one giant in the American Navy.'

'No,' she said. 'There is only one giant in the American Navy.'

Idris came back across the room quickly before she could gather her wits. 'And you know of him. Perhaps you *know* him.'

'I . . .'

His fingers twined in her hair, hurting her scalp, pulling her head back so that her eyes stared up into his. 'Perhaps you once shared his bed.'

'I came to you a virgin,' she gasped. 'You know this.'

127

'Ha,' he sneered, and threw her away from him, so that she fell across the cushions. 'You know of this man, and now he marches upon us. Ha ha! Perhaps he seeks to rescue you, my pretty pomegranate. Well, we shall see. My army will swallow up his force in seconds. But I will make sure he is taken alive, that we may have sport with him, and that you may watch him die. Why, do you not suppose that a giant will take longer to die than an ordinary man? That will be sport.'

To their right, there was the sea, blue, unchanging, and salt. To their left, there was another sea, the Great Sand Sea, stretching for hundreds of miles down to the mountains of Tibesti, yellow, unchanging, and arid. In front of them, there was brown stony desert, stretching it seemed forever, treeless and indeed featureless, except for the ravines, old dry river beds which the Arabs called wadis, which suddenly appeared at your feet and into which entire companies of men could tumble if taken unawares. Yet the wadis were of vital importance; in some of them there sprouted little desert flowers, yellows and greens and pinks and purples – and where the flowers sprouted, there was water, sometimes inches, sometimes several feet beneath the surface. The wadis, and the flowers, were the signposts of life in the desert.

Signposts which were just sufficient to sustain life. For the moisture dug from the soil was hardly sufficient to replace that sucked from their bodies by the ever present sun. It was early spring, and apparently the best time of year for a desert march. Every afternoon great black clouds rolled out of the sea, and often there was thunder – but never any rain. And the thunder-storms only increased the heat which lay on them like a physical burden.

Preble had said, 'Thank me when you are dying of thirst in the desert.' Well, Toby did not suppose he would actually die of thirst; the men with whom he marched were all experienced desert travellers, who knew enough to camp during the heat of the day, to turn their backs on the wind, wrap themselves in their cloaks, and remain motionless for hours when it was not necessary to move, conserving every

128

ounce of energy, and therefore sweat, so irreplaceable in this climate.

But even these men had never undertaken such a march as this, to such an end. Eaton had been able to raise no more than a thousand men in Egypt, willing to risk their lives for the rewards Hemet Karamanli promised them once they reinstated him on the throne of Tripoli. Toby had felt this was an utterly inadequate force, but he had allowed himself to be reassured by Eaton's optimism.

'We are but a diversion,' the ex-consul had insisted. 'We are to distract the Tripolitanian defences while your ships blow them apart from the sea.' But even he had had his doubts. 'If Congress had sent me any of the money I had asked for, so that I could have hired worthwhile men . . .' he had sighed. 'Ah, well, we must do the best with what we have.' And had given that huge, cheerful grin. 'Has that not been the cry of military commanders since time began?'

It had been impossible to be impressed by their recruits, but Toby had found it difficult to be impressed by the deposed Dey, either, so anxious to regain his throne. His way. Hemet Karamanli was, as his name indicated, a Greek by descent – but a Turk by upbringing and inclination. He had wished to march across the desert with all his women at his side; even while living on the charity of Mehemet Ali, ruler of Egypt, he had yet managed to accumulate a harem. Eaton had had to be very firm with him, as well as very enticing. 'There will be women enough, when you are again ruling Tripoli, Lord Karamanli,' the consul had said. Karamanli had grumbled, but he had realised Eaton was his only hope of ever regaining his former glory, and had contented himself with selecting four handsome pages to while away the lonely hours.

The recruits were, as Decatur had suggested they would be, the sweepings of Cairo and Alexandria. If they certainly knew how to use their weapons, they had seen little point in the weeks of training Eaton had insisted they undergo before commencing their march, the manoeuvres by which they learned to deliver volley fire and to form square to receive the onslaught of hostile cavalry – Mohammed ben Idris was apparently justly proud of his regiment of spahis, or Moorish lancers – or the mock battles he had made them fight beneath the shadows of the Pyramids, watched by crowds of amused Egyptians.

Gradually, reluctantly, they had been turned into a reasonably disciplined fighting force, men who at last understood what the various commands and bugle calls meant, and had some concept of fighting in a body, each man shoulder to shoulder with his comrade. But they also remained men who, Toby had no doubt, would cut the throats of their American officers and flee into the desert at the first check. There had not as yet been a check.

If Toby had been dubious about stepping aside to assault Derna, Eaton had revealed more knowledge of human nature. 'Morale, Toby, my boy,' he had said. 'That is the most important aspect of warfare. Our morale must be higher than that of our enemies. It matters little how such morale is gained. The important thing is that our people should become convinced of their invincibility.'

Thus they had swept down on Derna before their presence had been suspected, and the little fishing village had been taken with hardly a shot fired. Not that that had prevented a good deal of rape and pillage before the Americans had been able to get their men in hand, a difficult task as Hemet Karamanli had been the most determined rapist of all. But Eaton had gradually restored order, with the aid of Toby and his six seamen, to be sure, but principally by the exercise of his invariably good-humoured firmness. He really was a most remarkable man, Toby was coming to realise, a born leader, who, had he been of a generation earlier might have earned himself a famous name during the War of the Revolution, but who was too much of an independent spirit, of an adventurer, to be happy within the bounds of close discipline and rigid orders he would have known in the Army. Or the Navy. Perhaps he was a military equivalent of Decatur. Toby counted himself privileged to have known two such men.

Just as he hoped, when the time came, he would prove himself their equal. Certainly Eaton appeared to have complete confidence in him, and they very rapidly became fast friends, so much so that Toby soon hesitantly confessed his true reason for so quickly volunteering.

130

Eaton had laughed, and clapped him on the shoulder. 'A truly romantic story, and where would we all be without romance? Why, dull as ditchwater drones, to be sure'. Then he had grown serious. 'You do realise your chances of rescuing this girl are slim. Or of, shall we say, finding what you seek, even if you do free her.'

'I know that,' Toby acknowledged. 'Yet I must try. And if she is beyond recall, then must I avenge her, on Mohammed ben Idris.'

'And that, my huge friend, is all I wish of you,' Eaton said.

From Derna, they had despatched a felucca, commanded by one of the American sailors, to find the American squadron and give them a progress report; it would be the last contact they would be able to make with Preble's command until they appeared outside Tripoli. And already they had been falling slightly behind the schedule necessary to make the rendezvous by the beginning of April, with the greater part of the desert still to be crossed.

It was now that the march had become truly terrible, as the men had grumbled and even fought with one another, as the water holes had been discovered further and further apart, as their pack mules died one by one and they were forced to abandon even the half dozen ancient field pieces they had called their artillery.

'Ah, well,' Eaton had said with his unfailing confidence and good humour. 'It is our intention to capture Tripoli, not blow it to pieces.'

But a week later they became aware that they were being watched by patrols mounted on camels, who never attempted to interfere with them, but rode away as they approached.

'They are from Tripoli,' Hemet Karamanli grumbled. 'Mohammed ben Idris will have his army waiting for us.' His silks and satins were soiled, as was his temper; he had become bored even with the company of his page-boys. 'He will swallow us up like the sand, supposing any of us actually reach the walls of the city.'

This was a true enough consideration. The thousand men who had left Cairo numbered no more than six hundred now, and most of those missing had simply deserted. But the rest hung on, lured by the promises of rewards beyond their wildest dreams once they retook Tripoli. So they cursed at Eaton and Toby as they were driven onwards, with Eaton every day marking it off in his diary. 'Preble will be in position,' he said. 'How long will he stay there, do you think, before sailing away in disgust? It is already past the appointed time.'

It was actually the end of the second week of April before they finally topped a last rise, and saw Tripoli in front of them, bathed in the rays of the early morning sun. Best of sights, they could also make out the American squadron out at sea, blocking the channels to the port.

Toby shaded his eyes. 'He is still there, Bill. Now we are certain of victory.'

'Then why are they not bombarding the port?' Hemet Karamanli demanded.

'No doubt they are waiting for us,' Eaton said. 'They will commence firing as soon as they realise we are here.' He pointed at the city. 'Our destination,' he shouted at his men.

'Tripoli!' the army shouted with one voice. 'Tripoli!' Several men fired their muskets into the air.

'Now recharge those pieces,' Eaton commanded.

'Now we will camp, and consider our situation,' Hemet Karamanli decided.

'Now we attack, Lord Karamanli,' Eaton said.

'Attack? Now! After such a march? And against such a place? The men must rest.'

'For how long, do you suppose, my lord?' Eaton demanded. 'After such a march, will they be any the less exhausted tomorrow, or the day after? We must assault the citadel now, while the men are still excited by the prospect, and while the Americans are there to aid us. Who can tell when they will sail away? Toby, you will take two hundred men and capture the east gate. Lord Karamanli and I will take the main body and go for the south gate. Remember now, Toby, it is all or nothing.'

'Look there,' Toby said.

The south gate of the city was opening, and the army of Mohammed ben Idris was coming out. Even Eaton stared in momentary dismay at the brightly uniformed spahis, the pennons on their long lances fluttering in the breeze, and at the companies of foot, performing intricate musketry drills as they took up their positions.

'We are lost,' Hemet Karamanli whined. 'Lost. They will spreadeagle us on the sand and smear honey on our genitals.'

The pageboys began to weep, and clung to each other.

'He is making life easy for us, my lord,' Eaton asserted grimly. 'Now then, Toby, nothing need be changed. I will assault that force in front of me, and clear a way to the south gate. Do you make for the east gate, and force it.'

'But there must be three thousand men there,' Toby objected.

'To our six hundred. But I doubt their quality is as high, no matter how brilliant their uniforms. We will distract them by our manoeuvres. Besides, as soon as Preble discovers what we are doing he will open fire and that will send those fellows tumbling back into the city. In any event, we have only the one course open to us; to hesitate is to die. Come, we will march in two columns, and you will separate when I give the order. Will you accompany us, my lord?'

Hemet Karamanli mounted his camel. 'I will remain here to oversee the battle. That is the proper duty of a commander-in-chief. Not to lose himself in the hurly burly. You will leave me an escort of twenty men, Mr Eaton. And the camels.'

Eaton hesitated. But there were only twenty camels left in any event – and Karamanli was certainly not going to be an asset in a fight. 'I must have your sacred word that you will remain here, my lord,' he said. 'Our men look to you as their leader.'

Hemet sniffed. 'I have every intention of dying at the head of my troops,' he declared. 'Should it become necessary.'

Eaton nodded, and beckoned Toby to his side.

'Do you believe him?' Toby asked.

'No. At the first sign of defeat he will be off like a scalded cat. Therefore we must allow him no signs of defeat.'

'Does it really matter whether he is here or not? I will tell you straight, Bill, he and those lads of his sicken me.'

Eaton tapped his nose. 'Legitimacy, Toby. Legitimacy. Next to morale, it is the most important belief an army can possess. Legitimacy means God is marching with us, and all

133

the angels. Legitimacy means we cannot lose. Of course, when both sides believe right is on their side it is apt to be confusing.' He shook Toby's hand. 'Now we do or die. Are you ready for it?'

Toby grinned. 'I might wish I'd been able to bathe and wash some of this sand from my crotch, and perhaps change my uniform from this collection of rags. But I am ready for it.'

'Having you at my side has been a pleasure,' Eaton said. 'Knowing you are there now makes me confident of victory.'

He drew his sword, as did Toby, and together they put themselves at the head of their men. If anyone behind him felt as exhausted as he did, Toby doubted they would even reach the walls. Nor had they found a wadi this day, and he was already parched with thirst. On the other hand, there was, as Eaton had said, nothing left for them to do but fight and conquer – their only alternative was to die.

'Tripoli!' Eaton shouted, and pointed his sword at the walls, perhaps two miles distant.

The tiny army moved forward, losing sight of their enemies for a moment as they entered the dip, then re-emerging again and plodding onwards. The rebel forces had now formed their position, and awaited them with a clashing of cymbals, the steady beating of drums, and shouts of derision; Toby presumed Eaton's army was fortunate in that their enemies had decided against bringing down any of the cannon from the walls to form a battery. They had, as Eaton had remarked, indeed taken up their weakest position in offering to fight out on the desert rather than from behind their walls.

The loyalists had nothing to offer in reply to the noise of the rebels but a single, menacing drumbeat as they advanced; they were too thirsty to shout. But their approach, so silent and purposeful, had its effect; when the armies were separated by about half a mile, the rebels also fell silent, and Toby saw horsemen galloping to and fro between the city and the troops, relaying orders, or perhaps asking for them – which seemed to indicate that Mohammed ben Idris was not actually commanding his men in the field.

Mohammed ben Idris! Toby had spoken with Hemet

Karamanli on the march, and the Dey had told him that if he had indeed seen Felicity on the battlements of the citadel, then she had to be in the harem either of his cousin, or of the Vizier. Toby had no doubt to whom she belonged. That was one score he certainly meant to settle, come what may.

'Now, Toby,' Eaton shouted. 'On the double.'

'Wheel right,' Toby bellowed, turning smartly himself, and setting off at as fast a trot as his weary legs and cracked boots would allow. Sand crunched beneath his feet, and although he would not look back, he heard the stamping of his two hundred men behind him. Suddenly he felt a wild exhilaration, a certainty that they had but to dare, to win. Yet he kept his wits about him, watching the momentarily bewildered rebel army changing its deployment. While the infantry moved forward to receive Eaton's charge, the cavalry, some five hundred men, were being detached, obviously intended to scatter his small force before it could reach the gate, now half a mile away.

'Form square,' he bawled, checking himself and facing the approaching horsemen. 'Form square.'

This was one of the movements they had practised repeatedly outside Cairo, and his men responded without hesitation, forming a tight square, fifty men to a side in two ranks, twenty-five kneeling, twenty-five standing immediately behind, shoulder to shoulder, their muskets presented.

The spahis came on at the trot, shouting their war cry: 'Ul-ul-ul-Akhbar.' They made an impressive sight with their red cloaks streaming in the breeze. But Toby grinned at them. He had seen pretty sights before, as he had heard that shout before, and then, too, had gained the victory. He and the two petty officers who were his lieutenants had taken their place inside the square, patrolling from side to side, while the oncoming horsemen spread out into a vast crescent as they quickened their pace into a canter and then a gallop, their lances swinging down into the horizontal, the pennons still streaming in the breeze.

'Wait for the command,' he called. 'Wait for the command.'

A hundred yards, he estimated. Seventy-five yards. He looked left and right at his waiting men, and felt suddenly proud. They *were* cut-throats, and they looked the part; they

135

had never had uniforms, and their clothing was now nothing more than a collection of rags. But their weapons were bright and clean, and they were awaiting his command with the patience of guardsmen; however much they had grumbled during the past four months, they had learned to have total confidence in their American officers. How could he fail?

Now the ground shook to the drumming of the hooves. 'Front rank, fire!' he bawled, and with scarce a pause for breath, as the musketry rippled around him, continued giving orders. 'Front rank, two steps back and reload. Second rank, two steps forward. Kneel. Aim. Fire!'

The lancers had been shaken by the first volley, but by no means checked. They were now right up to the tiny square, dust clouding from their hooves, when the second volley exploded, sending men and horses crashing to the earth, the dead and dying bringing down several of those still unhurt and they fell to and fro. Yet for this moment, with the first rank still not reloaded, the loyalist flank was exposed, but the devastating effects of the volleys, together with the barrier formed by their own fallen comrades, had driven men and horses to either side, as water flowing downhill will seep around a solid obstacle. There they came into the sights of the next two sides of the square, and the petty officers were giving the commands. 'Front rank, fire! Second rank, advance. Front rank, retire and reload. Second rank, fire!'

Once again white smoke clouded into the air, horses screamed as they fell, men shouted and yelled, and died, and a dustcloud drifted across the furious scene. Some of the spahis actually reached the kneeling men, and hurled their spears. Several of the loyalists fell to terrible wounds in the chest, and lay screaming on the ground. But Toby and his sailors had their people well in hand, totally confident of victory. As the lancers turned away to regroup, the muskets were reloaded and the orders were repeated. Hit by another hail of flying lead, the spahis galloped out of range, their ranks disordered, their men gasping fear. Some sixty men and an equal number of horses lay writhing on the blood-stained sand, so deadly had been the execution of the mus-

136

kets; at so close a range it had been almost impossible to miss.

'Company will advance in square,' Toby called. 'On the double. Mr Strong, detach twelve men to guard the wounded, but I want you with me at the gate.'

'Aye-aye, Mr McGann,' the sailor called.

This was another maneouvre they had rehearsed often enough. The men ran forward, keeping their alignments as well as they could, so that should the cavalry re-form they could again receive them in square. But the cavalry clearly were not going to re-form; thoroughly discomforted they were making their way, at a walk, back towards the main battle. And now the gate was only a hundred yards distant. It appeared undefended. Where Toby had expected to see a head in every embrasure staring down at him, he saw only one or two. They, having overseen the destruction of their much-vaunted cavalry, were shouting and gesticulating, but clearly the remainder of the garrison were more interested in what was happening at the main gate. Or were distracted by the American squadron. Yet strangely, and disturbingly, as there could now be no doubt, even from several miles distance, that a battle was being fought outside the walls of the city, the American ships had not opened fire.

'Up the walls,' he shouted at the same time taking from his shoulder one of the ropes with which he had provided himself and the two sailors. The ends of these were swiftly made fast to the small grapples hanging from their belts, and thrown up at the embrasures. Lodgments made on the rough stone, Toby sheathed his sword and went up hand over hand without hesitation, as he might have climbed a mast, while the two seamen followed, and the Arabs behind them stood and shouted their appreciation, several even attempting to climb behind the Americans.

Toby was first into the embrasure, looking left and right. The last Moor had abandoned the parapet, and beneath him were the houses of the town. He swung himself through, ran for the steps leading down to the street and the east gate. At the foot, half a dozen men, undecided whether to flee or stand their ground, stared at him; he let out a tremendous whoop and swung his sword round his head, and they turned and ran. He put his shoulder to the huge wooden boom,

137

assisted now by the sailors panting at his heels, and slid it through the steel rings to leave the gate swinging free. A push, and his men were flooding through. He paused for a moment, to listen to the noise from the south, where, from the screams and the shouts he estimated that Eaton was gaining a similar victory, and then dashed along the narrow street with his followers.

'The citadel,' he bellowed. 'The citadel.'

The windows and doors of the houses to either side were barred; there was no telling if anyone was actually inside, for which he was utterly thankful. Undistracted, his men debouched into a square, only a quarter of a mile from the captured gate. Here there was a crowd of people milling about, restrained from approaching the citadel gate by a company of soldiers. Both people and soldiers made off with shrieks of fear as they saw Toby and his men bearing down on them.

'Break down that door,' Toby commanded, and a moment later the heavy door went crashing in. 'Mr Strong, you'll hold this against all comers. Mr Allen, you'll follow me. To the roof.'

He led the way, running up wide marble steps, using his sword to slash away priceless brocade drapes, reaching through empty hallways and magnificently appointed reception rooms, all strangely empty. His heart pounded and his breath came in great gasps as he found himself in a succession of even more splendidly appointed bedchambers, which gave access on to a flat roof with crenellated battlements. On to this he ran, and from the embrasures looked down on the harbour and the disordered shipping that drifted there, the men and women trying to board the boats, fighting each other in their determination to escape the marauding horde bursting into their city. While out at sea the American ships remained silent onlookers. But it was from here that face had looked down on him, nine months before. She had to be in this castle somewhere.

'Mr Allen, you'll hold this roof,' he snapped. 'Do not fire into those people unless they attack you, but should they do so, use everything you have, including these cannon. You and you and you . . .' he picked out three of the most reliable of the Arabs. 'Come with me.'

He ran back down the steps, seeking new corridors, saw two black men guarding a doorway. They stood immobile, statuesque, formidably disciplined despite the chaos going on around them, the fact that they had clearly been deserted at their posts. Toby ran at them, shouting at them to stand aside. Instead they presented their scimitars, and were cut down in two savage, swinging blows. He put his shoulder to the doors behind them, burst them in, and knew he was in a harem. Screams arose to mingle with the scents to either side. Women in the scantiest of costumes rose from their divans, or scattered from the groups they had formed to listen and discuss the noises they could hear from the street; now they all ran screaming back towards the inner compartments. The men at Toby's back gave whoops of anticipated pleasures and ran behind them.

Toby had no time to check them now. He tore open door after door, saw only terrified faces, some black, some nearly white, most brown, none familiar. He seized one girl by the arm and dragged her close to him, trying not to look at her exposed breasts and slender, hairless body, while her musk surrounded him like a cloud and her mouth drooped open in something between an attempted smile and a supplication, ghastly to behold.

'The English woman!' he bawled in Arabic. 'Where is the English woman?'

She goggled at him, shaking her head. 'No English,' she gasped. 'No English here.'

'Is this not the harem of Mohammed ben Idris?'

Again a shake of the head, accompanied now by a quick flick of the lips round her mouth; she was regaining some confidence. 'This is the harem of the Lord Karamanli, Dey of Tripoli.'

He swore, and she gave a scream of pain as his grip on her arm tightened. 'Then where is the harem of Mohammed ben Idris?'

'There. There!' She pointed back the way he had come.

Further yet into the recesses of the palace. he threw her away from him and ran back into the outside hallway, vault-

139

ing the bodies of the two dead guards, leaving his men to do their worst – or best, as the women had not seemed all that displeased to see them, once they had gathered they were not to be murdered – and ran along the empty corridors, until he reached more barred doors. But these were unprotected, and even unlocked – a push had them swinging on their hinges.

His heart lurched with the fear that he might be too late as he threw them wide, gazed at a scene even more chaotic than any he had already witnessed this day, that of a harem packing up. Women and children ran to and fro, bales and boxes were heaped higgledy-piggledy, eunuchs barked commands, lap dogs yelped, cats mewed, babies wailed. Unlike his puppet, who had obviously abandoned his women in his haste to escape the vengeance of his cousin, Mohammed ben Idris was intending to take his harem with him. If he could.

All the hustle and bustle stopped as the terrified people turned to face the huge, bloodstained intruder. None of the women wore yashmaks, and Toby could tell at a glance that Felicity was not amongst them. He strode forward. A eunuch attempted to stop him and was hurled aside with a sweep of his hand. The women fell to their knees, and he ignored them and threw open the doors to the inner chamber, looked at an elaborately furnished room, in which there were several more women and children, all now turning to face him. At their rear, there stood Felicity Crown. And at her shoulder there waited Mohammed ben Idris, scimitar drawn.

'Toby!' Felicity gasped. 'Toby McGann!'

'Stop there, American,' Mohammed ben Idris commanded, also speaking English. 'Or I will cut her throat.'

Toby never hesitated. He charged straight at Idris, his sword thrust in front of him like a lance, his flailing left arm sending eunuchs and women tumbling against the walls as they endeavoured to check his progress. Idris stared at him, tightened his grip on Felicity's hair, then realised that if he killed her he was certainly going to die himself. He threw her aside and ran for an inner doorway.

Toby let him go, stooping beside the fallen woman. 'Felicity,' he said, 'Felicity Crown.' She had been wrapped in a haik, but this had fallen open, and underneath she wore only sheer silk. Hastily he wrapped her up again, and raised her to her feet, while she stared at him, eyes wide, as if she could not truly believe what had happened. 'You are safe now,' he said, reassuringly.

'Idris?' she whispered.

'Oh, he has fled.'

'Fled? Oh, but, he must be ...' she bit her lip. 'As long as he remains alive, he will seek to avenge himself on you.'

Toby grinned at her. His determination to kill Idris had quite vanished with the joy of finding her, alive, and so far as he could tell, unharmed. He did not want to analyse his emotions at this moment, knew only that he was happier than ever before in his life. His first duty must be to make her as happy.

'He will never be a danger to you again,' he promised. 'You have my word on that. Now come ...' He looked around him at the women and eunuchs, most of whom had fallen to their knees to beg mercy on being abandoned by their master. 'Stay here,' he told them in Arabic. 'And no one will harm you.' His arm round Felicity's waist, he helped her to the door, heard his name being called.

'Toby McGann!' It was Eaton, hatless, and with a blood-stained sword in his hand. 'By God, but I am glad to see you.' He stared at Felicity. 'Is this the woman of whom you spoke?'

'Yes,' Toby said.

'Miss Crown!' Eaton touched his forehead. 'But our work is not yet done. There is something amiss here.'

'Amiss?' Toby frowned at him. 'But as you are here ... have we not gained the victory?'

'We have scattered Mohammed ben Idris's army, and you have seized the citadel. I have brought my men in here with yours. But the Moors are being rallied in the streets, and we may have to defeat them all over again. We must signal the ships to resume firing. Why they have not already done so I cannot say, unless they were afraid of hitting us. But that is a risk we must accept to disperse those fellows.'

Toby hurried out of the harem, still half carrying Felicity. 'I thought you had already signalled them.'

'Not I. Listen to that noise from the square. They are

certainly preparing a counter attack; we shall have a fight on our hands very shortly. However, I am holding the gate in strength. The rest of our people must be deployed on the roofs. Perhaps you would care to place Miss Crown in a position of safety.'

'Do not abandon me, Toby', she begged. 'For God's sake do not abandon me.'

'I'll never do that, Felicity,' he assured her, and squeezed her hand. There was so much to come. Hurdles to be overcome, certainly. An understanding of what she had suffered. Of what she had become. But these were only hurdles, to be vaulted at full speed. He had rescued her. If she had been, in his mind, a symbol of what this war was all about, then it was now won, conclusively.

Eaton had been studying them, and he was an understanding man. 'Well, then,' he said, 'why do you not play the guide, Miss Crown. Our very first duty must be to locate and release Bainbridge and his men, supposing they are in the citadel. But I would think it is their most likely prison. If we can secure them, we have achieved the object of *our* enterprise, at any rate.'

'And Karamanli?' Toby demanded.

'Oh, I have no intention of abandoning him, to be sure. He is still sitting on his hilltop with his guards, awaiting word from me. He is best off remaining there until we have settled the business here. But we will be in a much stronger bargaining position as regards Mohammed ben Idris with Bainbridge at our side. While with a hundred odd American sailors thirsting for revenge on their captors ... why, we will be able to withstand any assault, even if we can make no contact with the ships. Take Miss Crown and find them, Toby.'

'Aye-aye, sir,' Toby cried, and turned to Felicity. 'Do you know where the dungeons are?'

She shook her head. 'I know nothing of the palace save for the harem and this chamber and roof. But I am sure I can find them.'

'Then lead me. Mr Strong,' he called, for the petty officer had been released from his duties on the gate by the arrival of Eaton's men, and had come seeking orders. 'Follow me, with six men. William,' he said to Eaton, 'be sure to summon me back if we are needed.'

'I will do that. But I look forward to seeing you accompanied by Bainbridge and his people.'

Toby nodded, and followed Felicity down the stairs and through the lower corridors of the palace. She continued to hold his hand, perhaps to reassure herself that he was flesh and blood and not some dream, while he watched her move in front of him, seeing her for the first time, as he himself came to appreciate that the dreams were over, that he had actually found her and rescued her.

The haik fluttered in her self-created breeze, and as she was hurrying she had gathered it from around her ankles; he could see traces of crimson pantaloons, sheer to reveal the contour of her calves, sometimes fluttering to reveal knee and even thigh, as her breasts had been momentarily uncovered when Mohammed ben Idris had thrown her to the floor, and he had been afraid to look. She was virtually naked in his presence, but for the thin folds of linen. Her hair was loose and flowing. It was more beautiful, in its rich brownness, its silky texture, than he remembered. As was her face, which had filled out and lost the gauntness which had been the principal characteristic of her parents and brother. Obviously she was entirely well, and had even put on weight. He could hardly believe it, any more than he could believe that she had remembered him as well as he remembered her. His heart pounded with anticipated joys.

They continued to find no one in the palace, not even when they left the sunlit upper areas to descend cold stone steps, into darkened and damp passageways illuminated by flaring torches. Now Toby summoned Strong and his men closer, in case of ambush. But there was no one down here, either. Or ... no free men, that was certain. Because now they smelt the stench of unwashed bodies and rotting wood, and now, too, they heard the cries of men confined, aware that something dramatic had happened above them, but unsure of what.

Toby paused at the top of the dark corridor, where even the torches no longer guttered. 'Captain Bainbridge!' he

143

called. 'Are you there, Captain Bainbridge? This is Toby McGann.'

'Toby McGann, by God,' Bainbridge replied. 'Toby McGann!'

There came a ragged cheer from the darkness.

'Fetch those torches,' Toby commanded. 'Stand aside, Felicity.' He himself attacked the first locked door, smashing it open in seconds, shaking hands with the gaunt, bearded figure in the tattered blue uniform who awaited him.

'Toby McGann,' Bainbridge said again. 'How I have prayed for a sight of you. But ... the squadron ...'

'Has still to be reached. We may need your assistance.' Toby left him to help Strong smash the locks on the succeeding doors. 'What you say, lads? Are you ready to break a few Arab heads?'

'Just show us the bastards, sir,' one of the seamen called.

'Are you all here?' Toby asked, looking over the emaciated scarecrows in front of him, illuminated by the glare of the torches his men held above him.

'Jimmy Round died,' one sailor said.

'And Harry Belcher,' said another.

'We have lost five in all, Toby,' Bainbridge said. 'And I doubt the rest of us could pass a medical at this moment. But we can fight, man, we can fight.'

'Then let's go.' He took Felicity's hand once more. 'Our guide,' he explained to the bewildered Bainbridge, as he led them up into the light of the palace, listening to a loud noise, but strangely to no shots.

'Toby! Toby!' Eaton was waiting for them on the roof.

'I'd have you meet Captain Philip Bainbridge, Mr Eaton,' Toby said formally. 'Late captain of the USS *Philadelphia*.'

'Captain Bainbridge!' Eaton clasped Bainbridge's hand.

'You have saved our lives, sir. Be sure that we are grateful, and will remain so. What you have accomplished here today will go down in history.'

'Well, as to that,' Eaton said, 'I do not know what I have accomplished, exactly.'

Toby frowned at him, and then past him at the still silent ships. And at the boats now entering the harbour, flying the Stars and Stripes from the stern and white flags of truce from the bows.

'Has Idris surrendered?' He looked left and right; the green flag had been hauled down from the citadel by one of their own men, but other green flags still flew from the forts on the breakwaters. On the other hand, although a large crowd had gathered on the waterfront, shouting and gesticulating, no effort was being made to prevent the American sailors from landing, and no shots were being fired.

'There is some kind of a parley going on,' Eaton said. 'But I have interrogated some of our prisoners, and they claim the parley had begun several days before our assault.'

Toby stared at him in consternation, then ran to the battlements. Beneath them, the crew of the first American boat had disembarked, and were clearly being greeted by a party of Moorish dignitaries, for whom the crowd had parted. His heart lurched as he made out the figure of Mohammed ben Idris, expostulating and gesturing at the citadel.

And then realised that commanding the sailors was Stephen Decatur. There at least was cause for relief. 'Stephen!' he shouted. 'Stephen! We have gained the day.'

Decatur looked up, and some of Toby's elation dwindled. Even at a distance he could tell his friend was not looking at all pleased. But now, after another discussion with Mohammed ben Idris, Decatur advanced on the citadel itself, the crowd continuing to part before him.

'You'll let me in, Toby,' he called. 'There are matters to be discussed.'

Toby himself went down to open the gate, and Decatur stepped through. 'God, but I am glad to see you,' Toby said. 'Even if I have no idea of what is happening.'

'Happening?' Decatur shook hands. And then at last grinned. 'You are to be congratulated on you coup,' he said. 'A brilliant assault. Unfortunately, it was also an act of international brigandage.'

'What?'

'You were not to know, but only a week before you arrived, Congress signed an agreement with the Dey,' Decatur told him. 'To our everlasting shame, our government has paid the sixty thousand dollars demanded as ransom for Captain Bainbridge and his crew. The details of handing them over were in the process of being worked out when

145

your force appeared. But there was no way we could signal you, although we tried. Believe me, no blame can be attached to you, Toby, or to Eaton; rather the fault is Mohammed ben Idris's for immediately deploying his army to confront you, rather than sending an envoy to acquaint you with the situation. On the other hand, now that you do know the situation, well ... you no longer have the right to hold the citadel.'

'My God!' Toby led Decatur up to the battlements, where Eaton and Bainbridge waited. 'You'd best explain it.'

Decatur did so, while the other two officers and the assembled men listened with incredulity.

'Preble agreed to this?' Bainbridge demanded. 'I cannot believe that.'

Decatur sighed. 'Captain Preble no longer commands, sir. It seems that Captain Barron presented too good a case for himself when he returned to Washington, and in addition ... well, matters were complicated by the loss of the *Philadelphia*. Captain Barron had never lost a ship, at the least. So ...' He shrugged.

'You'll not pretend James Barron has been returned as commodore?' Eaton demanded.

Decatur shook his head. 'But Preble has been recalled.'

Toby gasped. He could not imagine the feelings of the squadron when that had happened. As for what poor Preble must have felt ...

'Captain Rodgers now commands,' Decatur said. 'But he was left with no choice other than obey orders. The war is terminated.'

'What happens when Mohammed ben Idris decides to take another American vessel?' Bainbridge asked bitterly.

'The peace treaty provides American ships with safe passes for all Tripolitanian waters.'

'And you believe these pirates will honour such safe passes?'

Decatur sighed. 'Congress believes it, Captain Bainbridge. My opinion was not called for.'

'And what of my people?' Eaton inquired.

'I believe it will be possible to do a deal with Idris,' Decatur said. 'Your feat of arms has mortally frightened him. He will have his ransom paid, and he needs the money.' His smile was sad. 'If only to repair the damage you have done, and attempt to raise a new army. It is also obvious to all that you acted in good faith, and there is the additional point that you have in your company the rightful Dey. However, I must stress that the United States Congress is apparently determined to end this war now, and thus it intends to give no support to Karamanli either, nor will it allow any American serving-men to take part in what is essentially a Tripolitanian civil war. As I have said, if you will agree to withdraw, Mr Eaton, I believe that Idris will allow your Arab people to march out of here under a flag of truce, and make their way back to Egypt.'

'Unrewarded?' Eaton was aghast. 'They will turn into brigands. And I will have broken my word to them.'

Decatur gave another sigh. 'Believe me, Mr Eaton, I would have ordered it differently. But as things stand now, your alternative is to lose all hope of further employment by your country. If, indeed, you are not named as a traitor.'

'I will not desert my men,' Eaton said. 'At least until I have led them back to safety. As for employment, sir, I shall seek none from such a government. You may be certain of that.'

Decatur gazed at him for several seconds, then saluted, and turned to Toby. 'You are commanded to rejoin your ship, Toby, together with your volunteers. And you are welcomed back on board, Captain Bainbridge, with your people. Do not look so crestfallen, Toby; you have played an honourable and innocent part in these unfortunate proceedings. It will look good on your record.'

'And Mohammed ben Idris?'

Decatur shrugged. 'He is no longer our enemy. Congress says so.'

'He is certainly still mine,' Bainbridge growled.

'And mine,' Toby agreed. 'I had promised myself to hang him.'

'You will have to postpone that pleasure, at the least. Now come, we must make haste. I will leave it to you to do as you think best, Mr Eaton. These sailors are my responsibility.'

'Toby . . .' Felicity whispered.

'Miss Crown will accompany us,' Toby said.

147

Decatur appeared to notice her for the first time. He raised his hat. 'Miss Crown? So Toby found you after all. Alas, I am afraid our negotiations were for the release of American nationals only.'

'Stephen,' Toby said, speaking quietly, but leaving no doubt as to his determination. 'Either Miss Crown comes with me, or I ride off into the desert with her, and become a brigand myself.'

'Spoken like a man,' Eaton said; he was clearly very angry. 'I'll accompany you.'

Decatur hesitated. Then he grinned. 'You will accompany us, Miss Crown, and you may take up the matter of your future with Captain Rodgers. Find Miss Crown a man's robe to wear, Toby, and wrap her up well, so that no one can tell she is a woman. I can offer nothing more than that. Now, let us make haste, and get away from this hateful place.'

Chapter 7

The Mediterranean – 1805

'Sit down, Toby,' John Rodgers invited. 'I think this chat should be off the record, as it were.'

Toby removed his hat, and cautiously lowered himself into the chair in front of the commodore's desk in the after cabin of the USS *Constitution*. He was back in a proper uniform, and the squadron was back in its base port of Syracuse. The long march across the desert need never have been, in these so familiar surroundings. And Rodgers was being as charming as he always was. Well, he was an old friend. But now he was the commodore, with a duty to perform, however distasteful. And Toby was determined to resist to his last drop of blood anything that might be injurious to Felicity, or indeed again separate them – even if it meant quarrelling with an old friend.

He did not doubt that Rodgers himself felt in an equivocal position. He had carried out his allotted task, and his ships were preparing to go home. Tripoli was only three days behind them, but already it was merely a bad nightmare of recriminations and fury, of betrayal and disgust. Eaton had taken himself off, determined to maintain his honour to the last, to escort the shattered Hemet Karamanli and his four pages and the remnants of his army back to the safety of Cairo, resolved that he would never again work for the United States Government. Toby wondered if he would ever even reach Egypt again. In that, too, he was aware of a sense of betrayal: perhaps he should also have gone with the men

he had led across the desert, turning his back on his career
... but not on *his* honour.

But that would have meant turning his back on Felicity
Crown as well, and that he would not do. Now or ever. And
he had no doubt that a crisis was at hand; he had seen the
Tripolitanian felucca enter the harbour earlier that morning.
He had seen nothing of Felicity since she had been hurried on
board in her masculine disguise, as she had promptly been
confined in the commodore's own cabin, Rodgers gallantly
moving next door to the captain's cabin: poor Stephen
Decatur, promoted captain in reward for his feat in burning
Philadelphia, had had to move into the wardroom with his
officers. Felicity had been kept in rigorous seclusion during
the short voyage to Sicily, and had there been taken ashore,
once again heavily wrapped up so that no one could possibly
identify her, to the house of Signor Pucchini, the squadron's
victualler. Toby had not even been allowed to say goodbye
to her, and had, on the advice of Decatur, to practise a
frustrating patience. But for all their efforts at concealment,
Mohammed ben Idris had had no doubts what had happened
to his favourite concubine, and now he had come to reclaim
her.

Toby girded his mind for battle.

'I want you to be sure of one thing, Toby,' Rodgers said.
'That I, and the entire fleet, are overcome with admiration
at the remarkable exploit of Eaton and yourself. I have no
doubt that the nation itself will thrill to learn of your march
and glorious victory. We all wish circumstances had turned
out to enable you to enjoy the fruits of that victory. Unfortunately, the decision to treat with the Tripolitanians had
been taken by Congress before you actually set out on
your march from Cairo – on the recommendation of James
Barron, needless to say. It was sheer ill fortune that the ship
bringing that decision across the Atlantic was delayed by bad
weather, and that your own march was equally delayed. I
was in an quandary when I assumed command of the squadron, quite apart from being thoroughly disgusted with the
treatment of poor Preble. Had your people been in position
outside Tripoli on 1 April I am not sure what I would have
done. However, they were not, we had no further word of

150

you other than the assault upon Derna, and I felt compelled to act as instructed and open negotiations with Mohammed ben Idris, negotiations which he was happy to conclude as rapidly as possible.'

'Because he knew he would emerge the victor in every sense,' Toby remarked.

'Of course you're right. But that doesn't alter the facts of the situation, which are that our negotiations were conducted on the basis of freeing Captain Bainbridge and his people, and any other American national held by the Moors. They did not include nationals of any other country, which would have entailed an enormous ransom, and which Congress holds, correctly in my estimation, to be the responsibility of the mother country involved. You exceeded my authority, inadvertently, I am sure, in bringing away Miss Crown. Were you aware that she was a member of the harem of Mohammed ben Idris?'

'I realised it when I rescued her. Mohammed was actually present.' Toby shook his head. 'And I let him go, over Felicity's protests. What a fool I was.'

'Yes,' Rodgers agreed drily. 'Well, I think we can legitimately claim that you were confused in the heat of battle.' He preferred not to specify as to whether he considered the confusion to have caused the escape of Mohammed or the rescue of Felicity.

'However,' he continued, 'it appears that Miss Crown was Mohammed ben Idris's favourite concubine, and has been so for the past four years.' He stared very hard at Toby, willing him to understand just what that must have meant. 'And now the Vizier is demanding the return of his property.'

'Which is obviously out of the question,' Toby declared.

'I agree it presents us with a most difficult situation. The point is, Miss Crown is not an American citizen.'

'There is a simple remedy for that, John,' Toby said. 'I will marry her, and make her one.'

Rodgers frowned at her. 'You have approached her already about marriage?'

Toby flushed. 'Well ... no. I haven't been allowed the opportunity, have I?'

151

'I think you had better tell me just how well you know this young lady, Toby.'

Toby's flush deepened. 'I met her once, five years ago. You remember, John, the day after the battle with *La Vengeance*.' He snapped his fingers. 'Of course, you stayed with the *Constellation*.'

'I remember you being fairly moonstruck when you returned from that breakfast,' Rodgers remarked. 'I put it down to the rum punch. But Toby, five years ago . . .'

'It's not as simple as that,' Toby explained. 'I thought a lot of her, yes. Then she was taken off that ship following the gale outside Gibraltar, remember? Somehow that made her more important to me. And then, seeing her again, last week . . . John, I love her. I think I fell in love with her the moment I saw her, and since then . . .'

'Toby . . .' Rodgers flushed, and was clearly most embarrassed. 'You do realise, well, it doesn't make a lot of sense to claim to be in love with a girl you have met only twice, five years apart. Of course her circumstances were unusual, and as she is a most lovely woman, I can understand the impression she made on you, but the fact is that she has been the mistress of another man for four years. And more than the mistress. As used by the Arabs, the word concubine virtually means wife.'

He held up his finger as Toby would have spoken. 'Hear me out. And I am afraid I am going to have to say some unpleasant things. It may well be that you are acting from sheer gallantry, in which case I salute you. But there is the matter of your career to be considered. Up till now, you have acted not only gallantly, but in good faith. No man can argue against that. Eaton was good enough, before taking himself off into the desert, to set out your achievements under his command, and I do believe you may have a great future in front of you. However, now that you are fully cognisant of the true situation, to persist in this mad course would not only be to disobey the orders of Congress, but quite possibly to re-embroil us in the conflict with Tripoli. Over a woman who . . . my God, what can I say? Do you know anything of the Moorish way of love?'

Toby stared at him, and Rodgers grew even more embarrassed. 'Well, I can tell you, it is very rarely conducted in what we might call a Christian manner. Worse, the women are forced to take an active part in the proceedings. They are quite wanton. I really cannot attempt to put it into words, but I can assure you that any Christian lady would rather die than submit to such mistreatment, and as for, well, reciprocating, the very thought is impossible.'

Toby had no idea of what he was speaking; since entering the Mediterranean he had kept himself aloof from all women, of whatever race or colour. Even in Cairo he had not succumbed to the dusky charmers that Eaton had been anxious to supply, and whom the consul had certainly enjoyed himself. But he could not be angry with Rodgers, who he knew was only trying to help.

'If you mean, John, that Miss Crown should have committed suicide, rather than surrender to a man like Idris, I am sure it is a step she contemplated. However, I am utterly happy that she chose to survive, and await her rescue. I do not concede that she is another man's wife, but even if she were, it would make no difference. She was forced, and therefore there can be no true bond between them, and even less if she has indeed been mistreated as a woman. And I love her. And shall love her, no matter whose orders I have to disobey.'

Rodgers stared at him for several seconds. 'I think you want to be terribly certain of that, Toby. It could involve your commission.'

'If the choice is between my commission and sending Felicity back to that scoundrel Idris, then my decision is already taken.'

Rodgers sighed. 'Had you made any other decision, Toby McGann, then you were not the man I knew you to be. Well, I must help you so far as I can.'

'Will you?' Toby cried, unable to believe his good fortune.

'In so far as I can,' Rodgers repeated carefully. 'But nothing we do must in any way exacerbate an already dangerous situation. Now, *Enterprise* is leaving Syracuse this evening. As she is the fastest ship I possess, I am sending her ahead of the main squadron to relay to Congress the news that our quarrel with Tripoli has been brought to a successful conclusion. Hull will command, but I will detach you to accompany him as supernumary, so that you can give to Congress a first-hand account of the land operation in which you played so conspicuous a part.'

'Thank you, John, but I will not abandon Felicity.'

'Kindly allow me to finish. I have told Mohammed ben Idris's envoys that Miss Crown is at present ashore, as she is, staying with old friends of her family, and that if they insisted upon her return, as they did, I would have to undertake the distasteful task of persuading them to part with her. I have told them that I will do this when I go ashore this evening. If Miss Crown were to be placed, clandestinely, on board *Enterprise*, and taken with you to Gibraltar, where you will necessarily stop for victualling before crossing the Atlantic, I will be able to tell the envoys, when they come for her tomorrow, that she has already left Sicily, and indeed, had done so before I visited the Pucchinis to demand her return. I shall not of course specify which ship she left on. They will undoubtedly be angry, but I do not see what they can do about it; by the time they can regain Tripoli and mount a pursuit, you will have made the Rock.'

'John,' Toby cried. 'That is the most splendid thing I ever heard. I . . . I would like to apologise.'

Rodgers raised his eyebrows. 'For what?'

'Ah . . . for . . . for doubting, sir.'

'Did you think I would ever return a Christian lady to the hands of the Moors? However, I must warn you that they may well suspect the truth, and may even make representations to Congress. I cannot believe that any American government would consider returning a young white lady to the clutches of a man like Idris, nor will they be able to do so while she remains on British soil.

'However, if you do intend to marry the girl, it is absolutely essential that you conduct yourself in every aspect of this affair as a commissioned officer in the United States Navy should. Miss Crown will be in your care as far as Gibraltar. This is improper, but these are unusual circumstances. However, during the voyage, you must conduct yourself with the utmost propriety. You will not so much as touch her hand, even if invited to do so, and under no circumstances will you

154

allow yourself to be alone with her. I wish that very clearly understood.'

'Yes, sir. Am I allowed to speak with her?'

'Well, of course you are. There is no necessity to be rude to her.'

'I meant, am I allowed to propose marriage?'

'If you can ascertain that she wishes to entertain such a proposal, certainly. But again, you must behave in an entirely proper fashion. When you reach Gibraltar, you may visit her parents and formally ask for her hand in marriage, if that is what you truly wish. Once that is agreed, arrangements can be made for her to cross the Atlantic and marry you. It will, of course, greatly enhance your chances of receiving the blessings of Congress were you able to say that you are betrothed to the young woman. But she must not cross the Atlantic in *Enterprise*, under any conceivable circumstances. I wish this most clearly understood, Toby. Any suggestion of abduction or coercion in this matter and you are done. Remember that at all times.'

'Yes, sir.' Toby stood up, replaced his hat, saluted. 'And I wish to thank you again, sir, from the bottom of my heart.'

'I think you should pray that you have something to thank me for, at the end of the day. Now you may go ashore and inform Miss Crown of our arrangements.'

Signora Pucchini clapped her hands. 'Fine,' she cried. 'Fine.'

That was, unfortunately, one of only half a dozen words of English she knew, which had made conversation rather difficult, as Felicity knew no Italian. But she thought the gown did look rather fine, even if its colours were somewhat gaudy, deep reds and blues in huge bands, while the skirt was absurdly flounced. It was when she turned in front of the full-length mirror that she became aware of how heavy it was, seeming to weigh her down, and how noisy, as the taffeta underskirts rustled and crackled . . . and how clinging.

But the two Signorinas Pucchini, teenagers, dark haired and eyed, with flashing smiles and excited movements – younger editions of their mother – were also clapping their hands in admiration; they spoke no English at all.

So, Felicity thought, was she going to admit to herself that she missed the soft, cool, light and utterly indecent silk of the harem? She certainly missed the velvet slippers or the bare feet; the boots bought for her to go with the outfit seemed to have encased her toes in iron.

'Promenade?' Signora Pucchini suggested, revealing another word of her limited vocabulary. 'Buono, buono.'

She watched her guest anxiously. She had indeed watched Felicity anxiously ever since the English girl had been brought to the Pucchini house, and although well equipped with maids, had insisted on serving her herself wherever possible, as if she were suffering from some dreadful disease. But then, Felicity thought, am I *not* suffering from some dreadful disease in the eyes of everybody? Certainly in the eyes of the Americans, who had kept her locked away far more firmly than she been in the harem of Mohammed ben Idris. Not even Toby MacGann had come to call. He had rescued her – but his mission had been to rescue his compatriots. Having done that, he had had the time to think, and consider.

Well, so had she, both on the two-day journey to Syracuse and in the twenty-four hours she had spent in this house. The Pucchinis had been most kind, and had done wonders in having their dressmaker run up this gown so quickly ... but she was still diseased. Because once the euphoria of being rescued had worn off, thought had accomplished very little towards reassuring her about the future. She had had to contend, first of all, with a sense of unreality, compounded by memory. She had found herself in the security of the cabin of a ship at sea; it had been from the security of a cabin of a ship at sea that she had been dragged to Idris's harem.

When she had got over that initial, stark fear that her rescue had been nothing more than a dream from which she would awaken on Idris's couch, she had then had to contend with the reality of being utterly alone. She had not actually been alone for four years. The harem had always been a crowded place; even if the other women had hated her, and their children had been afraid of her, yet they had always been there, as the eunuchs had always been there. As Mohammed ben Idris had always been nearby.

So then she had had to reconcile herself to two consecutive nights, which had now become three, without having a man's hand sliding over her body, so regular had Idris been in his attentions this past year. She had actually awakened on the second night aboard the *Essex* – the first night she had slept the sleep of total emotional exhaustion – and wondered where she was, and why she was sweating with anxiety . . . Oh, she was diseased.

But there were other, more subtle reconciliations to be made. The right, for instance, to leave this house and go for a walk in public, as Signora Pucchini was now inviting her to do. But behind that suggestion of total freedom there lurked another, more terrifying reality. These people were all strangers. They knew only a refugee from a Moorish harem. If she was contaminated by her experiences, she was also an object of admiration, for her survival and her beauty, of anticipated laughter and good manners when she was recovered, of even that recovery, into a normal English gentlewoman. And in any event, the Italian, the entire Continental, attitude to sexual matters lacked the prurient censoriousness of the English. But soon she would be on her way to meet her mother and father. Both Captain Rodgers and Signor Pucchini had assured her of this. To meet Jonathan, once again.

She dreaded that most. Jonathan, in his ambitions to climb the ladder of success and promotion with no backing of either birth or wealth to support his abilities, was the most gentlemanly gentleman in all the world. His life was a series of established rules, within which a gentleman, and a lady, manoeuvred, as best they could. The rules could be bent and even evaded, from time to time, in a proper secrecy, and to a proper end; they could never be broken – anyone attempting to do so was immediately an outcast. She might not have broken the rules herself, but she had had them broken about her, brutally, violently, completely, and worst of all, most publicly. As she could not go to the bed of a gentlemanly husband as a virgin, she could not go to the bed of a gentleman at all. And as marriage was the only acceptable occupation for a gentlewoman, she would indeed be an outcast.

Last night she had almost acknowledged a most terrible

157

desire, that the best news she could now receive was that her mother and father and brother had all somehow died, leaving her totally alone in the world to make her way to hell in her own good way. Because of all the world, she feared seeing them again the most.

'Promenade?' Signora Pucchini asked again, looking hopeful.

Felicity smiled at her. 'Why not? Si, signora.' Because she might as well enjoy her new-found freedom, until the walls of propriety shut her away more conclusively than ever. And in Syracuse, no one yet knew who she was, or where she had come from.

Signora Pucchini clapped her hands, and held out a parasol, taking one for herself. Her daughters also hastily equipped themselves, then all four women turned to face the door to the parlour, on which there was a knock, followed by Signor Pucchini.

'A caller,' he said. Unlike his wife, he spoke English quite well. 'For you, Signorina Crown.'

Instincitively Felicity brought up her umbrella like a weapon. She knew who it had to be. Well, did she not want to see him? But however brief their previous acquaintance, he was the only man in all Italy who had known her before Mohammed ben Idris.

Toby stood behind Pucchini, his hat in his hands. He looked very smart in his uniform, as smart as she recalled him on that day at breakfast, aboard HMS *Lancer*. But she preferred the memory of the tattered, bearded ruffian who taken her from Idris's harem.

'Miss Crown,' he said formally.

Felicity looked at Signor Pucchini, and then at his wife, who shrugged.

'Of course,' Signor Pucchini said. 'The parlour is yours, signorina. But it is correct for the door to be kept open. You understand?'

'Yes,' Felicity said, and went into the room. 'I have so much to thank you for, Mr McGann,' she said, 'that I don't know where to begin.' She did not look at him as she carefully laid down the parasol, and took off her bonnet. She knew she was blushing; that his cheeks were also pink was no comfort.

'You have nothing to thank me for, Miss Crown,' he said. 'Rather should you hate me.'

At last she looked directly at him, in surprise.

'For leaving you to languish in that ghastly captivity for so long,' he explained. 'I would have you know it was not for want of trying.'

Only three days ago, in the excitement of the battle and the rescue, they had called each other Toby and Felicity. Now that invisible wall of propriety and genteel manners she feared so much was already erected between them.

Felicity sat down, her hands on her lap. 'I am sure you came to my aid as soon as was possible, Mr McGann,' she said. 'Far sooner than I had any right to expect.' She attempted a smile. 'My own people never sought me at all. Won't you sit down?'

He obeyed, on the far side of the room. 'I ... I knew where you were,' he said. 'And wanted ...' He sighed. 'How I wanted ... to help you,' he hastily added.

'And you are a man who does what he wants,' Felicity acknowledged. 'For which I am truly thankful.'

Toby licked his lips.

'Will you take a glass of wine?' she asked. She could see a bottle and glasses on the table behind him.

'That would be very kind of you.' He stood up. 'I will fetch it. And you?'

The thought had not occurred to her. But she did need something. 'Why, yes, thank you,' she said.

He went to the table, filled two glasses, glanced at the open door; he could have no doubt they were being overheard. He came back across the room, held out the glass. Their fingers touched as she took it.

'My I ask what happens now?' she asked.

'Ah.' He returned to his seat and sat down. 'It is for that reason I have come. Please do not be alarmed, but Mohammed ben Ìdris has sent to reclaim you.'

She stared at him, her brain refusing to accept what he was saying.

'You were not included in the ransom payment, you understand,' Toby hurried on, 'which was strictly for the release of our seamen and Captain Bainbridge. And although we took you by force, it was an illegal act, as peace had already been agreed between the United States and Tripoli.'

'And when the Moors took me by force' she asked in a low voice, 'was that considered a legal act?'

'Aye. These people have the most colossal effrontery, to be sure. However . . .'

'I shall not return to Mohammed ben Idris, Mr McGann.' She kept her voice even with an effort. 'If I have to kill myself.'

'Of course you will not return to Tripoli, Miss Crown. I gave my word as to that. And my people feel exactly as I do. But the commodore also feels it were best you were not in the vicinity at all, if we are to avoid an incident. In any event, we all know how anxious you must be to return to your parents. There is a ship leaving for Gibraltar tonight, and we wish you to be on it. An escort will come for you at dusk.'

'For Gibraltar!' That feared fate was rushing at her even sooner than she had suspected. Absently she drank, felt the liquid tracing its way down her chest.

'Do you not wish to go to Gibraltar? So far as we are aware, your father is still posted there. And your mother is with him. Even your brother visits there, from time to time.' He gave an encouraging smile. 'Your whole family, waiting to welcome you with open arms.'

'Yes,' she said softly, and finished her wine. For a moment the room revolved about her – she had tasted no alcohol in four years – then it settled down. 'Do they . . . do they know of my rescue?'

'Why, no. There has been no time. You will be the bearer of your own good news. Which will be to the good, will it not?' Toby was clearly at a loss at her lack of enthusiasm. 'I am to accompany you.'

'You?' She put down the glass.

'Well . . .' His flush was back, deeper than before, and his glass was also empty. 'I am to bear despatches for Congress.

160

But I have also been granted permission to see you safe to your family. It is felt . . . ah . . .'

'That I am your personal responsibility,' she suggested.

'Well, not in that sense.' Again he glanced at the open door.

'You will have to explain the sense you mean. And please have some more wine,' she invited. 'I will join you.'

'Oh yes, of course.' He refilled their glasses, remained standing this time by the fireplace. 'I thought, perhaps, on such a voyage, that we might to able to . . . discuss things.'

'Of course,' she agreed, her heart beginning to pound more quickly. But that might just have been the effects of the wine. 'What did you wish to discuss?'

'Ah . . .' He returned to his seat. 'You have probably forgotten, Miss Crown, but on the occasion of our first meeting, off Dominica, I expressed a desire to call upon you should I ever visit Gibraltar.'

'I remember very well.'

'I . . . well . . . ' He licked his lips. 'I wish you to understand that I know I am behaving in a most unmannerly fashion in raising this matter at this time, and in these circumstances . . . but I meant that request, and when I was posted to the Mediterranean, which would necessarily involve a stop at Gibraltar, I was overjoyed, principally because of the opportunity it would give me to see you again. I believe we even sighted your convoy just before . . . well, that gale, with its dreadful consequences.'

'I remember seeing two American warships,' she cried. 'Were you on one of them?'

'Oh, indeed, I was. Oh, Miss Crown . . . to think that we gazed at each other across a few scant miles of sea, and then . . . my God! Is there any justice in this world?'

'Perhaps, Mr McGann,' she said quietly, 'as you have now rescued me. Supposing you still consider that to have been a worthwhile act.'

'Worthwhile? My God!' He finished his second glass of wine, and sighed. 'Well, I carried out my intention, and called on your parents, and there learned of your terrible misfortune.'

161

'They knew of it? But what was their reaction?'

He raised his head. 'I do not truly know, Miss Crown. Shock and horror, of course. But I . . . I left immediately, to attempt to organise a rescue there and then. I failed . . .' He sighed again. 'It was pointed out to me, with some justice I believe, that there was no hope of finding you until we could discover where you had been taken.'

She gazed at him. 'Was that all that was pointed out to you, Mr McGann?'

'I had no interest in the opinions of others, Miss Crown,' he said fiercely. 'I have dreamed only of rescuing you, ever since.'

'Someone you had met only once?' She attempted to lighten his mood with another smile, with more success than before. 'You are a romantic, Mr McGann.'

His smile was genuine. 'I'll not deny that, Miss Crown.'

'But a successful romantic. Again, I thank you, and indeed, God, for making you so. If there is anything I can ever do to repay you . . .'

Toby drew a long breath. 'I . . . I had hoped that circumstances would enable me to conduct myself as an officer and a gentleman, trusting that the situation, of us both being in the Mediterranean area, would permit me to visit Gibraltar with some regularity. However, my intention was, I think, formed on the occasion of our first meeting, and has never altered. And now, my imminent departure for the United States forces me to sidestep the restrictions of propriety. Miss Crown, Felicity . . . I should be honoured if you would consent to be my wife.'

She gazed at him with her mouth open, taken entirely by surprise, even if her instincts had been warning her that he was going to make some claim on her. But marriage . . . She couldn't think, as the room was filled with people, kissing her cheek, embracing Toby, Signor Pucchini shaking his hand. 'Oh, congratulations,' he said. 'We are all so happy for you.'

Felicity continued to stare across their heads at Toby. Her knees felt weak, but she was determined that she was not going to faint this time.

162

Toby stared back. His cheeks were flushed, but there could be no doubt of his determination. 'I shall, of course, make a formal representation to your father when we reach Gibraltar, but . . . will you not say yes to me, now?'

She drew a long breath. 'Have you truly considered those opinions you affect to despise, Mr McGann?' she asked. She was being utterly foolish not to accept him without hesitation, but she could not take so easy a way out of her problems under false pretences. Even supposing marriage to so upright a character as Toby McGann really was an easy way out.

The Pucchinis looked from one to the other, their animation fading into anxiety.

'I care less for them now than I did four years ago,' Toby declared. 'Please believe that, Felicity.'

'I . . .' She bit her lip. She simply had to think. 'I will abide by my father's decision, sir,' she said, and left the room.

Marriage! To Toby McGann. But marriage, to any man? It was not something she had considered for a moment. But then she had considered nothing of what was to happen to her. She had been afraid to. She knew only that she wanted time to think, and evaluate, and understand, and perhaps recover from her disease . . . a great deal of time. Perhaps the entire rest of her life. A life which would slowly dwindle into lonely memories.

But marriage . . . To share herself, what she had become, what she had been made, by Mohammed ben Idris . . . To undress, and reveal herself . . . That at least would not be a problem after a month or so, and she could not possibly be married in less than a month. But to lie naked in the arms of a man and not reveal herself to be a wanton creature . . . The thought was impossible.

Toby stood at her elbow as the Rock loomed above the horizon. He at least had no doubt of her answer, even if he was too much of a gentleman to press the matter further; he had certainly celebrated with the Pucchinis that evening before leaving Syracuse. Since then he had been nothing more than a charming and ideal companion, never encroaching, never even attempting to take her hand, but always there when she ventured on deck – Isaac Hull had allowed her the use of the captain's cabin – to walk beside her, point out things of interest, answer her questions, exclaim with her at the dolphins which cavorted beneath the schooner's bows. He might have been her oldest friend, instead of the man who wished to marry her.

Why? Because she was beautiful? There were a great many beautiful women in the world. Because he had indeed carried her image in his heart for five years? That suggested a remarkable immaturity, or, more hopefully, a singularly constant nature. Or simply because he felt it was the duty of a gentleman to propose marriage to the woman he had rescued from a fate worse than death. That was the most frightening thought she had ever had.

But whatever the reason, there was the point; he was a perfect gentleman. Idris had not been a gentleman. She knew nothing of gentlemen. And she was afraid to learn. Afraid that, having learned, she might yearn for Idris? That was an even more damnable thought than to be married out of pity. But for a gentleman, even Toby McGann, to suspect that she could feel passion, that she had come to expect passion, that she *needed* passion ... and such passion!

'Are you nervous?' he asked. He took this as the main cause for her moods of silent introspection. It was a serious matter, and one he could understand, returning to one's parents after four years of separation in such circumstances. But in what circumstances? He had no idea. She knew that now. He simply had no idea. But he wanted to be her husband. Out of curiosity? There was another damning and damnable thought. But how she wanted to have his powerful protection for the rest of her life, even if it meant living a lie ...

'Yes,' she lied. Because in fact she was no longer nervous at all. The apprehensions of meeting her parents had been submerged by the greater apprehensions of responding to the man beside her.

'Do not be,' he told her. 'I intend to be at your side.'

No one in Gibraltar had any idea what they were about,

164

saw only an American schooner putting in for food and water. Heavily veiled, and wearing her Italian gown which effectively disguised her nationality, Felicity was escorted ashore by Toby, and a carriage hired for the ride up the hill. She looked out of the window with considerable interest; she had never seen Gibraltar before, and by concentrating on the unusual contours of the Rock she could maintain her pretence of nonchalance. Because now the apprehensions were mounting thick and fast. And yet, secure in his support, she was determined that she would be herself, no matter what . . . and pray that her family would accept her as such.

Yet she was surprised when he suddenly took her hand. He had not actually touched her since they had left the Pucchinis' house. But now he squeezed her fingers. Her head turned abruptly. 'Courage,' he said.

. She gave him a quick smile, then looked out of the window again. It was just dusk, and the setting sun was playing on this western side of the Rock, bringing flickers of light from the houses and the catchments.

'It was like this when I first saw it,' she said. 'From over there.' She pointed at the African side of the channel. 'I had not thought ever to see it again.'

'And to think that I was but eight miles distant,' he said. 'God, what tricks fate does play!'

'But you found me in the end,' she reminded him.

'Oh, yes,' he said. 'I found you. And I promise you that you will never have to look upon this Rock again, once you have left it in my care. Unless, of course, you wish to.'

The carriage was stopping, and he helped her down. 'Shall I go in first?'

'Please,' she said.

He went up the path, knocked on the door, raised his hat as it opened. 'Mrs Crown? Thank heavens I find you here. I am Toby McGann, lieutenant, United States Navy.'

'Mr McGann,' Mrs Crown said. 'Why . . . I had not expected to see you again.'

'Because the last time I was here you received such terrible tidings,' Toby agreed. 'But ma'am, if you will but brace yourself for a surprise, and a most pleasant one . . .'

But Mrs Crown had already looked past him, at the tall, veiled woman behind him, and had recognised her daughter. 'Oh, my God,' she said, and took a step forward. Then, as Felicity started to respond, she just as quickly took a step backwards. 'Oh, my God!' she said again, casting quick glances to left and right to see if any of her neighbours were looking. 'You'd best come inside.'

She was still retreating, down the short hallway to the door to the parlour. Toby waited, and after a moment's hesitation, almost as if she expected the door to be slammed in her face, Felicity came forward and passed him to enter the house. He followed.

Mrs Crown reached the parlour door, still retreating: perhaps, he thought, she feared to turn her back on them. 'Charles,' she said. 'Charles . . . Jonathan . . .'

'Oh God,' Felicity muttered.

Toby took her elbow and guided her into the room. Charles Crown and his son were on their feet; Jonathan Crown still wore the uniform of a lieutenant in the Royal Navy. Both were looking at once mystified and thunderstruck.

Julia Crown was panting. 'Felicity . . .' she gasped.

Felicity drew a long breath and entered the room. 'Mother could not bring herself to embrace me,' she said, and threw the veil back from her face. 'Would you be so bold, Father?'

Charles Crown stared at her, then looked at his son.

Jonathan took a step forward. 'Felicity?' he whispered, and looked at Toby as he might have done at a magician. 'But how?'

'It's a long story,' Toby began.

'But soon told,' Felicity countered. 'I have spent the past four years in the harem of Mohammed ben Idris, Vizier to the Dey of Tripoli. From there, but just a week ago, I was rescued by the American Navy, in the person of Mr McGann.'

'Oh my *God*!' Julia Crown said a third time, and sat down heavily on the settee.

Charles Crown came forward to stand beside his son. 'My dear Felicity,' he said, and took her hands. Once again she seemed about to move forward for an embrace, but checked herself as he hesitated. 'My dear, dear girl. We had thought you dead.'

'I thought it best to live,' Felicity said. 'For as long as possible. I considered that the most Christian thing to do. Was I wrong?' She gazed at her father, who was speechless.

'Now you ...' Jonathan Crown changed his mind about what he was going to say. Toby suspected it might have been something like, 'have come back, to our horror and disgust. No, dear sister, it would have been more convenient had you been dead.' Instead of saying the words, however, he looked at Toby. 'Perhaps, sir, you would be good enough to withdraw. This is a private family affair.'

'Affair?' Toby demanded.

'I would prefer Mr McGann to stay,' Felicity said. 'He has a right to do so.'

Her family gazed at her; they could remember no such firmness in the girl they had lost and forgotten.

'I ... ah ...' Toby licked his lips. 'I am aware that there must be a great deal you wish to say to your daughter, Mr Crown, Mrs Crown ...' He ignored Jonathan. 'And I am equally sure there is a great deal she has to say to you. But as my stay here must necessarily be short, I must ...' His turn to draw a long breath. 'It is my great honour to ask for Miss Crown's hand in marriage, sir.'

The three gazes had been transferred to him.

'Oh my God!' remarked Julia Crown for the fourth time.

'Marriage?' Charles Crown was dumbfounded.

Jonathan Crown gave a short laugh. 'You mean you are seeking a just reward for your gallantry, Mr McGann. Or are you performing an act of charity?'

Toby kept his temper. It was no part of his plan to quarrel with his future brother-in-law.

'Or did "rescuing" involve some other act of which we are unaware?' Jonathan Crown went on.

Felicity stepped forward at last, passing Toby, to slap her brother on the cheek. It was a forceful blow, and Jonathan staggered.

'Why, you little whore?' he shouted and raised his own arm, but was checked by Toby's giant hand on his wrist. 'Let me go, sir. Let me go.'

'I shall,' Toby promised him, 'if you agree to behave

167

yourself. I will say, sir, that I am amazed and disgusted by your reaction to your sister's return.'

Jonathan stared at him, undecided how to respond.

'It is certainly not an occasion for quarrelling,' Charles Crown said. 'But my dear Mr McGann . . .'

'I know it must appear a sudden and perhaps prejudiced decision to you, sir,' Toby said. 'But I would beg you to believe that I have been in love with Miss Crown since the occasion of our first meeting, off Dominica, in 1800, which you may recall.'

'Bless my soul,' Charles Crown remarked. 'Bless my soul.'

'There's a tale, if ever I heard one,' Jonathan observed, prudently removing himself behind the settee.

'This,' Felicity asked at large, 'is a welcome?'

'My dear girl,' Crown said, taking her hands again. 'Oh my dear girl.' Cautiously he kissed her on the cheek. 'We are shocked. Welcome . . . why, we are overjoyed. Your boxes . . .'

'I have no boxes, Father,' Felicity said. 'I have what I am wearing.'

'Oh my God!' Julia Crown remarked.

'Toby,' Felicity said, 'will you please take me away from here.'

'Ah . . .' Toby had no idea what to do. Felicity of course had no inkling of the instructions given him by John Rodgers. And surely these people were going to get over this initial, rather unpleasant reaction, and remember she was their daughter?

'Now, Felicity,' Charles Crown said, attempting to take her hand again, and being rebuffed as she stepped away. 'This should be a joyous occasion. Yes, indeed, a joyous occasion.' He appeared to be attempting to convince himself. 'As for Mr McGann's gallant proposal, well . . . why do you not retire with your mother and leave us men to discuss the situation . . . ah . . . man to man.'

Felicity looked at Toby. 'I should prefer to stay,' she said. Her cheeks were pink.

'Now, you look here,' Jonathan Crown began.

Felicity sat down. 'You cannot harm me with words or

168

opinions, brother. If Toby wishes me to leave the room, then I shall do so.' She looked at him.

'Of course I wish you to stay,' Toby said. 'As this matter concerns you as much as anyone.'

Julia Crown began to weep.

'Here, I say . . . well, what a kettle of fish, eh?' Charles Crown remarked at large. 'I think what we need is a glass of wine, eh? Jonathan, would you be so kind?'

Jonathan Crown hesitated, and then went to the sideboard and poured three glasses of sherry.

'I would like one too, please,' Felicity said.

Jonathan looked at his father, who gave a hasty nod.

'Now, then,' Charles Crown said. 'Let us all toast your safe return. Oh, indeed, it is a joyous occasion. The most joyous occasion I can recall. Will you not join us, Mother?'

His wife gave a loud sniff, and Jonathan snorted.

'And I would also like to drink a toast to you, Mr McGann,' Crown pressed on bravely. 'For having restored our daughter to us. That was behaviour above and beyond the call of duty, as they say, and we shall remain forever in your debt. However, I do wish you to understand that we expect nothing more of you. And neither does Felicity, I am sure . . .'

'I happen to love your daughter, Mr Crown,' Toby said quietly. 'That is why I wish to marry her.'

'Love.' Jonathan gave another snort. 'Another man's cast-off whore? By God, sir, your tastes do you no credit.'

Toby stared at him, but continued to speak quietly. 'Were you not about to become by brother-in-law, sir, I should ram those words back down your throat with my fist.'

'You would, would you? What do you suppose gives you the right to march into our house and announce that you are about to marry my sister, simply because you picked her up from the floor of some filthy harem? What are you, McGann? You are not even a gentleman. Oh, you wear a uniform. A uniform which is the laughing stock of Europe, treated with contumely even by the Moors. Why, sir, I have no doubt you and your compatriots are the laughing stock of the entire world. But yet, yours is a uniform which befits a man who is the son of a dirt farmer and sometime Irish smuggler. Oh, I know all about your *illustrious* forebear, sir.

169

A deserter from the Royal Navy, a known pirate, and a red-handed revolutionary. Do you suppose my sister would even consider marrying into such a brood, had her Moorish master left her with any senses?'

Toby allowed him to say his piece, although it was difficult not to throttle the scoundrel there and then. When Jonathan appeared to have run out of breath, he replied, continuing to keep his voice and his temper under control. 'My father fought for freedom, Mr Crown. And he won it, too, from stiff-necked tyrants such as yourself. No doubt that sticks in your craw. As for whether or not I am the man to marry your sister, should we not allow her to make that decision? I assure you that I can discern nothing the matter with her senses, save that she would appear to me to have more courage than the average woman.'

'Ah . . .' Charles Crown began, but he was interrupted by his daughter.

'Yes,' Felicity said. 'I think I am old enough to make that decision. I would like to marry Mr McGann, Father.'

'Hurrah!' Toby cried; it was the first time she had actually said yes.

'My dear girl,' Charles Crown protested.

'You will marry him over my dead body,' Jonathan snapped.

'If that is a necessary condition,' Toby said, now totally jubilant where before he had been unsure of himself, 'be sure I will be happy to accommodate you.'

The two men gazed at each other, Jonathan's face rigid with anger, Toby's smiling – and then Jonathan looked away. He could estimate that even if he were a better swordsman, and he did not know that, he would never get near enough to prove it, such was Toby's reach, while as Toby was also a serving officer he might well be a good pistol shot.

'Why are you so anxious to retain me, brother?' Felicity asked, 'as you find my experiences so distasteful? Is it so that you can lock me away for the rest of my life, as an awful example of woman's misfortune?'

'Leave this house,' Jonathan declared, determined to retrieve some of his prestige, 'and you need never come crawling to us again. There will be no dowry, and Father will cut you out of his will. Is that not so, Father?'

'Why, I . . .' Charles Crown scratched his head, displacing his wig.

Julia Crown wept more loudly than ever.

'I shall not trouble you again,' Felicity said. 'You may suppose that I am indeed dead, or that I have remained lying on the floor of my filthy harem, as you put it. Mr McGann, I most humbly apologise for my family. But if you do indeed love me, I beg you to take me away from here.'

Toby hesitated for a last time, as once again Rodgers's words came back to him. What would Father have done? Why, Father would have said the devil with Congress and John Rodgers's strictures. This is the woman I love, and will have, come what may.

'Immediately,' he said. 'The *Enterprise* sails at midnight.'

Chapter 8

Gibraltar and Long Island – 1805–7

Isaac Hull stood on the quarterdeck of the USS *Enterprise*, gazing at the man and woman in front of him, and scratched his head. He was several years older than Toby, but having begun his sailing career in the Merchant Navy was no senior; the two had known each other all their service lives.

'I know what I want to do,' he admitted. 'But I also know what I should do, for the good of your career, Toby.'

'That is probably finished now, anyway,' Toby said. 'But I may be able to relieve you of any responsibility in this business. What date were you commissioned, Isaac?'

'Why, 1 March, 1798.'

'I was commissioned on 1 *February*, 1798,' Toby said.

Hull frowned at him.

Toby grinned. 'Oh, I shall make no attempt to relieve you of your command. But as your senior officer, I am requesting passage on board your ship for this young lady and myself to the United States. I will take full responsibility for my actions, and that will be recorded in the log.'

Hull hesitated, glancing at Felicity. Her veil was back in place and it was difficult to decide her expression or her mood. 'It will be difficult,' he said. 'I had planned no such accommodation for so long a voyage. Miss Crown is welcome to use my cabin, of course, but we shall be some thirty days at sea, and, well . . .'

'You fear for propriety,' Toby agreed, 'in private matters. But that problem, too, is easily solved. You are master of

172

this ship. As soon as we are beyond the three-mile limit, you can marry us.'

Felicity gave a gasp.

Hull's frown deepened. 'Is that legal? Truly?'

'If it is not, then the matter can be set right the moment we reach home.' He turned to Felicity. 'Will you accept such a form of marriage, as a temporary expedient, Felicity?'

'I . . . I had expected nothing so sudden,' she muttered.

He could understand her hesitation. He had been so pre-occupied with what he had to do that he had hardly uttered a word of endearment since leaving Tripoli. But she could hardly change her mind now.

'If you do mean to marry me, Felicity,' he said gently, 'then it really were best done immediately. There will be several factions seeking to prevent it. And I do love you, and wish you to be my wife.'

He heard her inhale. 'If . . . if that is what you are sure you wish, Mr McGann, I will willingly marry you here and now, having regard to all the circumstances.'

'And thus,' Isaac Hull said, 'by the authority vested in me as master of this vessel, I pronounce you man and wife. You may kiss the bride, Toby.'

Toby turned to Felicity. It had taken them only an hour to clear the port and glide down the Strait on the ebb tide; Gibraltar was still a mass of lights on the eastern horizon, and lights winked to either side of them on the Spanish and Moroccan coasts, as well. But they were certainly more than three miles from land.

Carefully he lifted the veil she had continued to wear throughout the ceremony, while the watch below, assembled in the waist, cheered and clapped their hands. He stared into her deep blue eyes, darker than ever in the midnight gloom, so dry, so watchful. And so apprehensive? 'I love you, Felicity McGann,' he said.

She bit her lip. 'As I shall love you, Toby McGann,' she promised.

Holding her hands, he slowly inclined his face towards her. Her eyes shut, and her fingers tightened on his as his lips brushed hers. No more than that, yet it sent thrills racing

173

up and down his spine. And doubts? How many men had known those lips? Or was kissing not a Moorish habit?

It was not a question he would ever dare ask.

'We'll drink a toast,' Hull declared, and his steward, previously briefed, hurried forward with a tray of glasses containing rum. 'To a long and happy life, for you both.'

'I thank you, Isaac,' Toby said.

'And I, sir.' Felicity sipped hers cautiously – she had tasted nothing like it before – and gazed forward at the twinkling lights on the starboard bow. 'Is that not the open sea? Yet it looks like a city, floating there.'

'It is a British squadron off Cape Trafalgar,' Hull explained. 'Watching the Spaniards in Cadiz.'

'Are the British commanded by Lord Nelson?'

'No, Nelson, I learned in Gibraltar, is chasing the French in the West Indies. The commander here is Admiral Collingwood. The Spanish would like to unite with the French, and it is his task to prevent it.'

'He will never let them move,' Toby said. 'Now there, Isaac, is a fleet. And a purpose.'

Hull sighed. 'We will have one to match it one day, perhaps. But do you intend to keep your bride on deck all night?'

Toby looked at Felicity; her expression was lost in the gloom. But she did not immediately reply, as if she might indeed have preferred to remain on deck all night. Then she seemed to gather herself. 'I shall retire,' she said. 'Perhaps you will join me, in due course, sir.'

'Yes,' he said. 'Yes.'

She went to the companionway, and disappeared from sight. Hull refilled Toby's glass; if strong liquor was strictly forbidden on board an American warship, and the captain himself had barely allowed the drink to brush his lips, Toby was not actually a member of the crew and had no watch to keep. Besides on this night they had broken so many rules one more hardly seemed to matter.

'She is a most beautiful woman, Toby,' Hull remarked.

'But no woman is sufficiently beautiful to cost a career,' Toby mused. 'Is that what you are thinking?'

'It is what *I* am thinking, certainly,' his friend agreed. 'But each man on this earth thinks for himself – or most certainly should do so.'

Toby nodded. 'Then I will go and make my decision irrevocable.'

'A strange way to put it,' Hull observed.

'Aye,' Toby agreed. 'But then it is a strange business.'

He went down the companionway, paused outside the door of the captain's cabin, which Hull had insisted they use for the voyage. A strange business. Hull had no idea how strange. How backwards, where he stood here, an anxious virgin, and she lay within ... but to think thoughts of that nature would be disastrous. Rather should he be reassured that she would know how to welcome him, would not be shocked, or afraid ... but did she really want him? How the doubts suddenly clouded his mind, as he recalled her hesitation of an hour before, her suggestion almost of a desire to delay their union.

Perhaps she had been acting, afraid to appear too eager. All his doubts would be resolved in her arms. If only he knew ... But whether she truly wanted him or not, he certainly wanted her. It was more than just the growing sexual urge. It was also the knowledge that she had turned her back on her own family, now depended entirely on him. And surely his desire was all that mattered at this moment. His desire, his love, would overcome all their doubts.

He knocked.

'The door is unlocked,' she called.

He turned the handle, stepped inside, closed the door behind him. There was a single lantern swinging from a deck beam as the ship rolled in the low swell. He could look at the bed, which in this small a ship was no more than a bunk, set against the bulkhead. Felicity was already in it, lying down, the sheet pulled to her throat, her hair, which she had dressed for the visit ashore, now loosed and scattered in dark brown profusion to either side of her head. She looked utterly entrancing.

'I have no nightclothes,' she said.

'I seldom use a shirt myself,' he said, 'in this climate. Should the weather turn cold as we make to the north-west, I will lend you one of mine.'

He listened to her breathe, perhaps a sigh of relief. He

175

hoped so. His principal task must be to put her at ease. And his passion was now all but overwhelming, as she was so close he could smell her, and as he knew what lay beneath that sheet.

'Would you like me to turn down the light?' he asked.

The sheet rose as she inhaled. 'Perhaps it would be better to leave it on.'

She gazed at him, eyes enormous, perhaps realising, he thought, that her reply had not been what he would have expected. Because she was revealing passion of her own? Or because she had never made love in the dark before? If the phrase 'made love' could be applied to a Moorish harem. But if it could not, what other phrase would he choose?

'There was talk,' she said, seeking to find some pattern of normality between them, 'of your career being affected by your marriage to me. I would hate to think that.'

'My career is what I choose to make of it,' he replied. 'It is nothing for you to concern yourself about at this moment. You are my wife, no matter who may object to it, and I desire you more than I have ever desired anything in my life before.' He bent over the bunk to kiss her mouth again, inhale her breath again. He straightened, as her body had seemed to grow rigid. 'But I must ask you to be my tutor in love, dear Felicity.' He removed his jacket.

Felicity sat up, still holding the sheet to her throat. 'No,' she said, almost angrily. 'That cannot be. It must be as *you* wish. Your every wish.'

Toby turned his back on her to finish undressing. 'My every wish shall be your every wish, my darling girl. I must confess that I lack the experience to know any better.' He faced her. 'I seek only to please you.'

She stared at him, her face stricken, and he knew she was not concerned at his size, although he doubted she had ever seen anything bigger. 'But . . . you mean you have never . . .?'

'No,' he said.

'Oh my God,' she whispered.

He returned to stand beside the bunk. 'Our roles are reversed,' he said, refusing to admit the despair which was

176

lapping at his heart and mind. 'I had thought perhaps that might please you.'

'Please me. Oh God,' she said again, and turned away from him violently, the sheet forgotten as she lay on her side and stared at the bulkhead.

Cautiously he sat down. Her buttocks were exposed. The first woman's buttocks he had ever seen, and surely the most perfectly shaped he would ever see. His hand hovered, and then touched the velvet flesh. She rolled back again, once more moving violently, so that he stood up in alarm. But some of the consternation had left her face. 'You do want me?' she asked.

'Want you? God, I have dreamed of no one else for four years.'

'Is that why you kept your virginity?' Her tone had softened.

'I guess so.'

She sat up, the sheet now entirely thrown back. Cautiously he lowered himself to sit facing her, take in the seriously lovely face, the swell of the breasts, the pointed nipples, pink against the white, the flat belly through which the shape of her ribs surged as she breathed, the widening of her hips, the . . . He caught his breath before he could stop himself, taken entirely by surprise.

'Does that disgust you?' she asked.

'I . . .' He licked his lips. He simply could not interpret his emotions. Nothing else had happened to indicate her past, save this.

'I had not expected us to be married so soon,' she explained. 'In a month's time it will have grown out, and no one will ever know it had happened at all.'

'Is that why you hesitated on deck?'

She sighed. 'You have been so gallant to me from start to finish, Toby McGann, I was almost glad that I would not be allowed to lie to you. And then I thought . . . I hoped, that you would know of the Moorish customs, as you have served against them for four years.' Her voice had become toneless as she watched his expression. 'It is the usual practice in harems,' she said. 'Moorish men prefer their women to be hairless.'

He gazed at her. She had deliberately precipitated this

177

confrontation. It could have been avoided, at least until morning, and thus until after their union had been consummated, had she asked him to turn down the lantern. But she had not wanted to lie. Her honesty was, no doubt, to be admired. But at this moment he hated it.

He sucked air into his lungs. There was so much to be admired, to be loved, about this superb woman. The length and shape of her legs, the curve of those buttocks he had just stroked, the touch to which she had responded, the velvet texture of her skin, those nipples he longed to touch ... but all were suddenly overlaid by the thought of her being shaved; she could not have carried it out so thoroughly by herself.

'It will grow again,' she promised, with a touch of desperation. 'It is already doing so. I only pray you will not find it abrasive.'

He had never supposed to hear a woman talk so candidly on so delicate a subject. Never hoped? Or feared? With equal desperation he sought to match her mood. 'Did your master never find it so?'

She stared at him, eyes enormous. 'No,' she said. 'My master used a different way of sex.' Her tongue stole out to lick her lips. 'Would you like me to show you?'

Again they stared at each other. Yes, he thought, show me, that I may match him. But no, do not show me, for fear the act disgusts me. He did not know what he truly felt, truly wanted. He only knew that he must either take her now, with desperate anxiety, with a mind shut to everything save his sexual urge, or leave this cabin and never return.

He threw himself upon her, and she spread her legs to receive him. He sought her mouth, and that, too, was opened for him. Their tongues touched, and she kissed him almost savagely, while moving her body beneath his, so that he entered before knowing it, vaguely wondering that it was so easy, that she was so damp and smooth. He was spent, too, before he was ready, while her arms held him tight, and her cheek moved against his. It was only when he raised his head, afterwards, that he realised the cheek was also wet, with tears.

178

'Captain McGann! Captain McGann, sir!' The hired hand hurried up the drive to the timber house. 'Mistress Elizabeth! Mistress Elizabeth! Master Toby is here.'

Toby supposed that if he lived to be a hundred, and became the senior captain in the United States Navy, Robert the farm hand would still call him Master Toby.

But he was never going to be the senior captain in the United States Navy. Not now.

Well, then, there were other things in life, to be sure. He could look around him at the trees and the meadows, listen to the birds, know there were fish in the stream and the Sound. And look down at his wife, seated beside him in the pony-trap.

'It is beautiful,' she said. 'Everything I had expected it to be. Will you be happy here, Toby?'

'I always was before.' He flicked the reins, and the trap moved through the gate.

She did not even sigh. Nor did she weep, when in bed with him, nowadays. They had been married for four months, and knew each other too well, as they did not know each other at all. Felicity knew only a man who gazed at her, and wanted her, and took her. That she knew he was also a man of gallantry and kindness, of determination, who had sacrificed his career for her, had no relevance to the purely physical relationship they enjoyed. If together they had smashed through the walls of propriety to marry at all, on their wedding night new walls had suddenly sprung up. He had become afraid of her past, simply because he had never taken the trouble properly to consider it, to understand the implications of it . . . and thus he wanted to shut it out. They could only talk of the future, and the future now lay here in this Long Island valley. Nowhere else.

And he knew only a beautiful woman. What she thought and felt and wanted, he did not know, dared not attempt to find out. He made love to her with a desperate intensity, which only seemed to grow. She could understand that he had kept himself away from women for too long, and that here was a whole seven years of manhood crying out to be released. She could also appreciate her own beauty; as it had so fascinated Mohammed ben Idris, should it not even more

179

fascinate Toby McGann, who had no harem of willing girls at his beck and call.

But she also suspected he was driven more than anything to want her because he had burned his bridges even more thoroughly than she. Yet the very power of his desire, as well as the unchanging orthodoxy of his lovemaking, made her wish to respond. And she dared not. She had chosen total honesty, total revelation, on her wedding night, but that was before she had realised he was a virgin. And then it had been too late to stop herself. Since then she had practised only acquiescence, in his words, his lovemaking, his decisions. She had admired Washington and Philadelphia and New York, and the country in between, because it was his country, and she had become angry at the reactions of his superior officers to his apparently flagrant disobedience of orders, because he had been angry. Where she had studied only to keep herself a separate entity from Mohammed ben Idris, now she studied only to merge her personality into that of her husband – because he was all she had in the world. She did not know if he was aware of that or not. He gave no indication either way.

Did she love him? She did not suppose so, truly and with all her heart. She knew nothing of love, and only the worst of men. She could recognise that he was a far superior man to any she had ever previously met, and valued his courage, his determination, as much as she relied on his strength, so strangely tempered by his manners and his gentleness. She had never a doubt that she was better off as the wife of Toby McGann than in any other circumstance that could possibly be available to her, after her experiences. And while she paid lip service to his bitterness at having been asked to resign his commission, she secretly was glad of it – she knew she could not have borne the long separations that would have been necessary as he took his various ships to sea.

But love? Love had to be an emotion experienced without the slightest reserve. She dared not lower her mental guard to that extent until she knew how much he still hated and loathed her past, how much he still resented, even if subconsciously, the fact that she had been the cause of his personal catastrophe. He never alluded to either – but he was a very human being. For love, she could only substitute pleasing him, and snatching at odd moments of happiness, and hope for better times.

But always she had known there was an ordeal awaiting her, which could end even her inadequate contentment at a stroke: her meeting with his family. And for all his apparent confidence and his constant reassurance that she would be welcomed, she knew that he was equally unsure of himself, remembering perhaps the reactions of her family.

And now the moment had arrived.

A dog barked, a huge Irish wolfhound which came bounding down the steps to start the hired horse rearing, made Felicity clutch the dashboard anxiously. But Toby controlled both animals simultaneously, the horse with a tightening of the rein, the hound with a single word: 'Boru!'

At the sound of his voice, the huge beast panted and wagged its tail.

'Toby!' There could be no doubting that the man at the top of the steps was the famous Harry McGann. Toby had told her of him, and here was not only the size he had transmitted to his son, the straight black hair and twinkling blue eyes, the huge mouth widening into a welcoming smile – but also the crippled leg which dragged at his side, the effects of a duel.

It was the smile she welcomed most, although at this moment it was directed at Toby rather than herself.

'Father!' Toby jumped down, tethered the horse, and then turned to lift his wife down; the dog licked her hand.

Harry McGann looked over his shoulder. 'Liz!' he bellowed. 'Liz! Toby's home.' He limped down the stairs. 'By God, boy, when last I heard, you were setting off to walk across the Libyan desert. We had given you up for lost.' He squeezed his son's hands, at the same time cautiously glancing at Felicity.

'No risk of that, Father.' Toby placed Felicity's hand in that of the older man. 'This is Felicity.'

'Felicity?' Now Harry was frowning.

'Felicity McGann. My wife.'

'Wife?' Harry's brows grew even closer together, and her knees became weak, as Toby suddenly released her hand

181

and went running up the stairs to greet the tall, blonde woman who had come out of the house. 'Ma! Oh, Ma!'

'Toby!' They embraced, a long, loving hug, accompanied by a succession of kisses, leaving Harry and Felicity to gaze at each other.

'I am sorry to be sprung on you like this, Captain McGann,' she said. 'But we knew we would travel faster than any letter.'

'You're English,' he accused.

'Why, so she is,' Elizabeth McGann agreed, coming down the steps. 'And that is at least admirable. But your wife, Toby? Is this not rather sudden?'

'We have known each other for five years,' Toby explained.

Elizabeth raised her eyebrows. 'And never a word to your parents? There is a mystery here. But you are welcome, my dear girl, so welcome.' She held Felicity close, looked into her eyes. 'If you make our Toby happy, oh, you are welcome here.'

'Mystery?' Harry McGann boomed. 'What mystery?'

Felicity looked at Toby, who sighed, and nodded. 'One which is best recounted as soon as possible, Father. Shall we not sit down and have a jug of whisky, and talk?'

As Toby told their tale, the sun sank into the trees west of the farmhouse. Occasional mosquitoes whirred out of the gloom to be slapped, and whipperwills cried in the trees, while the evening breeze brought the hemlock pods clustering on to the steps. Soon it would be autumn, with all the menace of winter to follow, but on these late summer evenings Long Island was at its most beautiful. He had to remind himself of this, to reassure himself that it was possible to be happier here than anywhere else in the world, with Boru lying at his feet, his parents to either side, the jug of whisky being passed round and round – and his wife close by. No man could ask for anything more.

That, too, had to be constantly remembered. Just beyond the trees was the Sound. He would walk down there tomorrow to look at the water where he had learnt to sail. He would enjoy taking Felicity fishing on the Sound, he thought. He would enjoy doing so many things with Felicity, could he possibly feel that she did anything more than accept him, because there was nobody else. Sometimes her quiet acquiescence in all his moods, her ready acceptance of all his likes and dislikes, all his desires, near drove him to despair. But no, he thought, she did not acquiesce in all his desires, because she did not know all of his desires. It was he who kept those locked away, for fear of reawakening those memories which must be so dreadful to her, even if his instincts warned him that they could never truly be married until those memories had been exhumed, and washed clean in the purity of their love, and then reburied, forever.

But that supposed they loved. That she loved. He did not doubt his own. Every time he looked at her he thought he fell more in love with her. But it also supposed that he could unlock her mind, that her hateful brother was not quite right, and some part of her senses been damaged beyond repair by Moorish mistreatment. But that was another reason for holding back; he did not really wish to find out.

And that was certainly for the future, at this moment. There were more important matters to be dealt with.

'You poor girl,' Elizabeth cried when he finally ceased. And flushed. 'There's an inadequate statement. To have survived so much ... you must possess a rare amount of courage and determination.'

'I waited,' Felicity said simply. 'I knew someone would come for me one day. I even supposed it would be Toby, in my dreams.'

Toby sighed with relief. But less at her words, than at his mother's acceptance of her. He had not shirked this confrontation, any more than he had shirked the confrontation with the Navy Board: he had never doubted for a moment that his every action had been dictated by all the ideals both his mother and his father had instilled in him long before he had taken the oath of allegiance. Equally, he had always looked to his mother for his surest support ... but presumably a white girl taken and held by the Moors was not very different from a white girl taken and held by the Red Indians – and there were few American families prepared to welcome one of *them* back.

'But to be forced to resign the Navy?' Harry McGann growled. 'A McGann? That is preposterous, Toby. And after such a feat of arms as taking Tripoli virtually singlehanded.'

'Now, I never claimed that, Father,' Toby protested. 'There were several hundred good fellows at my back, and Bill Eaton was the finest of them all.'

'Nonetheless,' Harry declared, 'I'll not stand for it. I'll travel to Washington myself, by God. I'll knock some sense into those blockheads.'

'No, Father, please,' Toby insisted. How to tell the old man that no one in Washington even remembered what he looked like? He was only a name in a history book, like his even more famous friend John Paul Jones, with whom he had played so glorious a part in securing the independence of this country. 'What is done, is done. I'll not go crawling back.' He forced a smile. 'And what purpose would there be in pursuing a naval career? Congress has given best to the Barbary pirates, settled its differences with France . . . there is no one left to fight.'

'You have Truxton's intransigence,' Harry commented. 'And as you have no ships to sail, what do you propose to do with yourself?'

'Why, can you not use another pair of strong arms about the farm?'

'You'll stay here? Oh, Toby!' Elizabeth cried, clapping her hands and then leaving her chair to embrace her son. 'Oh, Toby, that would make me so happy.' She looked above his head at Felicity. 'Promise me that he means what he says, Felicity, and I will love you like the daughter I never had.'

That's a squall,' Toby commented, pointing up Long Island Sound to the north-east, where lowering black clouds were starting to fill the afternoon sky. 'Maybe more than that. There were those mare's tails last night. We'd best put back. Take the tiller now, and keep her steady.'

Felicity, seated beside him on the transom of the twenty-foot long open boat, tucked her skirts beneath her – they were inclined to fly in the breeze – and obediently grasped the heavy wooden spar, while he made his way forward to trim the sheets of the gaff mainsail; the boat was cat-rigged, that is, she had only the single large sail, with her mast mounted in the very bow.

'Starboard your helm,' he called over his shoulder, and

she pulled the rudder up against her stomach, causing the boat to turn to the right, towards the shore, perhaps a mile away, as Toby hardened the sheets.

'Shall I take in the line?' she called.

He shook his head as he belayed the sheet. 'Let it trail awhile; there's no fish in this sea anyway, I'll be bound. We have entirely been wasting our time.'

Yet he was happy, even with an open boat to command, and her as his only deckhand. She loved to watch him handling the sails, caring for the brightwork, scouring the tiny foredeck just forward of the mast. This truly was his metier, the sea and a ship. Just as every time she watched him being happy, she felt the misery churning inside herself. He should be at sea all the time, wearing that uniform of which he was so proud, and which now hung and gathered mould in his closet.

She could still remember the expression on his face, two years ago, and indeed in the very autumn after their return to the farm, when news had been received of a great sea battle off that very Cape Trafalgar abeam of which they had been married, between the British fleet, commanded by Admiral Nelson, home from his chase to the West Indies, and Collingwood, and the combined fleets of France and Spain. The British had won a shattering victory, and Nelson had set the seal on his remarkable career by dying in the moment of victory.

Toby had turned his back on any such achievement for her, even if she dreaded every post, which might bring news of a war in which the United States Navy would be engaged, and which would further tug at his heart strings.

What had she given him in return for such a sacrifice?

Because he had given her so much more than a sacrifice. She had not supposed it could be possible for her ever to be happy again; Fate seemed to have set its face firmly against such a dream. Yet how could she not be happy in such surroundings, and with such people? Harry McGann, gruffly confident, gruffly contemptuous of modernity and the soft-spirited children he claimed it had produced, whose eyes twinkled whenever he looked at her. Elizabeth, so warm and gentle, and yet so strong, physically as well as mentally.

185

Aunt Jennie, Harry's sister, and Uncle John Palmer, her husband, Sally Canning, their daughter, and her husband Jason. Boru, the dog . . . She understood that there had been several Borus, stretching back to Harry McGann's childhood. Here was a happy, independent, self-sufficient clan, who existed for each other, and for whom even a journey to New York was a venture into a foreign country, who viewed the slowly spreading town, which now encompassed both sides of the East River, with suspicion.

And into whose hearts she had been taken, with never a word about her unhappy past. Of them all, she loved Elizabeth McGann most. Because they shared an unspoken bond: Lizzie had also abandoned family and friends and background to be a McGann, and if her experiences before finding this haven had not been quite so unspeakable, yet had she once been married to a harsh and violent man, perhaps even worse than Mohammed ben Idris.

Elizabeth had sought a shared intimacy with her daughter-in-law, a long-awaited luxury, Felicity knew. Elizabeth's was an entirely masculine world; she had little in common with Jennie Palmer. However, they presented a united front to the world and rallied to each other's side at the slightest call for assistance, and she had no daughters of her own. But now she not only possessed a daughter, but an English daughter with a social background very like her own. Felicity knew she had it in her power to make Elizabeth McGann the happiest woman in the world. But it was not a power she could exercise. Because she had first to make Toby the happiest man in the world, and that accomplishment was totally beyond her.

That first night had been a disaster. She knew it was a miracle she had not again found herself cast out into an empty world. And it had set the pattern for all the nights since. She had allowed him no more than a glimpse into the life she had lived for four years, and he had been at once fascinated and repelled. He could not resist her body . . . but was that love, or a distorted imagination seeing her at the mercy of the Moors? It had to be a distorted vision, because he knew nothing of the truth. He had not sought, and she could not tell him until he did seek. She did not know she could, even then.

The tragedy was that he was afraid to probe even into her mind, her present personality. In the beginning, she had been grateful for that. Now she was desperate to share some part of herself with him. Instead, she took from him all the time, by endeavouring to fit herself into his life. She would have chopped wood beside him, or managed the plough, had he been prepared to allow her. But as her labours were confined to the house, which Elizabeth thought sufficient for a woman, she could only share his leisure moments as best she could, always aware that she was a total novice at the things like fishing or shooting or handling a boat which he did instinctively.

All could be put right were she to have a child. This she knew. She was not sure if Toby gave a great deal of thought to the subject, but Elizabeth certainly did. But as she had not conceived for Mohammed ben Idris, so it seemed, even after two years, that she could not conceive for Toby McGann. She was an utterly useless hulk of femininity, she supposed. Sad to think that Jonathan had been right all along, and she was good for absolutely nothing, tarnished in both mind and body. She wondered where Jonathan was now. Or her mother and father. She had heard nothing from them throughout the two years since leaving Gibraltar, either. To them, she was as dead as if she had remained in Tripoli.

Toby came aft to sit beside her and take the tiller. She looked at the approaching storm. 'Will we make it?'

'Oh, aye,' he said. 'We'll be at the beach in ten minutes, and that wind is at least half an hour away. What's that?'

The line had suddenly tightened.

'It's a bite!' she screamed in excitement.

Toby seized the line and gave it a quick jerk, felt the powerful strength at the end of it tugging away from him. 'A big one.'

'What can it be?' She turned to kneel on the transom.

'Could be anything. We sometimes get sharks down here. But it's more likely to be a bluefin tuna. Now there is a fish. Got you ...' He managed to haul in two or three yards of line, and took a turn round a cleat. Immediately the line hardened again as the fish fought to get free, and now the force dragging on the stern was causing the boat to yaw

187

about from side to side, and the sails to flap as the wind was spilled from them.

'Maybe we should let it go,' Felicity suggested, looking at the black clouds, which were steadily approaching down the Sound; now she could make out the flurry of whitecaps driven up by the wind.

'Not this one,' Toby muttered, managing to haul in some more line and secure that as well; the fish, whatever it was, was only fifty feet astern now, and suddenly Felicity saw the fin, sharply triangular.

'It's a shark!' she cried.

'Aye. There's a gaff forward. Fetch it aft.'

She started to obey without hesitation, then checked. The squall was very close. So was the land, not more than a hundred yards, but the boat was not moving at all. 'Let him go, Toby. What'll you do with a shark?'

'I reckon it's a mako,' he explained. 'That's good eating. And he's a big one, six feet, maybe. There's a lot of food. Anyway . . .' He gave one of his tremendous grins. 'I mean to mount his head over the mantelpiece. His jaws, anyway. Fetch the gaff.'

He took in some more line, while the water astern of the boat boiled as the angry fish sought to free itself. Felicity crawled forward, reached beneath the short foredeck to find the iron gaff, and heard the whistle of the wind rising above even the tremendous splashing from astern. She turned to look aft, saw Toby with both hands on the fishing line, the tiller wedged against his stomach, while the sails filled and the little boat heeled to the gust.

'Toby!' she screamed. She knew nothing about boats, but she knew something was wrong.

Toby turned his head as the boat continued to list. He released the fishing line and grabbed the tiller, pulling it against him to turn the bow up into the wind and spill the force from the sails, at the same moment as he released the sheets. But fast as he moved, he was too late. The little boat had heeled far enough for the leeward gunwale to dip into the water, which now came pouring over the side.

'Oh, my God!' Felicity screamed, as she felt herself being thrown across the thwart and thence farther, water already surging round her waist. 'Oh, my *God*!' Desperately she clutched at the sheets, but the rope slipped from her grasp.

The wind was increasing in force all the time, and although Toby had now freed the sheets, the boat was already on her beam ends, and going over. Felicity struck the surface with her hands, flailing the water with impotent urgency. She had never told Toby she couldn't swim; it had not seemed important. 'Help!' she screamed. 'Toby!'

She felt his fingers grasp her shoulder. 'Easy, now,' he said. 'Easy.'

She spat water from her mouth and panted, her reassurance at his touch being tempered by her fear. 'The shark . . . ?'

'Has problems of his own.'

He was on his back, propelling himself with his feet while he held her shoulders with his hands, keeping her above the surface as he made for the shore, which had disappeared beneath the blanket of teeming rain which had followed the wind, and through which the thunder sounded like hammer blows and the lightning cut like a series of knife thrusts.

Felicity turned her head from left to right, saw the mast of the boat disappearing beneath the wavelets whipped up by the squall, saw the fin of the shark behind it, the big fish was still hooked and was unable to free itself from the sinking vessel. Then Toby laughed as his feet struck the bottom, and he scooped her into his arms and waded through the water, rain drops bouncing off his head and slashing into her face, the lightning carving vivid patterns across the afternoon around them.

'The boat!' she gasped.

'Is gone. Sunk by a shark, by God!' He gave a bellow of laughter. 'And my own carelessness, to be sure.' He splashed on to the beach as a streak of lightning sizzled into the trees before them and they heard the splintering of wood.

'We'd best not shelter beneath those,' he said. 'That's the way to get struck.' He set her on the sand, and when her knees gave way, caught her round the waist.

'But if we stay out here . . .'

'We'll get wet,' he shouted, giving another roar of laugh-

189

ter, as the water ran out from her hair, dripped from her sodden gown, rolled down her legs. 'Take it off.'

She stared at him.

'What's the use of it? It's soaked through.' He tore off his own shirt, dropped his breeches.

Her heart began to pound. There was something about the storm which had touched off a mood in him . . . a mood she was desperate to share. She gathered the gown and raised it over her head, threw it on the beach, threw her equally wet shift behind it.

'You are a Valkyrie,' he shouted, and took her in his arms. 'No, you are my prisoner. I am a Moorish dey. Please me. Please me!'

He held her close, their bodies slithering against each other, while she caught her breath and her brain tumbled. Because this mood of madness would pass, and then . . . but if she dared not, then the moment might never come again. She inhaled, allowed her body to slide down his, so that every part of her touched every part of him in turn, dropped to her knees, still pressed against him, and took him into her mouth. His body stiffened, and she almost let him go, then she felt his hands on her head, gently caressing her as he held her close. But she allowed him only a moment, before she moved back, and rose to her feet.

'Felicity,' he gasped, his voice thick as he reached for her.

'Everything,' she said. 'Everything, my lord. Do you not wish to possess me?'

He gazed at her in bewilderment as she fell to her knees again, her back to him.

He could not doubt her intention, and it was something he had always dreamed of anyway, but to see her there . . .

'I will break your back,' he whispered, coming down on her with great caution.

'I will bear you, my lord,' she promised.

'I . . .' He bit his lip as he caressed her, for the moment out of control.

She laughed, her confidence growing every second, as she reached behind herself to guide him. 'The other, too, on occasion. But not between you and me, Toby McGann. We have no need of that.'

She felt him in her, huge and growing, filling her more completely than she had ever been filled before. Then his weight did prove too much for her, and she fell to her face on the sand, but he remained in her, as she had hoped and intended, surging to and fro. And bringing her to orgasm as well. She had not expected that, had not intended it, wanted to do nothing more than please him. And suddenly she was gasping and moaning, and when he rolled away from her, was throwing her body across his, using mouth and fingers to bring him back to hardness again.

'Felicity,' he gasped. 'My God, Felicity . . .'

'Everything,' she said, and sat astride him to take him into her again, surging her hips and buttocks to and fro. 'Everything!' she shouted. Because here at last was happiness.

'There is news from the east, great one.' The messenger bent low; he was only one of several men waiting to speak with the Vizier.

'Then speak,' Mohammed ben Idris commanded.

'Hemet Karamanli returns, at the head of a vast army, great one. I have learned that he has been to Constantinople, to the Porte itself, and solicited the aid of the Sultan. This aid the Sultan has granted him, in return for an oath that Tripoli will once again be numbered amongst the provinces of the Ottoman Empire.'

'How vast is vast?' Idris demanded.

'He commands not less than ten thousand men, my lord. Horse and foot. And the Sultan has also supplied a fleet of galleys, able to cross the sandbanks and assault Tripoli from the sea.'

Idris stroked his beard. If his fortunes had seemed to reach a pinnacle in possessing the English girl and defying the American squadron so successfully for several years, since she had been stolen away from him they had steadily declined. Now . . . ten thousand men, with the backing of the Sultan himself and the support of a fleet of galleys . . . He had no means of opposing such an army. And defeat would mean execution.

No trace of his thoughts appeared on his face as he gazed

191

at the anxious man. 'To whom have you confided this information?' he asked softly.

'To no one, my lord,' the man protested. 'I came directly to you.'

'That was sensible of you,' Idris agreed, and looked past him at the other men, waiting against the wall. They were not close enough to have heard. 'Then do you remain here until I send for you,' he told the messenger. 'I will go immediately to the Dey. But remember, not a word to a soul, until we have made our dispositions.'

'It shall be as you wish, great lord,' the man promised, delighted to be in the confidence of so mighty a man.

Idris stood up, and all the waiting men dropped hastily to their knees. 'The audience is ended,' Idris told them. 'There are affairs of state.' He left the room, snapping his fingers to summon his personal chamberlain to follow; the chamberlain had stood at his shoulder throughout the interview, and had heard what the man had said.

The curtains fell into place behind him as he entered his private apartment, overlooking the roof and the harbour. 'We must prepare to leave Tripoli, Ibrahim,' he said. 'Tonight. And secretly. Prepare a small caravan. Six camels. Choose two of my favourite girls to accompany us. But do not tell them that they are leaving, merely that I will see them both tonight.'

'But . . .' Ibrahim was nonplussed. 'The Dey . . .'

'Will have to look out for himself. He may be able to reach some agreement with his cousin. I cannot. Hemet knows me to have been responsible for his overthrow, and he will have my head.'

'The Dey may prefer to accompany you, my lord,' Ibrahim suggested, 'when he hears the news.'

'He is not going to hear the news, Ibrahim. At least, not until after our departure. That would be to cause a panic and he might seek to restrain me here. I repeat, you and I will leave here tonight, with two girls, and two pack camels to carry my fortune. No one must know of this.'

'The messenger . . .'

'Summon him from the audience chamber. Tell him the Dey wishes to question him personally. And when you have him alone, despatch him. Is that understood?'

Ibrahim bowed. Idris was his master, and he acknowledged none other. 'May I ask where we are going, my lord?'

Idris shrugged. 'Who knows. Algiers, perhaps. I have friends in Algiers.'

Ibrahim hesitated. 'Will it be possible for my women and my sons to join us there?'

'Of course. We will send for them once we are established.'

Ibrahim bowed again. Supposing the Dey did not execute them in anger when he discovered the flight of his Vizier. But his decision was already taken: he could find other women, create other sons – he would never find another master like Mohammed ben Idris. 'Will you see none of the other messengers?'

'They no longer concern me.'

'One is from America, my lord. At least, he has news from that country.'

Idris frowned. 'Then send him to me. I will see no one else.'

Ibrahim bowed a third time, and withdrew. Idris grasped his beard again, and went to the windows, gazing out at the battlements until he heard the man come in. Then he turned. 'Speak. You have news of the woman?'

'I have news from the American agent you told me to contact, great lord. The woman is married, in the infidel style, to a man called Tobias McGann. It is said he is a giant of a man, who can pluck eagles from the sky, and lift horses from the ground. She now lives with this McGann, on an island off the city of New York. The island is called Long, great lord.'

'Tobias McGann,' Idris muttered. Toby McGann, he thought. The man at the sight of whom she had fainted. The giant who had marched with Eaton across the desert. And who had burst into the harem, after capturing the East Gate.

'Are there further instructions, my lord?'

Idris went back to the window, looked out across the roof at the sea. She had stood at those battlements and watched him, and fainted with joy. And now she was his wife. But now, too, *he* knew where she was – at the very moment he could do nothing about him. Fate was continuing to play

193

tricks with him, as she had done ever since Abd er Rahman has first shown him that pulsing white flesh.

'No,' he said. 'There are no further instructions.'

The man bowed and left the room.

At the moment, Idris thought, still staring at the blue waters. But when I am established in Algiers, then I will think of you, Felicity Crown. And of you, Tobias McGann. I will have you back, Felicity Crown, if only to watch that body twist in agony, hear that voice scream for mercy, as I torture you to death. Oh, I will have you back, if it takes the rest of my life.

Chapter 9

Long Island and the Atlantic – 1808–12

'It is a sad business. Truly sad.' Stephen Decatur leaned back in his chair on the McGanns' front porch, and took a sip of whisky. 'Although when was anything connected with James Barron not a sad business?'

'We have heard nothing but rumours,' Toby said, 'which are scarcely credible. You'll have to explain exactly what happened.'

'Well . . .' Decatur sat up, his lean face intense. 'I agree it is scarcely credible, from beginning to end. It was scarcely credible that he should have been reappointed to command the Mediterranean squadron, after the puerile efforts we remember so well from his first tour of duty there. He had been agitating for it for a long time of course, maybe to wipe the slate clean, and I guess he has friends in high places. Anyway, he behaved from the start in his usual confused fashion, reported his ship, the *Chesapeake*, as ready to put to sea twenty-one days before he finally sailed, and had scarce got off Cape Henry when he was approached and signalled by the British frigate *Leopard*, which had clearly been waiting for him. *Leopard* claimed that *Chesapeake* had three British deserters on board, and demanded their return.'

'That was an act of war,' Harry McGann growled. He had never either forgotten or forgiven his own impressment off an American ship into the British Navy, as a young man – and when that had happened, America had still been a colony.

195

'Aye, well, it is being debated as such in Washington, to be sure,' Decatur agreed. 'Debated, by God! After what happened.'

'You'll not say Barron allowed them to take the three men?' Toby was aghast.

'Worse than that, Toby. Worse than that. He began by refusing the British demand, with the result that the *Leopard* opened fire. Again, one suspects the Britisher had been out for blood from the start. Well, the *Chesapeake* was in no fit condition to fight. Ready for sea? Her decks were so crowded with unstowed stores she could hardly load a gun. So what does Barron do? He hauls down the colours.'

'My God!' Toby cried. 'He surrendered?'

Decatur gave a harsh laugh. 'But that was not the end of the affair. The *Leopard* refused to accept any form of surrender, continued firing, and then boarded the *Chesapeake*, and at gun point took several men out of her. She then sailed away, and Barron slunk back into Norfolk to complain, when it was discovered that his ship had suffered only the slightest of damage.'

'But . . . we are not at war?' Toby asked in bewilderment. 'After, as you say, such an action?'

'No, we are not at war,' Decatur said savagely. 'Congress is demanding apologies and reparations. From Great Britain, by God. They could as well demand an apology from the moon.'

'And Barron?'

'Oh, he was court-martialled. The initial charge was one of cowardice. But pressure was brought to bear to have it reduced to one of neglecting to clear his ship for action.'

'He should have been shot,' Harry remarked.

'I agree with you, sir. Instead, he has been suspended for five years, and has taken himself off to France, vowing he will sail under the tricolour. And vowing vengeance, against me, in fact.'

'Against you?' Toby asked. 'How were you involved?'

'Everyone who had ever sailed with Barron was involved. Rodgers, Hull and I were called to give evidence regarding his conduct in the Mediterranean. Had poor Ned Preble

196

been there, we'd have had Barron cashiered. But Preble . . . you heard about him?'

'Yes,' Toby said sadly. 'Forty-six is an early age to die.' Perhaps of sheer disappointment, he thought. Preble had been the finest officer in the United States Navy, but his superiors had been unable to discern his talent.

'Aye,' Decatur agreed. 'Awful early. Well, the other two temporised. I spoke my mind, as I thought Ned would have wanted. As you would have done, Toby.'

'Oh, yes,' Toby said. 'What would I have given to be there. And Barron took offence?'

Decatur smiled. 'He called me a liar.'

'What did you do?'

'He used the words in court, and was reprimanded by the judges. But as he had been privileged, so to speak, I was advised to let the matter drop, and did so. I have not seen him since the sentence.'

'I doubt you will ever see him again, if he has indeed gone to France,' Toby said. 'He will no doubt find the British blowing him apart again.'

'And what of the British?' Harry McGann asked.

'They will continue to treat us with contempt, sir, until we are prepared to face them on the high seas. As will the Algerians. You'll scarce credit this either, Toby, but your old friend Mohammed ben Idris fled from Tripoli when it was finally retaken by Hemet Karamanli, and is now in Algiers commanding a fleet of pirates, and proving himself as big a nuisance as ever. But I suppose that scarce concerns you now.'

'Mohammed ben Idris,' Toby mused. 'What a great deal of trouble I would have prevented by chasing him and cutting him down there in his harem. I regret that, truly I do.' More than you will ever know, Stephen, he thought. Oh, how I regret that.

'He can never trouble you again,' Decatur pointed out. 'And now you have all of this . . .' He looked around him. 'All that a man could ask. And . . .' His gaze came back to Toby.

'Oh, indeed,' Toby acknowledged. 'All that a man could ask.' He got up, went to the door, and opened it. Both

Felicity and Elizabeth preferred to remain inside when Navy men came to call – at least until the business of exchanging news and opinions was completed. 'Will you not come outside and meet Mr Decatur, Felicity? I am sure you remember him. He's a captain now.'

'Captain Decatur.' Felicity advanced from the hall, her hand outstretched. 'I could hardly forget you.'

Decatur gazed at her, taking in the swollen belly, then looked at Toby. 'My most hearty congratulations to you both.'

'We mean to call him Stephen,' Toby said.

'And I am most honoured by the thought.'

'You will be staying some days, I hope, Captain Decatur?' Felicity asked, sitting beside him.

'Alas, Mrs McGann, I must return south tomorrow. I have a ship to take to sea.' He looked past her at Toby. 'And how I wish you were sailing with me, Toby, as my executive officer.'

'How I wish I was too, Stephen,' Toby agreed. 'How I wish I was.' He glanced at Felicity, saw the cloud which had crossed her face. 'But I doubt I would be able to tear myself away.'

So, Felicity thought, happiness was not to be had simply by wishing it, and providing it. As she watched Toby looking at Decatur's uniform, on the morning of his friend's departure, her heart constricted as it had not done for three years. It was as if her husband had a scar across his personality which refused to heal, and could awaken the wound within to pain at the slightest touch.

Yet even deep wounds must heal, she told herself. Since that day on the beach, when the rolling storm had encouraged them to consummate their love, she had known nothing but happiness. Out of it, if not on that very day, had come the growing life in her womb. But out of it had come so much more than that. A growing intimacy with her husband, and because of that, with her parents-in-law. The McGann farm was a happy place. It had always been so. Now, she felt and hoped and prayed, their acceptance of her had made it happier than ever before.

As for Edward Preble, and Stephen Decatur, and Isaac Hull, and John Rodgers, and even James Barron, it was good for Toby to have known and fought beside such men: they had shared in moulding his character. But it was even better that he had turned his back on the sea, except as a hobby, and assumed the responsibilities of a landowner ... and a father. For Stephen McGann was born on 6 April 1808, only a few weeks after Decatur's visit, to the universal joy of the family. It was an event Felicity had refused to fear. However far removed she might be from doctors and midwives, she was secure in the reassuring experience of Elizabeth and Jennie, who performed all the necessary functions with total confidence.

The labour was longer than she had expected and more painful, and left her exhausted ... but the discomfort was more than compensated at once by the wail of the babe and the enormous comfort of having him placed in her arms, and then by watching the utter delight of her husband. Toby was transported, and Stephen was hardly two months old when he was being given a fishing line to handle, as well as a pistol, and being taken out on the Sound to get the feel of the fresh air on his face, a layer of salt on his skin. Felicity did not protest. That Stephen was what Toby so clearly wanted was enough for her – if it would replace the memory of the Navy.

She fed the babe for a year, and loved doing so, but she loved even more the ability to resume sexual relations with Toby, again to experience the joys they had so tardily discovered together, he for the first time, and she with even more wonderment because where in Tripoli she had supposed such desire was an outcome of perversion and sexual domination, she now realised how marvellous it could be when it was the result of love and mutual lust and shared intentions. She bloomed, and became pregnant again. Jane was born in January 1810, and Hannah at Christmas of 1811.

'You are blessed by the goddess of fertility,' Elizabeth said proudly. 'I never was.'

'But you were, Mother,' Felicity insisted. 'Save that the goddess of fertility crammed all of her gifts into the single body of Toby.'

'To make two women very happy,' Elizabeth agreed.

And not only two women, Felicity thought. It was in Toby's nature to lead, and he possessed an utterly tireless character. Harry McGann had necessarily been limited by his shattered leg, and as it had also been in his nature to lead, rather than drive, he had kept his acreage to an extent he could personally oversee. Toby intended nothing less, but with his powerful muscles to rely on he soon increased the farm by a third, himself walking behind the plough, while he employed two additional hands, a man and wife, to help with the milking and the reaping, as well as a nurse for the children, to allow Felicity more time to go sailing with him whenever the mood took him, which was often enough.

On most occasions Stephen would accompany them, as Toby was determined to make the boy as at home on water as on dry land as soon as possible, but Felicity liked it best when they were alone, and on calm days would drop the sail and let the new catboat drift, while they stripped off their clothes and sat or lay in the bottom of the boat, and just played with each other. She supposed they were utterly shameless, her Moorish experiences having demolished the strictures of her upbringing, and his rumbustious Irish lust for life performing a similar cauterisation on any New England puritanism he might have acquired in the Navy.

Of course he was as happy as she, she told herself, and allowed herself no doubts even when friends like Decatur or Hull came to call, as they did at least once in a year, carrying news of the Navy, of the new ships being built, of voyages around the world, of storms and ships and men and fish, and ports . . . all of which brought a gleam to Toby's eye, and left him thoughtful for days afterwards.

From these he invariably recovered. But his visitors also brought news of a more serious nature. For as Decatur had prophesied, the failure of Congress to force the British to compensate for their quite unwarrantable act of aggression in firing on an American warship in time of peace had encouraged the Royal Navy to treat the minuscule American Navy with contempt. While the American merchant fleet was entirely at the mercy of the whims of the British sea captains, who since the victory of Trafalgar ruled the oceans with a total dominance.

'I do not see how much longer it can last,' Isaac Hull remarked on a visit in 1810. 'The depredations against our people are far worse than any committed by the Barbary pirates.'

'Oh, come now, Isaac,' Felicity protested, anxious to defend her countrymen, however much she might have turned her back on them. 'There is no looting, or . . .' she met his gaze, 'raping.'

'Granted,' Hull agreed. 'The British are the most perfect gentlemen to anyone wearing a skirt, and they have the highest regard for another man's property, at least where they do not suspect it may be intended for use by an enemy. But the man himself . . . why, there is talk of ships losing two-thirds of their men because a frigate captain was short-handed.'

'Congress must act,' Harry McGann declared.

'And decree what?' his wife demanded.

'That our ships should open fire on the rascals,' Harry growled. 'I am sure not all of our captains are as pusillanimous as James Barron.' He looked at Hull.

He flushed. 'I assure you we are not, sir.'

'Yet would you be blown out of the water by the Royal Navy,' Elizabeth pointed out.

'That would be better than being made the laughing stock of the world,' Harry insisted.

'I doubt all of our ships would be blown out of the water, Mrs McGann,' Hull said. 'The French found that not to be so easy in 1799, eh Toby?'

'The French,' Elizabeth said scornfully.

'Those were great days,' Toby said, gazing at the trees. 'But Mother is right, you know, Isaac. The British . . . they have seafaring and sea-fighting in their blood.'

'Fiddlesticks,' Harry said. 'Is it not in our blood as well? I had to remind Washington himself of that, once, and it reassured him most powerfully. I tell you, sir, American seamen are every bit as good as their British counterparts, could they be as well equipped and led. They have lacked only the opportunity to prove it.'

Toby and Hull remained on the porch after the rest of the

201

family had gone to bed. 'Will it truly come to war, do you suppose, Isaac?' Toby asked.

'There is a powerful lobby in favour of it in Washington,' Hull told him. 'They call themselves the War Hawks, as opposed to the Peace Doves, and they talk of invading and capturing Canada while Britain is engaged in this endless war with France. They say President Madison himself is inclined their way. Now, to my mind that is a distasteful business, like seeking to stab a man in the back while he is fighting front to front with a superior foe. On the other hand, the Limeys do seem to wish to provoke us, Toby. Do you know that some six thousand American seamen have been impressed from our ships during the past ten years? That is coming close to two in every day. And even where impressment is not involved, the Royal Navy arrogates itself the right to stop and search any of our ships and, where there is the least doubt as to the composition or destination of the cargo, to escort the vessel to a British port, where some of them lie idle for months, awaiting clearance. Of course the British claim that they are engaged in a life and death struggle with Napoleon. But does that give them the right to disrupt the trade of the rest of the world? Mark my words, it will come to blows, sooner or later.'

'And then?' Toby asked.

Hull grinned. 'I am not so foolish as to suppose we can place our fourteen frigates in a line of battle against the Royal Navy: at the last reckoning they disposed of more than a thousand warships. But I also reckon your father is right, and ship to ship and man for man we are as good as any Britisher . . . save where we are commanded by men like James Barron.'

'If it came to blows,' Toby said slowly, 'I am only just thirty years of age. And I spend as much time afloat as anyone.'

'And I would be more than happy to have you on my ship, Toby.' His smile faded. 'But I have not the power to restore your commission.'

Toby nodded. 'I understand that. Just promise me a berth.'

Hull frowned at him, then waved his hand to encompass the farm. 'You'd abandon all of this, this prosperity and

202

comfort, that magnificent woman who is your wife, three splendid children, to sail before the mast?'

'If I can do no better,' Toby said. 'I once swore an oath of allegiance to the United States and to the Navy, Isaac, and I do not consider myself relieved of that oath because the Navy Board felt I had exceeded my jurisdiction. But promise me this conversation will go no further ...' he glanced at the door into the house, 'and that you will have a berth for me.'

Hull nodded. 'I am to take command of *Constitution* when she returns from her present duty.'

'*Constitution*! By God, that has to be the finest ship afloat.'

'I think she is. And I am to make her finer yet. She is to undergo a complete refit in Baltimore, and will probably be there until next summer. If war breaks out, Toby, and you have not changed your mind, come to Baltimore, and you'll have your berth. There's my word.'

If war breaks out, Toby thought. It was not something he dared discuss with Felicity: he could not imagine her reactions. And not only to his returning to the Navy. He would be fighting against her own countrymen. He could even find himself fighting against her own brother. And as a common seaman. Harry McGann had begun life as a common seaman, but he had very rapidly advanced, and had never looked back. By thirty he had already achieved his reputation and his immortality. His son could only be regarded as a total failure.

As a career officer in the Navy. Not, he was still sure, as a man. Indeed, as Hull had suggested would be the case, the hardest thought of all to contemplate was that of leaving the farm, and Felicity, and the children, however compelling the reason. They were the solid rocks on which he had built his life ... and Felicity was much more than that. From being a burden, however desirable and beautiful a burden, she had become his friend and constant companion and support, while remaining more beautiful and desirable than ever. While their mutual passion for each other continued to grow. They pursued each other's bodies with an unrelenting hunger, and if there was any truth in the old saying that a woman should be a hostess in the drawing room, a cook in the kitchen, a mother in the nursery, and a whore in bed, then Felicity was perfection itself.

How could he ever turn his back upon such bliss?

Yet he knew he could not remain snugly buried in Long Island while his old comrades were fighting for their lives. He took to devouring every item of news which came up from New York, and to making more visits than usual to the metropolis. He was there at the end of May, 1811, when news arrived of the action between the USS *President*, captained by John Rodgers himself, and the British sloop HMS *Little Belt*. The British ship had apparently taken some seamen from an American vessel, when the *President* came on the scene, gave chase, and opened fire with devastating results, killing more than thirty men and reducing the sloop to a wreck. New York was in a state of wild excitement, feelings extending from acclamation of the incident as a just retaliation for the *Leopard–Chesapeake* affair of four years earlier, and fears that the British would promptly mete out the most terrible reprisals.

In the event, the British, still locked in their life and death struggle with the Napoleonic Empire, and concentrating all their efforts on maintaining an army in Spain and Portugal, did no more than protest. But Congress, elated by such an example of American prowess, daily became more bellicose. Toby was walking behind his plough on a June day the following year when Felicity came running across the newly cleared field, having left the trap on the path. Little Stephen ran behind her as best he was able, and it was Stephen Toby heard first.

'War!' the five-year-old was screaming. 'War!'

Toby pulled the horses to a halt, drew his sleeve across his forehead to wipe the sweat away, and gazed at his wife, who stopped at some distance – even so he could see how agitated she was.

'Is that true?' he asked, as he swung the boy from the ground into his arms.

She nodded.

'With England?'

'Yes.'

'Whose declaration?'

'Congress,' she said. 'They claim it is to protect the freedom of the seas, but already there is talk of an invasion of Canada.'

'Well . . . no war was ever won by sitting on the defensive.' He placed Stephen on the back of one of the horses, then turned the plough itself back towards the houses. 'Hillditch can complete these furrows tomorrow.'

'What are you going to do?' she asked, her voice breathless, as if she could not see what he was going to do: the act of ceasing to plough was symbolic of abandoning the farm.

'I have business in Baltimore,' he said.

Felicity did not argue; she had known for too long that this day must come. Neither did Elizabeth, although the two women wept together, and joined together in reminding him to come back safe and sound.

Stephen gazed at him in rapt wonder as he prepared to leave, unable to understand why his father was leaving his uniform and sword behind, only dimly aware that this was a terribly important moment in all their lives. The two girls, fortunately, were too young to understand anything. But Boru hung his head in misery; he had seen his master depart before.

Toby felt just as miserable, but Harry was even more upset. For all his warlike utterances he had not truly expected to lose his son again: over the seven years since Toby's return from the sea, the older McGann had grown accustomed to relying on that strong right arm. 'But you'll give them best, boy,' he growled. 'You'll give them best.'

'On board *Constitution*?' Toby grinned at him. 'How could I fail?'

Only Felicity seemed to equal Stephen in noticing that he was leaving his uniform behind. 'Well, sweetheart,' he explained, 'it hardly fits me now. Besides, I shall be a volunteer. I shall have to wait and see what rank is offered me.'

She seemed content with that, and if, like the rest of the family, she assumed he would immediately be recommissioned, so much the better. But as he knew that was impossible, he was conscious of a considerable nervousness as he made his way down to New York, and thence, by various ferries and post-chaises, to Philadelphia and into Maryland. He had never stepped on board any ship in his life, save as at least a midshipman, with the certainty of authority and command in front of him. Now he had nothing to rely on save his experience and ability.

Yet his heartbeat quickened as he stood on the dock and gazed at the USS *Constitution*, two hundred and four feet long, and more than forty-three feet in the beam, drawing more than twenty-two feet of water, and carrying three masts, the highest of which, the main, towered some two hundred and twenty feet above the deck. He looked at the double row of cannon, the twenty thirty-two pounder carronades on the upper deck, and the thirty-two twenty-four pounders on the gun deck; there were also two twenty-four pounder bow chasers. This was the largest and most powerful vessel the United States Navy possessed. That she had never had the opportunity to carve her place in history, even when commanded by such a man as Preble, had to be sheer bad luck, which might be about to change: she was certainly far larger and more powerful than any British frigate.

There was a cluster of men at the foot of the gangplank, access to which was guarded by two blue-coated marines, bayonets fixed to their muskets. In front of them an officer sat at a desk, signing men on. But from the large group of sailors gathered farther down the dock, muttering amongst each other in obvious disappointment, he gathered that even more men were being turned away as not being up to the required standard of ability or experience. Toby caught his breath as he fell into the waiting line, less out of apprehension that he also might be rejected than because he recognised the first lieutenant.

'Name?' The officer did not look up.

'Tobias McGann, sir.'

'Experience ...?' Tom McDonough raised his head in amazement. 'Toby McGann? By God! You'd sail with us?'

'Yes, sir,' Toby said, looking into his eyes.

McDonough almost stood up, and his hand was already leaving his side, to grasp the fingers of his old friend. Then he recollected his position and sat down again. 'And right happy we are to have you, Toby,' he said softly.

'My experience consists of nine years' service with the Navy, sir,' Toby said. 'Seven of them at war, with France and then Tripoli.'

'Aye,' McDonough agreed. 'Aye.' He gazed at his sheet. 'What can I do with you, commensurate with your talents? Coxswain. That's it. I must sign you on as an able seaman, but you'll assume coxswain's duties immediately, McGann.'

'Aye-aye, *sir*,' Toby said in delight. He shouldered his sea bag and went up the plank and through the gangway, saluting the quarterdeck. Isaac Hull stood there, together with Mr Clements, his second lieutenant, and returned the salute. Hull could give no personal sign of welcome without risking his dignity as captain, but the two men gazed at each other for a moment before Toby turned and went forward of the mainmast, thence down the companionway to the crew's quarters, two decks below. Here standing room was limited for even ordinary men; Toby had to bend almost double.

'Christ almighty,' remarked the quartermaster in charge of equipping the new hands. 'What have we here? Gog, or Magog? Or the pair thrown together? We've nothing aboard to fit the likes of you, buster.'

'Avast there,' growled the boatswain, hurrying forward. 'Mr McGann.' He held out his hand. 'Welcome aboard, sir.'

'John Barclay,' Toby cried with pleasure, and shook hands. 'But I am a common seaman now, bo'sun.'

'There's nothing common about you, sir, and there never will be. I am right pleased to have you sailing with us.' He looked at the other men who had gathered around. 'McGann here is worth any four of you,' he told them. 'And don't you forget it. But the ship, sir, what do you think of the ship?'

'She's the best, bo'sun,' Toby agreed. 'The very best.'

USS *Constitution* was by far the largest ship on which Toby had ever served. With her two thousand five hundred tons displacement, her fifty-four guns, and her crew of more than five hundred men and boys, she was very nearly twice the size and strength of the *Constellation* or the *Essex*, and was indeed even larger and more powerful than *La Vengeance*.

Officially classified as a frigate, she was very near to being a small ship of the line.

But she was also perhaps the most beautiful ship on which he had served, and more than in just appearance. Built at Edmond Hart's shipyard in Boston, her timbers consisted of live oak, which had come from the coast of Georgia and was found only in the south-eastern United States, together with red cedar, white oak and pitch pine, and every knee, every joint was a work of art. Paul Revere himself had provided the copper sheathing for her hull. Her crew were at once experienced and eager, many having sailed with Hull before, and they had unbounded confidence both in themselves and their commander. As did Toby; he knew Hull's mettle better than anyone.

Almost he felt tears come to his eyes as he stood with his comrades in the waist to be addressed by the captain, when every berth had been filled. Hull reminded them that the honour and glory of their country and its flag were in their keeping. If Toby's uniform, white blouse and pants, tar-stiffened flat black hat, heavy shoes, was unfamiliar and tight, it seemed the more to express that sense of comradeship which was the greatest gift of the Navy, and if it was strange to sleep in a hammock instead of a bunk, to have to share his bag with two other men instead of having a cabin, with desk and wardrobe and washbasin to himself, and to listen to the sounds of merriment coming from the wardroom, which was at the after end of the same deck on which the crew messed, it was compensated by the friendship extended to him by his messmates, even if the rumour had already spread that he was a cashiered officer. *Constitution* was a happy ship, like all of those on which Toby had previously served, excepting only the *Essex* under James Barron, and the punishment roster was invariably brief. Everyone on board, like himself, was eager only to come to grips with their oldest enemy.

The ship was also a treat to handle, as he discovered the first time he grasped the helm, looking up at the great spars above him, the billowing canvas, responding to McDonough's commands as the first lieutenant mounted the horse blocks to con them down the sweep of the Chesapeake, past

Washington itself, and thence out to sea. If his hands were more calloused than ever on the farm from handling the tarred warps and sheets, and his nails were snapped off from the holystoning and cleaning of brightwork which was the lot of every able seaman, and if he already dreamed of the fresh meat and vegetables served at his own table, he yet felt curiously happy and carefree. What difference did rank make, or wealth, or comfort, he thought, when you can have the feel of a great ship beneath your hands, with the limitless ocean in front of you?

And a war to fight. Their orders were to join the squadron commanded by John Rodgers off New York, where it was supposed the British might attempt to land troops, or certainly blockade the port in order to cut the American trade. This concept was alarming to Toby, as he envisaged redcoats being landed on Long Island to burn and pillage – the British might be prepared to respect another man's property in time of peace, but this was war.

Hull well understood his concern. 'They'll not risk a landing until they have settled with our squadron,' he remarked, standing close by the wheel where he could speak in a low tone and not be overheard. No ordinary seamen were allowed aft of the mainmast except to carry out their duties or in action, and thus there was no one within earshot. 'You'll do your family more good fighting the British out here than waiting for them on the porch of your house, Toby.'

'The thought does make the blood tingle,' Toby agreed.

'And a man can be given a brevet promotion after an action in which he has distinguished himself,' Hull mused, apparently to himself. 'You'll remember that, Toby. I'd sooner have you conning this ship than anyone else in the world, even Tom McDonough. And he's the best.'

'I know it,' Toby said. 'And I am most grateful for those words, Isaac. I'll not forget them.'

They were off the New Jersey coast when the masthead lookout called sail ho, and the telescopes were brought out.

'Four ships at anchor,' Hull commented. 'Commodore Rodgers has four ships under his command.' He looked up at the sails, which were flapping lazily against the spars as the wind dropped. 'It'll come up again by midnight. We'll have joined the fleet at dawn, gentlemen. I will require all hands on deck at that time, and a salute to be fired.'

There was indeed a flurry of breeze during the night, but it died again at dawn, when Toby was on the helm. Still, the *Constitution*, her bottom only recently scraped clean of barnacles and weed, ghosted through the darkness towards the distant signal lamps of the anchored squadron. The heart of the American Navy was over there, Toby thought. Rodgers, and Bainbridge, and Decatur, his old sailing companions. He wondered what Rodgers would say on discovering Toby McGann was serving on board *Constitution*? It had been in disobeying the new commodore's orders that he had incurred his disgrace. Well, he thought, *he* certainly bore no grudge. But he could not forget that Rodgers, alone of his former shipmates, had never called at the McGann farm, which could of course mean nothing more than that an opportunity had never presented itself.

It was quite light now, and although he could not see the ships themselves from his position on the helm, amidships behind the seven-foot high bulwarks, the masts were clearly visible, and the ensigns were just being run up their staffs. He frowned. 'Mr Clements, sir,' he said to the second lieutenant, who was on watch. 'I will swear those ships are not wearing Old Glory.'

Lieutenant Clements, walking sleepily to and fro, and obviously counting the minutes until he was relieved, jerked his head, then stepped on to the port horseblock to use his telescope. 'Great God in the morning,' he gasped. 'But you have keen eyes, McGann. Boy,' he shouted at the midshipman of the watch. 'Summon the captain. We're sailing right slap into the middle of a British squadron.'

'Shall I maintain course, sir?' Toby asked.

Clements chewed his lip in indecision; if the *Constitution* was certainly more powerful than any one of the British ships, and probably equal to fighting two of them at once, four was a different matter. He looked gratefully at the after companionway as Hull emerged, still wearing his nightshirt, although he had added his hat.

The captain took in the situation at a glance. 'Four,' he said. 'Long odds. Too long.' He looked at the glum faces of

210

his officers. 'We do not have that many ships we can afford to hazard any of them, gentlemen. Our duty is to find our squadron, and *then* give battle to the enemy. Starboard your helm, McGann. Bo'sun, sound all hands on deck to trim sail.'

Toby had already put the helm down, but the ship was responding only very slowly in the almost complete absence of wind. And now, across the water, he could hear the rattle of drums and the strains of 'Heart of Oak', the traditional British summons to arms, as they in turn recognised the approaching vessel to be an enemy.

Hull was himself on the blocks, staring at the British; there was not sufficient breeze even to flutter his nightshirt, and yet the anchored ships were steadily coming closer. 'What is the tide doing?' he snapped.

'It is setting us down on them, sir,' Toby answered without thinking. 'Begging your pardon.'

'McGann is right, sir,' McDonough agreed.

'So they can afford to wait at anchor,' Clements remarked, 'for us to drift right up to them.'

'And if we also anchor, we stand the chance of the breeze reaching them first,' Hull mused, pulling his nose. 'Break out the boats, Mr McDonough. We'll have to try to tow ourselves clear.'

McDonough frowned. The *Constitution* was a very large ship to be towed by her boats, and if he put down all eight, he'd not have sufficient men left to man the yards, much less fight the guns.

'We could kedge her,' Toby suggested. 'It's shallow enough for several miles out to sea, and we'd only need two boats for that.'

Hull turned to look at him. 'Kedge her,' he said. 'By God, but you're right. And you shall do it, Toby McGann. Hand over the helm. Mr McDonough, put down the cutters.'

'Aye-aye,' McDonough cried with enthusiasm and hurried forward, Toby behind him. 'What of the bottom?' he asked over his shoulder.

'Good holding ground here.' Toby promised him. 'It'll do, if you man the capstan with a will.'

McDonough grinned and slapped him on the shoulder. 'I'll do that, Mr McGann.'

The two thirty-foot-long cutters were swung out, each manned by twenty men. Toby took his place in the stern of the first, and the seven hundred pound kedge anchor was carefully lowered into the boat, together with several hundred feet of stout manila cable. The second kedge, somewhat lighter, was lowered into the other boat, and a midshipman took the tiller.

'Give way, lads,' Toby commanded. 'We don't have much time.'

If the sailors wondered at being under the orders of one of their own instead of an officer they were the more enthusiastic for that fact. They bent their backs and pulled away from the ship, obliquely out to sea, as it was Hull's intention to get past the British if he could. The cable slowly uncoiled, splashing into the sea, while on board *Constitution* the drums beat and 'Yankee Doodle Dandy' was piped for the guns to be run out and loaded, while men also swarmed aloft to take in the sails.

Toby looked over his shoulder at the British, who were hastily raising their own anchors and launching their own boats to tow them out to sea. It was going to be a near thing, he knew. All depended on the holding quality of the bottom; he could only pray he had been right in his estimation, which had been based on memory.

The cables were almost spent. 'Rest oars,' he commanded, and went forward, exerting his own huge strength, with the assistance of three other men, to heave the anchor over the side. Down it sank into the dark water, while he took the flag from the jackstaff and raised it above his head. The second cutter had also dropped her anchor, and once both were well down, Toby waved the flag. That was the signal for the cables to be taken in. The men on the boats could not hear what was happening, but they could imagine the men sweating at the capstan bars as they marched round and round the huge drum amidships on the lower deck, the cable snaking up over the bows and thence down the hawsepipe to coil itself, dripping water, in the cable locker. And after several agonising moments when nothing appeared to be happening, the big ship began to move toward them: the anchors had bitten into the sand.

Slowly, but faster than the British ships could be towed, the *Constitution* inched over the ground, moving steadily out to sea.

'But look there, Mr McGann,' said one of the oarsmen, and Toby turned his head to see another sail approaching from the north, although well inshore. 'One of ours, do you reckon?'

Toby lacked a glass through which to inspect the distant vessel. If she could be an American, perhaps in advance of Rodgers's squadron, it would mean a complete reversal of the situation in their favour. And her appearance at all indicated that there was some wind, up there. But as he stared at her, he had no doubt she was British; he knew most of the American ships by sight.

'No,' he told the eager men. 'We'll just have to keep at it, lads.'

The *Constitution* rode up to them, the anchors were broken out and retrieved by the boats' crews, and the manoeuvre was resumed, the cutters again rowing out to the limits of their cables before dropping the anchors. Still the wind remained calm, and the approaching warship, which was identified from the masthead of the *Constitution* as HMS *Guerrière*, a British thirty-eight-gun frigate, soon had to resort to launching its boats as well.

Indeed, realising that they were beginning to fall behind, the British squadron eventually abandoned towing and began to kedge like the Americans, repeating the procedure time and again. But the *Constitution* continued to hold her own, although the tortoiselike race lasted for nothing less than forty-eight hours, and at one stage she and the *Guerrière*, which from her angle of approach was almost able to cut her off, even exchanged fire – but the range was too great for any damage to be done to either ship. The boats' crews were changed regularly, as the men became exhausted, but Toby never left his post on the first cutter, using his strength at the end of each leg to retrieve the kedge and once again resume rowing.

It was on the third morning that the British gave up, and

took in their boats. Then the American cutters were also recalled, and that night a breeze came up, enabling them to set sail and slip away into the darkness.

'The course will be north,' Hull commanded. 'Our squadron must be up there somewhere.' He then received Toby on the quarterdeck. 'That was fine work, Toby,' he said, and shook hands. 'As of this moment I am promoting you to the rank of warrant officer, and I intend to submit a report to Congress on these recent events as soon as we are safe to port; if they do not reinstate your rank I'll eat my hat.'

The American squadron was not to be found, either off New York, off Long Island – how Toby gazed at the shore as they sailed by, his heart aching at the thought of the happiness only a few miles away – or off Rhode Island. So the *Constitution* put into her home port of Boston, seeking news. There they learned that Rodgers's squadron had been driven off the coast by superior British numbers, and had, it was thought, sailed even farther north, to demonstrate off the Canadian coast. Thus they remained in port only long enough to provision, Hull still being determined to join the commodore just as soon as he could. The ship therefore sailed long before any replies were received from Washington, whence Hull had sent his despatches, including, as he had promised, his recommendation for Toby to be restored to commissioned rank.

Toby was happy enough, however. He had been able to mail a letter to Felicity, apprising her of what had happened and of his high hopes for the future, while as a warrant officer he was excused all the tiresome daily duties, from holystoning the decks to manning the masthead watch, which rotated amongst the ordinary seamen. And with Hull's support, the future had never looked so bright.

They had been at sea just over a fortnight, and were south-east of the Gulf of St Lawrence, ploughing through the heavy seas thrown up by a summer's gale, and still vainly searching for Rodgers's squadron, when a sail was sighted.

'At last,' Hull said, scanning the eastern horizon. And then frowned. 'A single ship,' he muttered. 'And . . . she's a Britisher, by God.'

McDonough had joined him, staring through his glass. 'I would say she's the *Guerrière*, our old friend from New Jersey. And she's recognised us, that's certain; she's putting on more sail, to escape us.'

'Thirty-eight guns,' Hull said with satisfaction. 'Now, we might say it's a pity she's not a fifty-gun ship, to enable us to show our true worth. But this situation is exactly that for which we were designed, Mr McDonough.' He stepped down, and smiled at his officers. 'Gentlemen, we are about to reduce the numbers of our enemies. Make no mistake, I want that vessel. Now to your posts. Mr McDonough, have McGann sent aft to the helm, and beat to quarters.'

The drums beat and the fifes whistled, the powder and shot were brought up, the nettings were spread and the sawdust scattered across the decks. Toby closed his hands on the spokes of the wheel, and waited for his orders from Second Lieutenant Clements, as all canvas was spread, despite the brisk wind and lumpy sea.

'Course is due east, McGann,' Clements said. 'We'll chase that fellow all the way into the English Channel, if we have to.'

'Aye-aye,' Toby acknowledged. He could see nothing but the sails and the sky from his position, and steered entirely by compass. But he could tell from the whistle of the wind and the way the ship rolled and from time to time gathered speed as she raced downwind that these were not the best conditions for accurate shooting. He could also tell, however, by the exclamations of pleasure from the officers, that the *Constitution* was hauling down the enemy. And soon enough there came the distant roar of cannon, and he could see water pluming into the air to either side.

'You'll hold your fire, Mr McDonough,' Hull ordered. 'In these conditions we'll not harm him, save at point blank range. All the rest were noise and air.'

The big ship continued on its way. The bustle of preparing for battle was over now, and the *Constitution* was almost silent as she breasted the waves, the only sounds the whine of the wind in the rigging and the hissing of the seas as they passed the hull. The gun crews on the quarterdeck shuffled their feet and attempted to peer through the ports, but of course could see nothing as the British ship was dead ahead. Then the *Constitution* herself trembled as one of the British shots struck home, and all heads turned to look aft, at the captain.

But Hull continued to gaze at the enemy vessel, and gave no order to return fire. 'Bring me a damage report, Mr McDonough,' was his only comment.

'Hardly a mark, sir,' was the reply a few minutes later.

Slowly a ripple of sound began to spread down the deck from forward, and Toby, arms growing weary now as he had been on the helm for some hours, realised that the *Guerrière* was coming in sight even from abeam. The British ship continued firing, and the *Constitution* was struck several times, but without apparent result. So much so that as the two ships finally came abeam, and scarcely more than fifty yards apart, one of the British seamen in the rigging shouted, 'Damn you, you Yankees; are your sides made of iron?'

Isaac Hull gave a grim smile. 'More than our sides,' he muttered. 'More than our sides. Now, boys,' he bellowed. 'Pour it into them.'

The ship exploded in flame and smoke, the entire hull reeling away from the recoil of the port broadside, so that Toby needed the assistance of the second coxswain to bring her back to course.

'Keep her abeam, Toby,' Hull shouted. 'Keep her abeam. Reload those guns, haste now.'

Toby could see the masts of the *Guerrière* begin to drop astern as the larger vessel surged past her, and he could hear, too, the screams and shouts from across the water; he turned his head to watch the British mizzen mast tremble and then collapse.

'Now,' Hull shouted, measuring the distance between the two ships by eye. 'Port your helm, Toby. Port your helm.'

They were very close, but Toby never hesitated. The wheel swung to the left, as both coxswains strained on the spokes, and the *Constitution* turned across the bows of the crippled *Guerrière*. The port-side guns had been reloaded in record time, and now the broadside again exploded, the heavy shot raking the length of the British frigate, sending men and wood and iron flying in every direction.

But so sharp had been the *Constitution*'s turn that she was

216

unable to clear the oncoming vessel. Toby looked up and saw the foremast of the *Guerrière* seem to rise above his head, even as it trembled in turn, and a moment later went crashing over the side.

'Stand by for collision,' he shouted, and before he could draw another breath the British ship smashed into the stern quarter of the American, the bowsprit charging across the quarterdeck like a lance and missing Toby's head by inches.

The impact threw most of the men on the quarterdeck from their feet, but they scrambled up quickly enough, staring at the Britisher, still locked against them, and at the marines assembling on her foredeck, red jackets gleaming in the sun, as they made ready to board.

'Boarders!' Hull shouted, drawing his own sword. 'Marines aft.'

The blue-coated American marines came hurrying along the deck, followed by a counter boarding party of sailors, led by Mr Clements – although as the two ships rose and fell on the swell, bumping and grinding against each other, it was obvious that getting from one to the other was going to be a perilous business. And before it could be attempted, all the guns on the *Guerrière* which could possibly be brought to bear were fired; the *Constitution* seemed almost to leap from the sea as the iron balls smashed into the captain's cabin immediately beneath the quarterdeck.

'Fire!' someone screamed. 'She's on fire aft.'

Hull, already attempting to swing himself on to the enemy by the ropes trailing from the British bowsprit, dropped back to the deck, and stared at the smoke issuing from the after companion. 'By God!' he said, as he envisaged his victory being snatched from his grasp by sheer ill fortune.

'You settle the British, Isaac, and I'll settle the fire,' Toby snapped. 'Take the helm, cox.'

He ran for the companion ladder, picking up four of the heavy buckets of sand – two in each hand – as he did so. Down the ladder he slid, holding his breath, while smoke swirled about his head and men stumbled past him, cursing and swearing and choking, anxious only to gain the cleaner air forward. Dimly he saw the glow of the flames thrusting through the gloom, and went towards it, emptying his

217

buckets on to the burning timbers. He turned, and found other buckets being pressed into his hands; a chain had been formed from the upper deck. Now, too, the pumps had been manned, and seawater surged by him to engulf the searing red. All his breath was gone, and his lungs were aching as if he were drowning. He threw four more buckets, and then the entire ship seemed to spin about his head and he crashed to the deck.

He was unconscious only for seconds, dragged forward to breathe relatively clean air, and sat up, gasping and choking. But the fire had been extinguished. Down here the noise of the hulls battering against each other was deafening; it hardly seemed possible for the wooden timbers to take such a battering.

He scrambled to his feet and regained the quarterdeck, saw that the British boarding party had been unable to make their assault, driven back at once by the sustained fire of the Americans, and by the seas, which were at last tearing the two vessels apart. And as the *Guerrière* fell back, her last remaining mast, the main, also went by the board, its stays cut away by the American shot, and leaving her a helpless hulk, rolling in the swell.

'Bring her about, Toby,' Hull shouted, and squeezed his hand. 'That was good work. Now let's finish him.'

'Aye-aye,' Toby cried, and spun the helm, himself directing Boatswain Barclay to the sails which needed trimming.

But McDonough was on the horseblocks, waving and hollooing. 'She's struck,' he shouted. 'She's struck.'

Officers and men ran to the bulwarks to watch the white flag being waved from the British quarterdeck: there was no mast on which it could be hoisted. In fact, Toby knew, there was nothing else they could now do. Without masts she could not sail, and the Americans would be able to circle her and destroy her at will.

'That will give them all something to cheer about,' Hull said, standing beside him. 'Oh, indeed, this is a famous victory. The greatest we have gained since Paul Jones, and your father, Toby, sank the *Serapis* off Flamborough Head. And you played your part most well. You'll have your commission back, by God, or I'll resign mine.'

'I'm just one amongst five hundred, Isaac,' Toby reminded him. 'They were all heroes. But it was the ship gained us the victory.' He grinned at his friend. 'And her iron sides.'

'Ironsides,' Hull said. 'By God, but you're right. That's not a nickname we'll ever forget.'

Chapter 10

Boston and Lake Champlain – 1812–14

There were fourteen men dead or wounded on board the
Constitution, but no fewer than seventy-eight casualties on
the *Guerrière*, the result of only half an hour's actual fighting. And the British ship itself was totally wrecked. Apart
from being dismasted, she was taking water from several
cracked seams, and the weather was deteriorating with every
minute.

'I am sorry, Captain Dacres,' Hull said to the British
commander, 'but I have no choice other than to sink your
ship, however much I would enjoy towing her into Boston as
a prize.'

Dacres nodded. From his point of view, total destruction
was clearly the lesser of the two evils.

The pumps were manned, and the two ships brought together, while the British dead were buried with due sol-
emnity, as were the Americans. Then the disarmed British
sailors and marines were confined below decks on board
Constitution; their officers, allowed to retain their swords in
accordance with best naval practice, were allowed the freedom of the ship – indeed, they had to be berthed amidships
as the after cabins were too damaged to be used – and it was
a treat to hear them muttering their wonderment at each
other at the size and strength of the so-called frigate.

Meanwhile, a boarding party was sent on board *Guerrière*
to set the trains. Then she was cast off and allowed to drift
away, slowly settling into the water, although it was no part

of the Americans' plan to leave her until they were certain of her destruction. Sail was set on *Constitution*, but she remained hove to, half a mile from her victim, until the explosions were heard, followed almost immediately by the gush of flame from below which rapidly enveloped the upper decks. Then, her already opened seams forced further apart by the heat and the force of the explosion, she went down by the head, disappearing from sight in a vast sizzle of disturbed water.

This was the second ship Toby had helped to burn, and although this one was an enemy, unlike the poor old *Philadelphia*, yet he had a lump in his throat as he watched the frigate settle into the waves.

Not that the crew of the *Constitution* were given much time to reflect on the fate that could possibly one day be theirs; once the *Guerrière* was seen to be sinking all hands were mustered to set to work and make at least temporary repairs on the stern of their own vessel, which was at once shattered by the British shot and blackened by the consequent fire.

Yet it had been a stupendous victory; the British were not accustomed to losing any of their vessels in ship-to-ship actions. And it had come in good time, as American morale, so high when war had been declared, had very rapidly plunged to an extremely low level. For by the time the *Constitution* regained Boston, the plans to invade Canada had gone dramatically astray. The Americans had set off in high spirits, actually commanded by General William Hull, Isaac's brother, but at Detroit they had been attacked by General Sir Isaac Brock, commanding a force of seven hundred Canadians and six hundred Indians, and two thousand five hundred men had laid down their arms without firing a shot.

The news of his brother's pusillanimity came as a terrible shock to Isaac, and his own sudden fame seemed rather to depress than cheer him up; he handed over the command of the ship – which would in any event take several weeks to be properly repaired – and hurried off to Washington.

But worse news soon arrived. A massive counter attack on Canada, launched by some five thousand men under the command of General Henry Dearborn, fought an abortive action at Queenston, and then the Americans, all of them militia, refused to cross into Canada, on the grounds that they had enlisted to defend their homeland, not to engage in foreign wars. The only American comfort was that the formidable General Brock had been killed in the skirmish.

In the circumstances, the *Constitution*'s triumph was the only solid cheer the American people had to enjoy; Old Ironsides became a catchword amongst the Bostonians, and her fame was trumpeted the length and breadth of the country. While her crew themselves thirsted to be returned to sea. And Toby more than any of them; it was galling to be lying only a hundred odd miles north of Long Island, and be unable to go home.

Equally was it galling not to know what offer was going to be made to him from Washington, how Hull was proceeding with having him returned to his former rank. He was nearly beside himself with excitement when at last the captain arrived, but it turned out to be an entirely new captain, although another old friend, William Bainbridge, who commanded Toby to his cabin for an interview, and greeted him most warmly – but could offer little cheer.

'I'm afraid the Navy Board feels that it cannot review your situation at this time, Toby,' he said. 'Your conduct, in disobeying the command of a senior officer, was really very serious, you know, and although they are prepared to acknowledge your considerable contribution to the victory over the *Guerrière* – and incidentally, despite the fact that John Rodgers has endorsed Isaac's recommendation that you be restored your commission immediately – they are only prepared to confirm your promotion to warrant officer. They feel it would be detrimental to discipline to restore your rank at this time.'

Toby gazed at him, his cheeks flushed with anger and disappointment. 'I doubt that is the best way to repay loyalty,' he remarked.

'I would say you are right. But there it is.'

'And supposing I say that I no longer wish to fight for them?'

Bainbridge sighed. 'You signed on for the duration of the

war, Toby. You cannot merely resign. You can only be dishonourably discharged. For a second time. I should hate to have a hand in that.'

Toby stood to attention. 'Then I had best return to my duties, sir.'

'Toby . . .' Bainbridge stood up. 'Your predicament commands the hearts of every man in this Navy. I will promise you that we shall seek a glory equal to that of the battle with *Guerrière*, and that your name will once again be presented to Congress for promotion.'

Toby saluted, and left the cabin. A week later the ship sailed for the Caribbean.

In fact, for all his resentment, he could not but be happy to be at sea again and for such a long cruise, and in those waters where he had first seen action, and indeed first met Felicity. And Bainbridge was as good as his word. After cruising the Caribbean to the total disruption of British shipping for the remainder of the year, in December he ventured as far south as Brazil on learning there were British warships in that area, and on the 29th, four days after his crew had celebrated Christmas, off Bahia he brought to action HMS *Java*, another thirty-eight, which like the *Guerrière* possessed no chance against the big American ship.

But this was a much sterner contest than the first. It lasted for some two hours, and the Britisher did not surrender until her commander, Lambert, was dying. There were thirty-four American casualties, and Bainbridge himself had been hit.

Once again Boston turned out to welcome their heroes back in the spring of 1813. Now they had to share some of their glory, for the USS *United States*, commanded by Decatur, had also gained a signal victory, over HMS *Macedonian*, proving yet again the wisdom of the Americans in building frigates larger than any possessed by their enemies.

Yet single-ship victories, while good for the nation's sagging morale, could have no effect on the overall course of the war, as the British began to exert themselves, and in addition to sending more warships across the ocean, took their earlier lessons to heart and commenced operating in convoys and squadrons. Worse, the major naval encounter of the year was an American disaster. In June, the unlucky *Chesapeake*, now commanded by James Lawrence, and moored in Boston only a few yards from where the *Constitution* was undergoing her refit, was sent a challenge by Sir Philip Broke, the commander of the lone British frigate outside the port, HMS *Shannon*, to come out and fight, ship to ship and man to man. Lawrence, who could well remember the disgrace brought on his vessel six years before, determined to accept the challenge, although warned against it by both Bainbridge and McDonough.

Technically, the two frigates were a perfect match, each mounting thirty-eight guns, and with similar sized crews. But the *Shannon* was well known to be the most efficient vessel in the whole British navy, and so it proved. The *Chesapeake* sailed amidst the acclamations of the Boston populace, who were convinced that ship for ship any American was better than any Britisher, while the crew of the *Constitution* swarmed into the rigging to see what they could of the battle. In the event they saw very little over the intervening islands, although they heard the ensuing cannonade. It lasted only a few minutes, during which time one third of the American crew, including almost all the officers, were killed or wounded, Lawrence himself being amongst the dead. His last words, 'Don't give up the ship!' were futile, as Broke put *Shannon* alongside *Chesapeake*, boarded her and triumphantly took her as a prisoner into Halifax, Nova Scotia.

Boston was plunged into the deepest mourning. But there was no prospect of avenging her loss. By the time *Constitution* was again ready to put to sea, there were no less than a hundred British men-of-war operating off the American seaboard, eleven of them ships of the line; not even the powerful American frigates could hope to fight a battleship with any chance of success. Boston was blockaded by half a dozen ships, and there was no hope of getting out at all.

As month after weary month drifted by, and summer dwindled into autumn the cause of the Americans seemed to go from bad to worse. In the west, things had promised well as the year had begun. General William Henry Harrison had marched an army of seven thousand well-trained men to recapture Detroit. But he had realised that the success of his operation depended upon control of Lake Erie, across which both his troops and those of the enemy had to move. He had requested a naval officer to assist him, and been sent Commodore Oliver Hazard Perry, one of the Navy's most brilliant young men. Perry had actually built a squadron on the banks of the lake, then put to sea, and gained a decisive victory over the also recently built British naval forces.

The news of the operation, perfect in concept, technical detail and execution, sent a thrill through the nation, and American morale rose even higher when Detroit fell, and Harrison inflicted another defeat on the British at the Battle of the Thames. It seemed as if all the disasters of the previous year were about to be wiped out, but now the error inherent in leaving the direction of the war to amateur politicians with no knowledge of strategy became apparent.

War Minister Armstrong decided that Harrison had done enough, and ordered his militia disbanded and returned home; his small remaining force of regulars were to concentrate entirely on the defence of Detroit. All the promised fruits of the victories of Lake Erie and the Thames were cast away, and Harrison, in disgust, resigned his command and himself went home. With him went the last American chance of success in the west.

In the north, American fortunes reached an even lower ebb. Generals Wilkinson and Wade Hampton between them commanded forces which were invariably superior to those possessed by the British, but equally were they repeatedly harried and beaten by the more mobile and better disciplined redcoats, always assisted by the Indians, who regarded the Americans as their chief enemies.

The nadir of American military prowess was reached at the Chateaugay River in October, when General Hampton, pursuing a much smaller British force, found himself lured into a swamp, and was so bedevilled by the British bugle calls and piecemeal counter attacks that he supposed himself in the presence of an outnumbering enemy, and fled after hardly firing a shot.

Yet no one talked of making peace. Utterly bewildered by the apparent ineptness of their leaders, both in Congress and

225

the field, the American people remained totally defiant, and dreamed of better days.

The one unit which could have done something to redress the balance, USS *Constitution*, remained bottled up in Boston throughout these dismal days, absolutely forbidden to attempt to break through the British blockade by a Navy Board still haunted by the catastrophe of the *Chesapeake*. But as the ship had orders to sail the moment an opportunity presented itself, the most galling aspect of their situation was the inability of Bainbridge to grant any leave to his crew, officers or men.

This, and the boredom of sitting in port, especially following the destruction of the *Chesapeake*, when the crew longed only to be in action, bred both discontent and ill-discipline, and for the first time the *Constitution* began to have its daily round of floggings as the men quarrelled amongst themselves. As a warrant officer, if Toby was largely uninvolved in the lower deck squabbles, it was his distasteful duty on more than one occasion to lay on the cat-o'-nine-tails – never had he felt so disgusted and even self-humiliated as the blood flowed and the victim screamed, and he had overseen punishments often enough as an officer.

To his surprise and total delight, his monotonous existence was at least relieved when, at the end of August, Felicity herself came to Boston to visit, and he was given two nights' furlough to spend with her in a local hostelry. Gratefully they fell into each other's arms, to renew the passion that had been forced to lie dormant for nearly eighteen months, and equally gratefully he heard that all was well with the farm, with his parents, and with his children – even Boru was doing well. While if she felt any disappointment that he remained only a warrant officer, she concealed it perfectly.

Felicity's personal news was less happy. Both her mother and father had died during the preceding year, and for all their estrangement she was deeply saddened by the event, and by the circumstances arising from it. It had taken several months for the information to reach her, and then it had been conveyed not in a letter from her brother Jonathan – indeed she had no idea where he was – but in a communica-

226

tion from the family lawyer. For to her amazement, and contributing to her unhappiness, after all that had happened, she had been left a half share in her father's estate.

'I truly wish I had made more effort to contact them after our marriage,' she said. 'Then who knows . . . we might have been reconciled. Now Jonathan has obviously taken deep offence.'

'He is far more likely to have taken deep offence at your father's generosity in leaving you his heiress,' Toby said, 'as I remember his character.'

She sighed. 'I'm sure you're right. But that, too, is a problem. The lawyer would like me to visit London as soon as possible to conclude the business. Apparently the estate cannot be released unless I am there in person. And I may say that it is by no means as small as I would have supposed; Papa seems to have died a relatively wealthy man. But I do not imagine that is possible as long as this war continues.'

'I'm afraid it isn't,' Toby agreed. 'You're an American citizen now, and might well be imprisoned.' He squeezed her hands, and frowned at her. 'Believe me, sweetheart, I am deeply sorry about your folks, and that we were never reconciled. And I am delighted that you are an heiress, even if your inheritance may have to wait a year or two before you can collect it. But I also think there is something else on your mind.'

She flushed. 'How well you have come to know me.'

He kissed her nose. 'Tell me what it is.'

'I suppose it is nothing, really,' she said. 'Nothing to concern you, Toby, at such a time.'

'Everything to do with you is of concern to me, Felicity,' he told her. 'At any time. Tell me.'

'Well . . .' Still she hesitated. 'I'll confess I was upset by an odd occurrence this spring.'

His frown returned. 'What odd occurrence?'

'Well . . . three men came to Long Island, and . . . well . . . they were seen riding round the farms. They were sort of inspecting everything. And they asked a lot of questions of the hired hands.'

His frown deepened. 'Three men? Inspecting the farms? By God, they must have been English spies, I'll wager. Planning an assault.'

227

'Your father thought so, too, and sent a report to New York. And indeed, Long Island has been fortified, so there seems little prospect of any attack succeeding. Nor is there sufficient there to make it worthwhile.'

'There's a relief,' he said. 'I have been worried about you, I'll confess.' He gazed at her. 'But that's not all you have to tell me.'

'It is all,' she insisted. 'Except that ... I don't think they were English spies. Two of them were most certainly Americans.'

'Which, unfortunately, doesn't prove a thing. What of the third?'

She left the bed to stand by the window and look down at the street. 'He was a dark man.'

'A Negro, you mean?'

'No, not a Negro. But an African, I am sure. I only saw him at a distance, but I thought he looked like a Moor.'

'A Moor?' He leapt out of bed to join her.

'It is only a supposition.' She leaned against him as his arm went round her. 'I still have nightmares, you know.'

'I know.' His arm tightened. 'A Moor, in Long Island? You should have had the fellow arrested.'

'For being a Moor? Anyway, they are gone, and as I said, we are now fortified and there are soldiers everywhere. It's just that ... the questions the men asked were less about the farms, it seems, than about me. Whether I ever travelled, how old were the children, and so on. When I heard that, I was frightened. I thought of Mohammed ben Idris. If I supposed he might wish to harm the children I'd ...' she sighed. 'I wonder if he is still alive.'

'Yes,' Toby said grimly. 'I have heard a report that he is still alive, and even prospering. How I *wish* I had settled the fellow there and then in Tripoli.' He turned her into his arms and held her close. 'But not even Mohammed ben Idris can harm you, here in America. Especially on Long Island. Or the children,' he added as an afterthought.

And in fact he did not have any doubts on that score himself, even supposing the Vizier still remembered the girl who had been snatched away from him – which was unlikely.

But never had he been so anxious for this war to end, and

enable him to resume his life at the farm, watching over them.

The very day after he rejoined the ship, he was summoned aft. Bainbridge had by now been replaced as captain, in accordance with the Navy Board's policy of reassigning their captains every year, by Charles Stewart, who was only two years older than Toby himself, and had gained a considerable reputation during the French war. Until recently he had been captain of the old *Constellation*, but had been so tightly blockaded in Norfolk, Virginia, by the British that he had not as yet actually been to sea, and was obviously hoping to do better with *Constitution*.

With him in the captain's cabin was McDonough.

'Close the door, Toby and sit down,' Stewart invited.

Cautiously Toby obeyed and lowered himself into the chair before the table, facing the officers. Stewart was one of the few of his contemporaries he did not know very well; they had never served together, and although he had been in the Mediterranean, as executive officer of *Constellation* in 1805, he had arrived just as Toby had been leaving – to disgrace.

'Have you heard the news from Europe?' the captain asked.

'I have heard rumours, sir.'

'Well, I can tell you that there appears to be the most tremendous overturn in events going on over there. Why, only two years ago, if there was one thing in this world of ours that seemed eternal, it was the grip that Napoleon Bonaparte had on Europe. Now it seems clear that the invasion of Russia last year was every bit as disastrous as rumour had it at Christmas; people are saying that only six thousand men of the Grand Armée, which had started out at six hundred thousand strong, remember, ever regained France. And this year has seen nothing but a series of French defeats, culminating in an immense battle at Dresden in Germany, last month, in which the French were opposed by just about every other nation on the continent. And were soundly beat. Added to that, Wellington's British army has just about conquered all of Spain, and is getting ready to cross the Pyrenees. Our agents over there are suggesting that

Bonaparte may well have to accept a negotiated peace if he is going to save France from invasion. I need hardly tell you what such a development would mean to us.'

'It would mean, sir, that Great Britain would be free to devote all of her men and ships to fighting us.'

McDonough nodded. 'We are talking of more than a thousand ships of war, remember. And in addition, this time we shall not be fighting hired mercenaries commanded by men who were more than a little sympathetic to our cause. Britain now boasts an army of tried professionals the equal of any in the world; her people are inured to twenty years of war – and we challenged them in the first instance.'

Toby smiled. 'That could be said to have been one of Congress's many errors of judgment.'

Stewart coughed. 'You may well be right, Toby, but that does not alter the fact that we are likely soon to be fighting for our lives.'

Toby waited. He had no idea why he was being included in such a discussion.

'Now,' Stewart continued, 'our masters in Washington feel, and I suspect that in this instance they may very well be right, that if the British do decide to fight this war with all of their strength, they will adopt roughly the same strategy as they did in the War of the Revolution, and while they will most probably assault both the Atlantic seaboard and the south, will make their main effort down the line of the Hudson, to shatter the New England States. In effect, to complete what Burgoyne started thirty-seven years ago.'

'Burgoyne was stopped and forced to surrender, sir,' Toby pointed out.

'It was a badly bungled campaign,' Stewart agreed. 'But one which has been extensively analysed since. And all the mistakes Burgoyne made are on file at the British Ministry of War, you may be sure of that. And as I have said, I fancy that this time we will be opposed by somewhat sterner stuff, both as regards men and commanding officer. However, Congress has also shown some ability to profit by past mistakes, especially since they have got rid of Armstrong as War Minister. They recall that Harrison's recapture of Detroit was only made possible by Perry's victory over the

British squadron on Lake Erie, and have concluded, again rightly in my opinion, that no British army can come down the Hudson if we retain command of Lake Champlain, which that army, or at least all of its transport, would have to cross.' He looked at McDonough, who took up the tale.

'There are actually no naval craft at all on Lake Champlain at this moment, Toby. And of course there is no means of transporting any there through the wilderness. There is an American army dug in around Plattsburg, on the west shore of the lake, but it is felt that this force is insufficient to withstand a determined British thrust. I have therefore been commanded by Congress to proceed there as quickly as possible, and construct a squadron of large gunboats, with which it is hoped we can deter any British attempts at invasion. To do a Perry, in fact. I assume I have been chosen because I qualified in shipbuilding as a midshipman. Now, Toby, I would be most pleased if you would accompany me.'

Toby looked at Stewart.

'I have agreed with Mr McDonough's request that you be allowed to volunteer, Toby. I shall be sorry to lose you, to be sure, but I, and I am sure every officer in the Navy, feel that you have been hard done by through Congress's refusal to reinstate you to your former rank. Nor do I see how any change in your situation can be affected while we languish here, cooped up by the British. Here is a chance of further distinction.'

'Hewing wood,' Toby remarked, but without rancour. The idea was most attractive. It would almost be like clearing land on the farm.

'Hewing wood in defence of your country,' McDonough reminded him. 'And I may add, that at a distance from any political control, out there in the wilderness, I may make my own appointments. Agree, and you are acting second lieutenant on this instant.'

'You should also consider,' Stewart put in, 'that should the British attempt that invasion route, you could well find yourself in one of the most decisive theatres of this war.'

'Oh, I volunteer, sir,' Toby said. 'I enjoy hewing wood. Besides, I've always wanted to see the wilderness.'

231

And he had more than enough of being confined to Boston, and even the old *Constitution* herself.

Neither Toby nor Tom McDonough had the slightest idea of the immensity of the task they were being asked to undertake. 'Hurrah!' Toby wrote to Felicity. 'I am being sent off into the forest to cut down trees and shoot bears and have a taste of the pioneering life. After these long weary months in Boston, relieved only by your visit, my own dear heart, I feel like a boy let out of school. You may now rest your mind in peace, as I am being removed so far from any theatre of war.' There was no need to tell her of the fears Congress had of an English invasion.

He soon discovered that the reality was a good bit different to his imagination of it.

In the first place, they found out that the five hundred men McDonough was to command had been very hastily assembled. Some hundred of the men were experienced seamen, garnered from the various blockaded American ships – there were four other volunteers permitted from the *Constitution* herself. But the remainder had never been to sea in their lives. Congress apparently felt that patrolling a lake was a service which could be carried out quite adequately by any man capable of handling a boat on a river. As these 'volunteers' were also basically militia, it was obvious that discipline was going to be a problem. Fortunately, amongst those volunteering from the *Constitution* was Toby's old friend Boatswain Barclay, who promised to be a tower of strength.

In the second place, while they were told they could expect an endless supply of fine timber around the lake, they could expect almost nothing else; the army at Plattsburg was itself short of supplies. Thus all the guns the naval force might need, all the powder and shot, all the food and side-arms, had to be transported up the Hudson in a long raft of small boats, at the oars of which their men had immediately to prove their worth as they toiled against the fast-running current.

At the least they proved that they could row, however much they grumbled. But by then McDonough and Toby had other things on their minds, principally with regard to their guns. As no heavy cannon could be spared, these consisted entirely of light calibre, long-range culverins. 'Culverins, to fight on a lake,' McDonough remarked in disgust.

In the third place, the journey was considerably longer than Toby had estimated, as they pulled their way past the fortress of West Point on its bluff overlooking the river, thence almost due north into the woods until they reached the villages of Albany and Schenectady. North of Schenectady the wilderness really began, as they followed the valley between the Green Mountains to the east and the Adirondacks to the west, surrounded now on either side by primeval forests which loomed above the river, silent and hostile. Every man of the expedition was well aware that the Indians supported the British, even if they could also feel that five hundred well-armed men were too formidable a body to be attacked.

By now all the provisions with which they had left New York had been consumed, but the river so teemed with fish, as the woods did with game, that they never went hungry, while there was all the water they needed to drink. It surprised Toby to realise that although he had lived in America since the age of three he had never truly understood the immensity of the country, as day succeeded day with hardly a change of scenery, hardly an indication that they had travelled at all during the previous twenty-four hours – save for their blistered hands and aching backs. And places like Buffalo and Detroit were another several hundred miles to the west, although still within the boundaries of the United States.

At last they came to rapids, and were forced to leave the river. 'It is only twenty miles from here to the lake,' McDonough told them encouragingly. 'That is not far.'

It was a huge distance, as they had to carry everything with them, boats and cannon included. The men cursed and swore as they covered perhaps two miles in every day, an advance guard hacking a path through the woods while the remainder toiled over the long cables which dragged the boats. Tempers flared, and Toby and Barclay had to use their fists more than once to quell an incipient mutiny.

233

'One day, perhaps, there will be a canal linking the Hudson with the lake,' McDonough suggested.

'If there is ever sufficient traffic to make it worthwhile,' Toby countered. 'We would not want to build one purely for the use of the British whenever they feel like invading us.'

It took them more than a week to reach the southern end of the lake, and then they could not help but wonder if they were actually merely approaching another river. The stretch of water in front of them was certainly wider than the headwaters of the Hudson, but was still bounded on either side by the thickly clustered trees. Soon they passed the famous old fortress of Ticonderoga, now virtually abandoned, then had to pull another thirty miles before Champlain opened in front of them into a truly magnificent body of water.

Now the trees were distant, and the fish seemed to wish to leap into the boat. Nights and days were silently splendid, the harvest moon leaving the hours of darkness almost as bright as noon.

'This is a paradise,' Tom McDonough exclaimed. 'We could be the only men in the world.'

Next day they saw their first elk, standing by the water to drink, and so unused to humanity that he merely raised his regally antlered head and stared at the boats as they rowed by, then resumed drinking.

They proceeded up the lake until they reached the narrows caused by Grand Isle to starboard and Cumberland Head to port. In the bay created and protected by Cumberland Head on the west shore of the lake, they found the new sprawling American fortress of Plattsburg, and were welcomed by its commander, General Alexander Macomb, who regarded the by now somewhat ragged seamen with distaste.

'Aye,' he acknowledged, when McDonough presented his credentials and the letter from Congress outlining the situation as it was seen in Washington, 'I have heard the rumours. But there is naught going on out there. The British have a post at Rouses Point, that is only fifteen miles away, but I am content that they should stay there. 'Tis only a further twenty-odd miles to Montreal, and I have no desire to stir them up. I have a mere four thousand five hundred men under me here, Mr McDonough. Fifteen hundred of them are described as regulars, but they have never fired a shot in anger, save at the odd bear or stealing Indian. The other three thousand are militiamen who will probably turn tail at the sight of a red coat. I need all the time I can manage to turn them into fighting soldiers. So you'll keep your men under control.' He eyed Toby's bulk, as if suspecting that here was a natural born berserker.

'I am here to build a squadron, sir,' McDonough assured him. 'I certainly have no intention of engaging anyone until that is done, at the least.'

'Not even then, sir,' Macomb barked, 'without orders from me.'

'He could be difficult,' McDonough confided to Toby that evening. 'But we have enough to keep us busy throughout the winter without locking horns with the military.'

He had considered the problems with which he was faced in considerable detail, and most nights on the journey up from the coast he and Toby had discussed their best course of action; their thoughts were confirmed by what they found on reaching the lake. Although there was a good deal of deep water, and to control the entire area it would be necessary to have some true ships available, there were also many shoal areas, with only a few inches above the bottom. In addition, the winds playing over the lake, so far from the sea, were for the most part light and variable – although there could be sudden squalls of frightening ferocity.

But they had to accept the possibility that when the time came for action, they might be left with no means of man-oeuvre save for oars. They therefore determined to reach back into history, and build a dozen galleys, flat bottomed and fast in even calm conditions, with which they could patrol every inch of the lake. As their main defences, they chose to go for four sloops of war, the biggest to mount twenty-six guns, which in fact made her into a very small frigate. That would give them a squadron of sixteen ships, which was the maximum number they could man or arm, but which would certainly also give them complete control of the lake – as things now stood.

Macomb was willing to co-operate to the extent of detaching various platoons of militiamen to help them – his little army was suffering in the main from boredom – and the cutting of trees and shaping of timbers and laying down of keels commenced in October. They had barely started when the first frosts of winter descended on them, and within a couple of months large areas of the lake had become sheets of ice. Not that McDonough allowed that to deter him. With Toby in command of the equally determined lumberjacking squads, work continued even as it got colder and colder: they were often working in snow drifts up to their waists, and McDonough so far broke with naval usage as to allow each man a pint of grog on his return from the woods.

But the news from the outside world also grew colder and colder. American operations in the north-west, under the incompetent Wilkinson, stumbled from bad to worse, the campaign at the year's end culminating in the British burning of the ship-construction yard at Buffalo on Lake Ontario, some three hundred miles away to the south-west.

On Champlain itself, all remained quiet until the new year, when, with the snow still thick on the ground and the ice equally thick on the water by the shore, a patrol seeking meat returned from the northern end of the lake to say they had been fired upon by a party of British and Indians, and that there was a great deal of activity around Rouses Point.

'Activity?' McDonough enquired.

'They are cutting down trees, Mr McDonough,' Macomb told him. 'It would appear that they mean to build ships to oppose yours.'

Tom McDonough stood on the edge of the lake and stared across the ice to the north. 'What do you reckon?' he asked.

'We have to be three months ahead of them,' Toby said. 'We'll be ready for launching as soon as there is a thaw. I don't reckon we should wait a moment beyond that.'

'You mean sail over there and burn everything they have,' McDonough mused.

'Better than sitting here and waiting for them to come to us.'

'I'll have a word with the general,' McDonough decided.

But Macomb would not hear of it. 'My orders are to sit on the defensive and bar the British passage,' he declared. 'Not

236

to undertake any offensive action. I will tell you when you may attack the enemy, Mr McDonough.'

There was nothing for it but to obey; Congress had not even promoted McDonough to captain's rank to give him more authority. Nor could they undertake the simplest answer, and keep ahead of the British by building more ships – they would have neither the guns nor the men to put in them. So they completed building their squadron, and as soon as the ice began to melt launched them.

McDonough, revealing a fine sense of history, elected to name his flagship USS *Saratoga*. 'That should cast their minds back a bit,' he grinned. For it had been at the nearby village of Saratoga that John Burgoyne had been forced to surrender his army in 1777.

The squadron was anchored in the bay formed by Cumberland Head, and settled down to wait . . . and listen with increasing disquietude to the news brought back by the army scouts. For it seemed that the British commander, now identified as Captain George Downie, was also in possession of facts concerning them, and had determined to ape their dispositions: he also was building four ships and twelve galleys. But as he had the advantage of hindsight – and they had thrown away their advantage of being first in the water – he was constructing a true frigate, which was apparently to be named the *Confiance*, and which would mount no less than thirty-seven guns, and be by some distance the most powerful vessel on the lake.

'Truly,' McDonough grumbled to Toby, as they shivered in their greatcoats and listened to the tremendous cracks of the ice breaking up out on the main body of water, and watched Macomb riding his horse up and down his fortifications, 'our Congress seems able only to give commands to men who do not understand how to wage war.'

Things went from bad to worse as the campaigning weather returned. At the end of April news was received that Napoleon Bonaparte had been forced to abdicate, and that the long European war was finally over. There could now be no doubt that the British would turn all of their attention to the upstart republic which had dared to challenge the lion's right to rule the seas to his own advantage. And so it proved.

237

Everywhere the American forces soon found themselves opposed by veteran regulars who had beaten even the famous French moustachios.

On the Niagara front, the long stalemate erupted during the early summer of 1814, in a series of sanguinary encounters, in which the Americans actually held their own, but could make no further headway into Canada. Further south, the British carried out a devastating raid into Chesapeake Bay itself, ascending that great waterway, shattering an American force – in which only a hastily recruited band of sailors, commanded by Commodore Joshua Barney, proved themselves worthy of the uniforms they wore – and then occupying and burning Washington itself. Barney was another of those brilliant officers who had quarrelled with the Navy Board, and like James Barron, had taken himself off to serve with the French. He had fortunately returned, unlike Barron, in time to fight for his country.

Finally, rumours came that a huge British expeditionary force was fitting out in Jamaica to invade the very south, capture New Orleans – where the creole population were not yet assimilated Americans, and being of a royalist inclination might well help the British – and ultimately wrest from the infant republic the whole of the Louisiana Purchase made from Bonaparte ten years before.

Most ominous of all was the news from Montreal, brought by American spies, that fourteen thousand British veterans of the Peninsular Campaign in Spain and Portugal were being disembarked there, under the command of General Sir John Prevost, to take the route of the Hudson into New York itself. This then, was what they had all known must one day happen – save that as Congress had feared, this army was twice the size of that commanded by Burgoyne thirty-seven years before, and more than twice as experienced and well armed.

'Yet they cannot reach the Hudson save by way of the lake, General,' McDonough told the thoroughly alarmed Macomb. 'Not without abandoning their guns and supply trains.'

'Then do you put out and destroy that British squadron,

238

Mr McDonough,' the General said. 'It was what you have always wanted to do. Now I am giving you permission.'

'With respect, sir,' McDonough replied, 'I must decline. Our chances of doing that with success no longer exist. Four months ago that would have been our best course. Now I think your original orders to stand on the defensive represent our only course.'

'You refuse to lead your ships into battle? By God, sir, I should have you arrested as a coward and a disgrace to the uniform you wear.'

'I refuse to lead my ships to certain destruction, General Macomb,' McDonough replied evenly. 'We will carry out our instructions, and bar the passage across the lake to the British. By standing on the defensive.'

'Standing on the defensive?' Macomb cried, and flung out his arm to point at his cantonments. 'I have but four thousand half-trained men there, sir . . .'

McDonough sighed. It seemed that Macomb's men were doomed to remain half-trained forever.

'. . . and Prevost has fourteen thousand regulars. Fourteen thousand, by God! And you say I must hold Plattsburg?'

'Sir John Prevost will know, sir, that even if he defeats you, he cannot proceed down the lake and across the wilderness without water transport. That transport must use the lake. As long as my squadron is intact, it cannot do so. Therefore Downie must seek to destroy my squadron first. He must come to us, in this instance, and that is the only way we can defeat him, as he possesses the larger ships. I do most earnestly beg you to consider these points, sir.'

Macomb frowned at him. 'And when he comes, you think you will defeat him?'

McDonough looked him in the eye. 'Yes, sir,' he said. 'Or I will die trying. And so will my people.'

'Words,' he commented to Toby, as they surveyed their tiny fleet, anchored within the protecting arm of Cumberland Head.

'But strategically sound words,' Toby reminded him. He was feeling personally elated. He had written to Felicity the previous autumn, sending the letter with the last despatches

239

able to go south before winter set in, and had received no reply. He had not expected one before the spring, but there had been none then either, and he had written again the moment the river was usable. But still there had been no reply, and as the summer had worn on he had become somewhat alarmed. If the British had been so bold as to penetrate into Chesapeake Bay, landing a marauding force on Long Island would mean nothing to them.

But yesterday a letter and a package had at last arrived. It had been sent before the destruction of Washington, but up to then at any rate all was peaceful around New York, save for the blockade, just as all was well with the farm and the family – and in addition, as he had told her he was now once again a lieutenant, albeit an acting one, she had got out and pressed that uniform which had hung in his closet for nine years, and sent it to him. He was wearing it now, delighted to find that it still very nearly fitted him. Certainly he felt totally confident.

'Now, Tom,' he said, 'all we have to do is make sure we *can* beat Downie when he comes.'

'As if any man could ever foretell the course of a naval battle,' McDonough sighed.

'Well . . . one or two have tried, with some success. Nelson, for instance. He tried to envisage how each battle might go, and worked out his tactics in advance, so he hardly had to give an order during the actual action.'

McDonough nodded. 'Sure. And he had the whole wide ocean on which to manoeuvre, all the wind he could use, and a fleet of the very finest seamen in the world. What have we got, Toby? A stretch of water so narrow that if you forget where you are for an instant you're aground; hardly any wind with which to manoeuvre our ships; and crews consisting of river pirates, for the most part.

'Our only advantage, if it can be called an advantage, lies in those culverins; we'll be able to hit Downie before he can hit us. But you know as well as I that culverins at extreme range aren't going to stop a well-found ship. And when he gets close and can use his carronades . . . It's going to be an old-fashioned killing match at point blank range, in which he will have both the heavier metal and the more experienced crews.'

240

'I reckon we have sufficient advantages to outweigh all of that,' Toby argued. 'You say Nelson always had the wind and the sea at his disposal. But that surely made the battle, where it would be fought and in what conditions, the more unpredictable. We at least know exactly where our battle is going to be fought; right here in this bay – simply because Downie dare not sail past us and give us the opportunity to rush out at his transports. Then, we also know the battle will be fought in very light airs; Downie isn't going to chance his arm in these shoal waters if there is the slightest prospect of a thunderstorm or a squall. That means everything is going to happen in slow motion, as regards working the ships.'

'Which merely gives the British more time to smash us with their heavy guns,' McDonough pointed out. But he was looking distinctly happier. 'Our best chance is to put out as soon as we know he is coming, and take our chances.'

'No,' Toby said vehemently. 'That would be suicidal. Make him come to us on our terms, Tom.'

'And when he gets close?'

'Well ... what about begging some shore-based cannon off Macomb?'

'I could try it. But don't you suppose Prevost is smart enough to attack both on land and sea at the same time? We must assume that he is, anyway. Macomb will need those guns to hold Plattsburg. No, Toby, however you look at it, we are going to be shot to pieces once Downie gets in this bay. If only we had even two more ships ... our culverins may be lighter metal, but if we had enough of them ...'

Toby snapped his fingers. 'You shall have four more ships, Tom.'

McDonough stared at him.

'At least, you will have the fire-power of four more ships,' Toby said, grinning. 'Aren't we going to fight this battle at anchor, in almost windless conditions? That means, after each broadside, the English have to either reload, or wear ship. Each of those is going to take several minutes. While we ...'

McDonough's face slowly broke into a smile in return. 'Kedges, by God,' he shouted.

'And springs,' Toby reminded him. 'There'll be a set.'

Because even on the lake, when the winds had been blowing in one direction for several days, as they invariably did, a current was set up along the wind direction. 'Properly cabled, I reckon we can wear ship twice before any vessel under sail can even begin to come about.'

'By God!' McDonough said again. He got up, walked to and fro, snapping his fingers. 'We'll have the use of four extra broadsides in seconds. Properly timed . . .'

'Oh, aye, timing is the secret,' Toby agreed. 'And then, concentration of overwhelming fire-power. That is the whole secret of warfare, Tom. Maybe we've a thing or two to teach the Limeys yet.'

August dwindled into September, and the Americans waited. But now they did not waste their time, as McDonough had them at gunnery practice six hours a day. He could not let them actually shoot – he lacked the powder and he did not wish to alert the British – but he trained them at loading and reloading their guns until Toby doubted there could be any more efficient crews in the world. But in addition they also practised the kedging manoeuvre, until every man knew just what he had to do, and each ship could turn itself completely about in thirty seconds. Here Barclay was at his best, and he personally selected the foredeck squad for each vessel, in charge of the vital business of cutting the main cables at precisely the right moment.

The men's morale was tremendous, as they realised not only that there was going to be a fight, but their officers had determined upon how to win it. This confidence was not shared by the army. No one on the shore had the slightest doubt, either, that the British intended to attack them, and soon. Their scouts reported an immense camp being set up close to Rouses Point, and that the British ships were daily out exercising. Rumour as to the strength of the opposing army was rife, and the militia were quite obviously terrified. Macomb daily became more agitated, and it was all McDonough could do to prevent him abandoning the field-works at Plattsburg and retreating to the Hudson.

'By God, sir, Mr McDonough,' he growled. 'If you are wrong, and cannot defeat the British squadron, the defeat

242

of the entire United states will rest squarely upon your shoulders.'

'To retreat without fighting, General, would be the same as a defeat,' McDonough insisted. 'And if we check them here, why . . . will not the honour of saving the United States rest squarely on . . .' he decided to be diplomatic, 'our shoulders?'

On the 7 September, an Indian appeared in the American encampment, bearing a message for 'Commodore McDonough and his officers, especially Lieutenant McGann.'

'From Downie,' McDonough commented, slitting the envelope. 'He is too kind to give me such an exalted rank. Ha! He sends his regards, and wishes to inform us that he will soon be paying us a visit. Well, well; quite the chivalrous foe. But what's this? There is indeed a special reference to you, Toby, a challenge within a challenge, so to speak, from a certain Lieutenant Jonathan Crown.' He frowned. 'The name is familiar. Do we know such a fellow?'

'You met him on board HMS *Lancer*, off Martinique, fourteen years ago,' Toby told him. 'He is now my brother-in-law.'

'The devil,' McDonough remarked.

'Oh, indeed,' Toby agreed. 'He loathes me as much as I loathe him. But . . . after fourteen years, he is still only a lieutenant, and he has been serving continuously, and been at war, throughout that time? Well, that sums him up.'

'He seems to wish your blood.'

'If he comes too close, I shall have his,' Toby vowed. 'The man is an arrogant fool.' But although he meant what he said, his heart had given a great lurch. This possibility, that he might one day find himself opposed to his own brother-in-law, had haunted him since he had first returned to the service. He had always supposed it would happen on the ocean, in a contest between two great ships. To have it happen here in the back of beyond, where no one even knew what they were about . . .

McDonough grinned, and slapped him on the shoulder. 'Well, at least we know we can prepare.'

Which they did, with great care. As the wind was out of the north-east, and however light, had been so for several

243

days, the ships were anchored with their bows in that direction. But from the bows, also, the kedge anchors were carried out, astern, to the extent of just sufficient cable to be certain the anchors held. The bower cables were secured on deck, and the kedge cables carried down to the capstans. But in addition, springer cables were attached to the bowers, so that the kedges also could be let go and the ships turned a second time, so that the squadron would indeed turn right round twice, in virtually the same positions, in a matter of seconds.

'But remember,' McDonough told his men, 'the enemy must not know, must not even suspect, our intention. He must be brought close by acceptance of his fire and our apparent adherence to ordinary tactics. If he smells a rat and puts about, we are done; he will not fall for such a ruse again.'

Three days later their scouts brought news that the British were definitely preparing to move. Macomb sounded the alarm, and his unhappy men filed out to take their places behind their earthworks, amidst a great deal of noise, as if they were whistling in the dark. Toby and McDonough went ashore to inspect the situation, and were not encouraged; the militiamen were in a state of high, almost hysterical, excitement, and Toby suspected there was a deal too much liquor circulating through the ranks – no frame of mind in which to oppose regulars.

The seamen, despite their hints that what was good enough for the army was equally necessary for them, were as usual refused all alcohol. But Toby had no doubt they would fight, and fight well, partly from a desire to fight, after all the weary months of waiting, and partly because they felt sure of victory. They slept by their guns, and next morning, just after dawn, they could hear, seeping across the stillness of the forest, the regular drum beat of the British infantry as it moved out.

Now even McDonough became agitated. 'Can Prevost mean to assault the fortress without sending in the ships?' he demanded. Because, although he had not dared tell Macomb this, such a tactic, followed by a British victory on land, while it would still leave his squadron controlling the lake, would also leave it in an untenable position, without a shore base.

'Not him,' Toby said reassuringly. 'Look over there.' He pointed at Cumberland Head itself, where the lookout they had posted was signalling, 'Enemy in sight.'

'Thank God for that,' McDonough said. 'Gentlemen, to your posts.'

The culverins were loaded and run out. The galleys took their places further down the bay, where they could engage British stragglers but also could run for cover should the battle go against the Americans. And now they could see the masts and sails of the *Confiance* and her three consorts, just carrying steerage way in the very light airs. Conditions were even better than Toby could have hoped; in this calm it would take half an hour to wear a ship under sail alone. But the wind was from the east, and however light, would still bring the enemy into the bay for that old-fashioned killing match at point blank range so dear to the hearts of the Royal Navy. Had not Nelson himself laid down the maxim, 'No captain can go very wrong if he lays his ship alongside that of an enemy.'

'Fire as they bear, Mr McGann,' McDonough commanded. 'We must act the part of complete orthodoxy to the very last minute.'

'Aye-aye,' Toby agreed, and a moment later he sighted the bows of *Confiance* coming round the headland. He gave the order, and the guns of the *Saratoga* began to boom. The culverins had a range of over a thousand yards, or better than half a nautical mile, and soon the men were cheering as they watched their shot striking home. But equally the twenty-four-pound balls were not capable of inflicting much damage at so great a distance, and the British ships came slowly and silently on, *Confiance* in the van, pennants hardly fluttering in the light air. Their galleys also soon came into sight, rowing at first to keep pace with the ships, but then quickening their stroke to proceed down the bay and engage their American counterparts, who watched them approach with cheers and jeers – but clearly it was on the outcome of the battle between the ships that the day would depend.

'God damn it, we might as well be throwing stones at them,'

245

McDonough fumed, walking up and down the quarterdeck of the *Saratoga*, and casting anxious glances at the cables to the kedges. Indeed, Toby felt the same. They were both seamen, and to remain at anchor to await the approach of an enemy was both galling and unnatural; the temptation to cut the cables and take their chances on the wind were enormous. But they had laid their plan, and must now have the moral courage to stick to it.

Gradually the range closed, as the British ships rounded Cumberland Head and stood into the bay, the wind astern now to drive them on. And now from the land there came the thudding of cannon and the rattle of musketry; Prevost had indeed timed his assault to coincide with that of the ships. But now was no time to worry about the fate of the soldiers. For the range was down to a quarter of a mile and closing, and signals were climbing to the masthead of the *Confiance*. Slowly, majestically, the four British ships turned to starboard, up into the wind, forming line abeam of the anchored Americans. As they lined up with their targets, the broadsides of heavy cannon exploded. The air was filled with flying shot, and with flying spars and ropes as well. And with men. The smoke was so thick Toby could hardly see what was happening.

'Fire,' he bawled, his voice hoarse. 'Reload. Haste, now.'

The culverins snapped back on their recoil ropes, and the men began to work with a will, even as they glanced at their comrades stretched on the deck. But for the moment the only sounds were echoes. The relevant broadsides of both fleets were spent, and it was a matter of who could reload first, or who could first come about to bring his other battery to bear. But as McDonough and Toby had calculated, the British were not attempting to wear their ships; they knew that would take too long in the almost calm conditions. With just enough wind to hold them abeam their enemies, they were confident of reloading and delivering another of those deadly broadsides, knowing that even if the Americans were as quick, the British shot was far the heavier.

'Stand by now,' McDonough called from aft. 'The moment is coming.'

The smoke was clearing, and Toby could see the British

ships slowly coming closer as they drifted before the breeze. Some of them had been hit, but not seriously, while the main deck of the *Saratoga* already looked like a charnel house, with at least fifty men dead or wounded, he thought, and more than one cannon dismounted; the foremast had been shot away. But that was irrelevant now. If their plan did not work, they were going to be destroyed long before they could set sail.

'Stand by,' McDonough repeated, staring at *Confiance*. 'Now!'

The notes of the bugle, sounded by the man at his elbow, cut across the morning to transmit the command to the other three ships. Toby looked forward, gasped as he saw that the men waiting at the cables had all been cut down. Amongst them was Boatswain Barclay. Toby ran forward, looked down in horror at the bluff features which had repeatedly proved so faithful a friend and ally. Then he seized the axe and with a single stroke severed the heavy rope, at the same moment as the kedge cable began to be taken up from below decks, where a special squad had waited on the capstan since the action had begun. Instantly *Saratoga* began to swing, and he could see the other three ships doing the same. He looked up, gazed at the astonished British seamen, only a hundred yards away now, their faces reflecting the knowledge that they had been outwitted. They had reloaded their guns at great speed, and the command to fire was even then being given. The guns exploded, but the *Saratoga* was already moving out of the line of fire. A few seconds later she had completed her first turn.

'Fire!' McDonough yelled.

The port battery exploded, enveloping the *Confiance* in a hail of shot, striking down one of her masts, sending men and guns flying in every direction. At such point blank range even the twenty-four-pounders could destroy.

Once again the bugle call rang out, and now the springs were brought into action to swing the American ships back to their original positions. The British port broadsides were again empty, and while the gunners toiled feverishly to reload, the Americans could again use their starboard guns without risk of reply. Once again the culverins raked the frigate. Another mast went by the board, and Toby could see that the entire quarterdeck of the Britisher had been swept clean, even the wheel had been shot away, while the dead lay heaped on the deck. A glance over his shoulder told him the other three ships had suffered hardly less.

'Reload!' McDonough shouted. 'We have them now.'

But even as he spoke, a white flag was being waved from the shattered bows of the big ship. The Battle of Lake Champlain was over.

Chapter 11

*Lake Champlain, Washington, Long Island and Boston
1814–15*

An English seaman sat amidst the blood and wreckage which strewed the deck of HMS *Confiance*, his head in his hands. Toby, picking his way amidst the bodies, stopped beside him. 'Are you hurt?' he asked.

The man raised his head, stared at him with eyes that clearly did not see him for what he was. 'I was at Trafalgar,' he said. 'It were nothing like this. It were child's play, compared to this.'

Toby stepped past him and went aft, gazed at the ruin of the quarterdeck. Captain Downie was there, shot to pieces by flying metal, and beside him, the tall thin body of Jonathan Crown, his features twisted in their invariable angry expression, even in death.

I killed him, Toby thought. I killed him just as surely as if I had run him through with my sword.

'A complete victory, Toby,' McDonough said. He was elated by the success of the stratagem. 'One of the most complete in all history.' For the galleys had also gained a victory; the entire British squadron had been destroyed. 'Now, if only Macomb can hold Plattsburg . . . '

But the sound of firing from ashore was already dying down. When they landed several hours later, after having supervised the grim business of assembling the dead and seeing which of the ships could be salvaged, they found a bemused but equally elated Macomb.

'They were all but through us,' he said. 'One of the red-coated columns was, anyway. Then the bugles sounded and they withdrew. It was a miracle.'

'You mean Prevost saw what had happened to his fleet,' Toby observed.

'By God,' Macomb said. 'Well, gentlemen ... we have saved the United States from invasion.'

'Aye,' McDonough said. 'We have saved the United States, you mean.'

The aftermath of a battle is always far more terrible than the event itself. Especially in a naval encounter, when the dead cannot be escaped, and where the ruination caused by the flying shot is everywhere in evidence. The casualties in so brief a conflict were staggering. No fewer than three hundred British sailors and officers had been killed or wounded, and some two hundred Americans; Toby could well believe the opinion of the Trafalgar veteran that this was the hottest fight he had ever been in. The dead were laid out and buried ashore, amongst them poor old Barclay.

'He was a good shipmate,' McDonough said, remembering their days together on the *Constellation* in the West Indies. 'But they were all good shipmates at the end.'

Several of the English vessels had to be burned, they were so badly damaged. For the others, they had not the men to crew them, but secured them on moorings in the bay. News of the victory had then to be sent to Washington. 'And you shall carry it, Toby,' McDonough decided.

'You should go yourself.'

'I must remain with my command. You shall bear the news, and my despatches, to Congress itself. And Toby, mind you take proper credit, wherever it is due.'

He took twelve men, and travelled light. Once they regained the Hudson, they cut down a tree, as they had become so adept at doing and fashioned a dug-out canoe after the India style. With this, and the current, they soon made Schenectady, where the church bells were rung, and a proper boat was supplied to them. Only a week later they were in New York, and Toby made his first report to the military commanders there. He had no time to visit Long Island, but sent a message, informing Felicity not only of the battle and its outcome, but of her brother's death, while

250

reassuring her as to his own good health, and then set off for the overland journey to Philadelphia, whence, as in 1776, Congress had assembled following the burning of the capital.

He had last ridden through here two years before, on his way to join *Constitution*, an unknown volunteer with a disgraced past. Now, the moment his mission was known, he found himself the hero of the hour. He was taken to see James Munroe, the new Secretary of War, who insisted that he read the despatches himself to the joint session of Congress, where he was received with acclamation. Then there was an audience with President Madison himself, and a gracious meeting with the famous Dolly, before, at last, an interview with Benjamin Crowninshield, who had recently replaced William Smith as Secretary of the Navy.

'Well, Lieutenant McGann,' Crowninshield said, surveying from his own somewhat limited height the giant before him. 'You'd best sit down, and tell me all about it.'

'With respect, sir,' Toby siad, 'I am but Acting Lieutenant McGann. I hold no commission, merely a brevet rank granted me by Lieutenant McDonough to facilitate our purpose.'

Crowninshield nodded. 'I am aware of that, Mr McGann. There is a thick file in that cabinet behind you, listing all your various achievements, and misdemeanours. But even an acting lieutenant may sit down.'

Toby lowered himself into the chair before the desk, his heart pounding. There was no hostility here. At Crowninshield's insistence, he related both the circumstances and the events of the battle over again, but now he had to be far more detailed than before Congress, for Crowninshield interjected a succession of questions which revealed him to be at once a seaman himself and the possessor of an acute brain.

'A singular tactic,' the Minister observed when Toby had finished.

'An obvious one, sir.'

'Think you so? Not to everyone. I am sure you can recall the famous Battle of Aboukir Bay, better known as the Nile, sixteen years ago, when Admiral Lord Nelson and the British fleet gained probably their most complete victory over the French. On that occasion, the French chose to fight at anchor, as did Mr McDonough and yourself, but passively so, enabling the British to engage them piecemeal and as

251

they chose, pounding them to pieces with their heavier shot and their skill at reloading more quickly than the French. Admiral Brueys and his people chose just to sit and take it, until they were destroyed.

'But suppose some imaginative French lieutenant had suggested the use of kedges and springs, to swing the French ships and prevent the British encircling manoeuvre, do you reckon Nelson could have gained such a triumph? You and Mr McDonough proved at Lake Champlain that you are seamen as well as warriors. And any navy, to be successful, needs men who are both. I am bound to say, Mr McGann, that it seems to have been your fortune to have been associated with the three most important naval events of this war, so far. The victories of *Constitution* over *Guerrière* and *Java* first made our people believe that an American could beat a Britisher. And now . . .

'I am not belittling Commodore Perry's great victory on Lake Erie, believe me. It was a superb feat of arms. But yet it produced no decisive results for our cause. But this skirmish on Lake Champlain, as it seems plain that it forces Sir John Prevost to abandon whatever plans he may have had to invade New England, may well turned out to be *the* decisive event of the entire conflict. You are aware that we have a team of commissioners at this very moment meeting with the British, seeking to terminate this senseless struggle?'

'No, sir, I was not aware of that.'

'At Ghent, in Belgium. We have of course given out the news of your victory along the whole seaboard, and have every hope that it will be reported in Europe in the very near future: ships do escape the blockade, and even if none of ours make it to sea, it will certainly be relayed by the British themselves. Such a failure on Prevost's part may well have a very benign influence upon British thinking, as our agents over there have informed us that they were hoping to use the cutting away of the New England states as a lever to bring us to our knees, and to the conference table as suppliants. Now they will have to think again. Thus you are doubly to be congratulated.'

'You should be aware, Mr Crowninshield,' Toby protested, 'that Lieutenant McDonough was also present at the events you mention, and in a much more responsible position than I.'

'Agreed.' Crowninshield nodded. 'You are both fortunate, and as poor Bonaparte was wont to say, a lucky general is better than a skilful one, any day. No doubt he presumed he was both, down to this year. And I have no doubt you are both. Mr McGann, may I take it that you are now old enough, and experienced enough, and ... ' he smiled, 'married enough, to be capable of avoiding the temptation to disobey orders in the future?'

'Yes, sir,' Toby said. 'I would say you may presume that.'

'Then we must see what can be done. This navy needs men of experience and courage and initiative ... and good fortune. Return to your Long Island home, Mr McGann. You deserve a furlough. Oh, do not worry. Lieutenant McDonough, who is of this moment Captain McDonough, will also receive a furlough at the earliest opportunity. You will both be reassigned: we cannot bury two such men away in the wilds of Lake Champlain where there is no need for it. You are confirmed in your rank as second lieutenant, Mr McGann.' He stood up and held out his hand. 'And will very shortly, I promise you, be promoted to a position more in keeping with your experience and talents and service.' Another smile. 'And fortune. For the time being, enjoy yourself.'

Enjoy myself, Toby thought, as he made his way north. But could it all be unalloyed joy? He had been promised a restoration to his rank, with even a hint that a captaincy might be in the offing. That was splendid news, but it would inevitably mean that he would be assigned a ship, and have to go to sea again. Even after the conclusion of peace? That would depend on whether he elected to stay with the Navy. And what would Felicity have to say about that?

Nor did he know how she was reacting to the fact that he had to all intents and purposes killed her brother.

More important yet, he did not himself know what he truly wanted. For so long had be dreamed of being reinstated in the Navy, and for so long had those dreams been shattered, time and again, by the determination of the Navy

253

Board not to forgive. The sudden change of heart was more than he could for the moment grasp. Who would manage the farm? But then who had been managing the farm for the past two and a half years?

Why, Father, with the assistance of an extra hired hand, and even of seven-year-old Stephen, who sat a horse like a cavalry general, and gravely dismounted to shake hands with his father. Not so the girls, aged respectively four and nearly three, who came tumbling down the front steps, accompanied by Boru, laughing and screaming, to be taken up into his arms.

Mother waited on the front porch to greet him, her eyes shining; more than just with pleasure at having him home. She, like everyone else, had heard everything about the victory of Lake Champlain, and the enormous possibilities that might arise from it. 'I had always known I possessed one hero in the family,' Elizabeth said through her tears. 'Now it seems that I have two.'

He held her close, but his thoughts were inside, as she understood. 'She waits for you, Toby.'

He released her, entered the house. The living room was deserted, and unchanged. He went down the hall and up the stairs, which creaked as he remembered them always doing. He crossed the landing and walked down the corridor into the wing which was exclusively theirs, and into the master bedroom. Felicity sat by the window in her favourite rocking chair; the room looked over the back of the farm, and she could not have seen his approach. But she had undoubtedly heard it. She rose as he came in, breathing quickly, pink spots in her cheeks, and faced him.

'How splendid you look in that uniform,' she said.

'And how beautiful you look, always,' he replied.

'Have you seen the children?'

He nodded. 'I would have supposed you heard them.'

'I did.' She still gazed at him, waiting.

He drew a long breath. 'I did not see Jonathan until after his death. He sent me a challenge, which I certainly meant to take up, but the matter was resolved while our ships were engaged. I cannot pretend I have any regrets, Felicity.'

She sighed. 'Neither can I, Toby. Neither can I.'

She was in his arms. After more than a year, and more than a year before that, save for those unforgettable two nights in Boston. 'Oh, Toby,' she whispered. 'Is it really over?'

'Well . . . that no man can say. There are peace talks going on, and we have checked their principal scheme . . . but their navy still blockades our coast, and I believe they are planning other invasions. We must wait and see.'

'Then you will have to go to sea again?'

He smiled, and kissed her nose. 'Is that likely? I have not actually been to sea for eighteen months. In fact, almost none of our ships have. I shall have to return to duty, I am sure of that. But not until I have spent a fortnight's furlough here with you. And Felicity . . . my rank has been restored, with promise of promotion soon to come.'

Her head moved back as she looked into his eyes. Then she released him and sat on the bed. 'For the duration of the war?'

He sat beside her, his hands dangling helplessly between his knees. 'That is something I shall have to consider. *We* shall have to consider.'

She turned her head to look at him. 'Do you really mean that?'

He opened his mouth, and then closed it again.

She smiled, then sighed and leaned over to rest her head on his shoulder. 'It is your dream come true,' she said. 'I have been spoiled, having you here beside me for so long. But now . . . I want you to be all the things you should have been already, do all the things you should have done already, earn all the fame you should have earned already, had it not been for me, Toby.'

'Really and truly?'

She sighed. 'No, not really and truly. But you must live your life. I shall always be here when you return home.'

But first, there was a fortnight in which they need do nothing but enjoy each other. They made love, and remembered, and made love, and laughed, rediscovering each other as if they were children. They went fishing, and made love in the bottom of the boat. They rode across to the Atlantic beaches

255

and looked at the British men-of-war hull down on the horizon, and made love on the sand.

'You will have me pregnant,' she warned.

'Would that be so terrible?' he asked.

'I would prefer it did not happen,' she said seriously. 'I have given you three strong and healthy children. If possible, I would prefer to remain strong and healthy myself.' She gave him one of those devastating looks. 'Is that very wrong of me to wish?'

'It is entirely right of you to wish,' Toby said. Besides, he understood what she meant even if she had not put it into words: she had things to do with her own life, especially if he was going back to sea. But what things?

She certainly wanted to talk about the future. 'Now that Jonathan is dead,' she said, 'I am sole heiress to my father's estate. And it is a tidy little fortune waiting over there, Toby. It would be senseless to allow it to rot away in England. I must get over there, as soon as this stupid war is over.'

He had to agree that she was right on every count. The farm provided the McGanns with all they needed in the way of subsistence, and there was usually enough profit to enable them to live in some comfort. But times had changed over the generation since Harry and Elizabeth had settled here, happy just to be able to escape from the hurly burly of the world which had caused them so much unhappiness. Elizabeth, daughter in her time of a wealthy and refined man, had done her best ... but both in the furnishing of the house and the clothes she wore there remained too much evidence of the homespun – acceptable certainly when Long Island had still been something of a frontier. But that no longer was true. Felicity brooded deeply every time she visited New York, where even during the war there was every evidence of a growing prosperity. She dreamed of the things she remembered from her own girlhood, both in England and the West Indies, wished for a harpsichord and a sewing machine, frills and furbelows for her gowns, new bonnets, store-made shoes for herself and the children, and an equipage which did not look like a farm cart because it had to double in that capacity.

There was also the question of the children's education. She dreamed of sending Stephen to an English public school,

256

one of those very private establishments which made a habit of turning out the world's leaders. And of course of marrying the girls into the best colonial families.

All of which, to be implemented, required money – and there was not enough of that to be had. If the farm was as productive as ever, because of the war there was less of a market for surplus than usual. And if he was going to resume his career in the Navy, then additional help would be required as Father grew older, and as Stephen became preoccupied with other things, which Toby naturally hoped would also include a naval career. A 'tidy fortune' would come in very handy at this time, and he was not such a fool as to have any doubts about using his wife's money for the family good.

'But you will not sail until the war ends,' he warned her. 'Not all the money in the world is worth risking you, my dearest girl.'

She pretended to pout. 'I do believe you do not wish it ever to end, Toby McGann. At least, not until you have gained even more glory from it.'

She was actually more than half right. He wanted to get to sea, one more time he told himself, and holding his proper rank. Just one more time. He was overjoyed when an official letter arrived from Crowninshield, informing him that he had been promoted first lieutenant, and far more important, that he had been given a command, the schooner *Eagle*, lying in Boston. Only a schooner, and mounting no more than six guns. But his very first command. He threw his hat in the air for joy.

Felicity was less pleased. 'I had hoped you would be here for Christmas,' she said. It was only a month away.

But she could see how happy he was, and kept her grumbling to a minimum. He left immediately, taking one of the farm horses to travel up the coast more quickly; he knew he could stable the horse in Boston, which he regarded almost as a second home, he had spent so much time there. And there was *Consititution*, still languishing in port.

Stewart was delighted to see him. 'I have been hearing so much about you, Toby,' he said. 'I but wish you could have been hearing something about me. Decatur now ... you'll know he got out with *President*?'

'No,' Toby said. 'What news of him?'

Stewart shrugged. 'Not a word. But you can be sure that wherever Stephen goes there the British will be confounded. We ... well, we must just wait our opportunity to follow his example. What do you think of *Eagle*?'

Toby would not confess his disappointment. The schooner lay close to the *Constitution*, about one quarter of the frigate's size. This did not depress him, but the condition of his ship did. She had been allowed to deteriorate sadly during her months of idleness, her previous captain having been taken ill some time before and the ship left in the care of an extremely slovenly young lieutenant named Mowat.

'Well, Mr Mowat,' Toby said, having carried out a careful inspection of both vessel and men, his heart sinking with every step, 'we are going to have to get to work. I will immediately arrange for the ship to be slipped. Meanwhile, as of this moment all liberty is cancelled, all men will remain on board, and all hands will fall to. I want those decks holystoned, that brightwork polished. I want the guns run out and in until they are moving freely. I want the capstan as well as the gun carriages greased. I want the canvas spread out for inspection. I want this ship ready to put to sea just as rapidly as it can be accomplished. I do not propose to remain in port beyond the end of December.

'With respect, sir,' Mowat protested, it is impossible to leave the port by sea. The British ... '

'Are there for us to fight, Mr Mowat, not to look at, or to be afraid of. Now get your people to work.'

How he wished he had Barclay at his side to lick the crew into shape. It was necessary to do so himself, but as captain that earned him a reputation as a martinet, whereas someone from the lower deck would have been able to lead rather than drive. He did his best, himself stripping to the waist to tear out some rotten timbers found in the hull forward, but was aware that his men regarded him as something of a freak, especially as word of his chequered past had leaked out. But none of them dared cross him; apart from his rank he towered over them and was capable of lifting weights it

258

took two ordinary men to attempt. They grumbled, but so had the backwoodsmen on Lake Champlain. And they worked, as had the backwoodsmen. If he could turn them into as willing fighting seamen he would not have been wasting his time.

As the snow began to fall he remembered more and more the previous winter in the wilderness above the Hudson, the difficulties with which they had been faced then - and the triumphant manner in which they had all been overcome. He wondered where Tom McDonough was now, and if he was thinking the same thought. And was then recalled to his present situation when on a misty December night, the *Constitution* quietly dropped her moorings and silently slipped through the islands. There could be no cheering at her departure, as that would have alerted the British, and Toby waited anxiously on deck until dawn. He heard some gunfire in the distance, but hardly more than a single exchange, and then nothing. It was not possible that *Consititution* could have been taken or sunk in a single broadside. So at least two American ships were at sea, and they were the two very best.

How he longed to join them! But he suffered disappointment after disappointment, the biggest being the discovery, early in the New Year, that the schooner's foremast had also been attacked by rot and would have to be replaced. This necessitated not only undoing much of the work already completed, but waiting on a new mast to be fashioned. January drifted into February, and the *Eagle* was still not yet ready to put to sea when the bells began to ring.

Peace had actually been signed at Ghent back in December, but it had taken some two months for the news to cross the Atlantic in the winter gales. Two months in which a great deal had happened. For the Americans, there was the resounding triumph at New Orleans, where the British southern invasion force had been brought to a summary halt by a militia army commanded by General Andrew Jackson, who at the loss of seven men killed had shot down several hundred of the redcoats and driven them from the field.

But for the Navy there was the doleful news that, again after the offical signing of peace but unknown to all concerned, USS *President* had found herself in the midst of a British squadron and been forced to strike her colours. This had happened almost as soon as she had left port, and before she had been able to accomplish anything of note. So during the weeks she had been thought to be disrupting British shipping, her people had been prisoners of war. How that must have galled Decatur, Toby thought. *Constitution*, on the other hand, had covered herself with glory, as usual, and following the escape from Boston had finished the already-over war by sinking two British sloops.

The Americans were jubilant, feeling that Jackson's victory had more than atoned for their earlier defeats and disappointments, even if the peace treaty settled nothing, merely restored the *status quo ante bellum*. Only the more thoughtful paused to consider that they had been hanging on by the skins of their teeth, and that the British had not had the time to develop fully the immense power they possessed. But all were agreed that the decisive battle of the entire conflict had been that of Lake Champlain, and that it had been the news that once again an attempted invasion of New England had ended in disaster which had made the British anxious for peace. Tom McDonough, and all his men, were the toasts of the country.

The blockading squadron was promptly withdrawn from outside Boston, but Toby was now required to await orders from Washington as to his future duties. He could not imagine what they might be, with no English ships to attack, and felt a considerable degree of frustration that two months' hard work should have suddenly counted for so little.

To aggravate his mood, a week later a letter arrived from Felicity. 'Dearest heart,' she wrote. 'You know how much I long to hold you in my arms, and indeed, to have you home. But I am informed that, despite the ending of the war, there is little chance of this happening for some months yet, and so I have sought and obtained a passage to Europe. Do not fret, I shall be travelling on an American vessel, the *Dolphin* out of Baltimore, and to a neutral port, although one which is allied to England, Lisbon. From thence there is a regular weekly packet to Southampton.

'I should be there in a month, complete my business

in another, and be back at Long Island long before the summer. Bringing with me, I hope, a fortune which will enable us to embark upon the second half of our lives with even more joy and happiness than we have known these past ten years.

'Elizabeth is more than happy to look after the children for me, and she joins me in hoping that you may be able to pay them a visit some time in my absence. In any event, until I return, I beg of you to keep yourself safe and well. Your loving wife, Felicity McGann.'

Toby sat for some minutes gazing at the letter. He had anticipated no such sudden decision, had supposed the matter of her journey would be discussed at length, and that he might be able to obtain leave to accompany her – certainly he would have found her a travelling companion. The thought of her going on her own ... His immediate reaction was one of annoyance, even anger. Then he reflected that she had always been very much her own woman, by sheer force of circumstances, and that he had allowed himself to forget how she might well also have found life on the farm somewhat restricting. But obviously she had planned this step back in November, as he recalled their conversation. Again he grew angry.

And yet, she was absolutely right in her prognostications of the future. For in the same post there was a letter from Crowninshield, reminding him that for all the ending of the war there was still a need for a United States Navy, and a navy at sea, and exhorting him to advise Washington of the very moment *Eagle* would be ready for sea. Well, she was ready for sea now, and Toby wrote back to say so. But clearly there was no possibility of his return home for several months, by which time Felicity would have completed her self-appointed mission.

The new mast had been installed and tested, and now it was merely a matter of awaiting orders. But instead of a letter from Crowninshield, there arrived, to Toby's great joy, Stephen Decatur himself.

'I am to inspect your vessel,' he said. Which he did, with great care and thoroughness. Toby had to wait until they were alone in the cabin to give vent to his feelings.

261

'Stephen,' he said, clasping his friend's hands. 'It is so very good to see you. I had supposed you were still languishing in some prison hulk on the Thames.'

Decatur smiled. 'It was a brief visit I paid to London, I am happy to say, as peace had already been signed.' His expression grew sombre. 'All those good men, killed for no reason. But you, Toby ... you have as usual covered yourself with glory.'

'I suspect I was fortunate in those I served under.'

'Ha! Then you will probably wish to pick and choose in the future. What would you say to serving under me?'

'You, Stephen? Why, nothing would give me greater pleasure.' Yet he could not help but look around him. 'Would you believe that I have never taken this ship to sea?'

Decatur laughed. 'Oh, I do not intend to ask you to give up your first command, Toby. You see before you the latest commodore of the United States Navy.'

Toby seized his hand to shake it. 'My most hearty congratulations. And I am to be part of your squadron?'

'Indeed. Save that I am to command ten ships. Squadron? Why, I would describe that as a fleet.'

'I agree with you. A United States fleet. But ... who are we going to fight?'

'Aha! A very old acquaintance of yours. But Toby, what of that magnificent wife and those splendid children you possess? Will they let you tear yourself away?'

'Of course. I am to resume my naval career, such as it is. Felicity is quite agreeable to that. Actually, she is herself at sea, and in Europe within another week, I should say. She has taken passage to Lisbon, and thence to London, to settle her late father's affairs. So you see, as the children are in the good hands of my mother, I have little to keep me here for a while.'

Decatur was looking grave. 'Felicity has gone to Lisbon, you say? When? On what ship?'

'The *Dolphin*, out of Baltimore. I do not know her myself, but her home port seems sound enough. She left not two weeks ago. Why? Is it important?'

'I hope not, old friend. By God, I hope not. This war we are to undertake, I hinted that it might stir your memory. We are bound for the Mediterranean.'

262

'Not the Tripolitanians again?'

'Amongst others. But they are the least. You'll understand that during the war with Britain it was necessary to withdraw all our ships from the Mediterranean. Thus the deys came to the conclusion that our sun had set and began preying on our ships once more. The worst of the lot is the most powerful of them all, the Dey of Algiers. And I leave you to guess who is standing at his elbow and urging him on, and indeed, it is said, commands his fleet.'

'Mohammed ben Idris,' Toby muttered.

Decatur nodded. 'The same. Well, we naturally have made our representations for redress. And this scoundrel has had the temerity to expel our consul in Algiers with every expression of contempt, and then has declared war on us.'

'Exactly as Tripoli did when he had control there. And so I suppose we are to commence a blockade of Algiers for the next three weary years,' Toby said bitterly. 'Until Idris names some fabulous ransom, which will then be paid to enable us to crawl home with our tails between our legs.'

'Not this time,' Decatur said. 'I am under orders to engage in no negotiations, Toby. Nor will there be any ransom paid. Congress is finally determined to settle this international piracy and terrorism by the only way it can truly be extirpated; our success against the British seems to have given the gentlemen in Washington some backbone. My dealings with the Algerians are to be carried out at the muzzle of a gun.'

Toby stared at him. 'Can that be true?'

'I have my orders, Toby. I am to demand the immediate release of all American hostages, the handing over of the guilty for punishment – and I intend that Mohammend ben Idris shall be amongst them – guarantees that there will be no further attacks on American shipping or citizens . . . or I raze Algiers to the ground.'

'By God!' Toby could hardly believe his ears. 'But what about the French and the British? The French in particular regard the western Mediterranean as their own sea. And the British regard themselves as the arbitrators of all the oceans. Will they stand idly by?'

Decatur's smile was grim 'From various conversations I

263

held with British naval officers, certainly, while I was in England. I have a notion they will be very happy to see that nest of cut-throats disposed of, however much they may protest. They regret that their own Parliament has not seen fit to act against the Barbary pirates before now. Anyway, I intend to carry out my order, no matter who protests. Will you sail with me?'

'Nothing would give me greater pleasure.'

'Then rendezvous with the remainder of my squadron off New York within a fortnight. We must make haste. You must make more haste than any, Toby. The Dey's ships are ranging up and down the coast of Portugal, seeking American shipping on the route from Gibraltar to Europe.'

'You mean Felicity could be in danger?'

'Pray to God that she is not. But the sooner we settle this matter, the better. Were she to be taken by Mohammed ben Idris, well . . . I prefer not to think about it. Haste Toby. We must make haste.'

Chapter 12

The Atlantic, Lisbon and Algiers – 1815

Felicity stood on the afterdeck of the brig *Dolphin*, feeling the wind ruffle her hair, flick the hem of her skirt, looking at the sea and the sky, and the horizon. Captain Carruthers had said they were just five hundred miles off the coast of Portugal; if the wind held they would be in Lisbon in two days.

Five hundred miles off the coast of Portugal! What memories that brought back. If she looked to the south, she could expect to see the two American frigates making a parallel course; to the north, the other ships of the convoy. But the sea was empty today. If she looked at the sky, she could expect to see great black clouds scudding out of the south-west to assail them; but the skies were blue today. And if she closed her eyes, she could hear Mrs Flemming chattering. But she was the only female passenger on board *Dolphin*.

Most of all, if she looked to the south-east, she could see the long, low hull of the Algerian raider coming over the horizon, and wished to scream. Fourteen years, and it all seemed like yesterday. But the south-eastern horizon was also empty.

She wondered if she would ever be able to forget that day, and what had happened afterwards, or treat it as nothing more than a bad dream. That was wishful thinking. One cannot forget four years of one's life. Yet in Toby's arms, or surrounded by the security of the farm, it had nearly been possible. Not here.

But that had been the main reason for undertaking this voyage at all, certainly for leaving before Toby could arrange things like travelling companions and agents to meet her. For nearly ten years now she had been content to be simply his wife, and the mother of his children. After the horrors of her Moorish captivity she had wanted nothing more, and it had been a delightful bonus that he had wanted her to take the lead in their lovemaking, to eradicate the last of her guilt and allow her to indulge her passion. Even two years before, when the strangers had appeared at the farm, her fear had been tempered by security. She was inviolable, because she was Toby McGann's wife.

She had never anticipated that circumstances would ever arise to enable him to resume his career. She loved the farm and her family, but it was as watered-down milk without his presence, just as her security rested on the knowledge that he was there. Yet it was going to happen, and she could not stand in his way. Thus she must find her own way, which inevitably would have to be the farm, without him. Then it would have to be the farm as she wanted it to be, not as she had found it, and accepted it. Her money would be important for that, of course.

But far more important would be the ability, indeed, the necessity, to stand on her own feet, to plan and do things for herself . . . and above all, to cease looking over her shoulder. This voyage was a first step in that direction. It was something she had long known she had to do, retrace her steps without giving way to the terror which lurked at the bottom of her mind. Of course, if she had been truly courageous, she would have taken passage to Gibraltar. It was something she almost had in mind to do. But just to sail these waters again . . . on her ability to do this without flinching might depend the entire rest of her life.

'You are pensive this morning, Mrs McGann.' John Marquand raised his hat, and she smiled at him. He had proved by a long way the most shy of the other passengers in that he had not even dared engage her in conversation until yesterday. But for that very reason she liked him better than

266

any of the others, each of whom in turn had attempted to indulge in at least a flirtation, despite the gold wedding band on her finger. But he had also proved a fascinating companion, during their conversation yesterday. He was a French creole from New Orleans, and claimed to have stood at Andrew Jackson's side during the now-famous battle which had so discomfited the English. Felicity could believe that: he had the hard, alert look of the man of action, although he also claimed to be nothing more than an honest trader, for whom the ending of the war was an enormous boon.

'I import, you see, dear lady,' he had explained. 'From La Belle France, eh? And that has been difficult enough these last ten years, with the British seizing all French goods they could find. To have them also seizing American ships, that was impossible. But now all the world is at peace, is it not? I may even be able to start making a profit again.'

He had not been very specific as to what he imported, but Felicity supposed it had to be wine or perfume, with perhaps some smuggling on the side, which would account for his reticence. Yet she appreciated his company, even if she felt that he was a man who would always seek to use, rather than share. And if she was sure that he was no different to any of the others, and had his own plans for furthering their relationship, she was almost tempted to indulge him, up to a point, if only as a reward for his patience and good manners.

'I am looking forward to reaching Lisbon,' she explained.

'Ah. You have relatives there? Friends, waiting for you?'

She shook her head. 'I shall only be there a day or two, depending on the sailing of the Southampton packet. I am really bound for England.'

'Ah, the fortunate English. Although I suspect, from your accent, that you are English yourself.'

He certainly would have ascertained that already. But yesterday, the topic had been him. Now it was to be her. He was clearly a man who laid his plans very carefully. She found it rather amusing. 'And you are correct, sir. At least ... I was English born. I am an American citizen, now.'

'Of course. And you say there is no one to meet you in Lisbon? A lady like yourself should hardly be travelling so unaccompanied.'

'I do assure you, sir, that I am perfectly well able to manage.'

'Nevertheless, will you allow me to offer a prayer that the Southampton packet is delayed? I should very much like to show you something of Lisbon and its environs. Cintra, Cascais . . . I know the Portuguese seaboard very well, and it is full of interest and some beauty.'

The approach she had anticipated. Made in the diffident, gentle manner she had expected of him. 'I would consider it blasphemy to pray for such an event, Mr Marquand,' she said. 'But . . . if the packet were not to be immediately available, I might accept your offer. Providing we are not assaulted by Barbary pirates before ever making land.'

She wondered why she had said that, even as she uttered the words. But Marquand merely smiled. 'No chance of that, Mrs McGann. Now that the Royal Navy has no more obligations than to patrol the seas, the corsairs are confined strictly to the Mediterranean. Besides,' his smile widened, 'am I not here to protect you?'

Would Toby approve? But Toby need never know. And in any event, once they had overcome the hurdle of her four years in a Moorish harem, there had been nothing for him to approve, or disapprove, of in her. If he had fallen for her at first sight, as she now accepted, he had fallen for her all over again that day on the beach in the rain. And since he had taken her on board the USS *Enterprise* on that never-to-be-forgotten evening in 1805, she had never looked at another man. Well, she was not doing that now. But she would enjoy a glimpse of Portugal, and she had no doubt she could cope with any advances Mr Marquand might choose to make. She told herself that conducting a mild flirtation with him was actually an essential part of the whole exercise, reminding her that she was a woman in her own right.

And he was at least right about the absence of pirates. The *Dolphin* made the Tagus without delay, and he was at her elbow to point out the Bay of Cascais, and then the palaces of Lisbon, and the monument to the memory of Prince Henry the Navigator, the man whose ambitions had first started the European people on their career of world conquest, as they slowly made their way up the river on the rising tide. She hurried ashore as soon as the ship was moored, seeking the shipping agent for the packet lines, Marquand at her elbow.

'A passage to Southampton,' the clerk said. 'Oh, indeed, nothing could be simpler, Mrs McGann. You have timed your arrival in Lisbon to perfection. The ship entered the harbour this morning, and sails at dawn tomorrow. If you could manage to be on board her by midnight . . . '

'The devil,' Marquand commented. 'The ship enters and leaves again within twenty-four hours?'

The clerk peered at him. 'Have you not heard, sir, that we are again at war?'

'War?' Felicity cried. 'You mean England? But . . . with whom?'

'Why, the French, madam. Who else? Can you not have heard that Bonaparte is loose?'

'My God,' Marquand commented. 'No, we had not heard. We have spent this last month at sea.'

'Well, sir, the monster landed at Cannes in the south of France at the beginning of this month, and promptly marched on Paris. It was supposed he would easily be stopped, as he commanded no more than a handful of men, but the force sent to arrest him, why, sir, madam, they threw their hats in the air and shouted "Long Live the Emperor". It was shocking. And then the common people welcomed him as a returning hero, and the towns were decked out in the tri-colour . . . The French will never learn their lesson.'

'But what of King Louis? And the Allied armies?' Marquand demanded.

'King Louis has fled Paris, I understand. Indeed, Bonaparte may already be sleeping in the Tuileries, as far as I know. The Allied armies, sir, well, they have been dispersed. I believe a new mobilisation has been ordered, but it will take time.'

'So we are launched upon another great war.' Felicity sighed, and paid the fare. 'I really must make haste; my husband will be worried about me in these circumstances.' She faced Marquand and held out her hand. 'I shall have to look at Lisbon some other time, Mr Marquand. But I do

269

appreciate your offer, and I have no doubt that if you ever find yourself in Long Island my husband and I will offer you all the hospitality we command. We may even do business with you.'

'I shall certainly remember that, Mrs McGann. And may well take you up on it. But ... you do not have to be on board the packet until midnight. And it is now but ten in the morning. Can I not at least entertain you this afternoon? And then, dinner?'

She hesitated. But she did have nothing to do with herself all day. Captain Carruthers had said there was no need to take her things ashore, as she could use the *Dolphin* as a hotel, if she chose, until she found herself a passage to England. So really, it was simply a matter of transferring her box from one ship to the next. And the prospect of spending a whole day sitting on the deck of the brig watching the stevedores at work did not appeal at all.

'Why, that would be very kind of you, Mr Marquand,' she said. 'If you are sure you can spare the time.'

'My time is yours.' He held up one finger 'Almost. If you will excuse me for an hour to see to my own arrangements, I will return for you at the ship at eleven o'clock. And *voilà*, I shall be at your disposal.'

She laughed at his sudden change of demeanour, and he was as good as his word, appearing at the reins of a hired trap, with which he took her first of all on a tour of the city, and then for a ride outside it, along to road to Cascais, from whence she could look at the huge Atlantic rollers creaming over the sandbank which guarded the southern side of the estuary. He had obtained a most pleasant picnic lunch, which they enjoyed sitting on the sand in Cascais Bay, after which they lay on their backs and gazed at the sky, and he told her the history of Portugal.

'It is remarkable,' he said, sitting up, 'how much of it has been concentrated within a few square miles of Lisbon. Alas, there is not even time to take you up to Cintra, if you are truly leaving tonight.'

'I must,' she said. 'I have seldom enjoyed a day more, Mr Marquand. I shall never forget it. But if you truly wish to entertain me to dinner, and yet give me time to be on board the packet by midnight, we should return.'

'Of course.' She sat beside him in the trap, cast a last look at the sun setting in the Atlantic amidst a blaze of gold and pink, and they drove back into town. 'I have an idea that you would enjoy sampling some real Portuguese cuisine,' he said, 'rather than eat in one of the fashionable places in the centre of town. They have become too used to catering to Englishmen, eh, and it is all boiled beef and cabbage. You will get enough of that in Southampton. But here . . . ' he guided the pony down a narrow side street. 'Here you will dine like a queen. Providing you like sea food.'

'I adore sea food,' she told him.

The restaurant was unimpressive, small and somewhat dingy and quite empty. 'Do the Portuguese not eat sea food?' she enquired.

'Oh, indeed. And this is one of the most popular eating places in the city,' Marquand assured her. 'But you see, this is the land of the siesta. Everyone sleeps until four, and then works until eight. No one thinks to dine much before ten o'clock, and it is only just after eight now. So . . . we have the place to ourselves.' He winked. 'That means we have first pick of the food.'

And first pick of the service, as well, Felicity thought, for they were attended by mine host as well as three smiling girls, whom she took to be the daughters of the house. They obviously knew Marquand.

'Well,' he explained, 'I eat nowhere else, when I am in Portugal. Now, let me recommend . . . the gambas.'

'Gambas?'

'They are shrimps. But shrimps such as you have never seen. Six inches long, and the sweetest taste in the world.'

She didn't believe him, but the shrimps were, indeed, six inches long. She supposed they were more what the French called langoustine, or baby lobsters - but they definitely tasted like shrimp and were quite delicious. They were followed by lobster, served with a very dry white wine. She had not eaten such a meal before, that she could recall, and felt quite light-headed when it finally ended.

'You will have a glass of cognac?' Marquand invited.

271

'Oh, really, I do think I should be getting back to the ship, Mr Marquand,' she protested.

'After a glass. Cognac helps to settle the digestion.'

And hers was suddenly feeling very odd indeed. Undoubtedly the lobster. Besides, she had seldom enjoyed a day more. He had been the most perfect companion, and the most perfect gentleman, too, never seeking for an instant to take advantage of being alone with her. She could not remember feeling so relaxed, even with Toby.

'Well,' she agreed. 'Perhaps a very small glass.'

'Of course.'

The words were scarcely out of her mouth when the glasses were presented. Marquand raised his. 'To our so fortunate chance meeting, Mrs McGann. I would like to drink to the success of your business affairs in London, and to say that if we do not meet again, I shall count myself the most unfortunate of men.'

'Why, thank you.' But when she tried to smile, she frowned instead, because his face had gone fuzzy. She drank the rest of her cognac, hoping to clear her vision, got to her feet, and felt the room begin to revolve about her. Only dimly was she aware that Marquand was holding her arm to stop her from falling to the floor, then she lost consciousness.

Felicity awoke to a gonging headache, and a good deal of discomfort as well. Principally it was movement, of several different varieties, all, it seemed, in conflict. Her brain moved to and fro inside her head. Her stomach moved up and down, and threatened at any moment to rebel. But in addition, her body was moving to and fro, and the entire world about it also seemed to be moving, bouncing and jolting, banging her head ... She realised she was in a cart, which was moving over an uneven road. She attempted to sit up, discovered that her wrists were bound together, as were her ankles – the reason why they were not hurting was that she had lost all feeling in them.

Yet she could sense that her boots had been taken off. She felt sick. At least partly this was because of the food and the drink and the drug which had obviously been fed her in the cognac, but equally it was at the thought of men tying her up, removing her boots, while she was unconscious. What else might they have done to her? She was so generally uncomfortable it could have been anything - she could pinpoint no individual pain. It was too many years since she had been manhandled, and then she had had the resilience of a girl. Now ... but over the sickness was a great cloud of uncertain horror. She had been kidnapped. For ransom? She had heard that these things did happen, and it had been generally known on board the *Dolphin* that she was an heiress. But that would mean ...

She opened her mouth, and sucked evil-tasting blanket between her teeth as she inhaled. Hastily she spat it out again, gasping and choking; she was not gagged but was covered in the cloth, which was lying across her face.

A man said something, and a moment later the blanket was pulled back. She stared at Marquand. As she had just thought, that would mean Marquand was involved. Marquand! The most perfect gentleman she had ever met. She opened her mouth again.

'If you scream, Mrs McGann,' he said, 'I shall hit you. And then I shall gag you. That will be unpleasant. Lie still. We have a long journey ahead of us.'

She got her breathing under control, and licked her lips, tried to focus. It was still dark, but chill to suggest it was close to dawn, and they were going ... she stared at the sky. Toby had taught her how to read the stars, and she could see the Plough. They were travelling south. But south of Lisbon was the river. Therefore they must have crossed the river while she was unconscious, and were going ... where?

She had to find that out. She had to find so many things out. But above all, she had to keep her wits and her nerve, and not give way to the blind panic which was clawing at her mind. If he wanted a ransom then she must simply agree to pay it. There was no reason for him to hurt her.

'How much do you want?' she asked.

Marquand turned round again. 'Want?'

'How much money?' she snapped, nerves already starting to fray. 'You are doing this for money, are you not?'

'Well, I suppose one does everything for money, Mrs McGann,' he agreed. 'But I am already well paid, thank you.'

'Well paid?' She could not stop her voice from rising. 'For doing what?'

'For returning you to your rightful master,' Marquand told her.

'To . . . oh, my God.' Then she did nearly vomit. This voyage had been intended to put the nightmare of her past behind her forever. She had been going to do that without any aid from Toby, to prove herself that she could do it. And she had been afraid on the sea. But once she had reached Portugal, she had been so sure all her danger was behind her. She wanted to scream and scream and scream. But she slowly, carefully, got both her nerves and her breathing under control again.

'But why?' she asked, her voice trembling.

'Because he is paying me to do so,' Marquand told her. 'As he has paid me to keep a watch on you for these past seven years, and seize my opportunity. He knew it would arise.'

Again stark terror threatened to engulf her mind; everything this man had told her, so convincingly, then had to be a lie. Far from living in New Orleans, and fighting shoulder to shoulder with Andrew Jackson, he had been waiting and watching, in New York. Desperately she fought to regain control of her thoughts. Only by matching him, brain for brain, could she hope to survive.

'You are speaking, I assume, of Mohammed ben Idris,' she said, amazed that she could even speak the name.

'Why, so I am. Do you remember him? Or should I say, can you possibly have forgotten him?'

'I remember him,' Felicity said. 'Just as I had supposed you were a white man with some aspirations to being a gentleman. Can you possibly consider returning me to . . . that?'

'Idris and I have had business dealings for many years,' he told her. 'I am by way of being his American agent, and you would be surprised at the amount of business he conducts with the United States. We trust each other absolutely. As for giving a white woman to a Moor . . . the thought amuses me. It has amused me throughout the voyage, as I have studied you. You are really a most delightful creature, Mrs

274

McGann. And I am sure Idris does not merely mean to return you to his bed, if that is what is bothering you. Not after you ran off with another man, and lived with that man for ten years. I think he will have some far more interesting ideas about what to do with you. So much so that I am going personally to accompany you to Algiers. I am sure he will let me watch.'

She gasped. He spoke in such matter-of-fact tones. Thus she had meant absolutely nothing to him during the two previous days, when he had been so attentive – except, as he had just said, that he had allowed his imagination to roam over the possibilities of mistreatment of her. She had been totally hoodwinked, and would now pay most dreadfully for it. Except ... that he was a man, and had said that his relationship with Idris was a business one.

'Listen to me,' she said. 'I do not know how much Idris is paying you, but I will double it. I am on my way to England to collect an inheritance. You know this. And it is a considerable sum of money, better than ten thousand pounds, I am informed. It will be yours if you will take me back to Lisbon and restore me to the *Dolphin*.' The packet would have sailed by now, of course, but Captain Carruthers would still be there. And perhaps even some of those passengers she had treated with contempt for making advances.

'Do you really suppose I believe that?'

'I will swear it,' she gasped. 'You may take any precautions you wish.'

He smiled. 'Ten thousand pounds. That is indeed a fortune.'

Her heart leapt.

'But no,' he decided. 'It is not sufficient to be worth the risk. As you may now be understanding, Mohammed ben Idris never forgives or forgets an injury. Had he not wanted to hear you scream, he would have had you assassinated long ago. He would certainly hunt me down, wherever I chose to hide, were I to betray his trust.'

'And do you not suppose my husband will hunt you down?' Felicity asked.

Marquand smiled again. 'Your husband.' He filled his tone with contempt. 'The famous Toby McGann. My dear lady, your husband is a nothing. Do you not suppose Idris could have had him murdered as well, at any time, had he wished it?'

'But he never dared,' Felicity spat.

'Dared? He wished him to live, Mrs McGann. He even worried, when McGann went off to war, that he might stop a bullet. Idris knows your husband will come after you, you see. It is what he most desires. I think he means that you shall die together, screaming each other's names, as you watch each other's bodies consumed. He is not a man to cross, Mohammed ben Idris.'

He turned back to watch the road, while Felicity felt as if she had been kicked in the stomach. Most damning of all was the understanding that for all their ten years of happiness, she and Toby had been under the surveillance of Idris's creatures, waiting and watching, biding their time. But the Moors were not as omnipotent as they thought. They had never dared attempt to abduct her from the farm. They had known they would never get away with that. Yet had they waited with the patience of a vengeful spider. And at last she had walked into their web like the most innocent of flies.

There was only one weapon left to her. But surely it was one she knew how to use: Idris himself had taught her. She waited until it was nearly dawn, and by then it was no subterfuge. 'Please,' she said. 'I need to relieve myself.'

Marquand looked back at her, appeared to consider, then nodded. 'Stop the cart, Pedro,' he said. 'We don't want the lady soiling herself.'

He jumped down from the seat, came round the back, flicked the blanket off her, and released her ankles. Then he seized her feet and dragged her towards him.

'Let me go.' She tried to sit up, and fell over again, while now blood was starting to flow back down her legs to the accompaniment of most painful pins and needles. 'Wretch!' Her gown had ridden up to her knees. But now she was at the back of the cart, and her legs fell down. He caught her under the armpits to lift her to the ground. Her knees gave way and she would have fallen, had he not caught her again, allowing himself to grasp one of her breasts. She was furiously angry, even if this had been a part of her plan.

'Stamp your feet,' he suggested. 'It will restore your circulation.'

She obeyed, panting because she was in real agony now. But after a few seconds that pain wore off and she could stand, her feet now aching from the pounding they had received on the uneven ground.

'There.' He released her.

'Did you enjoy that?' she asked as venomously as she could. He must not suspect what she had in mind.

'Very much.' He held her arm. 'If we go over there you will not be overlooked by the driver.' He pointed to some bushes, just visible as the dawn light began to spread across the landscape.

'Untie my hands,' she said.

He shook his head. 'No, no, Mrs McGann. You might run off.'

'Then how ... ?'

'I will assist you.'

She caught her breath at the effrontery of the man. But there was nothing for it ... and perhaps he was digging his own trap. She allowed him to gather her skirts as she squatted, staring at him.

'You are a remarkably beautiful woman,' he commented.

Felicity stood up again; her skirts fell into place. 'Whom you are proposing to have torn apart by Mohammed ben Idris.'

'I agree, it is a pity. But there it is.'

'Would you not like to own such beauty, Mr Marquand? And ten thousand pounds as well? Believe me, I will grant you all of that not to be sent to Algiers. And I have no doubt at all that between us we can escape Mohammed ben Idris's vengeance.'

He came close to her, and touched her breasts again, stroking them through the material of her gown. Then his hands slid round her back to hold her buttocks, and bring her against him. He stooped, his body sliding down hers, partly to bury his face in her breasts, partly to raise her skirts again. His fingers stroked the flesh of her legs, and it required all her willpower not to kick him in the groin. Then

277

he reached her buttocks again, beneath the petticoats now, and she felt sick with shame and disgust. But she kept still.

'I could take you now,' he said 'Idris could never know. You are not a virgin.'

'Do you not suppose I would tell him,' she asked, 'without a bargain between us?'

'Do you think he would believe you?' he replied, his eyes only inches from her own.

'But why should we fight over what we both so desire,' she said softly, 'when we could come to an arrangement suitable to us both.'

'And your husband? The giant?'

Felicity shrugged. 'He is but a man. I am sure he lacks your refinements, Mr Marquand. Indeed, I already have proof of it.'

Still he held her close, his fingers biting into her flesh, and she almost began to think she had won a victory. Then he suddenly released her, and stood away from her. 'You are a bitch,' he said. 'And you take me for a fool. You'll keep your mouth shut, from now on, Mrs McGann, or I'll stuff a gag in there. Now get back to the cart.'

Felicity wanted to weep, less with fear than with sheer angry frustration. She had failed. And the failure had entailed such self-humiliation. And such betrayal of Toby, even if the betrayal had been entirely false. And now ... Marquand lifted her back into the cart, and bound her ankles back together, and they set off again, travelling all day as they had travelled all night; her two captors seemed tireless. As it was daylight, the blanket was again thrown right across her, and she lay beneath it and sweated, while the bumping and grinding of the cart continued to bring her intense discomfort.

Worse followed when it appeared they neared other people, for the cart was then stopped, and Marquand climbed into the back to gag her. She wanted to promise him that she would not cry out, but she could not bring herself to speak to him, so instead glared at him with all the anger she could summon; he merely grinned at her, subjected her breasts and buttocks to another brief massage, and covered her up again.

Then she became truly uncomfortable, as even breathing was difficult because of the foul-tasting cloth which filled her mouth. She thought she was certain to choke, and was almost tempted to allow herself to do so. And then reminded herself, fiercely, that she must survive, as she had done fifteen years before. Had she succumbed then, she would never have had her ten years of happiness with Toby. If she succumbed now, she would never have all the other years of happiness with Toby. Because they were there, and she would reach them, or die fighting to do so. She must never give up.

Yet just keeping her breathing even was an immense and exhausting task, and when they stopped, just after noon, in a lonely valley, she could not stand at all. Marquand actually showed a hint of concern at this, released both her wrists and ankles, and carried her to the bank of a fast-running stream, where he laid her on the grass. She moaned and writhed as circulation returned, gasped with relief as he removed the gag as well, and hated the tears which rolled down her cheeks.

He gathered water from the stream and poured it over her head. It was cool and refreshing, and when he held a cup of it to her lips, she might have been drinking nectar. Then he gave her bread and cheese to eat, and some rough wine to drink, which she accepted very readily; she was going to need all of her strength, she knew, and she was intensely hungry after fasting for eighteen hours.

'Tonight we will reach our destination,' he said, squatting opposite her and staring at her.

She pushed hair from her face. She had no intention of speaking with him again. And when, as she knew he was going to, he came closer to lift her skirt, she kicked at him with all of her strength. But as before, her actions were futile. He caught her foot and twisted it, so that she rolled on to her face. Then he dragged her down the bank and into the water while she had to use her hands to stop her face from bumping on the pebbles and being torn to ribbons. She gasped and spluttered as the stream suddenly deepened and her head went beneath the surface, while he laughed, and still holding her foot, twisted her to and fro in the water, before clawing wet hair from her eyes, once again furiously angry and utterly humiliated.

'Now, Mrs McGann,' he said. 'I give you a choice. You may strip and ride the rest of the day naked, while your clothes dry, or you may lie in those wet things.'

She kept her mouth tight closed.

'Very well,' he said. 'I will make the decision for you. I think I will ... ' he pretended to consider ... 'strip you. I would not have you catching cold.'

'No,' she snapped before she could stop herself, and scrambled to her feet. 'I will ride as I am.'

'It will be uncomfortable.'

'I will ride as I am,' she spat at him.

He shrugged, and took her back to the cart, and tied her up again, lingering even longer over the task this time, as her clothes clung to her. She knew he was having a very difficult time resisting the temptation to rape her, his mind flickering between the thought that as she was not a virgin he could not be forestalling Idris, and yet too afraid that his master might consider anything as an infringement of his prerogatives. His master! She shuddered. Her master, too. She was being returned, a runaway. When she remembered the fate of runaway slaves in the West Indies, her heart nearly stopped beating.

Being wet through was actually something of a relief in the beginning, but as her clothes dried they became stiff and uncomfortable, and she could do nothing to straighten them. She was exhausted, and actually slept from time to time, but always awoke with a start to the realisation of the terrible fate which hung over her.

Yet she knew that it was her will which would matter in the end. Idris of course coüld cut off her head, or impale her, and then she would die. But if he really sought only to torment her, and wait for Toby to attempt to rescue her, then she could survive. Simply by gritting her teeth, whatever the pain and the humiliation to which she was going to be exposed, and closing her mind to everything but her rescue. She had done that before. And succeeded.

Despair always followed resolution. Before, she had been a girl, with the eternal optimism of youth. And besides, her rescue: how would Toby manage that? Oh, he would attempt it, she knew. But it would require him once again to throw up the career he wanted so badly. He would do that, too, she knew. He would recruit his own force, and come after her. And rescue her, or die in the attempt. But the one was at least as likely as the other.

She wept and nearly choked, and gasped with relief when the gag was removed with the blanket, and she discovered that it was again dusk, and that they were at the sea shore, in a secluded cove. But at sea there was a flashing light.

'As I said,' Marquand remarked, standing beside her on the sand while he released her feet and wrists, all danger of her escaping now being past, 'the British cruisers have made life uncomfortable over the past few months. But now they are distracted by the French, once again. And we have sea captains who can outwit even the British. This man you have met already. His name is Mansur.'

Mansur! He had been almost a friend. But that had been fourteen years ago. Now she stared at the grim visage as she was ferried out to the corsair in the boat, and then assisted aboard.

'Mansur,' she said. 'Do you not remember me?'

He gazed at her. He was older and more grizzled than she recalled, but he did remember her, that was obvious. 'I gave you advice once, white woman,' he said. 'Which you have not heeded. Now your death will be a long time coming. Take her below.'

'Mansur,' she gasped, prepared to try anything. 'I am sorely in need of a bath ... '

'Take her below,' he said again. 'And confine her there. I do not wish to look upon her face.'

Perhaps it was the same ship. Certainly it appeared as the same black hole in which she had been confined fourteen years before. But with the difference that she was no longer an object of value, to be pampered so as not to have her beauty tarnished. Yet she was fed twice a day. And she was not ill treated in any way. She was not even stripped, as on the previous occasion. Her destruction was to be the privilege of Mohammed ben Idris.

They spent four days at sea, as near she could judge, as she never saw daylight. More than once she heard the oars being used, to row the corsair away, she presumed, from the vicinity of a British frigate. But the British had the French to think about, as Marquand had reminded her, and there would be no visible evidence that Algeria had committed any crime. They would need to board her to discover that, and there was no reason for them to do so: Algiers was not at war with Great Britain.

On the fifth morning there were familiar shouts and commands, and she could feel the ship losing speed. Then there were sounds, and even smells, she recognised, the clatter of mooring warps being thrown, and the thuds of the ship being drawn alongside the dock. Then the clumping of feet above her. What should happen next? The eunuchs should come down to fetch her. She listened to feet outside the door, and braced herself. How their lips would curl at the sight of her soiled clothing and dishevelled hair.

The door opened, and she gazed at a lantern, held by Mohammed ben Idris.

She knew it was him before she even saw his face. Instinctively she rose to her haunches, and then her feet, and pressed her back against the bulkhead. Only then did he raise the lantern high enough to illuminate his own face.

'It is good to have you back, Felicity,' he said, 'after so many years.'

His tone was almost friendly. And yet she knew that the torment was already beginning. She gasped for breath, and licked her lips, which had suddenly become as dry as dust.

'Have you nothing to say to me?' Idris enquired. 'After so long a separation?'

At last, saliva. 'I . . . ' But she did have nothing so say.

'Do you not wish to beg for mercy?'

Almost she was tempted. But that would be to compound her misery and her humiliation. She had expended that line, with every hope of success, with Marquand. There was no hope of success with Idris. She met his gaze. 'I have nothing to beg for, Idris. It is you should beg my pardon for this crime.'

He raised his eyebrows.

'I was betrothed to Mr McGann long before you kidnapped me,' she said. Because surely, if Toby had truly fallen in love with her at first sight, then that was not a lie. 'Thus it is you who committed a crime, even then. And have compounded it now. You have taken another man's wife, Mohammed ben Idris. Allah will not look kindly on you for this.'

So now flog me, she thought, as he continued to stare at her for several seconds.

Then he said, still quietly, 'Allah looks kindly on those men who serve his cause to his best advantage. You were a virgin when I took you, thus you are mine, above all other men. You have betrayed my bed and my honour. For that you will suffer anything and everything that this brain of mine can imagine, before I take your life. Do not expect any mercy from me.'

'Mercy?' she asked. 'Does one expect mercy from a scorpion?'

Perhaps she hoped to make him lose his temper and kill her there and then. But she should have known better. He merely snapped her fingers to summon the men who waited behind him. 'Strip her.'

Felicity's head jerked. But it was necessary to remain in control of herself, and her fate, for as long as she possibly could. 'I can undress myself, Mohammed,' she said. 'If that is what you wish.'

He smiled at her. 'I wish you stripped.'

There were four men. She considered resistance, but decided against it. She would lose her dignity, and she might well be hurt. And she had no chance of success. Two of the men took an arm each, holding it behind her. The other two simply tore the clothes from her body. When opposed by gathers or straps they cut the material free with their knives, while they raised her legs to tear her sorely tattered stocking from her feet. She could not stop herself from panting with outrage and suppressed effort, and Mohammed ben Idris continued to smile at her.

But at last they were finished, and stood back.

'By Allah, but you are more lovely now than when I knew

you as a girl,' Mohammed said. 'I had supposed you might be old and fat. And you are a mother, I am told.'

'I am three times a mother' she said. 'My husband is a *man*.'

'We shall see,' he remarked. 'We shall see. Well, let us go ashore.'

'I have no haik,' she said.

His teeth gleamed at her. 'No, Felicity, you have no haik. What, are you afraid of the sun on your flesh?'

For a moment the full import of his words did not sink in. Only when the men had secured her wrists behind her back and were placing a noose around her neck, attached to a length of rope, did she realise that he meant to lead her naked through the streets of Algiers like the most miserable malefactor. But she was the most miserable malefactor, in his eyes.

He was continuing to gaze at her, awaiting a protest, or a plea for mercy. For a woman to be so exposed was the very worst fate that could overtake her in a Muslim country. Well, was it not one of the worst fates that could overtake her in a Christian country, as well? But she was not going to beg him, no matter what he did to her. She returned his gaze.

'Bring her,' he said, and went on deck.

One of the men went in front of her, the other three walked immediately behind her; it was clearly no part of Idris's plan to risk having her fall, or throw herself down, and attempt to strangle her there and then. She climbed the ladder and emerged into the waist of the ship, and hot sunshine. She had felt hot sunshine on her naked back before; but then she had been in Toby's arms.

She was surrounded by men grinning at her. Amongst them were Mansur and Marquand. She turned away from them, looked instead at the faces she did not know, and which were therefore meaningless to her. But then it was necessary to go ashore. Now the temptation to leap from the gangplank and either drown or throttle herself was enormous. But again she knew she would not succeed. The men were very close, and they would haul her back long before she could die. While the crowd would laugh.

Because there was a crowd, and it was laughing anyway. The women and children were worst. How she wished she had never learned Arabic. They called her names and then jeered at her when her bare toes scuffed stones and she stumbled. One or two even threw clods of earth, but these were chased away by Mohammed ben Idris's guards. She was still reserved. As long as she could remain reserved, she could survive.

She climbed that well-remembered hill, amidst the dogs and the donkeys, and the people. When last she had made this climb people had averted their eyes. Now they stopped to watch, and laugh, and jeer. Amongst them were men and women with pale complexions and blue eyes. I am one of you, she wanted to shout. Will you not help me? But no one could help her now. Only Toby. Once again, after fourteen years, she was back to that simple prayer, that simple belief.

She passed the doorway to Abd er Rahman's house, and expected to see him standing there. He was not, but in the crowd of women and children outside the door and looking down from the roof she assumed were his wives. They would remember her, and would be jeering as loudly as anyone.

On her first visit to Algiers she had not climbed higher than this, and she had worn sandals. Now the heated stones over which she stumbled seemed to be burning holes in her feet. She panted, and would have fallen from sheer exhaustion, but was jerked back to her feet by the men at her elbow. The sun seemed to be boiling her scalp, and her hair, trailing down her back, was sticking to her shoulders with sweat. But it was necessary to climb another hundred feet or more before they emerged into the open area before the gateway to a palace set only just below the citadel itself. Here at last there was blessed shade, and a bowing majordomo whom she recognised.

Painfully she licked her lips. 'Ibrahim,' she said. 'Do you mean he has not thrown you to the dogs yet?'

Ibrahim looked at his master, who gave a brief bark of laughter. 'She defies us to the end, Ibrahim. Well, if she did not, would there be any sport in it? Prepare her for me.'

So he did mean to take her after all. A spark of hope surged into her brain, and was fanned by the iced drink which was now offered her by a serving girl. Behind the girl there were eunuchs, waiting, She knew what they wanted, and heaved a sigh of relief. For an hour at least she would be cool, and even comfortable.

She was taken to the bathing chamber, shaved and shampooed. She desperately need a bath after her four days of confinement, and as she had anticipated, the cool of the water was heavenly. She could have lain there forever. The only sinister aspect of her situation was the presence of Ibrahim. A whole man would never have been allowed to be present had she been about to return to the harem. So, her respite was only a temporary one.

But Idris still wanted her. That was what really mattered, at the moment.

While her nails were painted, one of the girls gave her food to eat, dates and sweetmeats and honey. She had not realised how hungry she was, and was almost beginning to feel relaxed when Ibrahim snapped an order, and her wrists were bound behind her back again. Wellbeing fled in anticipated horror as she was led from the bathing chamber and up a flight of stairs, along another corridor, and then into Idris's bedchamber.

He stood by the window, looking out, but turned as she came in. 'Now you are more as I remember you,' he remarked.

'My lord is too kind,' she answered. 'Especially as I had not breakfasted.'

'You are a woman of great courage, Felicity,' he said. 'But I always knew this. I will be interested to discover how far your courage takes you. But first . . . '

He came towards her, loosing his robe as he did so. He wore nothing underneath, and had clearly been anticipating this moment.

'Can you wish me with my hands bound behind my back?' she asked.

'Oh, yes,' he said. 'That is how I want you, Felicity. Besides, being bound will remove any temptation you might have to scratch my face.'

He seized her by the shoulders and threw her across the bed. She had not supposed it could be possible to be raped by a man who had bedded her so often before. But rape is in the mind, not the deed. He savaged her, possessing every orifice she owned, hurting her even as he drove his own passion to its limits. The pain and the horror drove tears from her eyes, but she kept her mouth tight shut, except when he actually forced it open. She was not going to cry out, and she was not going to surrender to her temptations to the extent of biting him, which could only mean her immediate death. I will survive, she told herself. I will survive.

But at last even he was sated, and lay beside her panting, equally exhausted. Her wrists ached from having to take the weight of her body whenever she had been rolled on her back, and from sawing against each other as even she had not been able to prevent that instinctive movement. But at least her blood was still circulating. And he had not yet conquered her.

He sat up, pulled on his robe, went to the door. 'Attend to her,' he snapped.

The eunuchs hurried in, plucked her from the bed, applied powder where it was necessary to hide a bruise, combed and brushed her tangled hair into a smooth sheen, smothered her in perfume.

While Idris watched. Then he said, 'Enough. Bring her.'

He walked in front of her, and she followed, surrounded and urged on by the eunuchs. She dared not try to anticipate what might be going to happen to her now, because it was most likely, as he had avenged himself upon her body, that it was to summary execution. Then all her determination would have been in vain. But she would not have surrendered to him, and she would not have begged him for mercy. He would not have that satisfaction.

They climbed several flights of stairs, until she thought he was going to take her on to the roof, but he stopped on the floor beneath. This was a large and airy room, stretching the full width of the palace, with huge windows at each end. No doubt the inner windows looked out over the internal gardens. But the outer ... She caught her breath as she was marched to it, for it looked down over the square above the city, and there was a considerable crowd gathered down there. Was she to be thrown to them, like Jezebel, to be devoured by dogs?

Mohammed ben Idris smiled, and stroked his beard. He seemed able to read her thoughts. 'That would be too quick, my Felicity,' he said. 'No, no, first we must let them all look at you, and desire you.'

He snapped his fingers, and she discovered that the room was actually full of men, six of them bearing a wooden frame, shaped like an X. She was led across the room and made to lie on this frame, her wrists at last being freed, but immediately her arms and legs were extended and secured by wrist and ankle, so that she was, in fact, crucified, except that it was not a Christian cross, and therefore, when erected, she would not suffer the discomfort of having her shoulders dislocated: her feet would actually be touching the ground. But, again unlike the Christian cross, it left her as exposed as any woman could be.

While she was being secured, Idris stood above her, and now she realised that Ibrahim and Mansur and Marquand were also in the room, standing against the far wall. She cast them only a hasty glance, finishing with Marquand, and looked away again as she felt herself flush with humiliation. Instead she closed her eyes, but opened them again as she heard another man enter the room.

'Great Idris, is it true then? By Allah, but it is. You have regained her?'

She gazed at Abd er Raham, older and plumper and even more gentle-looking than she remembered him.

'Did you not always know I would?' Idris asked contemptuously.

Abd er Rahman stood above her, looking down at her. 'And now you torture her?'

'Now I intend to execute her, but in my own time. When she has finished amusing me.'

Abd er Rahman licked his lips. 'Would that not be a waste, great one? She is a most remarkably beautiful woman. Far more beautiful than I remember her as a girl. If she is for sale . . . '

'You would buy her?' Idris gave a peal of laughter.

Abd er Rahman looked embarrassed, but not abashed. 'Yes, great one. I would buy her. As you appear to have no further use for her.'

'Then you are a fool,' Idris said. 'Do you not realise this woman is thirty-two years old? She is a hag.'

'That is not so,' Abd er Rahman insisted. 'I have heard that infidel women do not age as do ours. And she has certainly not.'

'She is also three times a mother. By another man.'

'I care nothing for that.'

'She would also betray you, run away from you, without a moment's hesitation, if she is given the chance.'

'I shall not give her the chance,' Abd said.

Idris studied him. 'I do believe you are serious. Truly they say that there is no fool like an old fool. Suppose I asked . . . ten thousand dinars?'

Felicity caught her breath. The average price for a female slave was twenty dinars.

Abd nodded. 'I will return with that amount.' He went to the door, while the room was for a moment silent. Then Idris checked him with a bellow of laughter.

'You *are* a fool, old man,' he said. 'A besotted fool. But I will not rob you of your money, much as you deserve it. The woman is not for sale.'

Felicity discovered she had been holding her breath. Although she had been sure no man would pay a fortune to possess a single woman, to have been sold to Abd er Rahman would have seemed like being taken straight away to heaven. Abd's household had been filled with laughter, and his women had been happy. Now her body sagged in renewed despair.

'But you have no use for her,' Abd was protesting.

'I have a great many uses for her,' Idris told him. 'I mean to expose her, from that window, to all the people of Algiers. And any man who looks upon her, and wishes her, may do so, once he has paid for the privilege. Should I not make a profit out of her? She has cost me enough to regain. But Abd, old friend, you may place your name on the list. There are only two ahead of you: Mansur, my faithful captain, and the gaiour, Marquand, who has served me faithfully.'

Felicity found herself panting. She had anticipated extreme agony. Nothing like this.

'So you can be the third,' Idris said. 'There is only one

condition: I wish to watch.' He smiled. 'Just to prove to myself that you can still do it.'

'You are a monster,' Abd er Rahman said. 'And afterwards?'

'Afterwards? After she has serviced every man in the city? Then, my dear Abd, I am going to have her flayed alive.'

Felicity's brain seemed to grow cold.

'And her skin I will have stuffed and mounted, and placed in my entry hall as an ornament. As you say, she is too beautiful to be forgotten. The rest of her, the carcass, I shall throw to my dogs, still living. And you may come and watch the feed, Abd.'

Abd er Rahman stared at him, while the room began to spin around Felicity; she realised that for the second time in her life she was about to faint.

'You are a devil,' Abd said, correcting his former statement. 'Give me the woman, Idris. I will pay you twenty thousand dinars.'

Mohammed ben Idris stroked his beard.

Chapter 13

The Mediterranean – 1815

What memories these seas brought back. Toby stood by the helm of the *Eagle* and gazed at the sparkling waters of the Atlantic. He had just taken a noon sight, and placed his ship, and therefore the entire squadron strung out to the south-west, some three hundred nautical miles west north-west of Cape St Vincent, beyond which the Portuguese coast receded, via the Algarve, towards Spain. It was ten years since last he had sailed here, but then he had been going the other way. Memory was more inclined to return a full fourteen years, almost to the day, when he had first crossed the Atlantic.

He could remember the day before that never-to-be-forgotten storm as if it were yesterday, the ships of the convoy lying north of *Essex* and *President*, on one of which Felicity had apparently been, gazing at him, and the black clouds scudding up out of the western sky. He wondered what she must have felt as she had sailed over here, not five weeks before. What memories did she still have of that dreadful day which followed?

But no doubt on this occasion the ocean had been for her, as it now was for him, singularly empty. Save that he was part of the strongest squadron the United States had ever sent to sea, eight big frigates and two schooners as scouts. They made a magnificent sight, stretched away behind him; he guarded the port wing. And perhaps Felicity was less fanciful than he; certainly he had no doubt that she possessed stronger nerves. Her reaction to realising that it might have been agents of Mohammed ben Idris scouting the farm had been simply the protective instinct of a mother for her children.

Mohammed ben Idris! How he wished he had done as she asked, and killed him ten years ago. But not even Mohammed ben Idris could have been so fortunate as to assault the one vessel on which Felicity McGann would be travelling. He had told himself this time and again, ever since the news of this latest war with the Barbary pirates had become known to him. To suppose Felicity could have been captured at sea, for the second time in her life, would have been to accept that there was no justice in this world. And once she reached Portugal she would certainly be safe. While Mohammed ben Idris's days were numbered. There was a reassuring thought – he should have been dealt with long before Felicity commenced her return voyage.

Yet how he wished they were bound for Lisbon, instead of Gibraltar. Then he would be able to make sure for himself that she had arrived safely and had found her passage to England without difficulty. But of course she had arrived safely.

They saw no other ships at all until two days later, when they were within sight of the Rock, and overtook an English convoy beating up the Strait. The sight of the ships in convoy surprised Toby, as so far as he knew the Algerians had not been so foolhardy as to declare war on His Britannic Majesty. But as he was well out in front of the squadron, he contented himself with signalling the identity of the huddle of ships to the nearest frigate, for remittance to the flagship, then passed them to be first into the so-well-remembered harbour, dipping his ensign to the battery on the outer breakwater, and informing the harbour master, who was quickly out in his dory, that he sought berths for ten United States' warships on passage into the Mediterranean.

He was immediately piloted to the appropriate place, where several American vessels were already moored. His own ship secure, he swept these other ships with his telescope, and felt an almost painful sensation as he saw the name *Dolphin, Baltimore*, not a hundred yards away. There could hardly be another vessel with both that name and registry.

'Mr Mowat,' he said quietly.

'Aye-aye, sir,' was the ready response. Mowat, like the entire crew, had grown to appreciate his hard-driving captain, because of his consummate seamanship on the ocean crossing; they had encountered two full gales, and lost not a spar.

'There is a call I wish to make,' Toby said. 'Will you break out the captain's gig, if you please.'

'Aye-aye.'

Mowat hurried forward to give the necessary orders, while Toby paced the deck impatiently, looking towards the stranger every few seconds. But he knew his mood was not merely anxiety to have news of Felicity. It was also due to the fact that he was now virtually arrived at their destination, Algiers. He supposed he, and all his men, the entire fleet, indeed, were in a state of some excitement. No matter how the war with Great Britain had truly gone, the United States Navy had come out of it with enormous prestige. No one could doubt that had the struggle continued for a few more years, the British, with their tremendous resources in men and ships and material, would undoubtedly have taken or sunk every American vessel. But yet had the Americans not proved that, given even conditions or better, they were a match for any navy afloat?

But that was only the half of it. A good number of these men had served with Barron and Preble and Rodgers in the Mediterranean ten years ago, and not a man of that squadron but had deeply felt the humiliation of having to negotiate with the thugs who controlled the Barbary States, and pay them ransom for the release of American seamen, rather than treat them as what they were, pirates and murderers who deserved nothing better than the hangman's noose. But now at last, that was going to be put right. Commodore Decatur's orders were known throughout the fleet. There was risk involved, certainly, to those Americans now held captive in Algiers. But President Madison had weighed the balance, and concluded that such a risk had to be accepted, to prevent similar fates overtaking Americans in the future,

293

and to secure that very principle for which they had gone to war with Britain, the freedom of the seas. They were a fleet bent on retribution. That was enough to make the blood of any man tingle.

The jolly boat was ready, and Toby took his place in the stern for the short row across to the *Dolphin*.

'Who is there?' came the call from the brig's anchor watch.

'Lieutenant Tobias McGann, United States Navy.'

There was a brief silence from the brig, and Toby could make out three men in earnest conversation. He frowned, and his heart gave a curious thud. Then one of the men advanced to the open gangway. 'Welcome aboard, Mr McGann.'

'You'll wait,' Toby told the coxswain, and swung himself up the ladder to face the short, bluff man in the blue coat.

'Mr McGann? Carruthers, master of the brig *Dolphin*.'

Toby shook hands. 'You'll pardon this uninvited visit, sir, but I believe you may be able to give me some information I seek.'

Carruthers seemed to gulp. 'News,' he said. 'Oh, indeed, You'll have been some time at sea.'

'Three weeks, Mr Carruthers.'

'Aye,' Carruthers muttered. 'But I am showing no manners, keeping an American officer standing about the deck. You'll come below, Mr McGann, and take a glass of wine.'

He hurried for the companion hatch, and Toby followed, aware that the crew had gathered forward and were staring at him. The thudding of his heart increased. But what could have happened? There was no sign of any damage to the brig. Then an illness? He ducked his head to enter the cabin, where Carruthers was busily pouring two glasses of wine.

'Your very good health, Mr McGann.'

'And yours, Captain.' Toby did no more than brush his lips with the glass; he was out of the habit of taking alcohol at sea.

'Well, sir, sit down, sit down.' Carruthers sat opposite. 'You'll not have heard, then, that England and France are again at war.'

'The devil,' Toby said. 'So soon? What is the cause now?'

'Oh, the same, sir. Bonaparte. He has returned and taken

294

over the country, and is raising armies left and right, meaning to take on the whole world once more.'

'Well, well,' Toby said, relief flooding through his system. If that was the cause of Carruthers's agitation . . . 'That is important news, indeed, Mr Carruthers, which will interest my commodore. But it is advantageous to us, I have no doubt. There will be no officious interference with our plans. I thank you, sir. But what I really seek is news of my wife. She was a passenger with you to Lisbon, was she not?'

'Well, yes, sir, she was.' Carruthers's agitation visibly increased.

Once again Toby was aware of a peculiar breathlessness. 'Whatever you have to say, man, spit it out,' he commanded. 'She is unwell?'

'Now that, sir, I cannot say. We made a good crossing, and were fortunate, it appeared, in that we arrived in Lisbon the day before the Southampton packet was due to sail. Mrs McGann went ashore immediately and booked a passage on the packet, and then returned to the ship. She informed me that she was due to join the packet at midnight that very night. But it appears that she never did, sir.'

'What do you mean?' Toby refused to think for the moment until he knew what had happened.

'Just that, sir. She had left her boxes on board *Dolphin*. Indeed, sir, they are still in that cabin right over there. And as I say, when she returned from the shipping agent she told me she intended to fetch them before boarding the ship. Then she took herself ashore to look at Lisbon. But she never came back for her boxes. I was unaware of this, sir. My ship was securely in port, unloaded and awaiting a cargo, and I was early to bed and sleeping sound, having left instructions with the anchor watch that Mrs McGann was to be assisted in any way she wished. It was not until the next morning that I was informed that she had never returned for her boxes . . . and the packet had then sailed.'

Toby got up, opened the door to the cabin Carruthers had indicated. He did not recognise the boxes; Felicity would have bought them in New York, he presumed, during his absence. He released the straps and raised the lid of the first.

And immediately recognised her clothes, as well as her scent.

'Are you saying my wife went to England without her clothes?'

Carruthers licked his lips. 'Well, sir ... that was a possibility, of course. And one which had to be taken into account.'

'But you have something else to tell me.' He returned to the table and sat down, drank his wine without thinking. He still didn't want to think, right this moment.

Carruthers refilled the glass. 'Well, sir, my cargo was slow in appearing ... it was to be Portuguese wine, you understand, from the Oporto district to the north. It never did arrive, and so you find me here in Gibraltar, seeking freight to carry home, at great expense and inconvenience to my owners and myself. But I considered it my duty to remain in Lisbon until I knew for sure that the wine was not going to be delivered, and thus I was still in port when the packet returned the following week, when I learned for certain that your wife had not been on board.'

'You mean you sat in Lisbon for an entire week and more, knowing something had happened, but doing nothing about it?'

'Well, sir ... ' Carruthers flushed beetroot red. 'There were circumstances ... '

'What circumstances?'

Carruthers hesitated, and then sighed. 'Mrs McGann, when she left *Dolphin* for her tour of the city, did so in the company of a man named Marquand. An American gentleman, sir, and he seemed a very respectable person, too. He has sailed with me before, and always proved a most pleasant shipmate.'

'She went off with this man to look at the city. How long could this have taken?'

'That depends on how far afield they would have gone, sir. But they do seem to have spent the day together. When I attempted to trace them, I discovered that they had been seen together on the beach at Cascais – that is several miles outside the town, and ... '

'On the beach?' Toby snapped.

Carruthers sighed. 'Sitting together, sir, talking. And then I found out that they had dined together at a small restaurant in Lisbon itself. They were well remembered there, because they had come in early and been the only customers at that time. They left the restaurant together, the innkeeper said, to return to *Dolphin* for Mrs McGann's things. But they never did so, as I have said.'

Toby's brows were drawing together as he at last understood what the man was trying to suggest. 'Are you telling me that my wife had a liaison with this man?'

'Sir, I . . . I could not believe it was my duty to interfere.'

'I should break your neck,' Toby growled. But his stomach seemed filled with lead. Felicity and another man? It could not be possible. And yet . . . did he really know her any better now than he had ten years ago? He had thought he did, knowing all the while that her mind was a closed and private world. A mind which he certainly knew had been exposed to every foible of mankind by Mohammed ben Idris.

And equally, he knew that she had been becoming bored with life on the farm and her husband away, and likely to be so often in the future. He felt sick.

'Yes, sir,' Carruthers agreed. 'But then, when it was certain that she had not boarded the packet, I first of all feared that she and Marquand might have been set upon by footpads. But the authorities could find no trace of any such catastrophe. To my great relief, I may say. I then attempted to make some enquiries about Marquand, as to where he lived in Portugal, and so on, and could find no trace of him at all. He took his things from *Dolphin*, that I know, and then he entertained Mrs McGann for a day, that I know . . . and then he just disappeared.' Carruthers gulped. 'Along with your wife.'

Toby's whole being seemed to have become encased in a metal frame, pressing ever closer, calling upon him to leap to his feet and wreck the entire ship, in his anger and despair. But he kept control of himself with an effort.

'This man,' he said. 'This Marquand. You say he has sailed with you before? You must know something about him. He is an American, you say? From where?'

'Why, from New Orleans, I believe, sir. But he has lived in New York for some time, and conducts an agency there.'

'What sort of agency?'

'Well, sir, he acts as a buyer for certain European parties, negotiates sales for them and so on.'

'What European parties?'

Carruthers looked embarrassed. 'Well, sir, his clients are mainly Moorish gentlemen. You understand that with relations between the Barbary States and the United States being somewhat strained, these gentlemen prefer to conduct their business through agencies. As to the ethics of the agents themselves, certainly in time of open warfare between our country and these people, well ... I would have thought it was close to treason. However ... '

'By God,' Toby muttered, a huge white light seeming to explode inside his brain. Of course Idris would have known he had little chance of ever intercepting Felicity at sea. But he had had his creatures, led by this man Marquand, watching her and waiting for her ever to leave the farm.

'What I was going to say, sir,' Carruthers hurried on, 'was that you must understand that when I sailed from Baltimore with Mr Marquand amongst my passengers I was unaware that Algiers had declared war upon us. Therefore I had no reason to refuse Mr Marquand a passage ... ' His voice tailed away as Toby stood up.

'I thank you for your information, Captain Carruthers,' he said. 'I understand that no blame can be attached to you for what has happened. I would like you, if you will, to have those boxes sent on deck and lowered into my gig. I will attend to them. And haste, if you please, captain. I have a deal to do.'

Stephen Decatur drove his fingers through his receding black hair. 'The devil,' he remarked. 'By God, that creatures like Marquand should be accepted as American citizens ... it is a sorry life we lead, to be sure. However, Toby, we must do the best we can.'

'And what will that be?' Toby demanded. His brain still found it difficult to accept that Felicity might have been returned to Idris, with everything that would entail for her.

298

It was too nightmarish a concept for his imagination. But he had to look facts in the face.

'You intend to challenge the Algerians to fight or surrender. Well, with this force you command, they may well surrender. You then have a list, as I understand it, of all American vessels and all their passengers and crew known to have been taken by the pirates. These vessels, or adequate compensation for their loss and their people, you will require to be released on threat of a bombardment. You may well succeed in all of these aims, Stephen. But does any of that assist me? Felicity's name is not on any of those lists, simply because she was not taken from an American vessel on the high seas. Nor can we prove she is in Algiers at all. Carruthers, for one, is quite sure she is having an affair with Marquand and has simply run off, and you may be sure that is the prevailing opinion in Lisbon. But even supposing we could prove it, do you suppose, after having gone to such lengths to get her back, that Idris is likely to admit to possessing her? But even supposing he does, and then offers compensation for her as if she were merely one of the other American captives . . . my God, compensation? For Felicity? I think I am going mad.'

Decatur sighed. 'What would you have us do, Toby? This all happened better than two weeks ago. If Marquand was working for Idris, Felicity will have been returned to Algiers some time ago.'

'If?' Toby asked in a low voice.

Decatur flushed. 'I cast no doubts upon Felicity's honour, Toby, and you should know that. But it is at least a possibility that Marquand abducted her for his own purposes.'

'She is in Algiers,' Toby said. 'I know it.'

'I agree that if we do not accept that, then we really have no idea of where to start looking. But if she is in Algiers, having been returned there two weeks ago . . . '

'She is irrecoverable as my wife,' Toby snarled. 'I have heard all those arguments before, remember?'

'I was going to say,' Decatur's voice was quiet, 'that she very likely is dead by now.'

Toby stared at him.

'I doubt Idris meant to take her back into his harem,' Decatur said gently. 'He will have been after vengeance.'

'If he has killed Felicity,' Toby said, now also speaking quietly, 'if he has harmed a hair of her head, I shall throttle him with these two hands of mine, if I die in the act.' He stood up. 'I will submit my resignation in half an hour.'

'Your what?'

'I wish to be relieved of my command, sir,' Toby said formally.

'Now I know you have lost your senses.'

'Not at all. I know what I have to do is beyond the scope of your orders.'

'And what do you have to do? Raise an army and storm the city?'

'I must certainly get myself into Algiers, one way or another. It should not be difficult. I speak the language.'

'And once there you will rescue Felicity from the clutches of the dragon, and carry her off like some knight of old.'

'I will at least try to do so.'

'And if she *is* dead?'

'As I have said, I shall avenge her.'

'And then die yourself. Toby, Toby . . . Look, in addition to my list of vessels and crews taken by the pirates, I have also been instructed to demand the heads of those guilty for these depredations. I do not have any names, but one of them is most certainly Mohammed ben Idris.'

'Do you really suppose he will be handed over to our justice? Do you not suppose he wields as much power in Algiers as he ever did in Tripoli? You will find that he is mysteriously absent from the city, when you make your demands. No one will know where he has gone, but you may be sure his women and treasures will have gone with him. That is an added reason for me to have reached him before you commence your assault. Stephen, there is nothing you and your squadron can do which will regain Felicity. I know that. There is nothing I can expect you to do. This is a personal matter between Idris and myself.'

'And if I do not accept your resignation?'

'I will desert.'

Decatur scratched his head. 'So you are facing me with a

choice of putting you in irons, here and now . . . or detaching you to carry out a secret mission.'

Toby's heart leapt. He had never supposed his friend would fail him.

'So I had better detach you.' Decatur went on. 'It is, of course, entirely irregular to employ the captain of a ship on such a mission. However, I consider it necessary in this instance. It is essential that I obtain adequate information as to the Algerian defences and dispositions, and you are the only member of this squadron, apart from myself, who has fluency in Arabic. I must therefore ask you to accept this extremely dangerous mission, Lieutenant McGann, in the full knowledge that you may well be risking your life.'

Toby smiled at him. 'I accept, of course, sir.'

'Then I shall enter it in the log. Now, tell me what you will need. How much time, first?'

'I will have to be set ashore some distance from the city, and make my way into it as part of the normal comings and goings out of the desert. This will present no problem; I have walked across a desert before.'

'With six hundred men at your back.'

Toby grinned. 'Sometimes I wished there hadn't been.' Although, he thought, he would give a great deal to have William Eaton at his side on this occasion. 'Besides, that will give my beard time to grow, so that I will look like an Arab.'

'With those eyes? And that height? My God, that height.'

'No one in Algiers has ever seen me before.'

'Idris has.'

'When Idris and I come face to face, Stephen, my mission will have been accomplished.'

Decatur shook his head. 'I cannot allow you to consider this mission entirely in terms of suicide. If Felicity is alive, will that help her? I doubt you have thought it through at all, in fact. Well, listen to me very carefully, because these are orders. First, you will remain with the squadron for the next month, in command of *Eagle*, and taking part in our normal exercises.'

Toby stared at him open-mouthed. 'Month? But . . . '

'After the first week you will cease going ashore, no matter where we happen to be. This will give your beard

301

time to grow properly. Then I will have you set ashore on the African coast, a good distance from Algiers, as you say, and I will allow you one week to enter the city. Now, what are your plans for when you are actually there? How do you propose to gain access to Mohammed ben Idris's house, much less his harem?'

'Well ... I have not formed a plan,' Toby confessed. 'I cannot, until I see what the circumstances are.'

Decatur sighed. 'That is no way to plan a campaign, Toby, if one intends to win it. I can tell you exactly what the circumstances will be. There will be a great many closed doors and barred windows and armed guards, and an entirely hostile people at your back. There is no way that you can hope to enter Idris's house without a considerable diversion. Therefore listen. You will be set ashore on the night of 24 May. You will reach Algiers by the morning of 31 May. There you will remain as inconspicuous as you can . . . ' He gave another sigh. 'You, inconspicuous! But we must hope that there are such things as large Moors from time to time.

'You may reconnoitre the ground, but you will do nothing until 1 June, On the morning of 1 June I will make a preliminary bombardment of the harbour. That is when you will make your move, and gain access to the house. Having given them something to think about, I will issue my demands. Whether these are immediately accepted or not, I intend to enter the harbour the next day and force the surrender of the city. I will also reclaim you, and Felicity, if she is alive. All you have to do, having found her, is to stay alive until the next morning. You have my permission to reveal all of my plans to your captors, if you are taken, to use them, indeed, as a threat, because it will be a threat that will be faithfully implemented. But of course you will use your wits as well as threats to prevent Idris from fleeing the city, together with his women. And together with you, if you are his captive by then.

'I do not pretend that it is a very good plan, but it is the best I can offer you if we are to have the slightest hope of regaining Felicity. As for vengeance, Toby, if she is dead, and you discover this, which should not be difficult, I charge you to remain concealed until I take the city. We will get

302

Idris, never fear. But there can be no point in sacrificing your own life uselessly. Have you anything to add to that?'

'To add? That is a splendid plan. But ... a month? I cannot abandon Felicity for another month. She has already been in Moorish hands for some two weeks. Now you propose another five? My God ... '

'Toby,' Decatur said severely, 'above all else you must use your head, and keep your head, in this affair, and at all times think with absolute clarity, beginning now. If Idris meant to murder Felicity, then she is dead, and you have nothing left to you but vengeance. That, as I say, is timeless. If he did not mean to murder her, then she is still alive, and will remain so, no matter how miserable her condition. But she has been a captive of the Moors before, and survived. I understand that it must make your blood boil, as it does mine, to imagine what those devils may be doing to her. But she *has* survived it before. Thus you must believe that she will do so again. To take any foolish and careless chances could be to lose her forever. I have not chosen a month merely to give your beard time to grow. It is necessary to approach this whole business with finesse as much as force. You may be certain that Idris, and his master Yusuf Ali, are both well aware that a large American squadron has put into this harbour. They will now be poised for battle. And while I have no doubt we will win that battle, it would be at great cost. I intend first of all to lull them into a false sense of security. This squadron will behave exactly as did Barron's, back in 1802.

'We will put to sea, after a leisurely stay here in Gibraltar, during which I will negotiate with the Spanish government for a more suitable base, and we will demonstrate off Algiers, and mount a distant blockade, and fire a few shots from time to time, doing nothing more than that. We will also reconnoitre and, where possible, chart the passages into the port.

'But all of this will have been done before, outside Tripoli, to no result. Therefore Idris will believe that we are no more serious about prosecuting this matter than we were then. Who knows, he may even present us with a ransom demand. But on the first day of June, regardless, I intend to commence the campaign, and complete it, too. By then I have no doubt that the immediate state of preparedness in Algiers will have been ended, and our sudden urgency be the more surprising to them, and therefore terrifying. But Toby, whether or not you regain Felicity, I expect you to be alive when I enter Algiers.'

'I will certainly try to be so,' Toby promised him.

'Then be sure I will have you back, or I will truly lay that town in ruins, and you may tell Idris that, if you feel the need.' He stood up and held out his hand. 'When the time comes, hand over the command of *Eagle*, temporarily, to Mowat.'

Toby squeezed the offered fingers. 'Stephen, you are the truest friend a man could wish. And if there is any censure in this affair . . . '

Decatur grinned. 'Oh, there will be, Toby. There will be. But censure will be nothing when I have taken Algiers. You see, *I* am not taking any chances. There is no way that Congress can find out what I am about and send to relieve me of my command before the end of May.'

Toby nodded. It was obvious that it simply did not occur to his friend that he could possibly fail to take Algiers, if he put his mind to it – even if Algiers was much larger, and more strongly defended, than Tripoli. But Decatur probably possessed more resolution, added to courage, added, most importantly, to canny thoughtfulness, than even Edward Preble.

Therefore he must possess at least a share of all those qualities, and reveal them, too. 'I will see you in Algiers at the beginning of June,' he promised, saluted, and left the cabin.

Mowat was almost reduced to tears when he learned that his captain was being detached for special duties. 'But what shall I do, sir?' he asked.

'You will do exactly what I would have done, had I been here,' Toby said. 'And you will handle the ship as if I were standing at your shoulder.'

But he felt like tears himself. All of his life he had had one overwhelming ambition, that of captaining a ship of the United States Navy into battle. And now once again he was passing up that opportunity. Simply because it was not meant to be. Simply because he was a man in love with the most splendid woman who had ever lived, and who was now fighting for her life. Or already dead. But neither could affect his resolution now, and his determination to settle with Idris.

He obeyed Decatur and prepared carefully for his expedition. He was actually less concerned about his complexion than his friend. After his years of exposure to the wind and the sun his skin was hardly lighter than that of many of the Berber tribesmen who inhabited the African coastal areas. He could do nothing about his eyes, but there were even Berbers with blue eyes, throwbacks to the nameless ancestors of their race. His size was the most difficult problem, but the Algerians knew nothing of him, and he had to believe that there were occasionally outsize Arabs. He would dress as an Arab, and carry only an Arab weapon, a large, curved dagger. He intended to use his wits before his strength; when the time came to use his strength, he had no doubt he would be able to secure something more suitable.

For a week he, like everyone else, enjoyed the limited fleshpots of Gibraltar, allowing himself to be seen and known to be there, with apparently not a care in the world; undoubtedly Idris would have spies in the British seaport. That he had already stopped shaving was not at first noticeable, and then put down as American slovenliness, at least by the British.

True to Decatur's strategy, the squadron then put to sea and demonstrated off the Algerian coast, approaching within sight of the city, and even seizing two Algerians incautious enough to venture out. Then the squadron, leaving two vessels on guard, sailed away to their new base in Majorca, Spain remaining neutral in the resumed war between France and almost all the rest of Europe, and therefore most suitable for a visiting, and also neutral – as regards Europe – squadron, which soon lay securely at anchor in the vast Bay of Palma. But here Toby never went ashore, as his beard was now sprouting well, and his men were sworn to strict secrecy.

It was at times almost unbearable to sit in his cabin or pace the deck of the schooner, wondering what was happen-

305

ing to Felicity, wondering if they had not been entirely wrong, and where she might have been alive a week ago, Idris would have grown weary of her and cut off her head by now; dreaming of her, wondering why this fate had hung over them for so long, remembering all the gloriously happy days they had spent together on Long Island and promising himself that those days would come again – and all but going mad. Because he wondered, too, about the children. He had given Carruthers a letter to take home to his mother and father, and they would know by now what had happened. How miserable they must be, three thousand miles away from any chance at rescue.

He counted the minutes and the hours, welcomed every sunset and every sunrise, remained on deck all day wearing only drawers to burn his skin even browner. And the days did pass. From Majorca patrols were regularly conducted to Algiers, and on returning from one of these patrols, the *Eagle* at last put into a deserted cove some fifty miles east of the city.

Here, at the dead of night, Toby and Mowat shook hands, the crew whispered their 'God-speeds', and Toby was rowed ashore, wearing his disguise. The beach was backed by low cliffs. He waded through the surf, his haik held about his knees and his sandals in his hand, and made his way inland. By the time he had reached the top of the cliffs both boat and schooner had disappeared.

He had decided that his best course was to pass himself off as a pilgrim, and had equipped himself with a stout staff to back up his dagger, and another stick from the end of which he suspended the bag with his immediate food supplies. These were sufficient for no more than forty-eight hours, but long before that had elapsed he had reached the coastal road, and fallen in with a caravan on its way from Tunis to Algiers. Here he was welcomed by the camel master.

'From Cairo?' that worthy remarked, eyeing Toby's bulk. 'That is a long journey, friend.'

'I am a journeyer,' Toby told him. 'My life is composed of journeyings.'

'To what end?'

306

'How may a man know the end of his journeying until he reaches it?' Toby enquired gravely.

The camel master considered this, and decided it was unanswerable riddle. But he was prepared to obey the law of the desert, especially when Toby offered him some of the dinars taken from the two captured corsairs, and welcomed the big man into his caravan and gave him food and water to drink, inviting him to accompany them on their way. He had gained a foothold, Toby told himself, and more important, he had been accepted by these people as one of themselves. He considered that an important victory.

The camel master was a garrulous, friendly man, who confided that he operated regularly between Tunis and Algiers, and had in fact been in the latter city only two months before. It occurred to Toby that he would hardly discover a better source of information. 'Then tell me, friend,' he asked as they plodded their way along the coast road. 'How goes the war?'

'You wish to fight for the Dey?' the Arab observed. 'This is the true reason for your journeying to Algiers.' He glanced at Toby's bulk, as he regularly did, clearly unable to believe it was but one man in there. 'Anyone can see you are a warrior.'

'I seek a star to follow,' Toby confessed.

'Yusuf Ali?' The camel master was surprised.

'He is an old man, I have heard,' Toby agreed, 'and in many ways a feeble one. Yet his deeds are legendary. And now, to fight against the Americans . . . '

'The Americans, pouf!' the camel master declared. 'They are not fighting men; they do nothing more than demonstrate. As for Yusuf Ali, he has never left the safety of his palace to my knowledge. His strength is the strength of others.'

'I have heard this also,' Toby agreed. 'Men like Mohammed ben Idris?'

Another quick glance. 'You know of this man?'

'I have never met him,' Toby lied, 'but I have heard of his deeds. I know that he has fought for many of our leaders, and never been defeated. Did he not once defeat these very Americans?'

'Perhaps,' the camel master observed, somewhat sceptically. Perhaps he had heard of the battle outside Tripoli.

'Would he not welcome a strong right arm?' Toby asked.

'He has many strong right arms. But one such as yours . . . he would welcome it.'

'Then tell me of him.'

'I do not know him, pilgrim,' the camel master said. 'He has no time for such as I. But I do know that he is a mighty warrior, and no man to be opposed. I have heard that he well rewards those who fight for him, and that his justice is swift and sure to those who have done him harm.'

'That is as a warrior should be,' Toby said piously. 'Tell me of the woman.'

'The woman?' The camel master frowned.

Toby's heart gave a lurch. 'Even I have heard of the woman,' he insisted. 'The American woman, seized by Idris. Far away in Cairo, they speak of the woman and what Idris did to her.'

'The American,' the camel master said. 'Well, as to that, no one knows what he has done with her. I was in Algiers the day he brought her ashore. Naked she was, and her beauty was wondrous to behold. No man can ever have beheld skin so white, breasts so high, and belly so flat . . . and it is said that she is no longer a girl. Naked he dragged her up the hill to his palace, while the populace shouted his name and death to the Americans.'

'Naked?' Toby asked. 'He made her walk the streets of Algiers naked?'

'It was a sight to behold,' the camel master said again, clearly savouring the memory.

'I wish I had been there,' Toby said, wondering why he did not strangle the man there and then.

'You would have seen the greatness of Mohammed ben Idris,' the camel master said.

'But you do not know if she was then executed?'

'That no man can say. She was taken into Idris's palace, hard by the citadel, and never seen again. There was rumour that he intended to expose her again . . . ' The camel master sighed. 'And then to prostitute her to any man who could command his price.' He smiled. 'I was tempted. To lie upon such a woman would have been a memorable experience.'

'And did you?' Toby asked grimly.

The camel master shook his head. 'It was only a rumour. I have told you, she was never seen again. Some people said he had her flayed alive and her skin stuffed while her carcass was fed to the dogs in his yard. Others say he merely had her tied up in a sack and thrown into the sea. No one knows for sure.'

'What of the man who brought her to Idris?' Toby asked.

The camel master frowned. His new friend seemed to know a lot about the business and to be asking a great number of questions. 'The American man?'

'Yes.'

'He has been rewarded, and now sits upon Mohammed's right hand. It is said he fears to return to America, because of the vengeance of the white woman's husband. It is said this husband is a monster of a man, who kills men with his bare hands.'

'Can there be such a creature?' Toby asked, hunching his shoulders and trying to appear smaller than he was.

'I do not believe these things myself,' the camel master confessed.

'Neither do I,' Toby told him. 'I put my faith in men who are proven leaders. I will offer a prayer to Allah that this Mohammed ben Idris looks kindly upon me, and permits me to enter his service. He sounds like the man I have travelled so far to meet.'

Felicity was still alive. Toby felt sure of it. If Idris had meant to kill her, he would certainly have had her executed in the most public manner, after exposing her as he had. Therefore he was keeping her alive for some devilish purpose of his own, or simply because he had been unable to resist possessing again that beauty which had so powerfully affected the camel master. But whatever the reason, whatever she was suffering, she would survive, as she had done in the past, as Decatur had reminded him. Felicity was alive, and he was on his way to her.

Three days later they sighted the walls of Algiers. Exactly on schedule, because it was the morning of 31 May, 1815.

309

He had twenty-four hours to reconnoitre the city before Decatur made his move. Twenty-four hours in which he also had to keep out of harm's way, but he did not anticipate any difficulty in doing that. Although, looking at the matter from Decatur's point of view, he was somewhat concerned. He had only ever seen Algiers from a distance, and from sea level, before. Now he realised at once how much larger, and therefore presumably stronger, it was than Tripoli. Nor were there any signs of its being under siege – again like Tripoli.

From the hilltop which the caravan had to mount before descending to the gate, he could look out over the Mediterranean, and there were undoubtedly ships out there, perhaps three, he thought, squinting into the glare at the far-off patches of white canvas. Presumably they were American vessels, apparently being as ineffective as they had been outside Tripoli. He had absolute faith in Decatur's courage and determination and ability, had no doubt the rest of the squadron was poised just over the horizon, waiting for the twenty-four hours to elapse before they went into action, yet he could not escape a sinking feeling as he gazed at the several jetties creating a twisted entrance to the inner harbour, every one commanded by a battery of guns, at the strength of the walls, and at the numerous armed men, obviously soldiers although they wore no uniforms, who manned them. Everything of course depended on their will to fight. And that will depended on their commander, who, from all accounts, was scarcely the ageing Dey, Yusuf Ali, but his most prominent corsair, Mohammed ben Idris.

The caravan descended the hill side, and reached the gate. Here there were more soldiers, inspecting them carefully as they entered; Mohammed ben Idris had clearly not forgotten he had lost Tripoli to a land assault, and was taking steps to make sure that the Americans attempted no surprise attacks from that quarter.

'Who's this?' the sergeant of the guard demanded as Toby came up.

'He is a pilgrim,' the camel master explained; he stood with the soldiers to tell them what was inside each camel pack. 'He seeks to enlist in the army of the Dey to fight the Americans.'

'He should be worth a regiment,' the sergeant marked. 'I will myself escort him to the barracks.'

'I will find my own way to the barracks,' Toby told him. 'Am I not permitted to spend a last evening of freedom? I have heard that Algiers is a city where every pleasure known to man may be obtained.'

'That is true enough,' the sergeant agreed. 'If a man has money.'

'I have money,' Toby said.

'He has dinars by the dozen,' the camel master agreed.

'Then enter, friend, and enjoy your evening. Tomorrow we will set about making a man of you.'

Toby went through the gate, and found himself in the huddle of small streets which composed the kasbah. He was surrounded by narrow doorways and overhanging balconies, strange odours and loud noises, from the cries of men and women and the wails of babies, to the chatter of parrots and the barking of dogs. It was difficult to be sure just where he was, but he knew the harbour had to be downhill, and made his way there to gain his bearings.

'I seek the palace of Mohammed ben Idris, friend,' he said to a passerby. 'Can you direct me?'

'Up the hill,' the man replied, which was not particularly helpful.

Toby slowly climbed the main street, and halfway up found himself outside a most imposing house. 'Would this be the palace of Mohammed ben Idris?' he asked another passerby.

'This is the house of the Sheikh Abd er Rahman,' the man told him. 'The palace of the great lord Mohammed ben Idris lies up the hill, hard by the citadel.'

'I thank you, friend,' Toby said, and continued his climb, at the top remaining in the shadows of the houses of the kasbah, while he surveyed his goal. It looked formidable enough, with no windows overlooking the square until the fourth storey was reached, and access only through huge iron-barred wooden doors, outside which there lounged three very well-armed men. The castle itself, a hundred yards farther up and bristling with cannon, scarcely looked better defended.

Not for the first time Toby realised what a debt he owed to Decatur's cool judgment; there was no way he would ever get into that keep, undetected, without a mammoth diversion. It remained to be seen what the defenders would do when American shot started falling about them.

He went back down the hill, as it was by now late afternoon, and found a coffee shop where he was able to sit down and have something to eat and drink. 'I seek a lodging for the night,' he told the innkeeper.

'In Algiers? There are no lodgings to be had in Algiers, save you sleep in the street. We are at war, friend. Had you not heard this?'

'At war?' Toby laughed. 'Where are your enemies, then?'

The innkeeper smiled. 'It is true, they are difficult to see, because they keep their distance. They lie over the horizon, and pretend to interfere with our shipping. They are American ships of war.'

'Americans?' Toby asked. 'Who are these Americans? But wait . . . ' he frowned. 'There were people of some such name fighting against Tripoli some years ago.'

'These are the same,' the man told him. 'They are infidels from far across the sea who have the effrontery to sail past our harbours. The Tripolitanians defeated them, as they will be defeated if they attempt to attack us here. But the general of our lord the Dey, Mohammed ben Idris, takes no chances, and has commanded the outlying farmers to come into the city with all their produce, that we may be fully stocked and garrisoned in case these infidels come at us across the land.'

'But you said they were on ships, at sea,' Toby argued.

'Indeed they are, friend. But their ships cannot harm us. There is no ship in the world can enter this harbour without being blown to pieces. Our defences are too strong. No, no, only an army can hope to oppose us. Not that we fear an army, either.'

'All of this I have heard,' Toby said, wondering if it could be true. In which case he was indeed on a suicide mission. 'I have myself come to enlist.'

'But that is good news,' the innkeeper cried. 'They will make a man of you in that army. And if that is true, why . . . I might offer you a bed in my own quarters for tonight.' He eyed Toby's bulk. 'I should enjoy making a man of you myself.'

Toby got the message: he was well aware that most Moors were fairly ambivalent in their views on sex.

'I will thank Allah for your generosity, friend,' he said. 'But I have sworn an oath that I shall share my couch with no one, man or woman, until I have fulfilled a certain duty.'

'Then I shall pray to Allah that you are rapidly successful in the performance of this duty,' the innkeeper said. 'And I will not turn so honest a man out into the street. There is a stable at the back with clean, dry straw, where you may be reasonably comfortable. I offer you this, in the expectation that our friendship will outlast your oath.'

Toby bowed, hands pressed together. 'I assure you, friend, that if Algiers stands when I once again am free of obligation, our friendship will prosper mightily.'

So, Stephen, he thought, you now have to rescue me twice. But the stable was indeed dry and clean, and he slept soundly, awakening at the first cockcrow, feeling the adrenalin flooding his system. This was to be the day of days.

But there was time yet; Decatur would scarcely get moving before the beginning of the morning, if only to give him the time to position himself close to Idris's palace. There was time to eat first, and he was very hungry.

He went back into the inn, where there were several men already eating and drinking coffee, all stopping to stare at him, and then checked, as he realised that his friend the innkeeper was deep in argument with half a dozen heavily armed men standing in the doorway. Instinctively he knew they were seeking him. But how, and why?

If he immediately suspected the innkeeper, he realised he was almost certainly wrong as the men came into the building, pushing the alarmed man in front of them.

'I have no enemies of the state here,' he protested. 'In my establishment? Now Lord Mansur . . .'

The man he so addressed, a tall, lean, dark-visaged fellow with a savage expression, stared at Toby. 'Your establishment is a den of spies and infidels,' he growled and pointed. 'That is the man we seek.'

The innkeeper turned. 'Him? Why, Lord Mansur, that is a

313

pilgrim, a goodly fellow who seeks enlistment in the army of the Dey.'

Toby sized up the situation. The other seven men in the room were placing themselves against the walls in the hopes of staying out of harm's way. But he had no doubt that each of them was armed, and that all of them would support the soldiers if it came to a fight. Equally he knew he could not oppose even his muscles, and a single dagger, to the swords of six soldiers. And, as he had discovered last night before retiring, the stable at the back was a dead end. His only hope of survival lay in the flat roofs of the kasbah.

In a quick movement he stooped, picked up the nearest bench, and hurled it at the advancing soldiers. They gave shouts of alarm as they leapt backwards, in the same movements drawing their swords. But Toby was already dashing up the stone steps at the rear of the coffee house, throwing aside a man who attempted to block his way, and emerging on to the first floor into the midst of a crowd of half-dressed women and children.

He ignored them and took the next two flights of stairs, steep and narrow, past more women and children, and some men, all half-awake, half-dressed, and regarding him with total consternation, before emerging on to the roof, in the midst of a sea of washing flapping in the gentle breeze. For a moment he lost his sense of direction, stumbled, and nearly fell into the narrow crevice separating the next roof. He recovered himself, stepped across – it was only a distance of three feet – fumbled his way through more washing, and faced another six men, who must have entered from the street. Idris had surrounded the entire area.

He turned away from them, and saw the first half dozen reaching the roof he had just left.

He drew his dagger, and the twelve men slowly advancing hissed their anticipation of imminent danger. But Toby threw the dagger to the floor. 'I am your prisoner,' he said.

Mansur smiled, his teeth gleaming through his beard. 'My master will be pleased, infidel dog,' he said. 'He has long awaited the pleasure of your company.'

314

Chapter 14

The Mediterranean and Elsewhere – 1815–20

Mohammed ben Idris stroked his beard as he gazed at Toby McGann. Toby's arms were bound behind him, and he was surrounded by six guards, each with drawn sword. The Moors were taking no chances with such a giant. On the other hand, apart from binding him they had offered him no violence, as yet. They seemed too surprised to have captured him so easily.

'By Allah,' Idris remarked, 'but you are even bigger than I remember. Truly, watching you die will be the greatest sport a man could imagine.' He came closer and pulled Toby's beard. 'By Allah,' he said again. 'You have planned this venture –' his teeth flashed as he smiled – 'all to no avail.'

'Is the camel master to be rewarded, great lord?' asked the dark-visaged captain named Mansur, who remained at Toby's side, sword in hand.

'Bah,' Idris said. 'He did not truly bring us information. He merely bragged about town about the blue-eyed giant who had joined his caravan. It was I realised who it must be. He deserves nothing.'

'I see you are as honest as ever in your dealings with your people,' Toby remarked. He refused to despair, even if he had been catastrophically over-confident in not realising that a man who would talk so freely to him would talk equally freely to everyone. But he had at least gained access to Idris's palace, even if several hours early, and as a prisoner. And surely Decatur would soon be on the move. He had only to keep alive, and locate Felicity, for them both to be safe – and he felt sure that Idris did not intend to kill him out of hand.

'So tell me,' he went on, 'where is my wife, Oh abductor of women?'

Idris gave another flashing smile. 'Would you like to be reunited with her?'

'I have come here for that purpose and to demand her release.'

Idris nodded. 'The effrontery of your people never ceases to amaze me. But as you have come so far without an army at your back, and as I have anticipated your coming, even supported by an army, you shall certainly be reunited with her. I have waited for this moment for a very long time.' Another stroke of his beard. 'And when you are together, together you will scream so loud, that your ships out there on the horizon will hear you.'

Toby made no reply. The more he talked and threatened, the more was Idris digging his own grave.

'Now tell me,' Idris said. 'Have you breakfasted?'

'No,' Toby said.

'Ah. That is not good. I would have you sustain your strength. Very well. My own chef will prepare a meal for you. And for your wife. But now, let us go and find her, eh? Mansur ... ' He turned to the captain of the guards. 'You will send a messenger to awaken Lord Abd er Rahman, for assuredly he will still be sleeping at this hour. Your messenger will inform the good Abd that I am on my way to call on him, bringing with me Toby McGann.' He gave a bellow of laughter. 'Poor old Abd, he will be unhappy about that. He is such a fool. He does not understand humanity. Come, Mr McGann, let us take a walk.'

Toby's brain went round in circles. Nothing was as he had anticipated. 'My wife is with a man named Abd er Rahman? he asked.

'A rich fool,' Idris told him. 'Far too rich for his own good. Mansur here used to command a ship for him. But he gave his allegiance to me, when I settled here. That was a wise thing to do. Do you not think so, Mansur?'

'Truly, great lord,' Mansur agreed.

They were on the street now and walking down the hill,

while the crowd which had gathered round Toby when he had been led from the coffee house to Idris's palace, grew even larger as it followed.

'Would you not estimate that Abd become enamoured of Felicity Crown when you first brought her to him?' Idris asked.

'You brought her to this place?' Toby asked.

'I captured the ship on which she sailed, fourteen years ago,' Mansur acknowledged. 'She was the only worthwhile thing on the vessel. I brought her to Algiers, to my then master, Abd er Rahman, and he looked upon her, and desired her, and would have kept her in his harem, but that he was forbidden to do so by his head wife.'

'Ha ha!' Idris continued. 'A man ruled by his wife. Only a fool is ruled by his wife, Toby McGann. As only a fool would ever value a woman so high as to risk his life for her. You are as big a fool as Abd er Rahman. But we have arrived.'

Toby gazed at the house where he had paused the previous afternoon. Of course, the palace of Abd er Rahman. And Felicity was in there, almost certainly not as closely confined as he had anticipated. If only he had known that, he could have regained her and left the city by now.

The door was opened by a bowing eunuch, and they were taken inside to a luxuriously furnished reception chamber.

'Do you know,' Idris said reminiscently, 'this is the very room where I laid eyes upon Felicity for the first time, and wanted her. Ah, if a man could see the future, and know the trouble she would bring me, would I not have allowed Abd to place her on the common block? But then, it has all turned out satisfactorily, has it not?'

Mansur made Toby stand against the wall, still surrounded by armed men, while Idris waited in the centre of the room. 'I do not understand you, Idris,' he said. 'You claim to desire Felicity and yet you have sold her to this man?'

Idris smiled. 'Oh, indeed. I would have had her flayed alive and stuffed, and placed by the door to my bedchamber, but he wanted her. Even after she had belonged to me, and then you, and been a mother, he wanted her. I am a businessman. I sold her to him for twenty thousand dinars.'

'Twenty thousand dinars?' Toby could not believe his ears.

'I have told you, he is a fool. More than a fool, for he was so anxious to lay his hands upon her, he agreed to a certain condition in the sale, a condition which he did not believe could ever arise. Ha ha! He agreed that should you ever come to Algiers, seeking your wife, he would return her to me, on repayment of half the purchase price. As I say, he did not believe that could ever be possible, for it is the province of fools that they never believe any other men can be as foolish as themselves. So now, you see, I have you and I will have Felicity, and I have ten thousand dinars. Abd, my old friend,' he said, as the stout little old man hurried into the room, 'a pleasant surprise. I would have you meet Lieutenant McGann of the United States Navy.'

Abd er Rahman stopped and stared at Toby. 'I do not believe you.'

'Oh, it is McGann, Abd. Have you ever known me to lie? He has grown a beard, but we shall soon shave that off. And he is wearing Arab clothing, but we will discover that beneath his robe there lies an uncircumcised infidel. Anyway, I will prove it to you in the most simple of fashions. Fetch the woman.'

Abd er Rahman plucked at his beard. 'I cannot believe it,' he muttered. 'I cannot. And you would have me bring the woman here? Before these men?'

Idris gave a shout of laughter. 'Has she not already been exposed to these men? But let her wear the yashmak.'

Still Abd hesitated. 'You have not repaid the money.'

'It awaits you at my house.'

The little man's shoulders became more rounded than before, and he growled an order at the eunuch waiting in the doorway. 'There is some devilry here,' he said. 'Idris, you are indeed a devil. You mean to kill her?'

Idris chuckled. 'I will kill them both, but not until I have had my sport with them.'

He looked at the doorway, and Toby caught his breath. The eunuch had returned with a woman. She wore both a haik and a yashmak, as if she were about to go out on the street. But he knew immediately that it was Felicity. Oh, to be able to see outside, and know whether the American squadron was standing in!

She gazed at him in bewilderment for a moment, then gave a little gasp herself. 'Toby?' she whispered. 'Oh, Toby.'

'See how she calls his name!' Idris asked Abd er Rahman. 'There is a woman who loves. Yes, my dear, it is Toby, come to look for you. With my aid, of course.'

Felicity glanced at him, then looked at Toby again. 'You came alone?'

Toby decided it was time to make his play. 'I came with the United States' fleet,' he said, looking at Idris. 'Which is waiting to pull the city down about your ears, if either of us is harmed.'

'Ha ha!' Idris cried. 'Do you seek to frighten me? I would have thought better of you, McGann. That fleet is the same as waited three years outside Tripoli, and then gave in to my demands. It is manned by a pack of posturing cowards.'

'What will you do to the woman?' Abd asked gloomily.

'Many things,' Idris promised him. 'And you may watch. But to begin with, I would have them couple. I have long wished to observe the infidels' way of making love, for I have heard that it is truly a limited exercise. So, you shall possess your wife to my satisfaction, McGann, and before me.'

'And if I refuse to humour your filthy desires?'

'Then I shall commence flaying her before your eyes.'

'But you will spare her if I agree?'

'I will spare her being flayed alive,' Idris agreed. 'But this is a duty you should be pleased to perform, McGann. Not only because it must be a considerable time since last you knew your wife, but because it is the last time you will ever know anyone. I have an amusing programme worked out for you. When you have shown us what you can do, I will have Mansur show you how an Arab makes love. I have no doubt that he will send your Felicity into the utter realms of ecstasy. Then I propose to have you castrated. Felicity will watch. Then I am going to cut off your arms and your legs, where they join your body. Oh, do not fear, you will not die. My surgeons are too skilful for that. But when they are finished, you will watch your wife die, slowly. Then. when you have

319

screamed in agony and begged in vain, I will take out your tongue. So you will live, fed every day, rolling about my palace, that every time I pass by I may kick you out of the way. Does that not sound interesting?'

Felicity fell to her knees. 'Idris, my lord . . . '

Idris smiled. 'As I said, Abd, true love. Do you know that this is the first time in the fourteen years I have known her that she has deigned to beg me for anything, no matter how often I beat her?'

'Then savour your triumph, Idris,' Felicity said. 'For I do beg you to spare my husband.'

'Get up, Felicity' Toby said. 'He'll not harm either of us.' He had been listening to a steadily growing commotion outside. And now there came a banging on the door, and a moment later Marquand was admitted. He stared at Felicity, then at Toby, turning pale as he did so, then turned to Idris.

'My lord,' he gasped.

Idris was frowning. 'What is the meaning of this intrusion?'

'The Dey himself has sent me to seek you, my lord. My lord, the American squadron stands for the harbour.'

Idris's frown deepened. Then he snapped his fingers. 'Bring them both,' he told Mansur, and hurried for the street, Marquand at this side

'Once you served me well, Mansur,' Abd er Rahman remembered as the door closed. 'Now I would reward you more than generously, were you to serve me again. I would not have the woman die.'

'Now I serve a greater man than you can ever be, Abd er Rahman,' Mansur replied. 'Look to yourself. You . . . ' he addressed his men, 'Bind the woman.'

Felicity's arms were roped behind her back. As the knot was tied there was a rumbling crash, followed by several more, immediately accompanied by a chorus of screams from the street.

'May Allah strike down Mohammed ben Idris,' Abd er Rahman cried. 'He has brought this castastrophe upon us.'

'Be sure that I shall inform Lord Idris of your opinions,' Mansur promised. 'Haste,' he told his men.

Toby and Felicity were bundled into the street, to find themselves surrounded by a crowd of terrified people, running from their houses at the sound of the guns, although there was no evidence of any damage to the city as yet.

'Toby,' Felicity gasped.

'Courage,' he told her, speaking English. 'That is Stephen Decatur out there.'

If only he could free his hands, he had no doubt he could escape there and then. All around them was the utmost confusion, people running to and fro, screaming and shouting, dogs barking, asses braying, while the houses trembled to the noise of the explosions. Toby could not help but consider that it would be ironic were Decatur to smother Felicity and himself in the ruins of Algiers while endeavouring to save them, as just in front of them a wall collapsed into the street in a cloud of dust and rubble, its obviously rotten foundations shattered by the trembling of the earth.

They stumbled through the confusion, and reached the comparative fresh air of the square before Idris's house. From here they could look at the sea and watch the American squadron, flags and pennants flying proudly as the ships brought up, guns now silent. But that they had been fired with considerable effect was obvious – at last two of the batteries on the moles had been reduced to shambles.

'They are going away again,' Mansur said, in mingled relief and contempt.

'I wouldn't count on that,' Toby told him.

'Come,' the captain snapped, and led them into the house, hesitating there uncertainly as Idris was not to be seen. 'To the roof,' he decided. 'You may watch the defeat of your people.'

They were taken up several flights of stairs to emerge panting on to the roof, which was flat and reached by a large wooden trap door at the top of a flight of stone steps. Several times Toby and Felicity bumped against each other and looked at each other, but he could do nothing more than give her an encouraging smile. Whatever now happened, they would be together at the end.

Mansur stood at the parapet and stared down at the harbour. A boat could be seen leaving the American flagship and pulling for the entrance, a huge white flag fluttering in its bow. 'Does he think we will deal with him now?' the captain growled.

'I think he means to deal with you,' Toby suggest.

'They will all die,' Mansur declared.

As he spoke, one of the guns on the citadel exploded, the ball falling into the sea some fifty feet from the boat. Oars were at once checked, and the boat turned. Then the firing from the citadel became general, and several of the balls struck close to the ships, as Toby could see with concern. The harbour would not be forced without casualties.

But Stephen Decatur commanded the squadron, and he was not the man to be put off by a few cannon balls. He waited to regain his boat and his flag of truce, and then the ships were got under way again, approaching in line ahead while they accepted the fire from the citadel, and those of the harbour forts which had been remanned, before swinging up into the wind to present their broadsides when they were within a hundred yards of the shore; there were no sandbanks here, as outside Tripoli, to hamper their man-oeuvres. The naval guns exploded in unison, and it was as if Algiers had been seized by a giant hand and shaken. No doubt the Americans had elevated their cannon to the maximum to reach the hill fortress, but necessarily many of the shots fell short amongst the houses.

The city seemed to erupt into flying masonry, rising dust, and an enormous wail of misery which arose from its inhabitants. Idris's own house shook, and there came a tremendous crash from beneath them, while Felicity tumbled her length on the floor. Mansur gave a startled exclamation, and ran for the stairs, involuntarily followed by most of his men. Only one remained, glancing uncertainly from the stairs to the ships to the captives. Toby took a long breath, waited for the next glance away, and hurled himself at the man, feet up. He struck him on the side with such force that he flew across the roof and came to rest against the far parapet, blood streaming from his head.

'Toby,' Felicity gasped, trying to get up.

But she would have to fend for herself for the moment. Toby ran behind his victim, knelt, and turned his back, fumbling for the man's scimitar, locating the haft, and drawing the weapon from his sash, before turning the razor-sharp blade uppermost, and spreading his wrists over it. He could not of course see what he was doing, and his first effort sent the steel slicing into his flesh, but he gritted his teeth and found the right angle, and a moment later was free.

Then he ran to Felicity, freed her also, and faced the trap door and the steps, and the city was enveloped in another searing broadside, which, judging by the noise, caused even more havoc than the first. The sound of the explosions echoed into the distant mountains and was absorbed. The wails and the shrieks and the rumble of collapsing masonry continued, but the gunfire ceased once more, even from the citadel, and as Toby watched, the green flag of Islam came fluttering down from the flagpole, to be replaced by a white sheet. Yusuf Ali was surrendering.

'Toby,' Felicity panted.

A man was coming up the steps. Toby ran at him scimitar extended, struck him in the chest and sent him tumbling back down the steps with a dying shriek. Then he slammed the trap, and looked right and left for some means of securing it, but found nothing. And the man he had knocked down was beginning to move, writhing and groaning.

For the moment there was no one on the steps, so far as he could tell by listening. He ran back across the roof, tore off the man's belts; he carried a pistol and several spare balls as well as powder, and a dagger. These Toby laid on the roof, then he picked up the man, watched by Felicity, and returned to the trap, raising to to reveal three men cautiously advancing. He dropped their comrade into their arms to send them tumbling, and again closed the trap.

'What must I do?' Felicity said.

'We must hold this roof until Stephen comes for us,' Toby told her. It was the highest part of the building, and was far above the nearest rooftop of the kasbah. Only the battlements of the citadel overlooked it; he would have to hope that Yusuf Ali did indeed mean to surrender. 'I believe I can hold the door, but should I fail, can you support me with the pistol?'

'Yes,' she said, picking it up with the bag of powder and shot.

'Take the dagger too,' he said. 'And Felicity, use it this time if they do get past me.' She stared at him and he smiled.

'I will be already dead, and we must go together, if we have to go.'

'Yes,' she said. 'Together.'

He heard feet on the steps. He stood beside the trap, waited for it to be hurled upwards, and struck down with an enormous swinging double-handed blow. Blood flew, a man gave an unearthly shriek and went tumbling backwards. Several bullets were discharged at the opening, but they either struck the masonry or flew harmlessly into the air.

Toby reached round and threw the trap shut once again. So long as they could only come at him one at a time, they could not defeat him; his only fear was a marksman on the citadel battlement, but although that was crowded with people, they were all watching the harbour, where boats filled with marines and bluejackets were rowing ashore. Help was very close.

Then he heard Mohammed ben Idris's voice below him. 'Fools,' the corsair was shouting. 'Twenty of you, and you cannot take one man? Would you stay here to be hanged by the Americans? We must leave this place.'

'The giant is inaccessible, great lord,' Mansur protested.

'Bah! And the woman?'

'She is there with him.'

'Then charge that door and take them. They at least must be settled before we leave.'

'Great lord,' Mansur protested, 'are they worth our lives?'

There was a crisp sound and a gasp. 'I will be the judge of that,' Idris snapped. 'Well then, we will still listen to their screams.'

Toby waited, listening for some indication of what was coming next, but the voices faded.

'Toby,' Felicity said in a low voice. She was crouching by the inner parapet, looking down on the courtyard of the palace.

'Do not expose yourself to their fire,' he warned.

'They are hardly looking up,' she said. 'But they are packing up. Toby, a caravan is forming down there.'

'Well,' Toby said, 'if he wants to run, then we are safe. But he is not. I mean to follow him this time. The moment you are ... ' He checked, frowning, as he smelt smoke.

Toby!' Felicity's voice quavered.

Toby snapped his fingers. It had not occurred to him that Idris might consider destroying his own house just to be avenged on them. But if he was abandoning Algiers in any event ... He raised the trapdoor, looked down. As he had supposed, the floor beneath had been evacuated, but wisps of smoke were seeping up the stairs.

'Wait here,' he said over his shoulder, and went down the steps, cautiously approaching the staircase on the far side. A shot rang out and he felt the wind of the bullet as it smashed into the wall beside his head. He turned, his sword brought up, faced a second pistol, held by the same man, who must have volunteered for this suicidal post. And he would succeed in his task, Toby knew, as the pistol was levelled; he was too far away to be reached before he fired. But then there was another shot, and the man collapsed; Felicity stood on the steps, her smoking pistol in her hand.

'By God,' he said, 'but you would be worth dying for, my dearest girl.'

'I would rather live,' she said.

'And so you shall.' He went to the stairhead, looked down, and caught his breath; the floor beneath was a mass of flame. There could be no one on that floor, but there was no way past the fire; smoke was rolling up the stairwell in huge puffs, and breathing was already difficult – it could only be a few minutes before the entire house was engulfed.

He ran to the inner window, and looked down, keeping out of sight of the yard. The caravan was beginning to move towards the side gate, which debouched into the alleyway immediately beneath the roof. It consisted of several laden camels, and several more carrying howdahs for the ladies of the harem. But there was also a genuine wagon with a canvas roof; it was hitched to a team of oxen, and creaked across the yard.

'Toby,' Felicity said. 'If we made a rope of our clothes and hung it from the roof ... '

He shook his head. 'As a last resort, maybe. But everything we have would still leave us thirty feet short. Come.' He held her hand, took her back to the front window; here at least they could breathe – the room behind them was filled

325

with smoke. And from the window they looked down on the alley through which the caravan would have to pass to reach the square. 'That wagon.'

She drew a sharp breath.

'It is safer than dangling naked from the window,' he told her. 'And less embarrassing. Now!'

Before she could object, he picked her up, swung her through the window and dropped her. She gave a scream and went plummeting downwards, but landed exactly in the centre of the roof of the wagon, bounced, and almost rolled off, while her haik floated away to leave her only in her silk pantaloons and bolero – both her cap and her slippers had come off. She saved herself by desperately clutching at the canvas.

Toby was already falling behind her, holding his scimitar above his head. His weight proved too much for the canvas; it sagged and then parted. He went through it feet first, while Felicity gave another scream and this time did fall off and on to the road. But the canvas had broken their fall, and neither was more than shaken.

Men shouted, dogs barked, the curtains to the howdahs were parted to allow the women to see what was happening. Standing in the wagon, caught up in the canvas, Toby swung the scimitar left and right to cut himself free, bringing howls of terror from the dazed people who had been inside the vehicle. The driver stood up and turned, levelling a blunderbuss, but was thrown off-balance by the terrified oxen, who attempted to bolt and threw the wagon against the wall of the house. The driver fell one way, Toby jumped the other, landing close to Felicity, who was sitting up in a dazed fashion.

'Cut them to pieces,' Mohammed ben Idris shrieked, and Mansur led a charge of several men.

But Toby was now armed with a scimitar instead of a dagger, and he had waited for this moment for too long. He charged them equally, the razor-sharp blade whirling round his head. Mansur threw up his own sword, and had it swept from his hand before Toby's steel crunched into his scalp and left him half-decapitated on the cobbles. Toby was already swinging the blade back, and had struck down two more men long before any of them could reach him. The rest shrank back, glaring and panting.

'Fools!' Idris bellowed from a safe distance. 'Fetch pistols.'

Indeed, the wagon driver was now regaining his feet and his blunderbuss, which would be a far more effective weapon.

'Get down the hill to the harbour and our people,' Toby snapped at Felicity.

She hesitated only a moment, then ran into the crowd of people who were hurrying upwards, away from the dreaded Americans. Toby hardly waited for her to go before he charged again, once more scattering the swordsmen opposed to him to reach the driver before he could level his firearm. He fell to a single stroke, but then Toby was destracted by a shower of burning timber from above him: Idris's palace was starting to disintegrate.

The collapse of the wall and the accompanying surge of heat completed the rout; Idris's retainers dropped their weapons and ran, and were followed by the ladies of the harem, who abandoned their howdahs and the now-stampeding camels to run into the crowd. Toby looked left and right, but Idris had disappeared. He went to the front of the house and encountered Marquand, attempting to mount a terrified donkey.

'Mercy, for God's sake,' the renegade shrieked as he saw the huge, bloodstained figure approaching.

'Not for you,' Toby growled, and cut him down.

But still Idris was not to be seen. And there was Felicity to think of. He ran down the hill, scimitar in hand, thrusting people and animals to left and right. Parts of the city were also in flames, but the main street seemed to have suffered least, and in a few minutes he found himself in front of Abd er Rahman's palace, where the fat little man was supervising the loading of bags on to the backs of waiting donkeys.

He gazed at Toby in stark horror. 'Mercy, sir,' he cried. 'Oh, mercy.'

'Has Mohammed ben Idris come this way?' Toby demanded.

'He is inside my house, great lord,' Abd cried. 'Inside. With . . . ' He gulped.

Toby's brows drew together. 'Inside your house?'

327

'I thought you were dead, great lord,' Abd claimed.

Toby pushed him aside and ran into the house, looked left and right, and a terrified woman pointed at the stairs. He ran up them, gained the first floor, burst into a bedchamber, and saw Idris, holding Felicity by the hair as she twisted and fought him, and he forced her towards the divan.

'Idris,' Toby said.

Idris turned, his jaw sagging for a moment.

'Toby,' Felicity shouted. 'He . . . '

Idris swept her round into his arms, holding his dagger against her throat. 'I ran behind her, McGann,' he said. 'Because she is what lies between us. Thanks to you . . . ' his voice became a snarl, 'I have lost all. And now my life is forfeit. But you shall not prosper. I shall leave you your wife, McGann, to comfort your bed, lacking her breasts, lacking a nose.'

Toby stood in the doorway, sucking breath into his lungs. There was no doubt Idris could carry out at least part of his threat before he could reach the man; his left hand held Felicity by the throat, and his right hand, grasping the dagger, was resting against her chin. Toby's shoulders sagged. But vengeance would have to be abandoned yet again.

'Release her,' he said. 'I give you the word of a gentleman that you shall go free.'

Idris's lips drew back in one of his wolfish grins.

'Never,' Felicity gasped, and sank her teeth into the hand against her face.

Idris gave a yell a pain, and the dagger slipped from his grasp. Felicity elbowed him in the ribs and burst free, tripping and landing on her hands and knees in the centre of the floor. Idris reached for the dropped knife, and for her at the same time. But Toby was there before him, swinging the scimitar in a vast blow which sent the Moor's head spinning from his shoulders to crash against the wall. The trunk remained standing it seemed for a full second, before collapsing to the floor.

'Toby!' Felicity was in his arms.

'No more nightmares,' he told her. 'No more nightmares. Only you and me forever.'

He put his arm round her shoulders to take her down to

328

the street. They arrived at the front door to find the marines placing Abd er Rahman under arrest.

'Halt there, you rascal,' one of them shouted at Toby, levelling his musket.

'Put up the weapon, soldier,' Toby told him. 'I am Lieutenant McGann. And this is my wife.'

The two men stood to attention, while Abd fell to his knees between them. 'They mean to hang me, great lord,' he begged. 'Have pity.'

Toby looked at Felicity.

'He made me share his bed,' she said, her voice soft. 'But he treated me most kindly, and he certainly saved my life. Because he adores me. I suspect he adores me still. That was hardly a crime, Toby.'

'Let him go,' Toby told the marines. 'Of all these people, he is probably the most innocent.'

'Gentlemen.' Stephen Decatur addressed his assembled captains on the quarterdeck of the USS *Constitution*. With them were the masters of the ships held by the Algerians, and now released. The war was over, and Yusuf Ali had gratefully paid the indemnity demanded, to prevent the total destruction of his city. 'I give you Toby and Felicity McGann. You will all know that part of our plan was to create a diversion which would allow Lieutenant McGann to seek his wife, and if possible take her to safety. But gentlemen, Lieutenant and Mrs McGann themselves created the diversion, which so preoccupied Mohammed ben Idris that he neglected to take any proper means against our approach. They are to be congratulated on the parts they played in making our victory an easy one. So, may I say, Felicity, welcome home. And may you never be forced to wander again.'

'I thank you, Stephen, on behalf of us both,' Toby said. 'Be sure that we shall never wander again, either of us.'

Decatur frowned. 'That sounds a very final statement from you, Toby.'

'It is, Stephen. Much as I love this life, I love my wife more. I shall not leave the farm again without her at my side.'

'Oh, Toby.' Felicity squeezed his hand. 'Are you sure that is what you want?'

'Quite sure,' he said. 'These last few weeks have taught me that much. But gentlemen, if I may, I would like to give you a toast. To the United States Navy, and its future.'

'The United States Navy,' the officers said, raising their glasses.

Toby glanced at the Royal Navy captain seated beside him. The British frigate had come upon them soon after the surrender of Algiers, and its officers had been invited to join in their celebration. 'Will you not drink that toast, sir?'

'I shall, Mr McGann, with reservations,' the Englishman said. He looked at the smoke pall which still clung to the southern horizon. 'You have destroyed an entire city, sir, to make a point.'

'A point?' Toby cried. 'Why, have we not also secured the release of several British captives?'

'A few,' the captain agreed. 'And some Americans as well. At the cost of how many innocent lives?'

'There are no innocent lives in Algiers,' growled one of the American officers just released. 'There is no one in that city does not share in the profits from their piracy.'

'I am sure there are, sir,' the Englishman insisted. 'And now there are a host of innocent deaths, as well.'

'Are you suggesting that the matter could have been handled differently?' Toby demanded.

'Indeed, sir, I am suggesting that the orders given by the government of the United States in this matter, for I have no doubt that Captain Decatur was but carrying out his orders, that Algiers should be bombarded into surrender, were scarcely those of a civilised power. Such an infamous and indiscriminate massacre has not been carried out for over a hundred years with such deliberate forethought.'

'Which is why the Algerians have grown so arrogant, and so destructive,' Toby pointed out.

'Gentlemen,' Decatur said, 'I will have no quarrels on this day. Our guest is perfectly correct in assuming that I carried out my orders, as I am sure that he will always carry out his orders. As to the correctness of such order, every man is entitled to his own opinion. But in this regard, I will give you another toast, one to which I am positive our English friend will have no difficulty in raising his glass.' He stood up.

'Gentlemen, I drink to my country. In her dealings with other nations, may she always be right. But my country, right or wrong.'

The farm prospered, as did the nation, as world trade boomed following the final defeat of Napoleon at Waterloo, only a fortnight after Decatur's victory at Algiers. A victory which, followed by similar bombardments of Tunis and Tripoli, secured for American vessels the freedom of the Mediterranean. While the British, for all their criticism of American action in 1815, the very next year found it necessary to send a fleet of their own to bombard Algiers for the protection of the Union Jack.

The McGanns also prospered. Toby had indeed realised that however much he loved the Navy, he loved Felicity more, and was at last happy. Because they had experienced so much together, and at the end had fought, shoulder to shoulder, they had achieved a mutal rapport given to few, whatever their experiences. But the Navy was still in the McGann blood, and in early April 1820, Toby himself accompanied twelve-year-old Stephen to Baltimore, to see him taken on as a midshipman and continue the family tradition. It was in Baltimore that he met Thomas McDonough, now one of the senior captains.

'Toby McGann, by God,' McDonough cried, squeezing his friend's hand. 'But it is good to see you, even on so sad an occasion. You have come for the funeral?'

Toby frowned. 'The funeral? Whose funeral?'

'Why, Stephen Decatur's.'

'Decatur is dead? But how? My God, he can only have been forty.'

'Hardly more,' McDonough agreed. 'You mean you did not know? Well, how could you, buried away on that farm; it only happened a fortnight ago.'

'What happened?' Toby shouted. 'Disease?'

'A bullet, fired by James Barron.'

Toby stared at him, aghast.

'You'll remember that it was mainly on Stephen's testimony that Barron was suspended from duty, back in 1807,' McDonough explained. 'He went off to fight for the French, but when Napoleon finally abdicated, he returned here and sought reinstatement and a command, but was refused. I suppose this rankled. And to make matters worse for him, Stephen remained the hero of the hour, for his triumph at Algiers. You may believe that strenuous efforts were made to prevent them from meeting one another, but on 20 March last, at a dinner, both men happened to be present, and Barron accused Stephen, before witnesses, of bearing false witness against him at his court martial.'

'My God,' Toby muttered. 'But . . . that was no cause for a death, surely?'

'There was no necessity for a duel, even,' McDonough said bitterly. 'Everyone knew that Barron had spoken from sheer spite, and indeed, all the senior captains attempted to quash the business. But Stephen would fight. You know he never turned his back on an enemy in his life. What he did not know,' McDonough sighed, 'was that Barron had been practising for all of those thirteen years, and had become a crack shot. Yet he struck him in the thigh before being cut down himself.'

'My God,' Toby said again. 'The best officer in the fleet. With respect, Tom.'

'No offence taken. I agree with you.'

'And Barron?'

'Oh, he will recover from his wound, I would say. He will be remembered.'

'As the man who killed Stephen Decatur. There's immortality for you. Tom, when will this nation of ours, and this service of ours, grow to maturity?'

McDonough smiled. 'Why, never, I trust, Toby. And I think Stephen would agree with that. Nations, like people, need to stay young and vigorous and unafraid, and if sometimes they injure themselves from an excess of energy, that is better than dwindling from a lack of it. Do you remember Stephen's toast, outside Algiers? I think that will gain him more immortality that all his victories. And it is one we shall always honour, will we not, old friend?'

Toby clasped his hand. 'My country, right or wrong. The day we forget that, then indeed are we unworthy of his memory.'